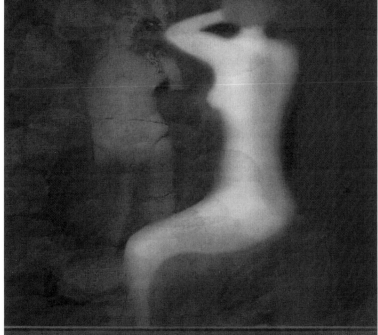

ARE BUT SHADOWS

M. Howald

ALL RIGHTS RESERVED

No part of this book may be reproduced or transmitted in any form or by any means, electronic or mechanical, including photocopying, recording, or by any information storage and retrieval system, without permission in writing from the author, except in the case of brief quotations embodied in reviews.

Editor in Chief: Nik Morton

Cover Art: M. Howald & Select-O-Grafix, LLC. www.selectografix.com

Publisher's Note:

This is a work of fiction. All names, characters, places, and events are the work of the author's imagination.

Any resemblance to real persons, places, or events is coincidental.

Solstice Publishing - www.solsticepublishing.com

Copyright 2013 M. Howald

Dedication
To Mom and Dad, beyond the divide

The best in this kind are but shadows,
and the worst are no worse,
if imagination amend them.
– *Midsummer Night's Dream*, Shakespeare

1

Someone died in my house. Ben Needham finally admitted it to himself as he stood on the leaf-stained sidewalk and looked up at the third story of his home. The November drizzle shivered into him. *Someone, not ready to leave this world, died in my house.* He felt an icicle forming inside of him, cell by cell, suffocating the warmth out of one another. *Someone, unwilling to pass, stayed.* Tiny micro-spasms took hold of his weakened gut. He felt thin-souled. He shivered again. *And stayed,* he repeated in bewilderment.

And on the covered veranda he stared at the lock on his front door. His lungs constricted. Breathing came shallow. A sudden fragrance, sweet and old, filled the air around him. His thumb and forefinger pressed against the small key with trembling hesitation. He knew in advance his home was being invaded. Each day he stared at the front door lock, wondering what new and disturbing evidence waited for him on the third floor.

The house was being invaded, but Ben Needham thought he had neither the experience nor the courage to deal with it. As he hesitated, he watched a perfectly round bubble of blood form on his thumb where a tiny cut had healed a week ago. The cut had healed without a scar. *Shit! Shit! Why is this happening to me?* As he drew it toward his mouth he watched the bubble disappear. *Shit. Now I'm angry.* His tongue curled behind clenched teeth as if snarling helped steady his hand. Calm his gut. He needed a horse tranquilizer to do the trick.

His dog, da Vinci, whined to get in.

And Annie complained, "Dad, it's cold!" She started to squirm. "I have to pee! Dad! Open the door!" She bounced and clapped her furry mitts together. "Hurry!"

As he fumbled with the key, he needed to tell Annie about his recurring nightmare. *I've been having this dream*, he wanted to scream. *Water. Splashing. Waves turning red. Perfume. Every night, the same nightmare since last Sunday. I can't breathe when I wake up. I can't move. I'm afraid to sleep. Kids have bad dreams, but I'm not a kid. I don't want to open this door. Don't make me! What should I do, Annie?* Ben had rehearsed what he wanted to tell her, but he was a good dad and did everything within his capabilities to make life feel wholesome for his ten year old daughter, so he kept it to himself.

He opened the door and picked up Annie's fallen, furry clothes as she raced to relieve herself and get ready for her mom's Saturday morning visit. Ben decided never to download his dreams into her manic, free-fall life, even though he wanted her to tell him he'd be okay. He would have liked the kid to have parented him this one time, but didn't ask.

* * * *

When Ben bought the two and a half story near Annie's school in the Roncesvalles area of Toronto's west end, one of the first things he did was soundproof the rooms, so they could talk and swap half-truths without the constant threat of distracting, invasive noises. Since Annie was born, ordinary sounds drove her into the darkest corners of closets – both hands and ear muffs welded over her sensitive, mis-wired ears. As a kid, she knew tears before laughter – more than most kids. But she did learn to laugh. Not always out loud.

Minimal soundproofing made life more comfortable for Annie. Music took on softer tones. Ben had purchased an audio minimizing system, so that mutually they could help each other with school work and Ben's graphic novels and hobbies. As she grew older, it seemed either she was coping better with intrusive elements or her system was self-repairing. Ben monitored her evolution with care – Annie was a gifted kid that had to be handled carefully. Like all rare gifts. Like all kids.

Annie's mom, Wendy, decided that raising a not-quite-labelled child wasn't functional in her life of comings and goings and goings-on and multiple comings. With only one functional parent, Annie needed Ben to be straight-talking (not straight-jacketed) in her wonderful world that Rousseau or Magritte could have painted. So he kept the third story disturbances that were getting out of control to himself, and his dreams, over which he had even less control – dreams that were deep invaders – he kept off limits to his daughter.

Annie's intelligence and talents were not assets in Wendy's busy life of lawsuits and indictments and court appearances. She visited Annie most Saturday mornings in Annie's room where they read and acted with puppets and watched a movie until Wendy's mothering session promptly ended. For Annie's sake the adults pretended to be on good terms. Ben never showed his absolute disdain for his ex-wife's rejection of them and for her new housemate, Ace, who insisted on remaining an only child in their busy, bubbly life.

It was Saturday, November 1, 2008. Saturdays were ritualistic. After Ben and Annie walked da Vinci, their Italian mastiff, and after Wendy arrived, Ben always slipped out for breakfast at Victoria's Bakery with his friends, Mark and the gang. On this Saturday morning the recurring dreams distanced him. He didn't want to fake it with friends, so he phoned with excuses. Instead he went for a long walk, going over in his head the details of the dream, the sensations, the invasion that was descending upon him in his own home. It didn't feel like a dream. It felt real, like doomsday. A final act of something really bad, not unlike biting into a rotten apple and finding a parasitic worm sliding down your tongue that you knew might not kill you, but might paralyse you instead.

The morning's palette ripped through the skies and over the frosty ground cover. When he arrived home he went through the sunroom and felt on fire with orange, flickering leaves on his face, the floor, the walls. *Apollo must have been a woman*, he thought, and closed his eyes in the warm haze. He loved the autumn light – low and playful. Wendy had already packed up her menagerie of bonding materials and was waiting in the family room while Annie quietly played a new composition for her on her keyboard. Ben thought Wendy would be checking her watch or cell, but she looked like she was actually enjoying their daughter's solo.

She told Ben what a great time they had and that she wanted Annie to come for a week-end before Christmas. It was hard for Wendy to wrap her arms around anything other than her computer and her boy/man, but she hugged Annie, kissed her forehead, smiled at Ben and left.

Ben joined the composer on the bench and listened to the song she was working on – a version of some old, jazz jewel, but couldn't fit a name to it. Wondered how Annie knew it. She insisted she had heard it before and it had completely taken over her brain, then it rolled off her fingertips a few days ago. She attached the audio cables and started transferring it into her computer to do some mixing.

"You're a brilliant kid, but you must have heard this somewhere. It's famous. You're not a psychic."

"No kidding. Yeah, I did hear it. From your studio."

"Well, it's really famous, not exactly like yours, but a whole lot like it."

"I can still mix it, can't I?" And she sizzled with the same passion she had for baking cookies and teasing the dog and collecting rocks and stones and pics of the Jonas brothers.

"Yeah, make it yours." Then he thought. "Hey, you heard it from my studio?"

"That blues lady you love. She was singing it."

"From upstairs? From my Kingpai system?"

"Yeah."

"Billy Holiday?"

"Yeah."

"The Kingpai is not even unpacked."

"I know I'm weird, but I'm not a magician. I know what I heard. How could I play it if I never heard it?" And she let her land of personal software seduce her into mixing mode. She didn't hear Ben grumbling on his way out.

Harlem Nocturne. That's the song. He was a jazz aficionado; he was sure he didn't have it downloaded. He turned around for a last look and watched the computer swallow his little girl. Tears flooded his eyes. *What ten year old kid would stay in on a Saturday to reinvent someone else's soul?* Silently he asked if it could be possible one day to have a normal week-end, but he really didn't know what that was like. He dabbed his eye with his shabby cuff and before he went upstairs he went back to Annie, grabbed her hands and kissed them and asked her about her visit with her mom.

"Really good, but maybe a bit too long," she said emphasizing each syllable equally. "She seems different. Like being the head person of this charity to save kids who got lost in some war is changing her. And she wants me to go to a big event with her and sit at the head table with her and Ace."

"That's really cool. She loves you." He slowly released her aching fingertips that flew back to playtime. He shook his head, wondered how she really heard the song and left.

* * * *

Two strange phenomena happened simultaneously that morning. The first was the song Annie had played. It wasn't unusual for Annie to play by ear. She was a prodigy. Had been playing since she was two. But to knock off a tune she hadn't heard before was something Ben couldn't grasp. And why would she lie about hearing it from the studio. The second phenomenon was the appearance of a pool of water in the middle of the studio floor between his easel and his art table. He had dreamed about it and there it was.

He didn't notice it until he turned on his work light and saw a reflective flash on the floor. Looking down he was amazed the water was self-contained. It hadn't run down the slight, natural slope of the floor. He was transfixed. The familiar dream flash-flooded his brain and sent tremors through his face until he shivered as if showering in ice water. He couldn't blink. He couldn't move. Then release came as if he were floating. This was the first time he had felt weightless, like particles of dust hovering in sunlight. He felt weightless, like when he was a boy and his dad showed him how to press his arms against the inside of a door frame, then step away and feel his arms floating upward. It was like that. Except it was his whole body. *Like particles of dust in sunlight*, he thought.

Shaken, excited, curious, he dropped to the floor and smelled the water. Something faint. Lavender maybe. Lavender and spice. Nutmeg? Ginger? Like the fragrance on the front veranda. Slowly he reached out to touch. *To touch or not to.* His fingers neared and hovered at the edge, then slightly caressed the surface. The clarity clouded. From nowhere, a drop hit the centre of the pool sending micro-waves to the rim. Then a collision and splashing.

Ben fell back as the pool turned red and his hand dripped with the scarlet liquid. It wouldn't shake off. It began to congeal. As he grabbed a towel from his table and wiped his hand, the pool disappeared. The towel turned white again.

What is fucking wrong with you? Are you crazy? he asked himself. His gasps slowed. He felt more grounded and warmer. He ran downstairs to check on Annie whose head bobbed and rolled to the gentle sounds that consumed her.

Taking a coffee back to the studio he checked the ceiling for leaks. There were none, and besides, it hadn't rained. He sat on the couch along the west wall and surveyed the space. His painting studio occupied the centre. Wide planked, original flooring glistened under the two, brilliant skylights that were on the west slope of the room. His bed, at the south end was opposite to his computer table at the north where he did all of his graphic work and networking.

His painting studio in the centre had an art table, an easel, and a free-standing table to store his art supplies. His wall space was uncluttered, but he had a small grouping of favourite artists – Degas, Chagall, Escher, Ernst, Hokusai behind his computer desk. And on his dresser at the far end by his bed, he had a picture of his twin, Jamie Needham.

Artefacts and collectables he had gathered on his world meanderings when he was twenty two were here and there – a donkey saddle in one corner, a camel blanket from Turkiye on the end of his bed, a woven blanket from Rhodos over the arm of his sofa, a rubbing from London on his wall beside the door.

He loved the Gothic Revival lines of the house. A little shabby. A lot stately. Original. He remembered the immediate chemistry and comfort he had felt as he had set about sketching the marble foyer, the ornate butler's pantry, the dilapidated gazebo in the back yard. It had been a great summer exploring the character of the house – its diverse, rich brick work, its old vines and ivy that had witnessed a hundred years of urban evolution, and the twisted, floral patterns in under-attended gardens.

He tried to remember subtle changes in the house before the dream started. There were some things - subtle things he had dismissed as imaginative flights or underfed hormones. There was this fragrance like bath talcum. Lavender again. And spice. It was stronger in the attic than downstairs. At one point it was so strong while he worked that his nostrils burned. He remembered that now and pinched his nose with his fingers, remembering the sensation.

And there was a shadow he had seen twice. Not anchored on the floor or wall like normal shadows are, but suspended in air. He had laughed and thought leaf patterns had been playing tricks on him. And the radiators banged – not on the first two floors. Just in the attic. Never where Annie was. He was grateful for that.

He remembered working late one night and falling asleep at his desk. When he awoke in the morning he was naked on his bed and felt he had been seduced like a drunken lover, asleep in a harbour-whore's arms. Ben decided that no one in these circumstances would have been suspicious and anyone would have at first, chalked it up to lack of sleep, loneliness, rebellious perceptions. But the dream, the music, the water he had witnessed was not perceptual pathology; it was some sort of invasion. He mused how all of these small details, out of the range of routine familiarity, got to him and made him wonder about his safety and if he'd live through another night or day in his house. Could a big guy – six-foot-plus - like himself be threatened by what others would think insignificant, self-directed incantations of an overdeveloped imagination?

Something had marked its territory in his space. *Am I at war? I don't want to fight you. I want to know who you are. Will you let me see you? What do you want? There's an abandoned house down the street. Try it.*

Ben considered the good, the bad and the barely acceptable. The good was that he and Annie were safe, the bad was the possibility of some paranormal disturbance that he didn't know how to handle and the barely acceptable was he was losing it. The pressures of deadlines, his constant need for perfection, the pressure of his commitment to Annie's success, and the stress of neglecting his own personal needs could be unhinging him.

He wasn't seeing the signs. He had heard of others who had breakdowns – saw snakes coming out of their saved drafts and contact pages – and slipped into schizophrenic states before they could log off. He didn't know if he were slipping into this place he had read about. At least he was aware he was slipping; he didn't know into what.

He never ignored the weight of his twin brother's accidental death when they were twenty one. His twin Jamie was born first and was stronger. Even though both were tall and strong Ben had been a weak kid who contracted every foreign invader that blew off the Saint Lawrence and into his Montreal home, his lungs and stomach. His mom had told him from the get go that he wasn't strong and he had to be overly cautious, to self-protect, so Ben became passive, was wary, was cowardly, was ill-equipped to handle trauma.

But it was Jamie who stopped breathing when his yearning tongue found peanut butter cookie crumbs in his girlfriend's mouth. A long kiss, a sweet taste. His girlfriend called the paramedics then in shock passed out beside him on the floor of the shower in her apartment.

After the funeral, Ben took a semester off and vowed never to love or be loved. He was terrified of its possible impact on his mom's delicate, emotional balance. His art and writing became his mistress until he met Wendy - strong enough for the two of them. Maybe he felt safe with her because she was half iceberg and half wolverine. He couldn't remember ever kissing her eyes or her hands or feet or inside her.

Ben shook his head. *No. No...no...no. This isn't right. It's not about Jamie's death. I handled that a long time ago. I love my work. I'm fucking happy! Fucking funsational happy!* he screamed silently. Jumping up, he turned to the west wall of the attic beside his sofa, along which was a large cubby – a compartment built into the slope of the roof. It was five feet deep and twenty feet long. When he moved into the house, he did a quick inspection of the storage space, and when its emptiness and cleanliness met his approval, his exploration ended.

Getting a flashlight he opened the sliding doors, fell to his knees and crawled inside. He inspected each empty drawer then moved to the far end to the open shelves. Almost beyond his reach at the last bottom shelf he found a tin box. Items inside rattled as he moved it out of the cubby to the skylight. On the front of it was a smiling young woman, could have been a teenager in a strapless, red stripe bathing suit sitting on a log at the beach. And on the back was the printed label for Walters Palm Toffee made in London, England in 1948. It was a toffee container.

Sitting on the sofa he emptied the contents beside him. There was what looked like a small gold-plate hand mirror that was broken, and on top of it several shards that had fallen out of the cracked frame, one of which was the largest. Standing up he turned to face the south wall and held the broken mirror up so that he looked into the remaining chard at the space behind him where his table and easel rested. Suddenly, a splash of light shot into existence then disappeared. Quickly Ben turned around to the empty space.

He looked again into the mirror. Nothing. And threw it on the sofa. *I'm sick of this shit. Do you hear me? Get out of my house! Get the fuck out!*

He paced to calm himself and stopped where the water had been. Then he examined the mirror more closely, packed up the pieces and replaced the tin box in the cupboard. He decided to check his playlist; he knew he didn't have *Harlem Nocturne*, but downloaded it for Annie. He checked Holiday's recording history and couldn't find the song on any label. Annie didn't need to know that somehow she had picked up a phantom song. *Wow, Ben, you bought a haunted house. Or maybe your brain's hemorrhaging....*

He needed to get out and decided to drag Annie into some fresh air when he found her hunched over her keyboard. He rubbed warmth into her stiff back that had been poised at her computer for an hour. She closed her eyes as her muscles loosened. Her physiotherapist had shown Ben how to pressure release stress points so that her air flow and circulation were more in sync.

"We're getting outta here. A walk. Some food. Italian or Thai?"

"Italian. Do we have to?"

"Yes, and we love everything Italian, don't we?"

Annie grabbed her special helmet (noise sensitive) and helped get their bikes out of the garage.
Ben looked up at the gabled roofline and thought he saw something at the small, arched window. Something and nothing. And Annie asked if he heard that. She pointed towards the attic. When he asked what it was she heard, she said something like breaking glass, like it was the same noise made twice.

He lied. Said he had heard it too.

She fastened her helmet and took the lead.

The attic slept. The light Ben left on dimmed. And glass rattled in the tin box as the young woman in the red, striped bathing suit smiled.

2

Saturday night had been without incident. Ben slept without threat of suffocation or air borne weightlessness. There were no fragrances, no invisible arms pulling him into some unscheduled rendezvous. And Sunday morning was blazingly beautiful. The air had turned warm – already November and so reminiscent of its summer origins.

Ben inspected the attic for its usual anomalies – perfumes, pools of water. Shadows. Shimmering lights. But there was nothing, and nothing appeared in the cracked mirror.

The radiators were politely quiet – cold but quiet. But not cold in Annie's room.

He let Annie sleep in until he got a call from Annie's art teacher reminding them of their field trip to the Art Gallery of Ontario (the AGO) to see the new art show and a puppet performance. Ten students and four volunteer parents were attending. Ben was one of them. The art exhibit especially interested him. There were twenty portraits of celebrities painted by lesser known 20th Century artists. Portraits of people like J.F. Kennedy, Einstein, Elvis, Roy Rogers, Babe, Trudeau, Pamela Anderson, Norman Bethune, Leonard Cohen and more. The kids were in grade six (Annie had skipped grade three) and were starting portraits in their art class, so Vienna Navarre, Annie's art teacher, thought the show would work well.

Ben had forgotten about it, but managed to get them ready and to the entrance of the gallery early, where they waited for the other kids. Both stood in amazement at Frank Gehry's architectural make-over. *I know how you think; I know what makes you do this,* Ben thought as he studied the building's lines and textures. Ben had always felt a close bond with Gehry's work and let it inspire his own settings in his graphic novels.

Annie was drawn to the Baroque staircase with its ascending curves, and said her brain felt like that. Like a spiral of anti-gravitational knowledge – her exact words.

"Spectacular, isn't it." Annie's art teacher found them and extended her hand to Ben. "It's good to see you again, Mr. Needham."

They had met once before at an open house at Annie's school. Ben couldn't remember her hair being that golden with shimmering, red strands in the morning light or long like the mane of his uncles' favourite mare on the farm in Arva near London. *Golden brown? Or brown. Light golden brown? Golden-red?* He couldn't decide on the colour and watched her bangs blow upwards in the breeze – bangs that were shorter at either end and longer in the middle.

He thought how the AGO was a perfect backdrop for her statuesque form. Tall. Straight. Almost curveless, but not without padding. Small breasted. He had mastered the art of a quick study – he had to for his gesture drawings in college and sketches on the road. He liked her square jaw and high cheekbones that were almost aboriginal and cradled her watery, indigo eyes and sallow skin. *Wow!* he almost found himself saying out loud. *And that hair. Gold or whatever it was!*

He usually didn't wander too far away from a person's eyes, but the hair held him and the open blouse beneath her jacket. Open and low cut, revealing skin with a hint of colour – maybe a tattoo near her left breast above her heart. Then the hair again and the black eyes. He was really stupid around women. He took her hand, but forgot her name and forgot he was still wearing his ear pads. Annie had already removed hers even though she had insisted she didn't need them anymore and replaced them with smaller devices for indoor silencing.

He held Vienna's hand, and when he came to his senses he released it. "It's nice to see you too, Ms. Danner."

"Hey, dad, this is Ms. Navarre. Ms. Danner is the librarian," Annie whispered, "with the unibrow," as discretely as she could.

"I'm Vienna," she smiled. She was fully aware she didn't mind Ben holding her hand or scrutinizing her hair. It had been two years since more than one man had held her – men she didn't need, but let them into her life anyway. Then decided enough was enough and let canvasses and paint instead of men hold her the way she needed to be held. But she liked this large, thick hand warming hers.

"Call me Ben." He was four inches taller than Vienna but compressed downward to lessen the difference. Not all women liked the six foot plus, dark and handsome type. A lot liked the Hoffman/Ponti/Devito type who made women feel maternal or dominant.

Vienna liked this slim tree with deep blue eyes who had held her hand. She smiled at Ben's scrutiny then turned to Annie. "How's my artist?" Annie smiled appreciatively then ran to join a classmate arriving with an older parent, probably her grandparent.

"And musician," Ben beamed. "Maybe she's too clever." He tried to look somewhere else - at the traffic, the concession booth, a mime artist – but couldn't stop looking at this woman. "Annie's told me you show your own works. She always talks about your art."

"I just finished a show in Calgary and sold six pieces, and before Christmas I'm opening a show here, at The Yorkville Studio."

It didn't feel awkward to Ben how the two of them smiled at each other without talking, how they seemed not to mind the silence, how they felt encapsulated in an invisible bubble, as if the streetscape was out there somewhere, and they were in their word-free zone, smiling without blinking - holding each other's stares.

Then conversation went back and forth comfortably. "Annie has brought in some of your graphic novels. They're really good. Dark. Witty. Really cool. I like 'em."

"Annie collaborates with me. I run things by her first, before my agent gets a look. I'll bring her to your art show if you send her home with the info. I know she'd like to take it in. We both would."

After the group convened, they found their tour guide who moved them from one work to the next in the three gallery rooms. Falling behind, Ben stopped at the fourth portrait and was transfixed by it. The anonymous painter had captured the subject in a way, Ben thought, no one had ever seen before. Ben drew close to the face of Billie Holiday - smiling and laid back. Eyes lit from a well of happiness. Lips like Millay on the verge of a love poem. As he gazed into her eyes, his own watered. *Why am I doing this? He couldn't help it. What's with all the tears? Why are you here? Why now? Did you ever sing Harlem Nocturne? Did you bring us here?* He looked into her eyes as if she had been cleansed by a brush and was waiting for him.

Vienna circled around and found him, as the others went on to the puppet theatre. "She's beautiful. I have her collected works."

"You do? Can I tell you something really weird?"

"Sure, but let's walk and do weird at the same time."

As they rushed to catch up, he told her about Annie playing Harlem Nocturne in her own style. Upbeat. A different signature. "She said she heard Holiday singing it over my system in my studio."

"Okay?"

"This is going to sound crazy, but the system's not connected. And Holiday never recorded it."

Vienna thought a moment. "You're right. The song's not in my collection."

They caught up and found Annie who had saved two seats for them. She moved over so that Ben and Vienna could sit together.

"So, what do you think?"

"I think that's beyond weird."

He didn't want to sound urgent, but whispered, "Do you think we could meet? Talk about Annie's progress? What things I need to focus on more? I need your advice."

"And you want to talk about all this other weird stuff too?"

"Yup. You don't know the half of it. I'm really concerned about Annie."

The audience quieted as the puppeteers worked their magic. When it was over Vienna said good-bye to the kids and parents, and Ben insisted on driving her home. Liberty Village was a six minute drive from his place.

Vienna didn't talk much. Often looked at Annie and wanted to probe, but didn't want her to think that her new music composition was a big deal. She had worked with highly gifted children for the past eight years and witnessed exceptional talent that resulted from equally exceptional sources. She loved Annie's spontaneous ingenuity. She would wait to broach the subject when she could get the whole story from Ben.

"Thanks for the ride. Do you want to meet tomorrow? Lunch?" she asked softly.

"Yeah. I really need to talk. Besides me, you're the only one who understands Annie's special qualities and can give me some direction here."

She didn't judge him. Wondered though if he teared up a lot. Maybe it was the art gallery-syndrome-thing that people experience when in the presence of master works.

But she thought his eyes had moistened. She didn't know guys like this. "See you at lunch. I have a really unusual work of Annie's you should see."

He watched her walk away. *What kind of a name is Vienna? Vienna Navarre. Austro-franco? Did her parents meet in Vienna? Make love in the Palais Hotel Wien or the Rudolf-Bednar-Park?* He drove home thinking of Holiday's full lips spilling a love song and Annie's funky plunking out some notes she couldn't possibly have heard. *I don't know how to do this. How to keep it together.* He drove by their house twice before parking.

Ben convinced Annie to cook dinner with him, so while she managed their wok, Ben probed for data on Vienna – the kinds of clothes she wore, foods she ate, favourite artists, music, animals. Did she colour her hair? Wear contacts? Have a tattoo? Have any sisters, a brother. Was she ever married? A boyfriend? A girlfriend?

"Stop it! How do I know if she wears Victoria Secret or if she flosses regularly or eats organic. You never asked about her before. Just stop!"

He had never spent an afternoon with her before. Smelled her hair so close. Or loved the way she talked about Annie. Then he brought up Annie's grade four crush to explain his feelings. "Remember Nat Newstead? That thin, cool dude with the dimples and wavy, blond hair? The kid who wrote poems to you with sticker letters?"

She blushed.

"Ah ha!"

Annie never knew two people could be that crazy about each other. At nine years old her heart had dissolved into jello when Highway 400 pulled Nat Newstead toward Georgian Bay. At nine, she thought she'd never love again, couldn't even find comfort in wrapping her arms around da Vinci. "You had to, didn't you?"

"I felt a spark this afternoon. Inside my chest. My heart sped up. My stomach got tickly. You can relate to that."

"Okay, I hear ya."

"My earlobes tingled."

"Dad!"

"My toes felt hot. Then numb."

"Dinner's ready." She turned off the burner and scraped the stir-fry onto two plates, while Ben grabbed Portuguese buns and wine. Quietly they ate in mutual understanding of love bites, and how they didn't draw blood but mauled you playfully, waiting for the kill.

"I'll never love again," she mumbled as if her lips were sewn shut.

"I doubt that." Ben's third glass of wine anaesthetized his face, as he spoke the words in slow motion. "You'll love again."

"I guess it took you a long time to get over mom."

Ben's stomach heaved. He suddenly felt a weight pinning his chest. "Yeah, your mom was really special. Ruined it for me. It's been six years already."

"That's sad – not having a girlfriend for so long. It's not even healthy."

"I have a lot of love in my life - you and da Vinci and my mom, I think, and Mark. That's all I ever needed, and now I've met V. Of course you matter most in my life," he emphasized, "but I really felt something with this woman."

"She's really nice, but mom's a Bond girl, don't you think? She has great boobs."

An image of a shark with lipstick and a 36 D-cup bulleted toward his flailing arms as he tried to swim to shore. "Mom's definitely Bond material."

"I...I just..."

"What?"

"I wish she'd take me out sometimes. Maybe over to her place. My ears are getting better. She treats me like a doll."

"Well, your mom feels safer here in your own familiar space. But she did say she wanted you for a whole week-end before Christmas." He poured a fourth glass which Annie removed to the kitchen before his tongue sloshed around in it.

She ignored what he had said. "Dad, I've got homework."

"Okay, I'll clean up. Do you need some help?"

"N...n...noooo. I have diagrams to label of female genitalia."

"I'll pass."

"I think I'll add some details - Frida Khalo style."

"You do that, but I don't want to see the finished product. I'll be out on the back porch. Need to clear my head."

"Of Vienna?"

"Of the wine, silly."

* * * *

The neighbourhood quieted by eight. He grabbed a coat, scarf and an old hat that had belonged to Jamie and sat in the crisp air. It had changed. Leaves like large snowflakes whirled about the yard. He loved looking at the gazebo – its roundness and well crafted, intricate lines. It had withstood decades of industrial soot, snow, hail and the remnants of southern hurricanes.

He walked to it through the falling leaves. The structure seemed unusually bright. He couldn't remember it being so fresh-looking and white. He searched the sky for a full moon, but there wasn't one. It looked newly painted, and flowers had woven their stems through the lattice. *Flowers, this late in the fall? No, it couldn't be.*

He heard laughter. Soft and secretive. A fragrance wafted by him. "Who's there? This is a private residence. Anyone there? I'm not leaving until you come out!"

Ben stopped walking and listened. Wooden floor planks creaked as whispers faded in and out of the night. Leaves rustled quickly behind him. He turned. The chair on the porch moved slightly, and then he thought he heard, *Good night.* He ran into the gazebo. The yard light was bright enough for him to see the cluster of leaves strewn on the floor and under the leaves by the steps, a shiny object – a piece of mirror. He stared at it, and then ran in to check on Annie.

His heart was racing arrhythmically when he found her asleep in bed with notes on the birthing canal and other O'Keefe and Khalo-like images scattered around her. He calmed and studied this miracle of sleep - the way it took hold of her. How she could close her eyes and fall so deep into this undisturbed night-womb, then the next day ride her bedazzling brain train for the next sixteen hours of non-stop creativity.

He never knew sleep could be so irreversible as when Annie succumbed to it without protest. He didn't know who to thank for that. But he knew if he had to choose between a kid who wasn't exactly peanut butter and jam through the day, but could sleep at night and a kid who was Jekyll through the day and Hyde at night, he'd want the first. He didn't want anything to change Annie's night world.

He watched her. Like a hibernating bear she breathed winter-shallow. *Annie, Annie, where do you go at night? What do you dream of?* She said she never remembered them.

He watched her sleep. Stood guard. Thankful she wasn't looking at him too close these days. *I don't want you to see what's happening to me. I'm gonna try so hard to be me. Not to let go. Sweet dreams.*

He looked for shards of glass on her floor. Smelled for perfume, and on the way out he felt the radiators. They were womb-warm. For now, he knew Annie was safe, that she was off limits to the shadows in the leaves.

* * * *

Friday nights weren't lonely, but Saturday and Sunday nights were. He had no significant other on Saturday nights when couples were supposed to shake off work aches and car repairs and dental appointments and engage each other in free expression. There was no one on Sunday nights by the fireplace, talking about the week-end and making plans for the week's work or holidays. At least that's what he imagined partners did on Sunday nights – watch the fire together, make plans. Smile. Whisper. Touch.

He grabbed a Stella and went up to his studio, stopping on the landing to look at the night sky erupting with tendrils of lightning. Then thunder. He always thought portals were opening when the weather got so deranged. Thunder. Lightning. And snow. They hadn't forecasted snow. It had become crisp, but still too mild for snow.

Turning on the electric fireplace he sat on his work chair and held out his hands toward the heat, letting the warm air blow on his arms and face. Mentally he barricaded himself against any disturbances and turned his focus on his new file: *The Secret Life of Milton Gage.* He navigated through the first ten pages – how Milton Gage (age 8), the prodigal son of Inter-dimensional Physicist, Phillip Gage had a childhood heart disease (Hypoplastic Left Heart Syndrome) and was dying; how Milton receives a high-tech, micro heart transplant and during the operation slips into coma; how two entities – the angel, Solaris and the demon, Maligo fight to empower Milton's soul; how Solaris defeats Maligo and weaves an immortal substance through Milton's body that causes him to morph into a humanoid droid with occult powers; how Solaris and

Milton fuse as one hyper-entity to fight for the good of mankind.

His frames were supposed to end at that point, but he noticed there were more. In disbelief, Ben stared at the next frame he knew he hadn't created. He closed his eyes then opened them – a prayerful blink, hoping the image would disappear, but it stared back at him. Maligo – not Solaris - like the Pieta, cradled Milton in his arms. And, whereas in the previous frames Maligo's face was concealed by his hood, in this frame his obscure mouth contorted into a malignant, smug smile as if his victory in winning Milton to him would warp history irreversibly. Ben stared in disbelief. *How in the hell did you get there?*

Ben hadn't drawn it. Never had the original idea for it. Never did preliminary sketches of it. It was Ben's style, but not his plot. Not his character. And Maligo's vague features stared with a wasteland of ice in his eyes. *What is happening?* he screamed, damming up his voice.

He highlighted it and pressed delete. It remained in his file. *Delete. Delete. Delete.* Quickly he opened a copy which did not have the additional frame. He closed it and stared again at this rogue frame and wondered if Annie had accessed it or someone at the publisher's.

As he stared at the monitor, he heard tiny, non-existent fissures cracking the surface of his imaginary sanctuary like delicate eggshell pieces falling away. He was losing his concentration.

The power of someone's residual memory, a power, an energy, a ghost left behind somewhere in his house was seducing Ben from his work and he let it. He felt naked and exposed to the presence of things gone by and now returning to do something needed. Fragrances like warm arms wrapped around his head and turned him toward his bed against the south wall. Not resisting, he followed while a burning heat like accelerated sunburn worked its way up his body from his feet to mouth, then held him in an intimate embrace. His clothes fell away. Lowering himself to the bed he welcomed the warmth, the smells, the pressure of intimacy weighing him down and moving him into pleasure's reach. He felt needed.

The wine, the sweet smell of intimacy subdued any fears. He heaved, rolled from side to side, kissed someone he couldn't see. Let his loneliness dissolve in the phantom's arms. Heard himself say, *I want you.* And, *Who are you?* And, *What do you want me to do?* He remembered falling asleep feeling like a calendar had kidnapped him into another year.

* * * *

"Dad!"

He tried to moisten his dry lips. He felt like all the liquids had been sucked out of him. His skin felt sandpapered and left in an unquenched desert.

"Dad! I called you four times – no five." She stared at his naked backside.

"Annie?" he asked wondering if she were something ancestral and resurrected.

"Who do you think I am? How come you're lying on the floor?"

He opened his eyes.

"What did you do with your boxers? So gross. You're not having any more wine. Ever!"

"What?"

"Your butt's goin' solo!"

"What?"

She shivered in the cold attic. "Why is it so cold up here?" And looked at the skylight. "That's really weird."

"What is?"

"There's snow on the window."

He got up and grabbed a blanket. "What's so weird about it? We had a snow storm last night. Rain, then snow."

"It didn't snow. I've already walked da Vinci. There's no snow. It's not even cold. As she turned to leave she picked up papers that had fallen around his table. "I made waffles. I'm going to be so late."

"Eat without me. I'll be ready in a few minutes. Hey, the thunder didn't wake you up?"

"What storm?" And she called back, "It's already 7:50!"

Quickly he panned the area. His bed was made. His clothes had disappeared. His computer slept. He looked up at the snow on his window. And even though the studio was fridge-cold, he felt warmth radiating under his skin.

* * * *

Before he kissed Annie good-bye in the school lane, he told her about his appointment with Vienna to check on her progress, then hesitantly asked her if she had fooled around with his novel file – maybe by accident and forgot to delete the doodles she had done. Her whispered protests absolved her from any suspicion, and when Ben tried to give her a hug, she bolted away indignantly.

* * * *

He found a cafe to research the genealogy on his house before municipal offices opened. He got kicked up on caffeine and Google. *Try to get blueprints, check chain of title search, check record of deeds and land and tax assessment records.* Then he turned to the topic of the occult: *Voices – In Your Head or Your House; How to Get Your Ghost to Pick Up After It; Should You Set Another Place at the Table;* and *Don't Anger It!*

He thought of Jamie and wondered if his twin had hung around after he had died and if he watched Ben. Did he know what was going on in Ben's house? Could he help Ben if he asked? He shook his head, logged off and went to the Ontario Genealogical Society first.

* * * *

Bernadette Costo, a CSR, steered him to the right government offices. And after listening to his reasons for wanting an ownership history she told him about her own encounters with ghosts when she lived on Euclid. That when no one in her house had been cooking, a mix of spices would waft through the rooms. Sometimes there'd be flour spilled on the wooden staircase and small footprints would appear and disappear in the flour dust. Sometimes there would be sticky spots on the countertops, like spilled lemonade.

When Ben asked how she handled it, she said she and her roommate had a séance with some people from The Canadian Parapsychological Institute of Research on Queen Street who said that it was okay if the presence hung around, and that it wasn't doing anyone any harm. Bernadette also said she had the house exorcised. Before the ghost had a chance to change or vacate, Bernadette moved.

* * * *

The clerk in the Land and Property Records office gave Ben copies of all the documents he needed that pre-dated 1910 until it was sold to Ben. The property originally belonged to a Catholic diocese and was used as a manse. The cathedral beside the house sustained massive fire damage in 1930 and was demolished and the property was sold to a Mr. Smithson who owned it until 1946. It was again sold in 1962 to a Mr. and Mrs. Bergman who owned it until 2002, then to the last owner who was a realtor who sold it to Ben.

He studied the chain of ownership. The years between 1946 and 1962 had no documentation. There were no land and tax records for those years. Mr. Smithson owned it until 1946 and the Bergmans bought it in 1962. *Who owned it between 1946 and 1962?* The clerk agreed it was odd and after searching through an extensive data base she found nothing. Ben circled owners' names and the names of the law firms that represented them. He had some time before lunch to go home and make some calls.

He stood on the porch looking at the front door. *Did you live behind this door, under this roof, after the war? Who are you? Why are you here?* He unlocked the door. Warmth and perfume and distant notes floated from an unknown place to meet him. He waved the documents in the air. *Did you live here from 1946 to 1962? Who are you?*

He ran up to the studio. The water had formed and remained contained. The clothes he had worn the day before were thrown beside the bed that had unmade itself, the sheets of which fell loosely on the floor as if someone rose and dragged them with him. He ran to the cubby and grabbed the tin box. Holding up the cracked mirror he saw his own face. Turning to the south wall he looked again. A shimmering light shot into focus. A face surrounded with red hair and bubbles of red lipstick curled on white skin lingered in the mirror.

He turned. The light-filled figure bent down and ran her fingers through the water on the floor. Holding them out to him, they reddened and dripped blood. He staggered back and fell on the bed. Reaching for him she kneeled in the centre of the room. Darkness loomed above her. Ben watched her disappear. He tried to breathe but couldn't. He waited. *Save me.*

A mouth found his. He felt his lips moisten. His throat relaxed. Air pushed in and out. A weight fell into his chest as if curling there for comfort. He wrapped his arms around it and rocked it. *Sh...sh...I'm here. I'm here. Sh...sh....*

3

He felt more needed by this thing than he had ever felt by Wendy in their under-stimulated, undernourished marriage. His lips still pulsed when he found Vienna placing two serviettes on her teacher's desk at the back of her room, that was like a gallery in itself. A wall for Masters, a wall for students. A corner for statuary. An antique book unit. A vintage rug with a comfortable chair beside it for reading or storytelling.

Serviettes. Sandwiches. Bottles of juice. Ben handed her a bag of Kolacki (Polish cookies) which she opened and smelled - fresh and nostalgic. She put them on the desk, then held out her hands to take his coat. After ushering him to his chair she offered the platter of sandwiches and poured the juice.

"Before I forget..." He got the documents from his coat pocket...."I did a bit of ownership history on my house this morning."

"And?"

"There are no documents from 1946 to 1962. Sixteen years of the house's history have disappeared. I'm going to take these records and do some probing; I need to know about those sixteen years. Who lived there, who loved there, who died there."

"I've been thinking a lot about what you told me yesterday. It's too crazy for logical answers. So, I gather something's going on in your house."

"A woman at the Genealogical Society told me to contact The Institute of Parapsychological Research. She said they had helped with a friend's problem." Ben passed another typed page to her. "I made out a list of things that have happened since I moved in."

She read them. "I know strange things happen, but...I knew you were too perfect."

"I'm not nuts. I promise. You're the first person I've really talked to about it. Because of Annie. I don't know how safe she's going to be. So far, nothing has affected her except the music she says she heard, but she couldn't have heard it from a real source."

Vienna read the fifth occurrence about the cut that happened when he was sleeping and looked at the tip of his thumb. "There's no cut now."

"It healed a week ago, then blood appeared and disappeared Saturday morning."

"Okay." She shook her head. "I don't know anything about this kind of stuff, but you should see Annie's latest art work." She went to her portfolio and got Annie's folder. "Neither of us knows what inspired her. She said she saw it in a dream; it's almost too good."

Ben took the lightly painted sketch. His breathing quickened. He paled. "Christ!"

"What's wrong?"

He stared at young woman in a strapless, red-striped bathing suit, sitting on a log at the beach. "This is way too deep for me! I really need some professional help. People who know about this stuff."

"What's going on?"

"This is the same picture that's on the old tin toffee box I found in the storage space in my studio."

"Maybe she found it."

"No. She would have told me. She always shares the things she finds." He thought he'd take a chance. "This is going to sound crazy, but can you come over tonight? Check things out? I can tell Annie you want to see some art for a show or something."

She grimaced. "Ben, you're a parent of one of my students."

"It isn't a crime, is it? I teach courses. I have students over sometimes."

33

She tried to be more encouraging. "Look, I know you're going through something that needs some work."

"It's just that, you know Annie. You're with her every day. I trust you. I can't speak to her mom about it."

"I really like her. I've never met any kid with her spirit. But I don't know how to help." She watched Ben fade into the chair. She felt guilty about seeming indifferent.

"Look, I don't usually refuse help." She thought about how desperate he was. "Okay. I don't know if I'm doing the right thing, but I'll come over. All I can give you is a little moral support. That's about it."

"It's a lot more than what I had this morning. Would 7:30 be okay?"

They finished lunch and went over Ben's list of disturbances. He tried to describe precise details. When he came to the point about his graphic novel he remembered he saved Milton Gage on his memory stick.

"Can I show you the last frame of my novel?" And he produced his file.

"Sure. My laptop is in my office."

The frame was still there. Maligo's face remained sickeningly bizarre in his youthful power and dominance.

"It's like a photograph. Not an illustration."

"I didn't draw it. It's not mine."

"And you think Annie did it?"

"No. I thought maybe someone, somehow accessed it - which is insane."

She examined the face more closely. "He's not old. Looks like an evil, baby-faced teenager." She shivered. "It's like he's looking into me."

Ben closed the file.

"I have about five minutes before my next class."

"Can I take Annie's work with me?"

"Sure."

"Do you want us to pick you up?"

"No. I'll take a street car. You can't be more than five...six minutes away. Ben, are you going to be okay?"

"I have to be." He gave her his address and a quick map to the house. "Thanks for listening. I want whatever's going on to leave Annie out of it. There are some things that I didn't put on the list. Personal things that I can't let happen to Annie. I'm afraid for her." He sensed Vienna's generosity. That she would not judge his fear as weakness.

She drew close to him and reaching her hands towards his collar turned it up and pressed it around his neck. "It's turned really cold out there." And smiled a smile with respect for what they both valued – the safety of a child.

He didn't go home, but cozied up at Second Cup and made a list of Canada 411 numbers for people whose names matched the ownership names: Smithson and Bergman. He made phone calls to the Smithsons first. Most were either out, hostile, or not the one he was looking for, but he left messages. It was the third Bergman he called who confirmed it was his father who owned that property from 1962 to 2002. The man was a teenager at the time.

When Ben told the man that he needed to know the name of the owner who sold the property to his father, the man said he didn't know and that his dad was deceased now and he was sure there was no current documentation on that property. Records had been kept while his dad was in a retirement home, but when he died the family went through his dad's papers and recycled the ones after probate was completed. He couldn't tell Ben what law firm did the litigation on the sale. He was certain it wasn't his dad's personal lawyer, and anyway his lawyer was also deceased.

Mr. Bergman was silent when Ben asked if anything was odd about the house. If there were any unexplained disturbances. He told Ben he only lived there for five years before he went away to university, but he couldn't remember anything weird happening. He thought the house had been vacant for a few years before they moved in and remembered his parents fell in love with it because it had been newly painted and new pine floors had been installed in the attic. In fact he thought the attic had been remodelled. As far as he knew, his parents never complained about the house. Then he paused.

"Mr. Bergman?"

"Uh...I was just remembering some wild dreams I had when I lived there."

"Like what?"

Bergman chuckled. "Nothing. Just teenage fantasies. I shouldn't even try to remember. My heart's not that good. If you need anything else, let me know. Good luck with your search."

Ben wanted to ask about his dreams. Were they sexy? Dripping with colour? Filled with monsters freaking out as if they were drowning under an iceberg? He knew he'd sound crazy if he called Bergman again, so he didn't.

His coffee was cold. He got a refill and left wondering how a house could lose sixteen years of its life as if it had vanished and no one had noticed.

4

Before going in, Vienna stopped to appreciate Ben's home – its ornate trim, varied roof lines, gabled windows and surrounding gardens. She wondered if she were being watched. Felt she was. She didn't doubt Ben's story and didn't believe in textbook explanations. She had reasons.

She had had an encounter as a child that was as vivid now as it had been when she was eight. No one had challenged it or disputed it, and her mom never accepted the fact that Vienna had been the chosen target in the encounter instead of herself. There had been a tragedy. Vienna's baby brother died from SIDS. The night after they collected his tiny corpse, Vienna climbed into his crib and curled up under his yellow and green quilt.

At dawn when the first dove cooed, Vienna awoke and felt his breath on her cheek and his heavy, soggy diaper against her stomach. The smells of powdered and stained skin made her forget her loss. He stayed with her for several minutes. Her eyes widened as his warm breath and wet bottom drifted away from her and upward and out the window. And the rattle he was holding dropped into the crib. *Come back, she called. Stay! Don't leave me! You can stay with me!* She shook the rattle to entice him back.

Her mom found her kneeling in the crib, her arms reaching towards the window. When she held Vienna against her, her shirt blotted the urine from Vienna's PJs. She begged her mom to listen and said she hadn't wet herself – her bottom was dry.

Her mom thought she was hysterical with grief and tried to console her, but Vienna adamantly retold the story - that it was Bobby's wet diaper that soaked her pyjamas when he curled into her. That he had come back. Her mother stroked her hair and said she had been dreaming. But she staggered back when she caught sight of the rattle that lay in the folds of the quilt – the rattle she had put in the body bag to comfort her baby.

After that her mom became reverent around her, treated her like a marble icon in the apse of a church, and the space between and around them remained almost monastic as Vienna grew up. In her mom's eyes, Vienna was an angelic conduit for Bobby's return. Throughout her childhood and adolescence Ms. Navarre lost sight of her daughter in the flesh.

Annie was eager to give Vienna the tour of the first and second floors then returned their guest to the family room where Annie played the new song she was working on. Even though she admitted it wasn't original, she beamed at its new arrangement and the praise that followed.

Vienna produced a book for Annie, *Bless the Beasts and the Children* and promised they could read it together at lunch time, and that Annie could invite a few friends into her class room for a small reading group. After Vienna talked about the theme of victory in the book, Annie wanted to start it before she did her homework and promised she would only read for an hour, then do school stuff.

Ben said they'd be in the studio if she needed anything and led the way to the third story, noting how the temperature was dropping even on the staircase. Vienna took his hand for moral support.

She looked from the south to the north end and shivered. "It is a lot colder up here."

"I've had the rads checked. There's no reason they shouldn't be giving heat. Hot downstairs - cold up here. I've had three companies check it out."

She walked into the space. "So this is it. Ben Needham's circus of paranormal, life-defying acts. It's way too Bradbury for me."

"Yeah, *Something Wicked This Way Comes*. That's a hard one to forget. Oh, I left Annie's art work downstairs. I'll be right back."

She wanted to reach out to stop him, but muscled up some courage instead. Seeing Ben's work on his easel, she walked to the middle of the room and stopped. Suddenly she felt immobile as if something were restraining her. She tried to move forward but was weighted to the perimeter around the easel. She tried to call out, but couldn't. When Ben returned she was released. Forty-five seconds of stasis. Unbearable paralysis.

She held her breath. Lost for words. Thought if she breathed, something would get inside of her.

Ben looked at her marblesque form. "Are you okay?"

Words came fast. "I wanted to see your work on the easel, so I started walking toward it, but something stopped me. I couldn't move. I couldn't talk. I felt welded to the floor."

"Welcome to my world." He wasn't good at this – not knowing whether she needed to be held. If it were Annie, he'd cradle her. Rock her back and forth. She was visibly shaken.

"What has that kind of power?"

"But you're okay?"

She nodded.

"I told you there was something going on."

"I know you did, and I believed you, but I didn't know it was this strong. Are we intruders or guests? What are we? Should we stay?"

"Do you want to go? I don't blame you if you leave now, but I really need you here to witness what I'm going through. Would you be able to do that? Just for a few minutes?"

She glanced sideways at the space around them. "What if it doesn't want me to stay?"

"I think that if I've invited you here, then you're supposed to be here. I don't know why." Ben understood how hard it was for her to relax. "You're sure you're okay?"

She shrugged. "I can't stop shaking."

"I can see that. I won't leave you again. I'll protect you. Damn, that was cheesy." They both laughed. "Are you going to stay?"

"Yeah, but I've never felt so helpless. I was literally anchored by something, like I had a mile of plastic wrap around me. Mummified by Gladwrap." They laughed again.

"I don't think we're helpless. It wants me to find out something. It's trying to build some trust."

"You think?"

"I'm going to let this thing take me where it wants to. And show me what I have to know. It's never hurt me. I'm beginning to trust it more."

"Any idea what it wants to show you?"

"No." He took her hand. "Come on." He led her to the sofa and gave her Annie's art work to hold, then went to the cubby and removed the old tin toffee box.

She examined the picture of the woman in the bathing suit. "Unreal. I wonder who she is and why Annie painted her."

"Annie has never seen the box. I won't show it to her. She'd freak out."

She opened it and saw the mirror fragments. "You said when you looked into this you saw something behind you?"

"Yeah. Between the easel and the table. A flash of light." They were silent. "Are you feeling gutsy?"

"Why?"

"Do you want to try something?"

"What?"

"If I walk you to the center of the studio and I come

back here and look into the mirror, will you do it? I won't leave you. I'll be here."

Vienna thought about the paralysis a few minutes ago. "I....can't."

"I'll be right here. Trust me."

She took a deep breath and let him escort her to the middle of the room, beyond the easel. Backing away slowly he turned from her at the far end and held up the mirror. She stood straight and smiled reassuringly at him. Then she felt light. Buoyant. Wet warmth rose around her body as if kneading her muscles and licking her skin. Her body relaxed. A spicy fragrance made its way into her lungs. Then she kneeled as if submerging herself in a warm lake. Cupping her hands she splashed her face with the imaginary water as Ben watched and wanted to join her.

Suddenly she lurched forward. Her arm dangled over an invisible barrier. She couldn't call out. Water splashed around her. Her mouth twisted open. A silent scream like a rogue squall undulated through the space. She reached toward Ben. Her arms dripped red. She reached. He dropped the mirror and bolted toward her, but couldn't step beyond the circle.

In horror he watched a shadow loom behind her – its arm striking down at her. Ben tried to break through - his fingertips touching an invisible wall a millimetre from Vienna's hand.

Suddenly the shadow spiralled upward and hovered above them. The wall broke and Ben enfolded Vienna in his arms. The water disappeared. And colours erased themselves. She remained silent, angry, abused.

Helping her up he released her. There were no stains on his clothes, but his hands that had pressed into her back dripped red.

She started crying and hung on to him. "My back!"

Consoling her he carried her to the bed and covered her. She pulled him beside her and held on to him. Through her sobs she asked what he had seen.

"A shadow, not much higher than you, stood behind you and over you. It looked like its arm was striking down into you. Fast. Powerful."

"You need to get help. You can't do this alone. Something attacked me! My back feels shredded. How do you explain what just went on? I want to know what happened in this house, but I don't know anything about this stuff. What do you think is going on?"

"Whatever it is, it needs me. I don't know why."

She tried to sit up, but flinched. "Maybe time's a factor. What if it's running out of time? You were right to be afraid for Annie."

Gently he turned her over. Her blouse was shredded. He rolled it up. "Let's have a look." There were no cuts or scratches or blood. "Nothing." His tender hand rubbed the invisible wounds. He bent close and kissed the soft skin as if healing one of Annie's scratched knees. "All better?" He pulled down her blouse and helped her sit up.

"Am I supposed to feel better? You're kidding, right? It's like a turkey buzzard was feasting on my latissimus dorsi."

"Latissimus what?"

"Art students do anatomy. You must have too." She tried to move the muscles in her back. "Yeah, it does feel better – you must have been a masseuse in a former life. Have you had a lot of practice in healing women's body parts?"

"I haven't rubbed a woman's back since 2005. And that was on the street car. A woman was going into labour and wanted me to rub her lower back. I haven't done any other body parts since 2006. I gave up trying to find anything worth rubbing or rubbing up against. Want me to do it again?"

"Maybe later," she whispered. "Did I just say, Maybe later?" And tried to smile as she stood up. She walked around the room, touching the walls, sliding her feet carefully along the floors, looking up at the sky through the skylights, then stopping at the easel and staring at the pale canvas that needed some historical detail.

Ben joined her. "You're still shaking."

"Really? I'm sorry. I can't help being sarcastic. I'm sorry. So, what's next?"

"More questions for the right people - professionals. I need some answers. Annie's safety comes first. Does that sound right?"

"Can we go downstairs now? I don't want to stay here."

Downstairs they lit candles on the kitchen table, drank wine and smiled at each other in the flickering vanilla light.

A new list was made. A plan was established to excavate the house's secrets and keep all parties safe in the process.

He called a taxi for her and while they waited they could tell each was feeling the same level of comfort in each other's plans.

5

Vienna was an early riser. At 4:30 she went on line to read news, art news, check her website, browse dog breeds (she was always a dog collar away from buying one). She knew she was too preoccupied to raise a pet and serve it unconditionally like Ben did da Vinci. But she still looked. Was partial to Boxers.

She never made early morning phone calls, but welcomed Ben's voice even though she didn't expect him to call. He was braver on the phone and told her how he liked having her around, especially when he was threatened by ectoplasmic clouds, and that if Annie knew her, like he knew her, she'd say she was a Bond girl. Vienna didn't know if that meant she was a Moneypenny or a Vesper Lynd type, but a combo of the two would be good.

She liked talking with Ben and felt they had awakened together, walked the
dog together, watched Annie wake up together. Needing to be propped up and held down at the same time was something she could get used to. She did know this could happen so fast.

At the age of eight, Vienna's mother all but canonized her – Saint Vienna. No child should have to bear the mark of the pious through her childhood. Whenever Vienna saw her mom, it was always on the verge of some revelation, as if Bobby's manifestation would be riding piggy back on her or hovering slightly above her.

Vienna was convinced by the time of puberty through subtle hints, that her mom never expected her to have sex or to marry, that her womb and birthing canal had to remain pure and uninvaded in case of an immaculate conception or reincarnation. But she desperately needed to feel human. So she let guys invade, fill the less-than-saintly space between her legs, between the imagined angel wings.

She let them grab her halo and throw it like a Frisbee into outer space. By her sophomore year she was tired of invasions, tired of being that human and decided to get turned on by the great masters, let their brush strokes and colours, and aesthetic sanctity touch her creative eros.

She never saw Bobby again.

Her mother thought she had betrayed them. She lived with this betrayal until Annie and Ben arrived in her life, and she thought she might have a second chance to get it right.

She wished she had encouraged an invasion. That space needed him. Ached for him.

On the phone they went over the agenda for the day and after lingering through small talk they said good-bye, as if in they had just kissed in the family car, before work.

* * * *

Vienna was eager to talk with her friend, Greg Miller, a serologist at a research company in Ottawa. She called him in between classes and explained the situation – that she had a mirror fragment with what could be blood on it from a violent crime. She had taken precautions to keep it uncontaminated; he agreed to analyse it.

At lunch she ate on the run, Fed-Exed the sample to Greg and got back to school in time for Annie's reading group. She started with a quote for discussion: *A living buffalo mocks us. It has no place or purpose. It is a misbegotten child, a monster with which we cannot live and which we cannot live without.* Annie thought all kids were like this, once, in their lives.

* * * *

Ben went to both the library and the police station to research violent deaths in Toronto's west end before 1962. He researched murders, accidental deaths, cold cases, missing persons and cases of family trauma. No one had died in his house except for an old priest who passed in

1925 from natural causes and there were no cases on file of family disputes. Ben was both relieved and perplexed.

Returning to the Art Gallery of Ontario, he wanted to have a second look at the Holiday portrait. He thought there was a definite masking of the artist's signature. Ben asked a security officer if he could speak with a supervisor. When an assistant curator joined him, Ben told her he was doing a book on Holiday and wanted to know the artist's identity. He asked if she could disclose who loaned the work for the show.

The curator got the list of donors from the program and drew Ben's attention to the Westing Collection and that it was on loan from Ms. Beverly Westing. When Ben asked if the collection belonged to the construction mogul, Bill Westing and his wife, the curator added that their art collection was insured for a hundred million.

Ben thanked her and found a quiet bench to Google the Westings. He sent an email to Ms. Westing's Art Foundation about the copyright of the Holiday portrait. Seconds later he got an automatic reply that thanked him for his inquiry. He decided to call Mr. Westing's company and leave a message for Bill to pass along to his wife. He didn't expect to hear from him, but a secretary called Ben's cell to set up an appointment. Ms. Westing would see him at Harbourfront Art Foundation at 2:00. It gave him enough time to go home and transfer Annie's music to a memory stick and decide what to tell Ms. Westing and what not to.

* * * *

Her office overlooked the lake that was muted and choppy in the pre-winter weather. There was a tray on her desk with bottled water and a dish with wrapped mints. She was a short, Tomboyish woman with bouncy brown hair and alabaster skin whose feet remained on top of her desk as she motioned casually for Ben to sit down. She stretched her hand out beyond her legs for him to take. Then clasping both hands behind her neck she arched away from her desk to stretch cramped muscles.

As Ben sat down he decided this mid-fifties socialite looked like she had come from Boheme and not from Lampton Baby Point in Toronto's west end. He had read that Bill Westing had recently completed renovations on an estate he had purchased in Baby Point for two million. The renovations included an indoor/outdoor pool with an adjacent bird sanctuary that extended to the banks of the Humber River. That the lighting system alone cost half a million. But this silky, loose-shirted art collector looked more like a visiting artist than the co-owner of the Westing estate.

After she buzzed her secretary and asked her to take her calls for her, she turned Ben's attention to the bottled water and mints. "They're Swiss. My one small indulgence. There's nothing here like them." When he hesitated, she unwrapped one and insisted. Laugh lines formed gently around her full mouth and eyes as she watched Ben experience the simple pleasure. And then handed him more for later.

"Where did you say you got them?"

"I'll have Joan give you the address – a small family business – in case you get to Switzerland. They're not an export. The family sends a special order for me from time to time."

She swung her legs off her desk, stood up and sat in a chair beside Ben in front of her desk. "I know your books. I took my great nephew to Indigo at the Eaton's Centre to buy one of your novels last year for his birthday. *The Ancient Astronaut*".

"Did he like it?"

"Can't stop talking about it. And wants to become a graphic novelist, even though my nephew - his dad and his granddad disapprove."

"He could do it as a hobby and see where it takes him."

"He's a smart kid. I'm sure he'll learn to compromise. Anyway, you have questions about the Billy Holiday portrait."

"Yes. I want to know the identity of the artist who painted it."

"We don't know who it is."

"I think the artist's name has been painted over. Bottom right hand corner. I was wondering if someone could look at it."

"It belonged to my mother. We don't know how she got it. Whether she bought it or whether it was a gift. But my older brother found it in an Ingles' warehouse and gave it to me for my fiftieth birthday. My mother was married to Harold Ingles."

Ben knew the Ingles family was a cornerstone in Canadian history, but didn't know much about them. "Ms. Westing...."

"Call me Bev."

"This is going to sound pretty crazy."

"You have no idea the inbound crazy and the stored crazy I have in me." A hint of pink surfaced in her unusually pale face. "I could write a book on crazy in two or three different languages."

Ben liked her attitude. He wasn't expecting to sit next to a moneyed icon like Beverly Westing and feel relaxed. "Okay, here goes. I live in a house that I think is haunted. My gifted daughter, Annie, rearranged a song she said she heard Billy Holiday sing on my sound system in my third floor studio. The song is Harlem Nocturne." He handed her the memory stick. "I brought it in for you to listen to – if you have time."

"I can do that. A haunted house - this is intriguing." Bev docked it and listened. "How old is Annie?"

"Ten."

"Really. This is good. If this is her own arrangement then she's very talented. But you've lost me. What is the connection between the song and the portrait?"

"Billie Holiday never recorded Harlem Nocturne and my sound system was never unpacked. She couldn't have heard her singing it. Then I went to the AGO with Annie's art class and saw the portrait the same week-end she started playing the song. I don't think it's a coincidence."

Bev could feel tiny response bumps form from her shoulders to her wrists. "And you think knowing who painted the portrait will help you to do what?"

"I don't know, but I think there's a strong connection between the two events and maybe other things going on in my house."

"We work with a reputable restoration specialist. I'll have him look at the portrait."

"I'll pick up any costs."

She shook her head and wanted to know more about his experiences. "Your house....how do you know it's haunted?"

"It's hard to talk about it. I really don't know what's going on. Things started to happen about a month ago. I began to investigate its ownership history, but I haven't talked with any professionals."

"You think Billie Holiday has something to do with it?"

"I don't know. Maybe the artist." He became silent. Felt uncomfortable.

"You don't have to talk about it, Ben."

"It's really hard to explain without sounding over the top. I feel so..." He stopped.

"I'll make some phone calls. I'll have to speak with my husband. But I'll call you."

Ben gave her his card. "If you can't do this, I'll understand. It's not easy to alter an artwork. You lose part of its history."

"And possibly gain some."

Ben stood and shook her hand. "Thanks for seeing me."

"What if I told you I'm interested in this house. What's happening in it. I've always believed in this paranormal business. My mother died when I was three and I always believed she watched over me and that one day I'd see her again. Find her in some way. It hasn't happened yet, but from time to time I feel her near – probably because I surround myself with so many of her things. I'm fascinated with what you're experiencing. Maybe at a later time you'll feel more comfortable talking to me about it. I want you to know that I'll listen."

"You want me to keep you updated?"

"Would you? I've never met a literally haunted human being."

He paused to look at her. "I want you to know I'm not crazy. What's happening is not normal, but there's got to be an explanation. I have to find out what it is."

She smiled and reminded him he had chocolate mints in his pocket and gave Joan his card to file on line. Then she called Louis Gabriel, the restoration specialist and arranged to meet at the AGO when she was finished.

* * * *

Ben left with a feeling of assurance that Bev Westing genuinely would help him. When he arrived home, the house was quiet except for da Vinci barking softly – a playful bark – on the landing outside of the studio. Like he barked when Ben and Wendy were having sex and da Vinci thought they were rough-housing over a dog bone.

While Ben's fingers nuzzled da Vinci's ears, he asked the dog what was going on. The barking subsided into whimpers as he begged to be let into the studio. Ben didn't know if he felt more or less secure with da Vinci by his side. He opened the door which he was certain he hadn't closed before he left.

"What do you hear, boy?"

The dog ran to the bed at the far end and knowing better than to jump on it, he crouched in puppy play stance and resumed barking softly. When Ben joined him he saw that his pillows were knocked about and that lipstick stains were on one of them.

Suddenly the dog trotted to Ben's easel and jumped up and down as if following an unseen hand holding a jelly bean for him. Then at the easel he sat and panted and looked up at the canvas that Ben had started when they moved in. The dog shifted his focus back and forth between the canvas and the area beyond it where the water had formed. Back and forth as if listening to a conversation.

"Do you see me?" Ben shouted from his bed where he had reclined and smelled the bed sheets for jasmine and lavender and white pepper. Buried in the threads, the fragrance held him, and Harlem Nocturne, like the last gentle drops of a warm rainstorm, fell on his ears. He stopped being afraid. Ben refused to alienate himself from this house's history. He wanted to be part of it.

He walked toward da Vinci and watched his ears straighten and relax as he listened. "Can you see me?" He waited. "I don't know who you are, but I'm trying to find out."

Delicate lines like faint water-coloured brush strokes formed in the foreground across his canvas on top of his own composition. Ben examined them. *Eyes. Nose. Lips. Contours of a woman's cheek and neckline,* he thought.

da Vinci stared as if struck by a live wire then bolted away. Fell shrieking by the door.

"What's wrong, boy? Come, da Vinci. Here boy."

The dog refused to come and a current of raw cold air dug into Ben's chest. Breathless but not afraid he backed away. A red stain ran down his canvas and on to the floor. Ben slammed the door behind him, but when he and da Vinci started down the stairway, the door creaked open. The dog turned to look and whimpered helplessly.

'*Fuck*' came with new tones and pitches until Ben was worn out. *I am not afraid. I am not afraid. I'm fucking mad!* Opening a drawer he looked at a box of matches and wondered if all this would disappear if he burned down the third floor. Just the studio. Of course he'd remove his equipment, make sure he'd have extinguishers ready and would put da Vinci in the garage. Or hire a contractor to demolish the attic. He had the money. Tear it down. Re-roof the second floor. A flat roof.

da Vinci barked at him. "You don't like my renovation plans?" The dog growled. Ben reached out to pat him. Gums and bare teeth warned him not to. *What the hell! All right! I get it!* He screamed at the ceiling above them. *I get it!* And to da Vinci. "It's okay, boy."

The studio door slammed shut and the phone rang.

Ben didn't answer at first, then picked up. "Hello.....yes....yes, I did call on the week-end. Who are you again? You're a nephew – a great nephew of the Smithsons who owned the house until 1946? I was phoning to find out who bought my house from your great uncle in 1946. Uh-huh.....yeah.....you think you'll be able to find out? It's really important to me. I'm doing its genealogy. I really need confirmation on its ownership.....uh... huh... if you find anything please feel free to call me anytime."

Ben was happy that Bryan Smithson thought that the much needed documents were filed somewhere – his parents kept every legal paper that had passed from great grandparents to great uncles to great grandchildren, but he needed a few days to find out if they still existed. Even though time was not running out, Ben knew the house was running into bad times. Times that were muddied. Times that fooled the senses into believing you could do something to get clear of it. Ben was the first to admit he had the imagination to get his characters out of the mud in their software world of workable solutions, but was not able to get clear himself. He needed help.

Before picking up Annie, he decided to check out the Canadian Parapsychological Institute of Research on Queen West. The building had been a small wallpaper company until the seventies when private interests partnered with the University of Toronto and purchased it. Along with offering undergraduate psychology and transpersonal psychology courses, the Institute recruited test subjects, did field testing, visitations, counselling, and lectures.

A receptionist welcomed Ben and after directing him to fill out a questionnaire she excused herself with his paper work and returned later with an appointment slip for 10:00 the next morning with Dr. Evan Fife. Ben commented that he guessed it wasn't the busiest place – try getting a next-day appointment with your dentist or vet for that matter. She smiled again and told him that Dr. Fife had a cancellation.

Briefly she explained that he would be asked to fill out a medical history and consent form before his consultation and testing and she invited him to visit their library on the second floor before he left. Ben thanked her and took some time to check out the library and a few other study and meeting areas to the rear of the building that enclosed an indoor courtyard where he noticed people were meditating. On his way out he thanked her again and said he was looking forward to meeting Dr. Fife.

* * * *

The two artists were standing together on the leaf-lit school walkway when Ben pulled up. The crisp air stung his nostrils, and Vienna had draped a shawl around Annie's jacket. It was a favourite shawl with a replica of Degas' *Dancers in Pink* screen-printed in its threads. Purchased at the Louvre. When she asked Annie if she'd like to keep it, Annie beamed and rearranged it theatrically around her shivering form.

They drove to Bloor West Village to a small Hungarian restaurant and let soup and good bread and better wine work their magic and one piece of cake that they shared. Ben watched the two artists, listened to their questions, answers and maybes and wondered how Vienna could climb inside them, understand their needs, agree to stay close after everything that had happened. He didn't have a lot of practice. Thought of women as arm chair or computer chair or lawn chair authorities on the standard success grid. Wendy was this ultimate chair-authorized historian, lover, mother.

He asked himself how Vienna learned the art of attachment. The art of tenure from inside a structure. Inside Annie. Inside him. He felt her there, weaving comfort algorithma through his troubles.

They watched Annie take her index finger and run it through the cake crumbs a few times before they dragged her away. Even though it was getting dark, they walked a bit in the park, huddled together like a moving Sumac on fire in the sunset.

* * * *

There was always that moment before unlocking the front door that Ben hesitated, looked up at the third story then went inside. Vienna rubbed his back knowing exactly how he felt. After Bobby's death, there was also a spiritual invasion – not like Ben's – that was always present in her house. An invasion that robbed her of her childhood and made an unwanted power the mastermind of her moral fibre through maturity.

There was no time for arm chairs or computer chairs or lawn chairs in Vienna's life. She plunged body and soul into the heart of canvasses, clay, kilns, city streets, beds (with and without sheets). What was different between Vienna and Wendy was that Vienna learned to enter when she didn't want to. To enter even though learning something prophetic would take its toll. Wendy had always retreated against poor odds.

Vienna understood Ben's turmoil. Every day as a child when Vienna got home from school she'd look up at Bobby's room, hesitate, then enter her home. She rubbed Ben's back and locked her arm through his.

While Ben and Vienna exchanged knowing glances of how the rest of the night was going to play out, Annie filled the family room with piano favourites. There was no homework, so she whipped her fingers into a musical frenzy until the moment of recognition that if she didn't stop, Ben would have to carry her upstairs and that disgusted her. She kissed her dad good night and thanked Vienna for the shawl, enwrapping herself with it as she danced out of the room and upstairs still humming.

They sat in silence. Ben knew that Annie would be enwombed in sleep's darkest cradle. He waited. Then patted the sofa. "It's a pull-out."

"Good. I didn't want to go to the studio tonight."

"Really?" he teased. "I'm definitely not up to any sudden anomalies tonight either. I kind of need normal - whatever that feels like. I've forgotten what that feels like. Are you normal?"

"Not too, but I can give you normal with a twist of the unexpected." And she moved closer to him. Moving her hand under his shirt she rubbed his chest and stomach. Laughed. "How abnormal do you want me to be?" His stomach made some noise. "You're rumbling."

"It was all that garlic, and wine and cake. I'm trying not to burp."

She kept rubbing. "Feel better?"

"My stomach's not objecting."

She noticed her hands still had paint and plaster on them even though she washed up at school. "Look at these." She held them up. "I need a shower. I'm filthy."

"I hope so. I need filthy."

"Filthy rich or filthy-minded?"

"The last one sounds good."

"Come on. Say it."

"Say what?"

"What you want."

"I need some – this is hard for me – I need some filthy-minded sex, but I don't really know what that is."

"That surprises me because you're crotch-wrenching gorgeous. "You're going to tell me that women haven't hurled themselves like javelins through your heart?"

"I haven't noticed. I've always been too preoccupied."

"Not even your wife?" She frowned. "Hey, you don't have to answer that. I'm sorry."

"Wendy was like a javelin. Liked to skewer my heart and eat it raw."

"I'm not interested in eating your heart, Ben." And moved against him. "Want to take a shower? We need this, don't we?"

They moved quietly to the upstairs guest en suite. They weren't like kids in a shower at camp. Or teens in the rain on a blanket beside their van. They were two hungry lovers who seemed to float into the delicious warmth of steam where they could barely see each other. Ben let her introduce him to sexual novelty like sex scenes in movies where he often wondered how much was real and how much was staged. But this was real. He took hold and forgave himself for making a vow never to love again.

Never to let the inside of a woman destroy him like it did Jamie.

As they left the steam and went naked to bed, he wondered if it was never Wendy. If he was the cold-eyed shark-like bastard never stopping for love. Then he corrected his momentary loss of sanity. No, it was always Wendy. And in spite of his vow, he had wanted that crazy love that kids had – their manic lips and hands and groins. He had looked for it, but never found it until now. Until one woman offered to help him.

* * * *

Even though Annie's bladder sat heavy like a water balloon, she made her way to the piano instead of the bathroom for a morning wake-me-up. She found the cold keys in the morning darkness and played and squirmed until the dam was about to burst.

Her hurried footsteps to the powder room got Ben up. "Annie?" He looked out of the guest bedroom and saw light coming from the downstairs hallway. "Annie?" He went down and found her fallen shawl by the piano bench. "Annie, why are you up so early?"

He had picked up the shawl when she joined him by the piano. "I couldn't sleep anymore. I kept having this dream about a doll and an elephant and lots of sun and flowers – I think they were roses. And I was riding the elephant with the doll in my arms. It woke me up. And I wanted to play."

"You never have dreams."

"So weird." And she found the soothing keys.

He was curious about the upstairs bathroom. He let the fallen, damp towels remain scattered on the floor. He searched for more evidence of their love-making. Saw the Prayer Plant knocked over and stood it upright apologetically. Found spiced apple and orange chips from the potpourri bowl strewn all over the countertop and in the toilet. Found the condoms. Two. *We did it only twice? I can't even remember putting them on.* Saw a tissue by the sink with *thank U* written on it in lipstick that he put in the vanity drawer.

He went up to the studio that was unusually was warm for a change. Noiseless. The scent of spice from the apple and orange shavings permeated the space. He sat in the middle of the studio and looked around and spoke. *Was that what you had with someone? Did you see us?* He paused to think about his appointment. *I'm seeing someone today who I think can help us. I have to know who you are. Why you're here.* He rose. *Don't give up on me. I'm just starting. I'll be back later. We'll paint together.* He broke away from the warmth and the fragrance and joined Annie who fired a barrage of questions about Vienna.

Did she hold his hand? Did she kiss him? Did she remind him of Wendy? Did she... did she? And before they parted for the day, Annie asked if Vienna could meet Wendy and if the three of them could spend a Saturday morning together. Annie always did try to fit together the seemingly unorthodox with orthodox pieces of puzzles. Ben wished he had that quality. To know that two opposites could reach an attractive agreement.

6

The Institute was quiet, unpeopled but inviting. The receptionist smiled warmly as Ben approached and told him what to fill out on the clipboard she provided and added she'd offer him a coffee, but he wasn't supposed to drink or smoke before the session. When the paperwork was completed, she led him into a small office with two larger, adjacent rooms.

Minutes after, Dr. Fife joined him with a firm handshake and a request to move to two comfortable chairs facing each other. Ben thought the doctor looked distinct – a tuft of carrot, wavy hair perched on top of his head, but when he talked, Ben thought he would need sub titles to translate Fife's staunch Scottish accent.

"Ben, call me Evan. This isn't Buckingham Palace. No titles here. No Her Majesty this or the Thane of Fife that."

Ben smiled and found his thumbs were revolving involuntarily around each other.

"And relax," Fife urged. "You're not on the Island of Dr. Moreau."

"My house feels like that. Like it's on some island."

"Yeah, I read your answers to the questionnaire. Some pretty bizarre stuff's going on. Before we get to that, I'll tell you a little bit about my background. I hold a tenured position in Bio Molecular Science at Glasgow Caledonian University and I taught Bio Chemistry in Europe. I share a passion along with many colleagues who are in mainstream science for psychological anomalies. I'm here on a two year sabbatical doing research on Bio Communication, Bio Feedback, and Transpersonal Psychology, all of which involves anomalous psychological testing. I conduct tests, but unlike my colleagues I don't go into the field. I've scheduled you for two hours of tests that I will go over with you in detail."

"They won't prove I'm crazy, will they?"

Fife laughed. "No. But first, tell me about these activities you're experiencing."

Ben relived the last month and didn't spare any details. Included the attack on Vienna, Annie's music, the portrait of Holiday and Beverly Westing's help, the gazebo, the snow without a snow storm, the mirror fragments. Everything.

What impressed Fife was the clarity in Ben's details. The clarity and lack of contradiction when Fife asked Ben to go over certain details. Here was a well-adjusted, contributing man with great creative skills and obvious exemplary parenting skills. A man comfortable with himself in spite of the anomalies that chose to visit Ben and not the previous owners for whatever reasons.

"Okay. It's not often I'm left almost speechless, but I'm finding it difficult to verbalize what I'm feeling about what you're going through."

"I'm relieved talking about it. I know it sounds incredulous, but Vienna has experienced it first hand as well."

Fife produced three sheets of paper and handed them to Ben. "We're going to do three tests. I'll discuss each one separately. If you look at page one, you'll see that the first test is a modified Ganzfeld ESP test aimed to test any telepathic abilities you have. You will be what we call the agent or the sender and you will try to send the images you see from the video you will watch to a receiver or target in another room. After three minutes the video will stop and the target will be shown a series of images, picking out the ones she saw most frequently, as well as making any notes she feels are necessary. When the tests are done, we'll review the results. Are you ready?"

"Let's do it."

Fife escorted Ben into a small, colourless room and sat him in front of a monitor. "When the video starts try to make strong mental images to send to the target. Like intense wishing. When the video stops, wipe the images out of your mind like a camera wipe. Just relax. Have fun."

Fife patted him on the shoulder on his way out and joined the target in an adjacent room to prepare the receiver for a mild sensory deprivation control. Fife placed two white eye cones that looked like halved ping pong balls over the target's eyes and shone a red light on to the target's face. After fitting ear muffs in place Fife instructed the target that the session would begin in one minute.

In the sender's room the video started. Ben focused on images of playful cats in a pet shop window. Cats in a jungle. Mice eating cheese. Monkeys at a zoo. There was distortion and flashes he could barely perceive through the audio/visual fuzz. Screams. Growling. Crying. A gun shot. A woman dying. Numbers. Blood. He was becoming uncomfortable and exhausted as he tried to transfer the images to the target. After three minutes the video stopped and Ben wiped his mind clear of what he had seen, but the distorted flashes persisted.

Fife rejoined the target who had taken off the eye shields, but was still making notes, drawings and names.

"You can stop now, Brenda. Our agent has stopped. Brenda?" Fife turned off the red light. Brenda continued as if she were unaware of his presence. Fife gently held her hand and removed the pencil. "Brenda?"

She turned to look at him. "I didn't hear you come in. Wow! That was something else! I wasn't expecting that."

And he looked at tears forming in her eyes. "Are you okay?"

"Yeah, I'll be fine."

Before looking at her notes he held up cards with random images, not all of which were presented on the video and asked her to identify the images she most frequently saw. She didn't receive any images of giraffes, snakes or birds. She did receive strong images of cats, monkeys and mice.

"But there were even stronger images – more like a story."

"A story?"

"Yeah, look at my notes and sketches."

She wrote about a large, wild cat-like beast slinking into a farmyard where a young, red-haired boy was playing with a water gun. There was a barking dog. Then she did a sketch of the cat attacking the boy and sinking his teeth into the boy's ankle. Then more words about the cat dragging the boy off into the woods. Next, the dog attacked the beast and killed it. And names like McDuff and Heather. And a description of how the mother got a gun and shot the dog who was dying from his wounds.

"Fuck me!" Fife was stunned.

"What did you say?"

"Uh...no. I didn't mean....no!" And grabbed her papers, running breathlessly out of the testing room.

She called after him. "Don't forget to look at the final drawing, Dr. Fife."

He called back, "I will. You're free to go. Thanks."

Taking a deep breath Fife joined Ben and pulling up a chair he stared into Ben's eyes.

Ben shifted uncomfortably.

"Am I crazy?"

"Before I show you the notes our target made, I want to know what you saw and imagined."

"Well, I saw cats playing and other animals, but especially cats. I closed my eyes – I didn't know if I was supposed to – for only a few seconds and really focused on them and tried to send them. Did the target get my images?"

"You didn't imagine anything else like a story?"

"No. I don't think so, but there were two or three sudden flashes on the screen like acute camera flashbacks of a lion-type cat and a kid – I couldn't see it and a wolf-like thing. Quick images. A blur almost. Oh and a name kept revolving in my mind. A familiar name. McDuff. That's it. McDuff, like in Macbeth."

"Before we get to that I want to show you the results of the testing and our target's notes." Fife went over how she had received ninety percent of the images he had sent and none of the images which hadn't been part of the video. Then he showed Ben the target's notes and sketches and asked Ben if they could have accurately described the flashes Ben saw on the video.

"Maybe. They're a lot more detailed. What does that mean? How could she provide detail if I wasn't sending it? I mean if she wrote down what I was sending – maybe on a subconscious level, then they would have to connect. But I can't say I focused on them. Can that happen? Seeing something for a micro-second and being able to transfer more of it to a target? Does that normally happen?" He shifted uneasily.

"Not usually."

"There was one last image that appeared in my mind. I don't know if I sent it or not."

"Of what?"

"A hooded figure that appeared in one of my novel frames that I didn't create."

"Was it on the video?"

"How could it be?"

"Let's look at the video."

And there it was. The original images, the flashes of blurred images and the hooded figure. Fife stared in disbelief and turned to the final drawing. "Is this what the figure looks like in your novel frame?"

"Yup."

Fife bit his lower lip trying to reach a decision as to how to proceed with Ben. "Okay, here's the thing. I want to talk to you about the target's notes, but I need to do one or two more tests and I don't want to prejudice you or disrupt your concentration in any way."

"I don't think that anything you say can distract me more than I've been for over a month. So give it to me straight. Now. Before we do the second test."

"I don't friggin' believe it myself, but the flashes you saw or imagined and the notes our receiver made were about me. I was attacked by a mountain lion when I was five on our farm. Our dog, McDuff killed it and my mom had to put the dog down." Fife rolled up his pant leg and showed Ben the scars. "Obviously these images were not originally on the video."

Ben shrugged. "I'm not the slightest bit surprised. No doubt you are. But for me, this is my life right now and I need help to deal with it. I don't want to jump ship. I just want to solve this problem and get on with things. But what's more important is my daughter's safety. This thing is powerful beyond my understanding. I want Annie to be as safe as I can make her."

"I've just had fifteen years of research and scholarship knocked around like a pinball in my head. I mean we do simple testing compared with what happened today. Important testing, but this ended up personal. I can't help you, but I know people who can. We'll get to that before you leave. Can we do one more test?"

"Let's go for it."

Fife drew his attention to the second sheet. "It's an MMI test, short for Mind/Matter/Interaction. We're going to test you for psychokinetic ability. We'll stay in this room. I am going to pin prick your finger and take some blood which I'll then put in this test tube with a saline solution, then I'll hook up the tube to a spectrophotometer and computer. This will test the breakdown of red blood cells or hemolysis as the process is called. You as the agent will focus on trying to lower the rate of hemolysis by imagining anything that decelerates. You're going to try to slow it down. You can see the long range benefits of this research."

Ben nodded as he watched droplets of blood drain from his finger into the test tube.

When everything was in place, Fife started the equipment and told Ben to focus on simple images that were decreasing in speed. He focussed on a car stopping. A train slowing in a station. Heartbeats slowing. Not only did the hemolysis show a marked decrease, but everything else slowed down – their heartbeats, their breathing rates, the clocks, their words that collided like turtles break-dancing in slow motion.

For one minute all systems slowed. The two men were caught helplessly in an MMI beyond their control. Then release. Normality.

Heartbeats returned. And breathing. And words bumped about with reckless frequency – *what the hell was that....I don't know....holy shit......I told you......It's not you, Ben...... something else....shit.....am I alive........I thought I was dying.....am I breathing.....shit.... I couldn't find my pulse...are you breathing....you're so fucked up!*

"Man, I couldn't be happier you've seen this, first hand. Do you know how great this makes me feel?"

"Let's go grab a coffee." Fife dragged Ben out of the room and back to the office where a fresh pot of coffee had just stopped gurgling. His hand still trembled as he poured the strong brew into two mugs, then ladled sugar and milk substitute into his and sat down unaware he had left Ben's on the counter.

When Ben got up, Fife remembered his oversight and apologized. "No, it's okay. I'll get it." Both men sat quietly and blew into their mugs.

It took a few minutes for Fife to get a hold on what just happened. Then shook his head. "I can vouch for my colleagues – and we've seen some strange stuff – when I say we have never seen or heard anything like this movie shit. You need to work with people who are not my colleagues but who handle this sort of thing."

"What sort of thing?"

"That's what we have to find out."

"How?"

"I'll contact some people who will set up the initial investigation at your house. There will be a team of four or five who will come with equipment – a lot of equipment – and do some mapping of your house. And other tests. They'll explain everything. Then they'll follow up with a more quiet, more focused investigation based on their findings."

"Ghost hunters?"

"Among other things," he smiled.

"Are you going to be there?"

"No. My expertise ends here. You'll be in good company."

"When is this going to happen?"

"I will really try to get them moving on it, but depending on everyone's availability, it could be anywhere from a couple of days to a couple of weeks."

"I don't think we have much time."

"Expect a call later today. Can they reach you on your cell?"

"Yeah."

Fife's hand shook as he tried to steady his mug.

"Are you okay?" Ben was calm and concerned.

"I don't know what's worse – being dragged away by a lion or being invaded by something I can't see."

"I don't think it wants casualties."

"Christ! Our hearts almost stopped!"

"But they didn't."

When Ben left, Fife grabbed his arm. "It's been a pleasure, I think. Someone will call later. Take it easy."

"You too."

* * * *

Ben went home, went up to the studio and stared at the canvas. He inspected the initial ochre undercoat and the faint lines of a second wash that wasn't his composition or colours or style. He looked around the room and nodded in acceptance that the entity had worked a second wash. *Okay, here I am.* He surrendered his talent. *Here I am. I said we'd paint.* Calmly he stepped into the challenge. *Let's paint.*

There was a warm surge that spread from his head to his chest and into his arms and hands. He was fully aware of the process – choosing the palette, the brushes. Oils and thinners which were not in his art supplies replaced his acrylics and glazes. He could smell the linseed and didn't know if his paint had morphed into oils or whether he thought they had. A heap of rags appeared on his table by the easel.

A commingling of sounds whirled around him on his speakers as he worked: *the sports world is mourning the loss of seven Manchester United soccer players... U.S. Nuclear Submarine, the Nautilus passes under the Ice Cap... crashed in Munich today... the Hula Hoop rage has hit America... I'm going to buy you a Ronson Electric... Arthur Miller is cleared of contempt of court by the Court of Appeals... Alaska becomes the 49th state... wife of Canadian millionaire dies of respiratory illness... Howard... Princess gives birth to son, Albert Alexander... Toronto socialite... Alexsis... seven soccer players... Ronson... Hula... Nautilus... mourning...* Words and names, songs and jingles faded and formed in the audio static. Ben tried to make mental notes of what he could make out while he worked.

Sweat ran from his hairline to his chin even though the room had begun to cool. From time to time he put his brush down and moved back to look at the tones and shapes. As he painted he looked from his canvas to the centre of the studio and back again. As lines and colours moved about the canvas that two artists were painting, a woman's form was taking shape – a young woman in an old claw foot tub. A woman with red hair and alabaster skin.

The brushes became heavy like hammers. He wanted to work longer but couldn't pick up even the smallest one. He tried to rag the tones with his thumb, but his hand hovered in front of the canvas. *You want me to stop? Okay, I'll stop.*

Beyond the easel there were muffled words and laughter. Then two figures rose from the floor, shimmering and androgynous. Enwrapped in a screen of light. As he watched Ben felt weightless as if a centrifugal force were turning him slowly around. Weightless like he was dissolving into the canvas and into her eyes and behind them where he could see Paris, an atelier and people – black and white - smoking, drinking, dancing. And jazz below. Musicians. Applause. And numbers, 4951 riding on the smoky sounds of songs.

Then gently he was lowered and felt the floor beneath his feet again. The figures vanished. The sounds stopped and Ben left feeling he was becoming an important part of a moment in history that had to be remembered. He wondered if it were a gift.

7

Louis Gabriel wanted Beverly Westing to see the results of his testing. Bev agreed to meet him at two in his lab. When she arrived he explained the scaling technique that involved an application of synthetic skin over the concealed signature then photo-lasering the tissue off with the overlay of paint.

Bev put on her glasses to examine the barely discernible signature. "What does it say, Louis?"

He shook his head. "It's unique, but I can't read it. We have options though. There are data banks for every professional artist for each decade dating back to the 1500s. We can photograph the signature and digitally try to match it."

"Okay. Let's start with the 1890s and work through to the sixties. It's really important to me that we identify this artist. Do you think I should fax the signature to galleries carrying extant Master works?"

"Yeah, you might get lucky."

"I'll take a copy of it with me."

"I'll do up to the 30s today, then from the 40s to 60s in the morning. I'm just as eager as you to identify this artist. It's a great portrait. If Holiday actually requested him or her to do it, then that's something."

Bev went home to her office and wrote a cover for her fax and attached the artist's signature. She sent twenty five faxes to dealers in Canada, the UK and the States. By dinner she hadn't heard from anyone.

Bev's husband was going to be late in getting home – something that seldom happened – so she planned a modest meal alone. Alone for an evening in her mansion that she helped redesign and decorate, not just for her and Bill, but also for the absent ones – especially for her mother, Alexsis Ingles (born Alexsis Chisholm). Bev always knew there was as much fantasy as fact in her elaborate fabrication of a perfect childhood even though she was orphaned - at the age of three with her mother dying of a congenital disease and at five with the passing of her father, Howard Ingles from a heart attack. By the age of five Bev had lost three people she loved – her parents and her half-brother, Harvard Ingles who was thirteen years her senior and a freshman at Oxford when his dad died. He left his baby sister immediately after his father's funeral. She couldn't remember him saying good-bye.

Bev's aunt and uncle, Jane and Thomas Ingles officially adopted her. Thomas was Howard's younger brother by fifteen years and he and Jane were only twenty five and just married when Bev came to live with them. They had always loved her from the time she was born and took her with them every opportunity they could to allow Bev a social life she embodied.

Bev was the first to say they were ideal parents in every way possible. They had been there for her through every nightmare, every phobia, every dream, every truth and every fictitious imagining along the way.

Alone for an evening. A novelty. She had surrounded herself with paintings and artefacts and colours she thought her mom would have liked. Paintings with red-haired women because Lexi (the name her close friends used) had red hair. A bronze statue of an elephant made in India graced the entrance from the grand foyer because Lexi Ingles spent her childhood in India where Katherine and Charles Chisholm, Bev's grandparents were partners in an export company. Lexi had had a pet elephant she rode like a pony.

It was in India that Bev's grandmother contracted a rare and serious lung infection from a rose thorn in her cherished garden when she was carrying Lexi. The disease left Lexi with a compromised CNS and a predisposition to anaemia. They returned to England when Lexi was eight to get specialized medical care. From what Bev's adopted parents told her about her mom, there seemed to be nothing that Lexi Chisholm-Ingles was threatened by – not disease, not money, not age, not separations, not love, not beauty.

Bev loved her aunt Jane retelling the story of how Lexi and Bev's dad, Howard met in London. He had been vacationing in England with his son, Harvard who was nine at the time. When they stopped at a milk bar to have a shake in Sloan Square, Howard Ingles caught sight of a poster ad selling Ribena syrup topping. In the ad a young woman with vibrant red hair and a chocolate mustache was eating an ice cream dripping with Ribena syrup. It took Ingles one day to find the model in the ad, ask her to join him and his son for dinner, go with them to the lake district where he proposed to her, shop for a wedding dress in London, walk down the aisle of St. Margaret, Westminster Abbey, and sail to Canada to start a new life as the wife of Canadian millionaire, Howard Ingles.

Lexi turned twenty on the day she landed in Montreal in 1952 and had Beverly in 1955 for three brief years of motherhood. Her congenital anaemia suddenly took her away when she was twenty-six. 1958.

Bev had chosen blue and green tones in her living room – blue like Indian skies and green to complement her mother's red hair. Besides the bronze elephant there were green and blue silk pillowslips from India. Bev felt a constant reunion with her mom in this home. She often had Jane and Thomas Ingles over – another way to stay close to her real parents. Even Jane admitted she felt Lexi was there. And that Bev was taking care of her.

Perhaps that's why Bev never had kids. You have them, then leave them. Fabricating Lexi's existence in Bev's life allowed her to feel connected, and now at the age of fifty five she felt she protected this wondrous young woman of twenty six who was very real to Bev – like a daughter.

Fifty five and prone to tears and introspection. She sat alone. Looking from one artefact to the other and cried. *Mom, I love you. I'll find you.* She didn't know why she said that.

When the phone rang she welcomed her brother's voice – the voice of a man who as a young boy had gotten to know Lexi Chisholm-Ingles as well as anyone and deeply mourned her death. Deeply.

"Harvard?"

"You sound congested, Bee." He had always thought calling her 'Bee' was appropriate because she was just as busy as one.

"Sinuses. The moulds are bad. What's new with you?"

"Mickey and I are planning a visit. Just for a week if that's okay with you?"

"When?"

"Soon. We're taking a flight out on Friday. Be there on Saturday. I know it's short notice."

"I...I can't believe it! Do you want me to call Jason and Mariah?"

"Already did."

"I'm really excited. Do you want our limo to pick you up?"

"No. We made arrangements."

"Is it all right if we plan something here for Saturday night? I know you'll be tired. Family and a few friends? Your old partners in crime?"

"We'd love to see everyone. Make whatever plans you want to. I have to go, Beverly. It's really late here. I'll send an email. Give you more details. I love you, Bee."

"Me too. Give our love to Mickey."

Harvard was always sailing or flying in and out of her life for brief periods of time. Bev took a deep breath and headed for her office to make a to-do-list for Harvard's homecoming: contact the family, friends, the caterer, musicians, cleaning service, the florist. And Ben Needham. She wanted Harvard's grandson to meet this eccentric, intriguing man. This man who had moved into a house, picked up the phone and arrived in her office. When she thought of Ben, something stirred deep in her memory, pressed in her memory like leaves in a scrapbook. Old, flat, but not forgotten.

8

1958. Elvis was drafted. Castro was invading. *Great Balls of Fire* was invading. The Ronson Electric was invented. Thirty million Chinese died in the great famine and Brazil won the World Cup. Beverly Westing's mom, Alexsis Chisholm-Ingles died, leaving a heart-broken, little girl to wander through life looking for her. But this was unknown to Ben.

When Ben was getting ready to meet Annie he was surprised at Bev Westing's call and her invitation to join her on Saturday night to welcome home her brother from Rwanda where he and his wife, Michelle Dupuis (Mickey) were instrumental in social and educational reform. And she insisted on Ben bringing a guest. She went on to explain Louis Gabriel's test procedure and identification process. She hoped they'd find something by Friday afternoon.

He accepted the invitation and phoned Wendy to beg her to take Annie for the week-end – something that only happened once a decade. This would be the second time. The full moon must have influenced her decision because she said she was looking forward to it.

Ben arrived at school early, parked and waited on the walkway. Annie was first out.

With a tone of feigned upset Ben announced he had some news.

Annie jumped in. "Is it da Vinci? Is he okay?"

"Of course he is," Ben added slowly and seriously.

"What's wrong?"

"I don't know. Something, because your mom wants you to herself for the whole week-end. Just you, though. Not the beast."

"This week-end?" she squealed.

"Yeah!"

"I spoke to her today to ask if she'd come over for a few hours on Saturday and she said she would really like you to stay the whole week-end with her."

Annie's eyes were like the night sky over the CNE on Canada Day. Sparkling with incredulity.

"I think she…she's changing? She's going to call tonight."

"Wow! I've got to get ready. The laundry….."

"I'll do it."

"Snacks."

"I'll get 'em."

"Are you sure about da Vinci?"

"No way. He's an award-winning shedder. He stays." Ben looked toward the door. "Is Vienna somewhere?"

"Oh I forgot, she said to wait. She has some news." Annie sat on the step, produced her PDA and started making a survival kit to take to her mom's: pack the grey sweater mom bought for me last Xmas, download her favourite Dixie Chicks, pack *Pride and Prejudice*, and *Atonement,* pack……

As Vienna rushed to join Ben she tried to keep hold of her briefcase and laptop while she struggled putting on her coat. She glanced at Annie and questioningly at Ben.

"She's making a list of must-haves to take with her to her mom's for the whole week-end."

"Annie, what did you do to deserve all this devotion?"

"Maybe mom's growing up."

"Meaning?" asked Ben.

"Maybe she's learning to have more faith in me. That I won't pull a Regan McNeil on her."

"Who is Regan McNeil?"

"You know. The girl in *The Exorcist.*"

"How do you know about *The Exorcist*?"

"Jenny's mom rented it for her birthday party last month."

"Really! For her tenth birthday party?"

Vienna rolled her eyes and Ben thought he'd let it go. Didn't feel like a discussion about relics and levitating beds today. He looked around at the other staff members leaving and decided it wouldn't be discreet to grab Vienna and bury his face in her neck and tongue her and rub against her. Then there was Annie. Instead he looked lovingly at her like a virgin after watching Liv Tyler in *Stealing Beauty*.

They both smiled and Annie asked coyly what they were going to do all week-end.

"Maybe take in a party at a millionaire's home. Drink the finest Dom Perignon. Talk with ambassadors..."

"Sounds boring," Annie teased. Then to Vienna, "Don't forget to tell dad your news."

"Thank you. I almost did forget."

"Good or bad?"

"My friend, Greg Miller, the serologist called." She drew closer and whispered. "He said the sample was blood and he emailed his test results. Do you want to have a look?"

"Not here. Can you come over tonight?"

She nodded. "Not until ten. What's this about a party?"

"What are you whispering about?" Annie complained. "It's almost rude."

"Hey! NYB. Let's go eat. Say good-bye to Ms. Navarre. You're rude!"

"Good-bye, Ms. Navarre. I'm not rude. You are."

Annie smiled and had to drag Ben to the car as he watched Vienna walk away, turning around once to see if Ben was looking.

"You're hopeless," Annie complained.

"I told you I was."

9

At ten o'clock there was water still in Bev Westing's eyes as she stepped out of her shower and bumped into the six foot man holding a towel for her. She was startled and screamed.

"Sorry! Didn't mean to scare you." He had heated the towel under the lamp and wound its warmth around her. Holding her small form close he smelled her wet hair.

"I checked your office first. I'm glad you weren't there." He found a hand towel and blotted the wet strands that he noticed had been trimmed.

"Did you see the list?"

"You know I did." He was the nosiest male Bev had ever met. "What's it for?"

"Harvard and Mickey are coming on Friday. For a week."

"Finally. How'd they swing that? I would have thought they would have left in '06 when Rwanda severed diplomatic ties with France. They're not running, are they?"

"He sounded all right. He didn't have time to elaborate. So, I thought we could have something Saturday night."

"Will they be up for it?"

"He said they would."

"I love short-notice things."

"Lucky for me. Nothing fazes you, Billy Boy."

"How about that quartet at the Ottawa theatre opening? Everyone liked them."

"Quattro....something. I bought their cd. What was it called?"

"*Pennacchio.*"

"How do you remember these things?"

"Because I remember what we did when we listened to it."

"Oh that night! I must have been possessed."

"Let me do the music. If they're not booked we'll get them here. And if they are I'll surprise you."

"You're one of those amazing husbands, aren't you? Are you hungry?"

"I'm starving."

"Don't go away." Her kitchen was a replica of the French kitchen she had cooked in as a teenager, except for the upgrades.

Before the age of thirteen, Bev's adopted parents, Clarence and Jane Ingles (Clarence was Howard's younger brother by fifteen years) received an income from Bev's trust fund even though they were independently wealthy. But at thirteen Bev received an annual allowance that she managed herself. She picked out the town of Aix-en-Provence as an annual July destination to soak up sunshine, listen to great opera and learn to speak and cook French.

For a month Maria Garnier picked Bev up at four a.m. and together they biked to her restaurant where Bev watched her cook. And as the summers passed Bev helped her prepare meals for the dinner tourists – salad nicoise, bourride, minestrone, ratatouille, hot oysters, lavender honey.

When she attended McGill she insisted on living on her own and never went without a good meal. She met Bill there when he was doing his first year in architecture and she was doing her doctorate on the Psyche of the Collective French Woman. He and a roommate shared the townhouse below Bev. One day he knocked on her door to ask what she was cooking and that whatever it was he'd buy some of it if she had any extra. Bev was four years older, almost as wise, a lot richer, and not quite as courageous.

Even though Bev had always been independent and matured earlier than most of her peers, Jane and Thomas Ingles were cautious when it came to boyfriends. They were overly cautious when Bev brought Bill home for

Thanksgiving after he moved from his town below to her town above and continued to contribute more food money than his share just to have her cook when she had time.

The Ingles didn't know much about Bill, but knew he wasn't rich. When he and Bev both finished their degrees, the Ingles strongly advised Bev against taking trust fund money and investing in Bill's architectural and development plans which at first involved smaller projects like bridges, performance centres, dorms and small strip malls.

The Ingles soon changed their minds about Bill Westing when he refused to get married until he had paid Bev back in full and had the money to buy a home of her choice. It didn't take long for Bill to create his own socio-economic signature and rise to an internationally acclaimed business icon. In 1988 they were married and moved into their Baby Point estate. What Bev loved most about him besides his towering height and rugged beauty was his honest appreciation for the uniqueness in others. He was the son of a boat builder and never forgot his roots. And kept his first hard hat, first safety goggles, breeze box window fan, blow torch, and the first set of nitrite rubber gloves.

They both were sentimental and would have made great parents, but as an adolescent, Bill contracted orchitis, a rare condition resulting from mumps that left him infertile. They talked about adopting, but never did. They had always been close to Harvard's kids and now their great nephew. And Baby Point became their cherished progeny.

After Bev set the tray down on a throw, they both reclined and Bev poured hot maple syrup over French toast made unholy with dark chocolate and wine-sautéd pork medallions. Bev lay back and linked her hands behind her head as she waited for Bill's preliminary response to run its course.

He closed his eyes and let the steamy smells do their magic. Eating in bed with this original wonder of womanhood made him feel young. At fifty-five Bev was the hottest woman he knew – one who loved her own body, took care of it and let it take care of him. She often caught him looking at her deep set, black eyes and full pink lips and one dimple embedded on her left cheek. He watched her walk – her muscled calves propelling her forward. He knew he could count on there being another picnic, another jazz album, another night like the *Pennacchio* one. And if they didn't have the estate on Baby Point, he was sure they'd still have all of this.

10

Ten o'clock brought people home. For Bev and Bill Westing they used their familiar space and cues to reaffirm their deep need of each other. It was a good story, a tale of two lovers without conflicts or sub plots. A story with climaxes and plateaus, close to perfection. Editing their lives became a passion.

Ten o'clock brought Vienna to Ben's door. He was checking on Annie, clearing away the remnants of her homework – pencils, a ruler, scissors. She was absent-minded about using her bed as a work station. Ben shook his head and as he left to answer the door, he noticed something red sticking out of Annie's blanket. Gently moving the comforter back Ben saw a doll he never knew she had – red-haired, dimpled, porcelain, vintage, expensive. The hair looked real. And wondered where Wendy had bought it. He was surprised Annie hadn't mentioned it. But she did say she had dreamed about a doll.

The door was open and Vienna slipped into the foyer, removing her shoes and handing Ben her coat. Reaching into her bag she got a candle and a cd and gave them to Ben. "It's a mix. A little slow. A little fast. A little far away."

"Far away?"

"Like music in places in other countries that end up in movies. And you don't care who's doing what to whom – you just want to hear the music over and over and do your own thing."

"Oh, that kind of faraway music. And are we going to do our own thing, over and over?"

"In the studio."

"In that far away land of crazy? Are you sure?"

"It's already invited us in. It knows who we are." She wanted to talk and be close. Unbuttoning her blouse she straddled Ben's lap and held him close trying to hook words together coherently between kisses. "How... (kiss, kiss)... was your appoint... (kiss, kiss)... ment?"

"Can we talk later?"

Half way up the second staircase, the studio door opened – another invitation. They stared and smiled at each other.

"Are you ready for this?"

Vienna loosened the drawstring on Ben's workouts. "Let's show it how we feel."

Ben gathered her into his arms. "Let's do this right."

"I know I'm so damn long, but I always wanted to be carried over a threshold. Don't drop me."

"I'm longer."

The studio was cool like spring water in a quarry or the breeze at the top of a mountain. Looking over Ben's shoulder as they passed the easel she looked at the obscure features of the subject and transparent washes of red hair falling in waves over the edge of a tub. The subject's arm like white marble dangled beside her tresses. Her fingers curled around flowers that had no name. Like a doll without a face she was waiting.

Ben released Vienna – her feet finding the cool floor beside the bed. Slowly they undressed each other and as their clothes loosened they felt like they were floating, like aerial artists under the big top. As they lay facing each other a force began to pull them into each other.

"Do you feel that?" asked Vienna.

"Yeah. Are you scared?"

"I... I feel like I'm dissolving into you."

"Me too. Do you want to leave?"

"No." Vienna tried to relax as she felt she was floating inside Ben's skin, through his veins, like driftwood on a gentle stream.

Then a sudden invasion of pin pricks shot through their faces, eyes, tongues, hands, ears. Like thousands of small needles diving and threading their way through each pore.

"What's happening, Ben? Ben?"

He couldn't respond.

They were being sewn together. Threads of energy shot with precision from one to the other and back – stitching their senses together until each other's memory transferred in fast-motion-channel surfing.

Vienna saw Ben finding his brother dead in the shower. Felt his rage, his fear, his isolation. Ben witnessed Vienna curled beside her brother's spirit. He reached out and cradled the baby in his arms. Their pores and cells were raw with borrowed memories of pain and acceptance. They reached into each other as they never could have. And knew their losses carried the same depth of despair and the same weight of responsibility – if only Vienna had taken Bobby into her bed and if only Ben hadn't changed plans to hang out with Jamie.

They wept at what they had lost. *It's okay to cry. I know.* And they knew happiness didn't belong solely to the living. That it was sought after desperately and pursued savagely by the departed.

They were enveloped by the spiritual energy of their loved ones that shot with precision aerobatics around the lovers. Then vanished. Vienna and Ben divided. Left each other's domain of tragedy, self-incrimination and healing. They lay motionless in a deserted world. The last two lovers with borrowed dreams. Motionless and silent.

When they left the studio they didn't shut the door. Ben knew nothing could contain that kind of power – not a door, nor an easel nor a wish. He led her to the family room and lit her candle. Put on the cd.

They sat on the sofa until Vienna spoke first. "We're good people. We have so much to give." She cried. "Maybe, that's why it's reaching out. To our goodness."

"Hey." Ben wiped away her tears with his sleeve. "I've never felt that close to anyone – not even to Annie. She's outside my past."

"What happened upstairs – was it a gift?"

"I've thought about all of this – the past weeks. Yeah....yeah. I think it's saying that love after death is necessary for the spiritual world to survive. It's a gift."

Vienna's lips trembled. Words clumped in her throat like hard candy. "There was such violence here. Ben, what if we can't give it the answers it needs?"

He drew her on top of him and pulling a cover around them he kept her close.

She knew he wondered if it was right to thread into each other in their own human way. She didn't care and kneaded his body to a perfect fit.

It was three in the morning when they woke up. Ben put coffee on. They knew they had neglected to talk about important things – Ben's testing, the serology report, Saturday night – but the questions still lingered.

And Ben's testing was no less explainable. "What possesses that kind of energy? To be able to manipulate the natural world around us." While she was amazed at Ben's experience at the clinic she was prepared for the unexpected. After what had happened here nothing surprised her.

The coffee was so good, so old world, part of a natural process that made them feel for a short time that they were earth-anchored. Ready to look at a new day, at a new sun while they sat in rocking chairs, rocking and sipping their coffee. Just the two of them.

Her fingers clung to the mug as she closed her eyes and breathed in the aroma. "My friend Greg Miller did a bang up job on the serology report."

"Yeah?"

"It was blood. Belonging to a female. Type AB. I memorized it all." And she took a moment to steady her voice.

Ben reached across and caressed her hand.

She took a deep breath. "The blood stain was long like an exclamation mark. It fell through the air from an arc movement. Like a swinging motion. Probably from a knife wound. The person with the knife was standing behind the victim. A small person. Left-handed. But there was a lot of energy in the attack that caused the blood to disperse the way it did. There was a high activity of an enzyme called LDH present in the blood that could be linked to a lung injury that caused pernicious anaemia. I don't know exactly what he means by that. He's locked the sample and report in a safe place."

"Good. But the mirror could have been planted. A joke."

"You don't believe that. With all that's been going on? Someone put it on that shelf a long time ago hoping that it would be found."

"I know you're right. But according to police files nothing happened in this house."

"Something happened that they don't know about."

"Okay. Enough. Let's talk about the week-end." Ben went over the details of Annie's get-away and the party at the Westings.

Vienna was looking forward to it, but couldn't see him Friday night because of her show the following week. She took a marker and wrote the show info on the bulletin board. "I hope you can make the opening." And saw a name. "Who's Mark?"

"A long time bud. He's been phoning. I should do lunch. See if he wants to come over on Sunday for a meal."

"Can I come? I'll cook."

"Mark's easy. We'll order in. We don't have to impress."

Their cups were empty. "A refill?"

"I gotta go. I can still catch a couple of hours of sleep." She let Ben put her coat on her, zip it up, turn up her collar and hold her one last time. Another taxi waited.

11

After Ben contacted his agent about being behind with Milton Gage, he got a phone call from Smithson about the ownership from the undocumented years. All transactions had been done through a trust fund. The owners' names were anonymous and the law firm of Mason and Goodyear changed hands in 1965. Smithson was sorry.

The day was as normal as Ben willed it to be. He missed his long-time friend Mark Chainy, a singer/musician who was glad Ben finally had time to do lunch in Little Italy at a favourite bistro, Coco Lezzone.

Ben let Mark vent about Ben neglecting the gang, about Mark's divorce proceedings (his third), about Mark's chick-tailgating-strategies, about Mark's new gigs and contracts, about Mark's Christmas and New Year's plans. When the Wild Mushroom Risotto with Porcinni arrived Ben had a captive audience.

"Don't you want to know why I haven't had time to hook up?"

"Are you going to eat your bun?" Ben handed it to him. "Why? Is it Annie? Is she okay?"

"No. It's not Annie? She's doing really great."

"Are you sick? You're definitely thinner. You don't look that healthy. Too pale. How do you feel?"

"Sometimes like shit that flies don't want, but today I feel good."

"So what's goin' on?"

"My house is haunted." Ben gave it to him straight up even though the Risotto was more interesting to Mark.

"Do you have witnesses?"

"Yes I do."

"No shit!"

"Yes shit."

"I believe you, man, because you wouldn't be pulling my woollies over my navel if Annie were involved. And this whole song thing and the portrait and everything else, you wouldn't kid about. Not with Annie in the picture. So I believe....I believe...that..."

"Thanks for the vote of credibility."

"I mean I'm haunted all the time – by my past fuck-ups – but I've never experienced a real haunting. I don't know if I believe it..."

"You just said you did!"

"No. I believe you, but I don't know if I believe in the source. The ghost thing. There could be other reasons."

"Well, you're coming over on Sunday for dinner, with or without the ghost. And you can meet Vienna, my friend."

"Vienna...Vi...V for victory. Okay. What are you cooking?"

"We're ordering in."

"So, what is V like?"

"Like nothing you've ever read about or seen in the movies or passed on the street or passed out on at a party or made a pass at."

"Ass?"

"Plenty. End of discussion."

"Are you going to eat all that or what?"

Mark took a doggy bag with him and held Ben's arm. "You're going through something, right? You can count on me. I was your best man, even though I warned you about Wendy's infatuation with the jugular. Right? I've been your best war strategist, your best heart doctor. I don't know how good I'll be at ghost busting. But I am looking forward to meeting your golden-haired Helen/Indira/Georgia/Theresa/goddess person."

"Okay, bud. Sunday, it is."

"Sunday at six?" They knocked knuckles and set off in different directions.

* * * *

When Ben got home he scribbled on the kitchen bulletin board beside Mark's name, *is on for Sunday.* He checked his messages. Bev called and asked him to contact her.

She was excited to share Louis Gabriel's findings: that the signature belonged to a Spanish/Italian artist by the name of Rigo Molinaro who had studied in Paris and emigrated to the States in 1955. Then disappeared in 1958. That Molinaro's Italian grandparents investigated his case and weren't satisfied with vague circumstances and inconclusive findings.

When the police told the Molinaros that a motorcycle they thought their grandson owned was found wrecked outside of Kingston, Ontario and there was a small artist's portfolio among the wreckage, Mr. Molinaro flew to Canada to identify the belongings. They knew the sketches and photos belonged to Rigo, but his body was never found. The police reported that there was no blood at the scene, that it was probably a hit and run and closed the case. Molinaro returned to Italy somehow believing his grandson was alive.

Ben thanked Bev and told her he'd be bringing a guest to the party and asked if he could bring anything.

"If you could part with a back copy of one of your novels for my great nephew, that would be appreciated."

"Done." And thanked her again.

He found a copy of *Bad Men Don't Cry* and left it out so he wouldn't forget to sign it and take it Saturday night.

Ben stretched out on the sofa and repeated the initials, R.M. R. M. Rigo Molinaro. He wondered if the police still had the hit and run case still on file or if the grandfather took it with him. It was a day of important calls. One ended. One began. Rose Henhawke called to say she had seen the tapes of his testing and had spoken with

Evan Fife. She wanted to do the initial investigation on Sunday at two. Ben was eager to meet the team and asked what he could do in advance.

Rose told him not to clean. Not to touch anything he wouldn't normally touch. And to make a list of everything that had happened since he moved in. He got the journal he had stopped updating and took it to the bottom of the stairway to the studio.

Sitting on the bottom step he started writing then looked up at the open door and decided not to go up. He didn't need this fusion thing – two colliding histories to happen right now. He could only be kidnapped so many times in a week. He called up, *People are coming to help you. Sunday. They're professionals. They want to meet you.*

Turning away he decided to purge Annie's room. He wanted to winterize it with a warmer comforter and flannelette sheets. Get it up to Wendy's inspection. He made a pile for Good Will after he bagged leftover summer stock. And packed a suitcase for the week-end. Even included the butt-ugly, corporate, grey sweater Wendy bought for Annie at Christmas. Annie insisted on taking it with her.

He enjoyed the cleaning ritual from opening a new bag of rubber gloves to wielding a Q-tip. He liked the ownership of wall, window, tile, tub and floor maintenance. When he reached under Annie's bed to clear a way for the vacuum, he found a school kit with a poster wrapped around it: Grade Five: Human Sexuality A student-friendly guide.

His hand trembled. Sitting on the edge of the bed he opened the kit and stared at the expected – one condom, a plastic banana, a comic book of how things worked down south, hygienic stuff, medical info. He took a deep breath and packed it in the folds of the infamous sweater for Wendy's maternal discretion.

He walked the dog before it was time to pick up Annie. He needed to clear away some thoughts to make room for new ones. Like the thought of moving somewhere else temporarily while the ghost squad did its thing. And thoughts about Vienna's permanent place in their lives. How he wanted to take her home to Montreal to meet his estranged mom – perhaps to get to know her again. And thoughts about how he had to learn to share Annie more with Wendy. And if his home would ever recover its soul.

* * * *

Wendy arrived with a smile and a plaid scarf (Burberry) in case Annie didn't have one. As Annie took her mom's hand she winked at Ben on their way to her room to check out how clean it was. A quick inspection. A mom's beaming approval.

On their way out, Ben could tell Wendy was looking forward to the week-end. *Fucking unreal*, he thought. Her face softened; the world had reached an accord with Wendy's centre. Her eyebrows curved gently, not hurled into soldiering. Her mouth was relaxed, ready to make pleasant. And when she was excited she fussed. She was fussing over the proper scarf look for Annie (tied at the front, the back, looped). Annie sucked it up.

Before they left, Wendy couldn't resist asking Ben if had a girlfriend.

"No."

"Yes," corrected Annie.

"Red hair?"

"No."

"Gold," added Annie. "Light gold."

"Why are you asking?"

"I saw a woman at your studio window when I got out of the car. She had red hair. She was staring at me."

"Probably a painting I'm working on."

"This painting moved." And she smiled a smile Ben didn't know.

"Her name is Vienna, mom. But she's not here, yet. She's my teacher."

"Oh. Your teacher?" And she smiled at Ben. Then to Annie, "Do you have your hearing diffusers?"

"Yup, but I almost don't need them anymore."

"Then let's head out." As Annie led the way, Wendy turned to Ben with a note of approval. "It's about time. And it's okay to have two, until you figure out which one's the keeper."

Ben threw up his hands. "No one's here."

"I saw her. We'll be back around eight, Sunday night?"

"I'll be here with my harem. Have a great time. Oh, where did you get the red-haired doll for Annie? It looks like an antique."

"What doll?"

"Porcelain. Very French looking."

"It wasn't from me."

"Okay. Forget it."

He watched them back out of the driveway, Wendy looking up at the studio window. Normally da Vinci would be spazzing out to go too, but he remained quietly aware that when he was around, Wendy's consonants were accented like a Taser. He stayed close to Ben, thankful he hadn't been invited.

"Come on, boy." da Vinci followed Ben as he quickly searched through Annie's room for the doll. It was nowhere. Taking two steps at a time Ben rushed up to the studio and stood in the doorway. *What the hell are you doing? You came into my daughter's room. Don't ever do that again! Stay the hell away from her!*

As he ran downstairs, the door slammed shut. Twice.

Ben submerged himself in a deep, hot tub with a chilled mug of *SkullSplitter*. He had been saving this sweet, malty brew for a special occasion. And this was it. Friday night alone – sort of alone. A rarity. He soaked, drank, read GQ and after he let anti-aging thoughts of Vienna carry him to bed, he slept soundly until dawn.

The phone woke him up. Vienna had time for breakfast and a quick tour of the Eaton Centre to pick up a new dress before her spa appointment. He had never done this before – watch a woman move into and out of clothing revelations. He had seen men from time to time sitting in comfortable chairs doing this, but he hadn't.

A black sleeveless on the second level, a possible knit on the third, a worsted, shoulderless, three-quarter sleeved back on the second. Cinnamon. And jewellery on the third again. She bought the worsted. And there was a ring. A single pearl protected by two mythical, silver leaves.

A maybe ring. A thank you ring that Ben insisted was an early Christmas present.

"What exactly are you thanking me for?" She studied its singular coyness.

"We both know I was starving. You've been fattening me up – emotionally."

"I'm a love carb to you."

"Nice. Yeah. You're sticky, subtly sweet, outrageously decadent."

"Can I wear it tonight?" She tried it on again.

"That's the plan."

"I have to go." One arm reached up and hooked around his neck drawing him close until her lips moved in. "Here's some outrageously decadent, sweet stuff." To her, his mouth was like a school boy waiting for a bus. Waiting for a ride. There was no other way to kiss Ben, but passionately. "How's that for subtlety?"

He stood still as she released him and backed away then disappeared in the crowd.

* * * *

He had avoided the studio Friday night, but he was ready to talk and write and paint and be in his space where he was most comfortable with himself, even with this unhappy tenant.

Talking. *Are you here? Are you Rigo Molinaro? Did you live here? Did you die here? I don't know what you want. There are people who can help you. Tomorrow afternoon they're coming here to find you. To listen to you.* He panned the room for company.

He walked around the space touching his familiar things. Picking up a book, an old photo of the gang, an award, an empty wine bottle, a tie that Annie had given him, a stuffed hippo Annie had outgrown, a picture of Jamie. And wished Annie could have met him.

Annie's a great kid, isn't she? You'll protect her, won't you? Just don't fool around with her. Leave her out of this. Will you do that for me?

Writing. He got his neglected journal and started to update it. Everything that had happened over the past two weeks he noted – even his night with Vienna. How they saw each other's pain from inside. How they dissolved into each other's soul. He went over the details and made some notes in the margins. Drew some diagrams. Made some thumbnail sketches.

Painting. He examined his canvas – the shadow woman with the red hair falling like diagonal ocean waves to the floor. *You're like a grey cloud. I can't see you.*

Then the urge to paint. Mixing a creamy palette he brushed skin tones over the linen. A jewelled comb formed by her left temple over her ear. A comb with green jewels in the shape of a seahorse. The woman's right hand and arm reached up, behind her head as if fastening the comb in place. Her left arm and wavy hair fell over the tub. White on white. Red hair and red lips and one red nipple on white skin. Then a brush of colour breathed form into petals scattered around the tub.

As he worked the expected music didn't disappoint him. A strange mix – chants, marches, opera and Holiday. Harlem Nocturne with words soft like a melting candle. Ben wanted to dance both of them – Holiday and the white-skinned lady from inside the house to the gazebo. Around and around until they convinced autumn not to pass into the dead season, but to stay colour-driven for a while. Ben wondered if they were his thoughts, his feelings or the artist's.

Talking again. *Did you feel like this? Did you dance with Billy? Who is the woman in the painting? How do I beg you to help me?*

Moments passed. Letters like shimmering heat above a summer highway blurred in front of the canvas. He grabbed his pen and like a lozenge it engraved letters through multiple pages in his journal: s i s i. He repeated them and turned to the painting. *Sisi. Sisi,* he whispered.

The model's eyes reached into him. Pleaded with him to rescue her. His fingers found her outstretched hand and pressed into her fingertips. Like a train derailing he left reason and safety, and leaving his safe place he plunged into a dark cell. *Where are you taking me?* Locked away. Forgotten. *I don't want to go with you. Annie needs me.*

He eyes felt detached, flying away like wireless binoculars into the cell's corners. There was a figure – unidentifiable in its age, its pain, its deformity.

Is it you? Ben asked the fragile form. *Are you real? Who are you?*

Ben panicked. He felt sightless groping in the dark without sight. *I want to see. My eyes!* He touched the concave sockets and backed away from the canvas, afraid to open his eyes. He stumbled to the door and carefully found the banister. Fumbling, he found the bathroom downstairs and faced the mirror. He forced himself to open his eyes.

Alternating in flashes he saw his own face, then the other. His own. The other. He touched his eyes, blinked, touched them. The other faded away.

da Vinci whined as Ben fell on to the sofa in the family room. *I know that whine, da Vinci. It's your empathetic whine. You know something, don't you?* When Ben reached out to massage his ears, da Vinci shot backwards, yelping and cowering.

"Come, da Vinci."

He wouldn't.

"What is it? Come on, boy!" Ben approached. "I won't hurt you." da Vinci bolted away hysterically leaving a path of urine in the hall.

Ben didn't pursue.

12

Just when he thought he had had one too many visions for the day and decided to distance himself from ocular clarity, Ben's eyes struck a match and held it close to this last, one vision – Vienna in autumn moonlight, gliding like a goddess on a bow of a Viking ship. Her hair like cool gold under the clear sky.

She stayed close to him in the car. Her arm wound through his, her lips caressed his face, her fingers erased the evidence. She asked about Wendy and Annie and said she was happy that Wendy kept her date and that Annie mentioned Vienna more than once.

* * * *

The Westings hired an attendant to help direct guests from the gate to the parking pad where they were greeted by a second attendant and escorted to the house. Ben was habitually early, but Bev was happy to have him and Vienna to herself.

She never fussed at these get-togethers. She was curled up with a book in the great room when they were shown in. She rushed to greet them.

"I'm always the first to arrive." He almost seemed apologetic.

"I hope not the first to leave." And she noticed he had lost weight. A little gaunt. And while she thought his eyes were brighter in the company of his friend, she noted sleepless rings encircled his Aegean eyes, and the corners of his mouth found it hard to curl upward.

"No. I'm not the first to leave; I pretty much have to be escorted out. Bev, this is my friend, Vienna Navarre."

Vienna was captivated by the Indo-British decor of the grand foyer: two bevelled, stained glass windows on opposite sides of the entrance with window seats that were appointed with colourful layers of embroidered turquoise, silk pillows, a modern textured Indian rug, artful tapestry treatments on each window framed with rich, natural walnut, a sandalwood chess set by one window, towering silk palms under which rested a large carved elephant at the far end of the foyer, and three carved birds with ivory beaks suspended from the twelve foot ceilings. She knew the Westing's home would take her on a journey in a way most homes didn't.

"What a name!" Bev commented as Vienna remained awestruck by the decor. "There's got to be a story behind that." Bev's eyes sparkled with curiosity as she addressed Vienna who was still connected to the mounted birds.

She had hardly heard a word, nor felt Bev take her hand and lead them to the great room where she asked the two of them to join her. She had felt the ring on Vienna's finger, took a look, but didn't ask about it. "So let's hear this story behind this intriguing name." And she offered space next to her on the custom, sandstone couch.

Vienna was speechless as she soaked in the aesthetics of the room. Such tasteful interactions of colour, motifs, and icons. "I'm so sorry. Your home is breathtaking. I've never seen anything like it – not even in magazines."

"Thank you. A joint effort." Bev was grateful for Vienna's genuine reaction that the rooms evoked.

"There's nothing earth-shattering about my name. College boy from New Brunswick meets college girl from Chicago on a language exchange in Austria. I was born nine months later to two very sweet, but totally irresponsible kids who managed to stay together for nine years. I was ten and my mom was all of twenty eight when my dad left for deep sea oil drilling. I've seen him twice since then."

"And Navarre?"

"My dad's family, I think traced back to the Bourbons."

"Quelle provence?"

"Je pense, Bearn."

"Bordered by Basque provinces and home of d'Artagnan."

"Oui." Vienna smiled. *The Three Musketeers* had been a favourite of hers. Sometimes she'd sit in Bobby's room early on a Saturday morning and read parts of the novels. She loved d'Artagnan. She imagined Bobby would have been like him if he had had the chance.

"What do you do, Vienna?"

"I'm an elementary school art teacher."

"And a represented artist," added Ben.

"Really. What's your favourite medium?"

"Both acrylics and oils. For different reasons."

"I'd love to see your work."

"She has an art opening in Yorkville in December."

"Ben!" Vienna protested.

"I can plug it."

"Yes you can, Ben. Send me the details. I'd love to go."

Ben placed a gift bag on the coffee table. "For your great nephew."

"You remembered. Alex will be so excited. He was named after my mom, Alexsis."

S i s i. Ben thought she had said and leaned closer. "What was her name?"

"Alexsis. Close friends called her Lexi. Alexsis Chisholme-Ingles." She looked toward a large portrait beside the French doors. "That's my mom and my grandmother. My dad commissioned an American painter to do it. It was based on a photo. My mom was five."

"That's a great name too – Chisholme-Ingles. Poetic," Vienna mused.

"The photo was taken in India. My granddad owned an exporting business."

Vienna was panning the room – its lines, colours, shapes, contrasts, art. "This is much more beautiful than Casa Loma."

"Thank you, but I never wanted to live in something that big. This is actually over-indulgent, but what's not to love?"

Vienna smiled. "My condo would fit into half of this room."

Bill Westing joined them with two drinks – one for Bev and one for himself. "I didn't know we had guests." And Bev made introductions. "What would you like to drink?" He used the intercom to have one of the caterers bring beverages.

Before the other guests arrived the four of them talked about everything Toronto, then Bev was called away and Bill took the two guests on a tour to the tropical aviary.

"Wow!" Ben was amazed at its landscape – trees, shrubs, feeding stations, walkways.

And Vienna pointed at a Toucan. "I should have brought a sketch pad."

"I have two Toucans, Honeycreepers, Bee-eaters, Bellbirds, Lovebirds, Tityra, Cockatoos and I'm sure others."

"Why all this? A boyhood dream?"

"I love flight. Things that fly. I'm mesmerized by it."

"It's incredible."

The men sat in the garden in the aviary and talked about design while Vienna went birding. Bill understood Ben's affinity to architectural images. Ben used the same principals in his graphic backgrounds in his novels. They shared favourite architects – Gehry (of course), Wren, Ming Pei, Wright, Rossi, Loos, Tange and others.

And later Vienna joined them, drawing from her extensive art history and travels. She had her favourite sites too that even Bill hadn't visited yet – Top Capi Palace, the Aya Sophia.

It didn't take Bill long to know why Bev had invited them. He had never known her to be wrong about people. It was a pleasure meeting these two decent, talented, passionate, grounded art lovers. He wanted to sit in his quiet sanctuary longer, but he knew other guests would be waiting. When they returned, the others had arrived. Old friends - Louis Gabriel, Amelia Strato, the singer, friends of Harvard Ingles, and the family, including Mickey and the kids. Music enlivened the night - he was able to book three musicians from *Quatro Amanti* to which Bev had already started singing. Bill nodded and raised his glass to them.

A small gathering. Twenty guests. Ben watched them – how Harvard walked with both his arms around his sister and his wife. And occasionally kissed Bev's forehead. Ben would have liked that closeness of family, even if they lived on separate continents – his parents divided their time between Montreal, New York and Florida.

When they came to Ben and Vienna, Bev introduced Ben as the graphic novelist who had captured Alex's imagination. A very popular writer of comic books.

Harvard smiled. "My dad wouldn't allow comic books, but I snuck them home anyway. *Black Terror, Rawhide Kid, Beware Terror Tales, Frontline Combat, Human Torch.* Ben, do you think they help to establish justice?"

"I like to think they do."

Bev called to Alex who was carrying Ben's gift. "Alex, this is Ben Needham."

"Your books are so cool, totally sick!"

"Thank you."

Alex shook his hand and ran off, and Harvard squeezed Ben's shoulder. "It was very kind of you. My son is just as hard on Alex as my dad was on me. A kid has to have his heroes."

Ben smiled and when Harvard withdrew his hand Ben noticed that it was deformed. Harvard caught his momentary glance and held up his left hand. "Lost three fingers in a boating accident when I was sixteen. 1958. And I was left-handed too. But it was a miracle I didn't lose the whole hand."

"He had to learn to write with his right," Bev added.

"Tennis is a bitch. And golf."

"And flipping pancakes," Bev laughed. "Actually Harvard was a junior Canadian tennis champion. He was driven by pure talent."

Ben was going to ask him about the Phantom Limb Syndrome, but was interrupted when one of Harvard's friends waved him over to another group. As Harvard left he shook Ben's hand again and kissed Vienna's cheek. Ben watched him go and wondered why he thought he had seen him before. But he couldn't possibly have.

Vienna and Mickey Ingles had moved to a seat to talk about their French backgrounds. Mickey had met Harvard in England when she was studying medicine. And Harvard chose to stay in France with her while she started her career and later decided to practice in Rwanda where her father was an ambassador.

Harvard who had graduated in Business managed family interests from abroad and became a Good Will Ambassador in a country with decaying moral mortar. They knew the land would not love them back, but they stuck it out, weathered the chaos and collapse of a land they had claimed as their home. They had learned to survive socio-politico shifts on every level.

By the end of the evening Mickey had invited Vienna to visit, to see firsthand the institutional recovery strategies of Rwanda and to encourage Vienna to think about a six month work op with the country's artisans to help rework their designs and get them marketable.

Vienna had always known this about her life. That doors were always opened. That she was strung to people like festive popcorn around Christmas trees, by metaphysical threads of need and passion. That she trusted invitations. Never took them lightly. And knew immediately the people she liked, like Michelle Ingles.

She didn't feel the same about Harvard. She had watched him throughout the evening and felt there was a hubristic tendency in his approach – could be a result of the family money, or a Messiah complex from his work in Rwanda or a defence mechanism because of his hand. But she didn't feel comfortable around his egocentricity. She thought most handsome guys were a little shy, but not Harvard. He moved into light and angles as if he were being filmed.

While Vienna and Mickey were deep in conversation, Bev looped her arm through Ben's and invited him to tour the main floor. Often stopping, Bev elaborated on many artefacts, art works and photos. And again they came face to face with the commissioned painting of Bev's mom, Alexis at the age of five, cuddled by her mother beside a temple in India.

"My dad commissioned it. Oh, I already told you that. My mom loved that photo because her mom was happy there, before she got really sick. My grandmother loved her rose garden, but who would have known that a simple thorn could cause such sickness. Like a viral tsunami. It hit her so hard. A respiratory illness. They had to go back to England. My grandmother spent the rest of her life fighting the disease. She was already sick with it before she had my mom. My mom was born anaemic."

"They look so happy." For a split second Ben paled as an image flashed across the painting. He blinked. Rubbed his eyes. Looked more closely."

"What is it?"

He drew close to the little girl's face. His lips dried. Another flash. He moved back as Bev watched curiously. "Ben?"

"Yeah, no. It's nothing. I..I thought...never mind."

"What?"

"I thought I recognized her," he lied.

"My mom? Well, when she married my dad and they moved to Toronto, she was a favourite in the social columns. She didn't really change much from this early picture. Her hair became redder. Her skin whiter. Maybe you've seen media pics of her. Somewhere. She's not that easy to forget."

"She's really beautiful."

"Yeah. I look more like my dad, I guess. Except for the pale skin - a slight predisposition."

As they moved on, Ben looked back. Didn't want to share what he had seen – an image of the little girl reaching her hand around her head as if fastening a comb in place. Her other hand dangling, as if over a tub. A barely-seen flash. An almost-blur. Ben wondered if it had really happened. Or if the little girl's red hair triggered the memory of his painting.

Bev stood at a table and picked up a photo. "And this is me at three with Alexsis."

S...i... s...i... Ben heard again. A soft voice echoed the sounds over and over. *Sisi... Sisi...*

She passed the photo to him.

He stared at the three year-old holding a red-haired doll with a porcelain face and expensive clothes. Her mom was crouched beside her – her head pressed into the child's chest. Her large sun hat covering most of her face.

"I love this photo. I can feel Lexi near me. I used to sleep with it. Press it into my heart, carry it to school."

Ben was fixed on the doll. "The doll – did your mom buy it for you in England?"

"God no. Nothing was store-bought or mass produced except for our cars. Everything was hand-crafted. Clothes. Rugs. Rocking horses. Beds. And this doll. One of a kind. It was a replica of Lexi as a child."

"Do you still have it?"

"No. This is going to sound weird, but my mom was buried with it. I can't remember it, but they say I put it under her arm in her coffin. Like I was giving her part of me."

"Oh."

"Are you thinking that Annie would like one? Or maybe start a collection? I have so many special dolls. I'll go through them and start her with a few I know she'll love."

"That would be really great of you to do that for her."

She took Ben's arm and walked him to Mickey and Vienna.

"It's so good to be here. I don't know if I'll be able to fly home after meeting this wonderful woman."

Bev turned to Ben. "Is Mickey right?"

"Nah. Vienna's one of these bitchy artists. Like Picasso. Rivera. Runs around on me. Stays high on two hundred proof ego most of the time."

Vienna laughed. "He's absolutely right for at least thirty six days of the year. But the other three hundred and....and...twenty seven....."

"She's pure geisha and Lizzy Barrett Browning and Lizzy Bennett and...."

Vienna reached up and removed his drink. "Okay, Tokyo Miyamoto. Club Soda refills only."

"... and..."

Vienna put her finger on his lips. "Sh..."

"Okay. Food."

"That's a good idea," Bev interjected. "I think you've lost some weight since last week. I'm going to fix a heaping plate for you. I'll be right back."

Bev patted Vienna's arm as she brushed by her. And Harvard stopped to envelope Bev for a hug on his way to join his wife and her new friends. "I'm reading your thoughts, Harvard. You don't want to leave either."

"Do you blame me?"

Mickey asked Ben and Vienna to sit with them. "I'm trying to persuade Vienna to come for six months and I'll set her up with the RAEA to help move our artisan's businesses into a world market."

"I'll really consider, but if I can't go, I can recommend a lot of eager, highly qualified artists who would jump at the chance to do something in that capacity. I'll spread the word."

Ben had been staring at Harvard. A handsome man, boyish for his age. Large, wistful eyes that were different in colour. Eyes, Ben decided, that guarded a mind full of hauntings, but his thoughts could have been liquor-induced. *Impurities and secrets*, his inner voice slurred. A history of secrets. Ben could always tell from the light deficit in a person's eyes if their history were locked safely away for eternity. Harvard was one of these people with deep eyes – dark like vertical caves that had prehistoric claims on his morality. *Again, liquor talk.*

While the women were deep in exchange, Harvard tried to ignore Ben's scrutiny until he finally addressed Ben's staring. "Is it the liquor or a mental disorder or my unique handsomeness?"

"Come again?"

"Why you're staring at me."

"I was staring? Sorry. Christ, I think I was sleeping. Was I snoring?"

The women stopped talking. Vienna who had already taken a dislike to Harvard from the moment she met him, quietly armed her defences.

"Sorry, man. Maybe I was staring. Maybe you remind of someone."

"Who?"

Ben shook his head. "I guess that's why I was staring. I don't know. Someone I've seen recently. Or maybe I was comparing you and Bev. I don't see much of a resemblance."

"Really? I think we have my dad's high cheekbones. Narrow upper lip. Widow's peak. But I have my mother's deep eyes, even though one is dark brown and the other dark blue."

"Bev's skin is much lighter."

"My mother – my dad's first wife – was part Armenian. I have her skin colour, but Bev has my stepmother's Dresden-doll skin."

"Did you know her?"

"Alexsis?'

Ben nodded.

"Knew her. Loved her. Worshipped her like everyone did. Everyone."

One of Harvard's friends, a retired Cabinet Minister found him and persuaded him to take a drive downtown for a drink at the Canoe in the Toronto Dominion Tower. Before he left, Harvard shook Ben's hand allowing himself to hold on longer than needed, while he stared into Ben's blurred perception and told him to take it easy. That he hoped to see him again before he left. And thanked him again on Alex's behalf. Before leaving he took Vienna's hand and kissed it. "Enchante."

She shivered when he let go. It bothered her why she couldn't explain her feelings.

Bev joined them and handed Ben an enormous plate of food. She didn't want Harvard to leave but didn't protest. She had seen Harvard kiss Vienna's hand and saw her less-than- enamoured reaction. "I think it's his age," she whispered to Vienna. "I apologize if he made you uncomfortable."

"No, don't worry about it. I'm not the touchy type around strangers, that's all."

"Well, I'm going to let you eat and I'm going to join the kids in the pool. Catch you in a while. Join us if this one can float." And she pointed to Ben. "Bill, will get you swim suits?" She rushed away, eager to be a kid again.

* * * *

As it grew late, everyone felt the buzz of fine-labelled cheer and easy conversation. Mickey circulated among friends she had known through Harvard - friends that never asked about her and Harvard's political rebirths during the genocide. And Vienna slid beside the pianist offering a spare pair of hands.

Together they jazzed up Van Morrison's *Moondance.* For an hour Ben had forgotten why he had become so thin. Why he breathed shallow. Why he had palpitations. Sweaty palms and a tiny cut that from time to time bled after it had healed. For an hour he felt he was in a Fitzgerald novel – the good times in it, without malice or trickery or guilt.

Someone cleared away his plate and offered him coffee. Much needed. Reminiscent of family gatherings after turkey and pie and card games. Or after the wedding shower. Or the baby showers with old aunts who knew how to brew a decent cup. Tonight was like that.

He watched Bev walk into the room from the opposite doorway. Her hair was wet. She found a settee and stretched out – her feet draped over the padded arm. As friends left they bent down and kissed her and told her not to get up. Ben had forgotten it was November, felt it was summer and he was on a vacation somewhere on the coast.

Ben clung to the coffee and the normality it had brought him. Coffee, a family time, a woman he thought he was falling in love with, leaning into a keyboard he didn't know existed in her life. He clung and savoured it, then decided it was time to collect Vienna, drag her away from this loop she was in, or they'd be there all night.

Trying not to fumble, he rubbed her shoulders and whispered incoherently into her ear. Vienna thanked the pianist for letting her jam, then took Ben's arm and put it around her shoulder to steady him.

"You're not driving home."

"Are we walking?" he asked puzzled. "It's too far to walk. Might fall into the river."

"No...no. I'll call a taxi." She walked him over to Bev. "Say good night, Ben."

"Are you leaving so soon?" Bev got up and took their hands.

"I'm beyond froper fronunciation," admitted Ben.

Bev reached up and put her hands on each side of his face, drew him close and kissed his cheek. "I'm so glad you came – with or without proper pronunciation. You are a prince in this world of dethroned royalty."

"Printh Ben," he slurred again.

Bill had nodded off in a chair beside Bev's settee and opened his eyes when he heard good-byes mentioned. "Are you leaving?"

"I can't hold my liquor. I think I over-indeluged tonight." Indeluged? Or indulged."

Bill shook his hand, while Bev went to get their coats. "It's not earth shattering to enjoy earth's produce from seed to sin."

Ben teetered. "The last time this happened was before a funeral, then after it. The after it went on for a couple of years. But tonight is all for the right reasons."

"I called a limo," Bev added when she returned.

"Thank you."

"It's been a magical moment in history," Ben managed.

Bev handed Bill the coats. He helped both his guests into them and started laughing at Ben's unruly arm, waving like a flag trying to find the sleeve.

"Come any time tomorrow to pick up your car. I wish we could do brunch, but we're all heading to the Falls early. When we get back, I'll call. We'd love you to come over before Harvard leaves."

Bev wrapped a throw around her shoulders and waved good-bye on the portico as Ben tumbled his six‑foot-plus frame into the limo.

* * * *

They didn't go back to Ben's. She had cleaned and candled her place. Made it man-mantis inviting, but knew once they stripped and fell into bed, Ben would taste only what deep sleep cherished most – loving arms. Hers and Annie's. And their smiles. And coffee and notes.

13

Three leather masks of women wearing burkas were mounted on Vienna's bedroom wall and stared down on Ben as he slept. When he woke he studied the trio with stiff veils that trailed sideways, like winter laundry drying in an arctic wind. He liked them.

Ben didn't know if his head ached because of a hangover or hunger, but one whiff of Vienna's morning coffee mixed with cinnamon buns and crisp smoked bacon seduced him back to health. Breakfast in bed with a glowing fireplace in the opposite corner and Jazz FM had Sunday with Vienna stamped all over it.

"Do all your guests get this treatment?"

"What guests?"

"When was the last one?"

"A while back. He wasn't even that good in my fantasies, let alone on my real skin."

"Did you do the breakfast thing for him?"

"He left before midnight. I've never seen him since."

They ate and talked about the party - how both Bev and Bill were more than just down-to-earth people. More than great hosts. Ben agreed that the Westings had a way of disabling your guard and replacing it with a two-way layman's confessional. They had an emotional authenticity in a class of its own.

"They're artful," added Vienna.

"That about sums it up. I expect they're artful in everything they do."

"What do you think of Harvard?"

Ben considered the question. "I know what you think of him. I didn't get a great first impression either."

"He comes off friendly, but he's cold. Something's not right there. I hope we don't see him before he leaves. But I really like Mickey."

When they got to Vienna's condo, Ben had stumbled into bed and missed the tour. After Ben helped her clean up, Vienna got an oversized hoody and made Ben put it on so they could go outside after the tour. There was a kitchen, a living/dining area in a great room and the master bedroom on the main floor. In the loft was a guest room and small den that doubled as her art studio that led to an outdoor deck and garden.

They put their hoods up and went out to look at the CN tower, due east, and the Gardiner and the Canadian National Exhibition drenched in hazy sunrise.

"It's an amazing place. I can see why you can work here. Of course there're no ghosts." He started to shiver.

"Yeah, don't think I didn't listen for one when I first went through. Cold and hot spots. Strange electrical activity. I look for them in every place I live."

When their clothes began to dampen in morning dew, they went in. "I always wonder what women have behind their closed doors and drawers. You know – all the things that get tucked away."

"Come on. I'll show you." From room to room, she opened up her life to Ben. Told him it was all right to soldier through her things. She didn't know what she had stored away and was surprised at the things he pulled out. Things Ben thought defined her as much as her bed facing west did, or the jazz channel, or the label on her coffee can. Things like ticket stubs, plane tickets, post cards, matches, menus, pens, stockings, a fake mouse, a fake beard......

They ended up in her studio – a small, bright space with an art table, and shelves instead of an easel, more shelves to hold supplies, a cd player, track lighting and an old, blue, corduroy tub chair with a worn, purple pillow on it.

"I usually don't show my work until the show, but here it is." She had turned the works away from viewing. One by one she turned them around for Ben's scrutiny. "Be honest."

He was drawn into faces and bodies of statues juxtaposed with people whom Vienna had sketched in Italy and Greece, then painted them on canvas. Even though time had chipped away the subjects' exteriors, each one passionately shared an activity with their human counterparts. He lingered on one – a statue of a little girl resting beside a woman playing a piano while flowers were growing out of the keys.

"Wow! What else can I say?"

"The statue was on a veranda in Italy. I fell in love with her."

"Is it Annie? The little girl?"

"I realized as I was painting her, that Annie was there – her skin, her eyes, mouth full of notes and wisdom."

"She's going to love it. They're beautiful. You're beautiful." Her art had taken him to an abstract place where his head, not his hands touched her. "You're so beautiful."

"Would you like to see a map of their original locations where I first sketched them?" She had marked them on a globe and guided Ben through each site – talking about the colours, the light patterns, the people, the food, wines and what it was like leaving each place. How the process impacted on her in different ways.

"I'd like to go there with you. When my novel's done, for a couple of weeks in the summer, and when Wendy is a hundred per cent with having Annie."

They had more coffee, showered affectionately, picked up the car, and as they drove to Ben's, they talked about the afternoon and the first investigation.

* * * *

Ben felt as he always did, when he stood on his veranda, holding his keys and staring at the lock on his front door, that if to unlock it would mean unleashing everything unwanted, everything that threatened his weakening stability, everything that challenged his rational reserves.

Vienna cupped her hand around his, removed the key and let them in.

The radiators were dead.

"Can we get some heat in here?"

"I don't think Rose wants us to touch anything." Walking through the house, Ben wanted to check for any disturbances. To see if things on the main floor and the second were as he left them. Nothing was out of place until he came to Annie's room. He had left the door open, but it was closed.

"I purposefully left it opened." He stared at it.

"Are you sure?"

"Uh-huh."

Vienna reached to open it.

"Don't!" he shouted. And grabbed her hand. "They said not to touch anything."

"I heard you the first time."

"Sorry, I need to change my clothes." They didn't go up to the studio, but found clean clothes in the laundry room. He got changed and helped Vienna into a fleece-lined top and found scarves which they wrapped around their necks.

Wrapped warmly, they sat in the kitchen while a veil of gloom – dark and clammy grew like a fog around them and blocked the sunshine that was heating up the entire city outside, but not Ben's house.

Vienna went to the back door of the kitchen and looked outside. "It's sunny."

"I know."

"There's no light coming in."

"I know."

"It should be coming in at this angle." Her hand traced an imaginary line from the window to the floor. "The trees are skin and bones." She shuddered. "Is it foggy in here?"

"I think so."

"It's like dark silk around us or like swimming in the Dead Sea. Do you feel it?"

"Yup."

Above them a door slammed shut. They reached for each other's hands and sat as if they were under water.

There was a knock at the front door, then Rose Henhawke entered and called for Ben. She stood waiting until Ben joined her, then introduced herself.

"Hi, I'm Rose. I hope you don't mind my letting myself in." She quickly took off her coat and placed it on a hallway chair.

"It's freezing in here. You might want to put it back on," Vienna suggested, then noted beads of sweat had formed on Rose's forehead and nose. "Or not."

"I won't need it." As her technicians entered, Rose introduced each one and the equipment each would be using: Martin would operate the thermal imager to pick up black body energy; Justin would be on the night vision camera and would work with Martin to rule out any anomalous shapes; Emma would work the magnetometer to record extreme hot or cold or mobile electric fields and the Ion counter to test for by-products of any presences; Burt was responsible for the video camera to capture any RSPK (recurrent spontaneous psychokinesis).

Ben listened quietly as the team passed by him. He watched Rose - this tall, androgynously-chiselled, model-like woman, who barely parted her lips as she spoke gently and rhythmically. She had pulled back her blond-streaked hair and had fastened it with a hair clip at the back of her neck. Her lips were thick and broad with two slightly protruding upper front teeth. As he looked at her long wide-set eyes he wondered how many men had plunged into their azure depths. She must have Scandinavian in her background, Ben thought.

She ended by explaining what they would do in the first sweep and that as a psychometrist, a person who learns a history of an object by touching it, she would only explore items that reached out to her. When they finished the first mapping they would consult with one another and compare notes. Then do a second sweep to determine if a psychic was needed.

She asked Ben to kill the power and to remain with Vienna in the living room. Then turned to leave.

"Can I ask you a question?" Ben called.

Rose stopped. Didn't turn around and quietly said, "It's called a 'moon wall'. It's like a fog, as if the moon's magnetic force is pulling dampness from graves. I felt it as soon as I entered." She hurried to join the others.

"A 'moon wall'. That explains everything," Ben whispered.

The team worked like miners searching for life after a cave-in. The main floor was without any questionable imagery or occurrence. The second floor as well, except for a room they couldn't get into. Before mapping the third floor, Rose joined Ben and asked him about the locked door on the second floor that had the name Annie on it.

"Do you have a key?"

"It's not locked. It's my daughter's room. When I left Friday night, the door was open. My daughter is with her mom this week-end. I left the door open. When Vienna and I got in this morning, the door was closed. Not locked. It has no lock. I didn't try to open it."

"We'll leave it to the end."

The others were waiting for her on the third floor stairwell.

"Another locked door?"

Cold air as if blowing over an arctic glacier shot across the hallway from under the door, then the door opened.

"Find out where the cold spot is most prevalent, Emma."

Slowly they entered and started enabling their equipment. From the north end to the south and from the west side to the east they mapped. When they had completed the circumference, they focused on the centre of the room where Ben's easel stood with an unfinished painting needing its maker. They stopped to make notes. Whispers criss-crossed the space to ask for clarification or confirmation on what they were finding: intense cold in the centre of the room, a self-contained pool of water, a fragrance, distant notes, sounds of breaking glass, distant laughter, a shadow lingering above the easel.

Rose slid open the doors of the crawl space. Nothing was there except the tin toffee box with mirror fragments inside. She examined the contents gently nudging each piece aside, then took a fragment of mirror and placed it in the palm of her hand until it grew hot. Taking the warm side she placed it flat against her forehead. As she closed her eyes she called to Burt to videotape.

A different world began to spin into existence. A world of relentless heat. Sweat formed over her body. Her blouse moistened and stuck to her skin. Something undid her hair fastener until her hair fell about her shoulders. She was in a world of elephant trains, and she felt as if she were being tossed atop a huge cow under a merciless sun. She reached out to grab at some invisible pole, perhaps an umbrella to steady herself as she jostled along. Streams of colourful silk fell about her. Flutes and nets and snakes charmed her.

An oval frame of gold with a relief of elephant heads and tusks floated into her hand. A gold frame with a mirror in it. She looked into it. Images floated in and out as she mapped its history. A date, 1947 and a number, 305 and the letters S I S I floated like carved feathers around her. She called them out as she saw them.

Then the image of a woman, powdered chalk-white lay with her hands crossed upon her chest. Satin folds of a coffin cradled her. A little, red-haired girl watched the dead woman, and as the woman's face faded, the child's face replaced it. The child stared at Rose from within this foreign world. As she stared she replaced the woman in the same coffin, pale and lifeless. She grew into womanhood in the coffin, and when she opened her mouth to speak, torrent of blood filled the mirror – transfusing itself through Rose's veins that swelled and bruised.

Blood, hot and wild broke through the membranes of Rose's eyes and raged down her face. Burt kept taping and counting the seconds of hemorrhaging.

The mirror fragment flew from her grip, as she tried to open her eyes, tried to breathe more slowly, tried to cool the blood boiling through her. She was choking.

Burt felt faint, panicked, stopped taping. Rose went into shock – her arms flailing, her throat choking on someone else's blood. Burt shouted for Emma. "Get the kit!"

Emma forced Rose to the floor and turned her on her side. An endless stream of red ran steadily from her mouth to a space in front of the easel, then stopped in a contained puddle. Rose lay gasping as if unseen fingers were choking life from her.

"She's going, Emma," he screamed. "Do a trach!"

Emma counted down the seconds as she snapped sterile gloves in place. Placing her thumb and finger on Rose's throat, she stretched the skin and readied the scalpel. She counted. One minute...*50...40...30...20...10...* Two minutes.

"Do it!"

"No!" *10..9..8..7..* The knife hovered ready to obey. The point found the membrane. As Emma applied pressure, Rose began to cough. A weak breathing returned, then became regular. Air filled her lungs, as her eyelids separated the coagulated blood and partially opened.

Softly, she spoke three words. "Call Joseph Hightower."

"Are you all right? Do you want ice?"

Rose shook her head. "This was a simple test."

"You call this simple?" Burt muttered in disgust at his helplessness and took off his sweater, rolled it up and placed it under Rose's head. "It's not simple to me."

"The Olympics will come later. We need Joseph. Ask if he can do a walk about today, perhaps this evening."

When the team finished their first sweep and Rose had witnessed the disappearance of blood on her and was ready to proceed, they went downstairs to the kitchen, examined their notes and compared. There was fresh coffee and cold mineral water. Ben left a note inviting them to something harder in the fridge. Burt helped himself to a cold Stella, even though he knew Rose would disapprove.

After going over readings and comparing notes, they agreed that there was a constant cold spot in the middle of the studio, and Ben's bed had fluctuating warm to hot temperatures. That they all had smelled fragrances. The shadow was distinct. They reviewed the numbers – 1947 and 305 that had no significance to them. Rose went over her notes, and Burt confirmed he had left a message with Joseph Hightower to contact her. That it was urgent.

Before she talked with Ben, the team reviewed once again her psychometric findings to help Rose define more clearly the sensory intake she experienced and possible denominators they led too. They examined the tape closely. They agreed they saw a shadow hovering ten feet away and above Rose. A shadow that looked like an old man watching them. When she joined Ben and Vienna, they offered her a well-padded chair and foot stool and were concerned about the transformation that had overtaken her earlier composure. Using her fingers as a comb she tried to style her ashen waves that had fallen into her face that was still wet.

She moistened her lips, cleared her throat and composed herself before she asked Ben to start from the beginning. As he recalled every detail, Vienna offered her own take when Ben asked her for corroboration. She also told Rose about Greg Miller's serology tests and report. Rose nodded from time to time, then when they had exhausted their list of anomalies, it was Rose's turn.

"What we're finding is not different from what you already know and because of that I've asked a colleague to join us – Joseph Hightower who is a survival evidence medium, among other things. I'm not going to do a second sweep with my team until Joseph can do it with us. We need Joseph to conduct a séance. It would be best to do it today. I'm waiting for his call." Then Rose went over the cold and warm spots, the heightened electromagnetic field by the easel and in the bed, and shared what the team found.

Ben nodded in agreement and added details that the team hadn't experienced.

Slowly, Rose gave a descriptive replay of her reading. When she finished she went over what they had to research: deaths of women in the house, maybe a red-haired woman, the name Sisi, and the numbers, 1 9 4 7 and 3 0 5 that she had no way of decoding.

When she finished she returned to the subject of the second floor door that was closed, then decided it wasn't the right time to see it - it would be hard for her. That they should wait for Joseph to join them. She requested that Ben keep Annie away from the house for another day for her own safety.

"So what do we have here? Do you have any idea?"

"After what you've been through and what I've just experienced, it won't come as a surprise if I said that a tragic death, a violent act was committed in this house. I'm sensing a woman and perhaps a man as well. Two tragic passings. You do have a haunting, an intellectual haunting, but there's something else here, another power I can't identify. I do know something violently tragic took place here. It seems as though there's a trail this powerful presence wants us to follow, to strap us into the past, to see the truth and expose it and purge it. I don't know what this power is."

She explained what the intelligent haunting was – a presence not wanting to leave this plane but remaining - in this case, with traces of death and love. Fragrances, the warm bed, the whispers of pleasure and screams of pain.

She held them spellbound when she hypothesized about the other power – one that raged and was waiting for release. One that was more than intelligent. An element of nature with premeditation. Like a catastrophic storm premeditating its course. "This second power is beyond the small disturbances you're picking up on. I think it orchestrated what you experienced with Dr. Fife and what just happened to me. It's demonstrating its power to let us know it expects us to deliver what it wants."

"And if I can't?"

"I think it lost its heart and soul a long time ago. I think it's ready to rip out someone else's. It's running on pure energy. That's my take; I might be wrong."

"So you think there might be two presences?"

"Yes."

Abruptly Ben stood up and walked away. "I'm going to my daughter's room."

"I wouldn't go in," called Rose as she quickly took Vienna's hand and followed.

"It's a test," he said. "To see how much I can take."

"Maybe we shouldn't," Vienna whispered as they stared at the closed door.

Ben tried the door; it wouldn't open. "It's not locked, Rose."

She placed her hand gently on the wood. A slight vibration moved against her palms. She looked at Ben. "It doesn't want you in there."

"How do you know?"

"Because it's waiting for me." She stepped back and it opened. "Come with me." She waved them into the room. "You can be my witnesses."

"Should I get the others?"

"No, but get Burt's camera. Would you tape?"

Nothing had been disturbed. Everything was as Annie left it, except for the porcelain doll in the middle of her bed and a cold, damp earth smell like a farmer's field after a rain. Ben started taping. They remained quiet as Rose walked around the perimeter staring at the red-haired doll in the centre. She moved to the bed and reclined. Taking the doll into her arms she lay back, closed her eyes, sensing the price she'd have to pay for a surrendered touch.

She held the doll, breathed in its perfumes, and the earth smells around it until the smells became damp clay on her. She knew what this place was – a grave. Her fingers felt the doll's face – plump and smooth. The red waves fell like filament silk between her fingers.

Drawing the doll against her face, her forehead, Rose slipped into another history, like a disjointed dream: images diffused and infused, women and men and lovers, doll parts floating on classical notes, machines whirring, empty sockets seeing into her, a young child crying, a warm bath she was lowered into, then cloth wrapping itself around her, mummifying her. Around and around. Rose knew she was breathing, but she couldn't feel her lungs expanding nor contracting, as if air was not being breathed in or out.

Then darkness came, darker than blindness. People were talking, saying comforting words like *at rest* and *at peace* and *God's grace* and *God's will*. But Rose didn't feel comforted. Was not at rest. She felt as though black glass surrounded her and she couldn't see out of it. Not at peace! Not at rest! Then she heard cracking. As if the black glass and the endless rolls of cloth were breaking apart and fissures like veins were spreading all around her.

Piece by piece the blackness broke away. She felt exposed. Cold. Unprotected. She lay motionless and braced herself for the next days of biblical memory – dust to dust. Rose had studied two cases in which two different men had encountered burial and decomposition in their sensory exploration. She held on to the doll, her link back to the land of the living. The doll spoke from the grave, from a woman who had died, had been buried and returned in residual memory to this house.

The process began. Rose hovered above the woman. Looked down at her auburn hair, her white skin, her shrunken form. Then she prepared for fusion. She dissolved inside the dead woman's body. Rose felt her own body shutting down, cooling, stiffening and losing its defences. She started to bloat with bacteria and gases. Then the creatures came and free-ranged on her body. Black putrefaction started in.

And as all of this was speed-tracking through time, Rose saw the woman through the doll's eyes. She had been a woman adored transcontinentally. A woman who liked jazz. Who slipped in and out of smoky places with a dark-skinned man, high-cheek-boned and thin-lipped. There was a woman who held a baby to one breast. And the dark-skinned man to another. A woman who wore flowers hand painted in the small arch above her backside. A woman held by a dark-skinned man who whispered over and over, Sisi... Sisi while blood ran down his hands. A woman who cried under the weight of a white-haired man when he touched her. A woman swaddled and laid to rest with a child's doll in her arms. A woman, not at rest, but waiting in the center of a cataclysm.

Then suddenly Rose felt the remains of the woman being lifted from her interment place. Lifted. Jostled. Transported. And thrown down. *Find me! Find me!* Words threaded through Rose's visit. *Find me!* And she saw a Madonna with two children gathered around her on moss-eaten stone, and the numbers again barely discernible, 1947 and 305.

Ben watched in horror; Vienna turned away. Rose's skin had started to darken with foul, uneven pigments like bruised ponies galloping over her. Ben buried his nose in the crook of his arm. He watched her nails darken and fall off.

Rose felt her body begin to liquefy, ferment. Her organs melted away. A pool of putrid liquid gathered on her back and under her legs. Then dry rot set in slowly skeletonizing her. The creatures had burrowed into every orifice and cavity.

She lay decimated and waited for release. Waited to breathe again. To feel her lungs and heart move again. Time was running out. She felt pinned, locked down, devoured by someone else's history.

Vienna had turned away in horror.

Ben shook his head. "It's all wrong!" And screamed that Rose was trouble.

Martin and Emma rushed in, but Emma stretched out her arms to hold them back.

"Do something!" Ben shouted.

"No! We can't! She can't be touched!"

Ben looked at his watch and counted the seconds. Then like Well's time machine shimmering into existence Rose returned, the doll still in her arms as if unearthed.

She choked into existence. Air like desert dust forced itself in and out of her lungs. Heartbeats like timpani pounded inside of her. She sat up abruptly then ran into the washroom and cried and heaved.

"Don't go to her!" Emma ordered. "She needs to be alone. When she's ready she'll come back."

"Can I get anything for her?" Vienna asked trying to steady herself as she stood.

"Blankets. A cup of hot water. Green tea, if you have it."

She left gladly while Ben inspected the bed that had no traces of Rose's trauma. "What kind of power can do this?"

"We've never seen anything like it, have we, Emma?" Martin shivered and stayed by the door.

"No." Emma thought it best to give them some space and left with Mark to join the team in the kitchen.

Ben cradled Vienna into the kitchen, then went to the guest room for blankets. The sun was setting. They made tea and Ben turned on the fireplace and dimmed the ceiling lights.

Gently Emma knocked on the bathroom door. "Do you need any help?"

"Yes." Rose answered weakly. And the door opened.

Emma looked at the stricken woman. "What do you want me to do?"

"I don't know how to clean up. Look at all this crap. I think it's larvae and insect parts. Let's save a sample for Joseph?'

"How do you explain it?"

"I can't. We don't bring things back from sensory infusion, from looking into the past."

"I don't think you brought it back. I think the other presence did."

Rose nodded. "Help me."

After Emma washed her in the shower she called down to Vienna for loose clothes. When Rose was ready she emerged wearing a pair of Ben's track pants spotted with paint and a warm sweat shirt that Vienna found folded neatly in a clean clothes basket in the laundry room.

Vienna fit the blankets snugly around her and handed her the cup of tea. "Do you want it warmer?"

"No. It's good." Rose's wet hair hung in thick strands on her sunken shoulders. A faint odour like decaying vegetation oozed mildly from her skin. "I smell it too," she said reassuringly. "Pull your chair over, Ben."

Softly, he drew near.

"It was gentle with me."

"You call this gentle?" He looked over at a cabinet against the wall. "Is it okay to have a drink?" He held out his shaking hands for her to see.

"Only one. I need you alert and sharp, but I know this was a little too sharp."

"You got that right." He poured himself a tall Drambuie and asked Vienna if she wanted one to toast something with him.

She nodded.

When all were seated Ben asked if Rose were in any pain.

"Discomfort. Psychosomatic metamorphosis." She finished her water and handed Vienna her cup. "I've never experienced anything like it. I've read about it. So, I'll try not to leave anything out." She tried to sit more upright to invite more wind into her lungs.

"This doll is buried with a woman in a family crypt. It would make sense that it's here, in Toronto. She was a young woman when she died. She was loved. And known. She left behind a little girl. I feel the woman died in this house. I sense her tragedy. I saw her face. It reinforces what I felt during the first session with the mirror."

"Would you recognize her if you saw a picture or a painting of her?"

"Yes, I would. But I didn't see her name. I heard what could have been a nickname – Sisi. Yes, Sisi."

"I've heard that name too."

"Something strange happened after I heard that name."

"What?"

"I felt like she was being lifted and carried away."

"After she was dead?"

"I'm not sure."

"Was it her energy departing?"

"I don't know. It's so important that Joseph conduct his own investigation. He'll be able to see much more. I know I suggested it before, but Annie should not stay here. It's risky."

"This is going to sound crazy, but I think I've met the little girl you saw. She's a married woman now. The doll belonged to her. I can get a picture of the woman and the little girl."

Vienna looked questioningly at him. "What picture?"

"At the Westings. I saw this doll in a picture with Beverly last night."

"The Westings?" asked Rose, amazed that Ben had been invited into their circle.

"Beverly Westing was three. Her mother died from a supposed asthma attack."

"You think all of this has something to do with them?"

"We were brought together by Billy...."

"Holliday," finished Rose. "I heard her singing in the transvisitation. I saw her face."

Ben nodded. "It can't be a coincidence."

"Who am I in all of this?" asked Vienna.

"I don't know, but I want to find out. Don't you?"

"Yeah. I want to know everything."

"I know you do. I'm glad you do." Ben went on to fill in the narrative blanks for Rose about how he ended up at Beverly Westing's party. And what he thought needed to be done.

Emma took a call from Joseph Hightower saying he'd be there around six, and at 5:30 Mark Chainy arrived with coupons to order in Chinese, Thai or Mexican.

Ben introduced Mark to the team with a brief overview of their jobs, and Rose felt strong enough to gather her people together in the family room and leave Ben and Vienna alone with their guest until Joseph arrived.

When Mark passed around the flyers with a short commentary on the quality of the food on each flyer, Vienna felt queasy and knotted, but tried to be appreciative. She held out her glass for Ben to fill up. "I need another."

"Me too," Mark added. The liqueur burned a smooth path down his throat. "Should I go?" he asked. "You guys look....preoccupied."

"No! I really want you to stay."

"I feel invisible, like you don't know I'm here."

"No. Sorry. There's this guy, this psychic coming over soon. Joseph Hightower. They phoned for him because whatever is here is too much for them to handle. He's a medium. Rose wants him to conduct a séance."

"Oh. I definitely wanna hang around for that."

And Ben went over what the first investigation turned up. And how Rose looked like she was dead. And how she had never witnessed anything like it before.

"I wanna go up there." And he pointed to the studio.

"You can't be an asshole up there. You can't piss it off. You have to be respectful."

"I just want you to show me what the hell's been going on."

"Okay."

"I'm staying here." Vienna curled up with her glass and put her cold feet under a pillow. "Don't call me if you need me."

"You don't like this ghost, do you?"

She raised her glass with one hand and her finger with the other.

When they passed the family room, Burt was examining the camera to see if it was damaged after Ben had dropped it, and Ben asked if he could borrow it.

Gently Ben opened the studio door and cautioned Mark to keep calm. They stepped in.

"It's cold in here, man."

"I know." And Ben cued up the footage from Rose's interaction. "Have a look at this. It happened in Annie's room an hour ago." Ben explained what Rose's field of expertise was and how it worked.

Ben noticed Mark was shivering and suggested they could sit up against his bed that was warmer at the other end.

"Where's the heat coming from?" Mark looked for hot air vents, but there weren't any. "Why is it so hot here?"

"It's the bed. The... bed."

"Really? It's not an electric blanket?"

"No it's just The Bed. Probably where they did it. You know the artist and this woman. Fifty years ago."

"Okay." They sat down and Mark let the radiant heat dissolve into his pores. As they watched the replay, Mark cringed and turned away.

When it was over Mark was stunned. "Yeah, at first she looked like she maybe was faking all this possession shit, but you can't fake fingernails rotting and falling off." Mark was disgusted. "And this happened right in this house?"

"In Annie's room. She wasn't being possessed – at least not in the Hollywood explanation of possession." Ben walked him to the centre.

Suddenly, Mark ducked when a shadow that had been crouched inside the skylight swooped down for a closer look. Mark fell at Ben's feet shouting. "What the hell was that? What should I do? Run? Aren't you scared, man? Don't let it get me!"

Ben spoke to the presence. "This is Mark. He only looks dangerous, but he's not." "Sh...don't get it mad! Here's the deal. When you say it's safe to run, I'm outta here. When you say it's safe, okay? Is it safe? Is it still there? Is it safe?"

"Sh....just stay calm. It's not a bee or an anaconda. It's just a presence. Harmless."

"Can I stand up?"

"Yup."

Holding on to Ben's shirt Mark pulled himself up. "I can't stop shaking. You've made a believer outta me. Do you want me to stay or should I go? Are you sure there aren't too many fingers in the pie? All those techies downstairs and your girlfriend? I could go. You won't offend me if you ask me to go."

"I want you to stay. Somehow you make me feel stronger." And Ben started laughing – little bursts at first. Then bigger eruptions until he fell down and drew his knees up to his chest to ease the laugh cramps. It had been the first real laugh since he met Wendy and her fiancée, Ace, and Annie asked Ben if he thought Wendy would pay her to babysit him. It was so unexpected that Ben went A.W.O.L., just like now, when he watched Mark shrink, as this smoky residue thing swooped down on him.

"I don't think you should be laughing, man. It looks like hard work. You're too thin already." He offered Ben his sleeve to wipe his tears. "Okay, I've seen enough. I need to drink or get stoned. Do you have anything?"

"No."

"It's okay. I brought stuff." He helped Ben up and dry his face.

"Watch this." They stopped on the stairwell and looked back. The door closed itself.

"Of course," Mark said without surprise.

14

As he walked down the street Joseph Hightower could feel what Rose was concerned about – a power source so strong that it had sucked her into someone else's physical history. He stood as Ben did every day, on the sidewalk and looked up to the third story. *I'm here. Don't bullshit me. Don't play games with me. You don't want to do that.* Something swayed him from the inside out like the first three bars of some Latin jazz classic. *I didn't come all this way to dance. When I'm finished here, you'll be dancing on the other side of the divide. That's what you want, right? I'm going to help that happen.*

He had never ridden a horse, had never been on a farm, but he felt like he rode to each visitation on a shiny steed, like a cowboy on a horse that would end up someday in the Smithsonian. His inner voice (his almost ventriloquist voice) took on a quasi-Texan drawl to compensate for his short, slight stature – an irony people didn't expect given his name, Hightower. This is how he saw himself.

Vienna let him in and felt an immediate warmth circumventing his awkwardness. A man who she thought was the antithesis of his name. At fifty he was boyish and round-faced with flat, long, bleached-blond hair combed to the side, as if ready for a school picture. His large, caricature-like green eyes, that were like diagonal almonds, were deep pools behind which Vienna knew the world in all its clarity resided. She felt him scanning her without judgement.

After introductions, Joseph requested a quiet place to talk with Rose in private and followed Ben to the family room and closed the door. After he warmly kissed both sides of her face he examined her colour. "Not good. You're almost blue." He placed the back of his hand on her forehead. "You're still cold. I can smell the interment on you. I don't like you taking risks like that."

"I'm not joking when I say I never want to do that again. Ever."

"That bad?"

"That monstrous! A monster led me there, kept me there. Almost didn't let me come home. I didn't tell the others that." She produced the tissue from her pocket and unfolded it. This came back with me."

Joseph examined the tiny, dead creatures that had fed on her corpse. "Did you see this monster?"

"No."

"Intelligent?"

"Excessively. A powerful energy fingerprinting itself in our world from God knows where. It won't leave. And I think there are two. There's another presence. An intelligent energy who is waiting. A woman who is waiting, but she wasn't the one who took me into the grave. It was this other power, a power like a demi-god who I feel is premeditating all of this. Like it's a self-ordained god on some mythical mission."

"Don't go poetic on me. Speak science. I don't know what you mean."

"I don't even have a handle on it yet."

"So let me get this straight. You think there are two presences - one that is waiting to be released and the other that is a manipulative energy who wants to do what? A poltergeist? Maybe wanting to help the other to pass?"

"It's totally possible. There was great love in this house. And even greater tragedy. I don't think either has passed. I think the tragedy is very much alive. After what Ben and Vienna have experienced and myself as well, I feel there is a manipulative energy, not only in this house, but in Ben's life." Rose went on to describe the lab tests that Dr. Fife did on Ben and how this power was present outside of this physical space.

Joseph smiled. "Not your usual run-of-the-mill haunting." He felt her forehead again. "You're getting warmer." And his hand travelled down the side of her face.

"I've never felt like this before."

"Like what exactly?"

'Like I was in the presence of something that might have been human, but isn't anymore. Like it has found a way to infuse its soul into some super power."

"It can be done. I have to see it for myself. Let me have a look at the studio before we start. Maybe your monster will introduce itself. I can find my way up. And I want you to get something to eat."

Joseph Hightower wouldn't be walking up to the studio, wouldn't even care to walk up to the studio if he hadn't gotten two doctorates - one in quantum physics and the other in neuroscience. If he hadn't spearheaded research at Queens University on mental programming, active visualization and engineered brainwave training, he wouldn't be walking up these third story stairs.

He stood outside the door. Waiting. Waiting.

It didn't open.

Oh, I see. I'm not here to tame you. You're here to tame me. I'll give you the respect you deserve if that's what you want. He opened the door.

There was a drawing table, a computer station, an easel in the centre, a bed at one end, a built-in storage space, wide, warm, pine floors and bright skylights. It was quiet. Comfortable.

Have a good look. I'm a small man. Boy-faced. Brain-evolved. Have we established something? I respect you; you respect me? Why don't you introduce yourself? I want to see you. I need to believe we have important things to do.

Joseph found himself moving in front of a mirror beside Ben's wardrobe. He stared into it aware that it held him for several minutes. Joseph didn't move. Handwriting

– not Joseph's – flowed slowly in lines, one after each other, unfolding a moment in history that was the last moment Joseph lived as a married man before his wife lost her battle with cancer. He repeated what was written, *I would give up every passion I've ever had for one last minute with you in my arms.* These were the words he had said before she took her last breath.

He stepped back and turned around. *Who are you? Am I that transparent? Who are you? I want to see you.*

As if a bomb detonated in the centre of the room – its brilliant mushroom sending shock waves of light throughout the space – a brilliance shone so powerfully that Joseph had to shield his eyes, felt the radiance burn his face, and quickly covered his skin with his shirt. As the waves subsided, standing in the middle and rising ten feet to the highest pitch of the ceiling, towered a mammoth body of shimmering particles that were both charged with heat and blinding light, the particles of which, moved about in mini-collisions with each other - bouncing, colliding particles of intense light.

Squinting and trying to look through the loose weave of his shirt, Joseph saw the shimmering particles form wings – feathered and muscular that folded and unfolded in their show of power. Wings along which fire travelled and made them appear to be burning. A cool, white fire.

Joseph reached his hand toward it. Rays licked their way down his hand. A cool, burning sensation drew him closer until he was surrounded by an enormous wing span. Standing below the massive form Joseph looked up into the unmistakable face of himself.

Do you think I am this powerful? Why are you doing this? Who are you?

The wings enfolded him.

* * * *

135

"It's been twenty minutes. How long does it take for a quick look?" Mark kept looking at his watch then at the ceiling as if expecting to see through two floors into the attic. "Should Ben go up?"

Rose tried not to show her concern and remained quiet.

"Do you want me to see if he's okay?"

"Ben, he'll be all right."

"What's Joseph's story? What's his line of work?" asked Mark.

"Research at Queens. Quantum physics and mental programming, brainwave training."

"What's that?"

"He was conducting experiments with active mental visualization that would impact on both our internal and external lives."

"Like the power of positive thinking," added Ben.

Rose smiled. "Something like that, but a little bit more complicated."

Vienna believed in mental visualization and how it could impact both negatively and positively on a person's life. She was convinced that through visualization she brought Bobby back for one night. And before she started a new art piece, she often visualized an entire painting. When she was ready to paint, it was like it was already there, like she was manifesting her vision.

"Some people can actually alter their physical surroundings by rearranging particles, displacing and replacing them through visualizing."

"Can Joseph?" asked Ben.

"He's conducted conclusive experiments."

Ben didn't probe further but checked the time. "I think I should go up."

"I'll come too," offered Vienna.

"I'll stay with Rose," Mark insisted.

As they started up the stairs, the studio door opened. Joseph backed out slowly closing it gently. He stood a moment, bowed his head and clasped his hands, then turned to go down.

Vienna rushed up to meet him. "You're burned. Your face, your hands!"

He was both weak and energized. He steadied himself on her arm and all of them returned to the family room. Rose inspected his hands as blisters formed on their backs.

"Do you need a doctor?" Ben asked.

"Not really. I'll be all right." And he leaned toward Rose. "We need to talk."

* * * *

Joseph asked Rose to send the team home and to ask them to reconvene Monday evening at 6:30 to tape a séance. He needed time to reflect. When everyone had packed up and said their good-byes, Joseph asked Ben if everyone could gather around the kitchen table to talk. Ben insisted that Mark stay for moral support, and while Mark would rather have been at home with TSN and MGD, RIS or ANPA (his favourite brews), he agreed to stay.

Ben thought Joseph was being theatrical when tears formed in his eyes and his voice cracked when he tried to speak. And Rose had never seen Joseph so vulnerable; so they waited until he could handle his emotions.

A humble smile formed on his trembling lips. "Everyone, I suppose, thinks scientists don't cry – real scientists don't cry." His smile broadened. "I can't help it."

Rose watched Vienna mother Joseph, even though he was a stranger – something Rose should have done. "Take your time," Vienna soothed. Moving to him she drew back his hair that had fallen over his forehead to see if there were burns and did the same with the collar of his sweater – unbuttoning the top two buttons and looking at his neck. There were none.

"Can you tell us what happened?" asked Rose gently.

"I want to. You've all earned the truth. It must have been terrifying for you, Ben. What you've gone through in the past month."

"I have a little girl. I just want her to be safe."

"Can I please have a paper towel?" Joseph felt the salty tears run over his burned face.

Vienna got one and handed it to him.

"I haven't cried like this since my wife, Clair, died last year."

"We've all lost someone we really loved."

"I haven't," said Rose. "Not a pet, not a lover, not a parent, sibling. No one close."

"Maybe that's why this energy didn't trust you to understand, but chose to give you the darker side of the past. You haven't loved and lost yet."

She didn't comment. "Did you see it?"

He nodded and hung his head low, his eyes closed in disbelief.

"What it did to me was gentle, but not kind," Rose said. "What it did was motivated by rage. I experienced dying. I felt all the sensations, but I wasn't in pain. I didn't know if I was going to come back."

"Vienna was struck too," added Ben. "In her back. It pinned her."

"But it let me go, Ben. And it gave us that night."

"Yeah, I heard about that," Mark said clearing his throat and trying to focus.

"We've seen both sides of this presence," Ben added.

"It's not monstrous."

"Joseph, how can you say that?" Rose was perplexed and waited for him to explain.

"Perhaps you went in with a bias, that made this presence hostile, and that's why it delivered what you expected in the manner it did, but what I saw, what I experienced was from a source filled with altruistic tendencies."

"What makes you think it's altruistic?" asked Ben.

"I saw it. I spoke to it. It's not a Hollywood monster or a demon - it's an angel."

"Get outta here!" Mark said.

"Did I not tell you it had a power that was like a demi-god?"

"An insightful feeling, Rose." Joseph tapped his fingertips together, then added. "But it's not a demi-god and angels supposedly were never human. This angel is man-made. A sixth-order angel, called a Throne, a bringer of justice. Very powerful."

No one spoke. Took a minute to consider what Joseph had said.

Then Vienna. "Man-made? What does that mean?"

"A poltergeist," clarified Rose.

"Yes," confirmed Joseph. "But much more."

"Like in the movie?" Mark asked.

"No."

"I really need you to explain what you're talking about." Ben didn't know whether he felt totally defeated or encouraged, but he was angered.

"In layman's terms, Joseph," suggested Rose.

He tried to simplify it as much as he could to explain that poltergeist activity is caused by living people who have experienced trauma and are manifesting their extreme emotions in telekinetic disturbances.

Ben shook his head in disbelief. Couldn't wrap his mind around the idea that some maniac outside of his home was doing all of this in his home. "No! No! Come on! I need another theory that will stick, because this just isn't!" He stood up and paced. His face reddened. "Come on!"

Rose understood his confusion, but reassured him that most modern research validated what Joseph said.

"And you saw this man-made angel? This Throne thing?"

"I saw it."

"What exactly did you see? Are you on meds?"

"Ben," Vienna whispered. "Try to keep calm. Please."

"How can I? I was hoping for something easy! Like it's some spirit that hasn't passed on and we can sprinkle some holy water on it and it'll disappear. I'm packing up and leaving. Tonight."

"Ben, let Joseph explain. This is his field. He's here to help you." Rose nodded at Joseph to continue while Ben sank into his chair, half listening.

"I was in its energy. It showed me things similar to what happened to you and Dr. Fife at the clinic. These disturbances are being released from the power of an individual who over a great period of time has studied and practised these visualization skills. I've never encountered anything like it before – power that goes into our brain waves to cause us to see things real and imagined. Power he can manipulate to recreate his visualizations in another space, wherever he chooses. This person has suffered the most horrible trauma anyone can endure, and I feel his time is running out. He's fighting for something he cherishes more than life itself."

"What is it?"

"I don't know. That's what I hope to find out." Joseph knew that all wars were relative in their pain and loss and destruction. Even though he and his wife fought eight years against her cancer and rehearsed all the cues for his recovery after she passed, he felt no one had gone to war like he had and had come home so scarred. "I don't know what it's fighting for."

"How do we find out?" asked Vienna.

"Rose said there was another presence. A woman."

"A red-haired woman?" asked Ben.

"Yes."

"I want to do a séance. I think this powerful energy is here for this other, intelligent presence that remains between two planes. I want to find out why he's here and how she figures in. I would like to do this tomorrow evening, if that okay, Ben."

"Yeah, it's good."

"I would like your daughter to be present."

"Emphatically, no! What's wrong with you?"

"What if I tell you she wouldn't be hurt. That if this presence, this woman connects to your daughter, we would be able to contact her better and to understand why she's still here."

"No! What don't you understand about *no*?"

"Ben is right. Annie's not going to be here," argued Vienna.

"Okay. I respect that. I had to try, but I understand your objections."

"I'd like to invite a friend," Ben requested.

"I don't want curiosity-seekers."

Rose patted Joseph's hand which was returning to its normal pigment. "Ben is talking about Ms. Beverly Westing."

Ben didn't ask Rose how she knew. He accepted her gifts however surprising they were.

"The... Ms. Westing? Why?"

Ben took a deep breath. "I think her mother, Alexsis Ingles, is in this house. I think she's the one haunting me."

Joseph eyes sparkled. "Really. I trust your judgement. I don't have to know the details." He took a moment to consider. "All right. Call her."

When they left, Mark tried to convince Ben to stay the night with him, but Ben insisted he needed his house even if it was under attack. Ben asked Mark to take Vienna home, but to hold back on spilling all of Ben's delinquent, near indictable offences on their European tour, when they were less than men.

As she took Mark's arm she turned to Ben and let her mouth form the words, "I love you." And watched his eyes fall on her like they never had before.

Ben went into Annie's room, changed her earth-soiled sheets, lit a pumpkin 'n spice candle (Annie's favourite) and sat looking at her family pictures pinned to her bulletin board.

15

Wendy refused to believe that Ben wanted her to keep Annie another night, because he had publishing problems and not girlfriend problems. She also confessed to Ben that she had gotten to know how funny Annie was and how giving she was, and that she never would have guessed that Ben would be such a great dad, because he had never been a great husband. She thought it was nice of him to want to pick Annie up from school, take her to an early dinner, then drop her off at Wendy's. She hinted at figuring out a new arrangement for mutual visits and shared responsibilities that Annie thought could work. It relieved him, and he told her.

* * * *

Even though Bev Westing had planned a full week of social and family events for Harvard and Mickey, Monday was open. Harvard was flying to Ottawa with friends, while Mickey was spending the day and night with her grandchildren.

Bev was glad to hear from Ben, but when he said he didn't want to alarm her, but he urgently needed to speak to her about her mother, and that Dr. Rose Henhawke, a renowned geophysicist would be joining him, she anxiously waited for their arrival at one.

Bev liked Rose as soon as she saw her. Mutually both women felt they were in the presence of each other's strengths. "I smell science in every pore of your body. Science seasoned with a pinch of mysticism," Bev commented.

"Ben told me you were honest and direct. I have two doctorates – one in Kinesiology and one in Geophysics. That takes care of the sciences. But I've devoted the last fifteen years to Psychometry. I work with clinics, law enforcement, and other clients, many of whom are in Ben's situation, to help them deal with psychological anomalies. She could have, but didn't tell them she worked with Scotland Yard in its investigation of the Princess of Wales' accident and with the investigation of the Antwerp Diamond Heist in 2003 and too many others to mention. She focused on Bev.

"Before we talk, is it all right if I walk around and look."

"Sure. Take your time."

The great room was a special place – like a personalized museum with an artistic, eclectic bent, with every wall showcasing multi-faceted histories. She stood in front of the large painting of Bev's mother at five and her grandmother wearing the signs of anemia and sadness under rich red lips and dark stencilled brows. Mother held her daughter close as they stood beside an intricately carved temple, the Hadimba Temple, surrounded by tall, shady Deodar trees on one side and an elephant saddled with colourful blankets and umbrella on the other.

Rose drew close. She had seen this child. She had watched this child lose all resemblance of youth and womanhood in an early grave. As she panned the room, a table caught her eye. She examined one artefact – the picture of Bev Westing at the age of three, holding a porcelain doll, the same token-object Rose had held in her investigation.

A tray of organic biscuits and teas arrived that Bev offered to her guests. "Take whatever you like."

While they steeped their tea, all three thought in their own way about the complexity of history and its aftermath – how things set in motion are like twisters spiralling to some destination, bringing with it and perhaps together people and their deeds and their valuables. And that inside this twister's centrifugal force important events get forgotten and buried and others get warped and rewritten, but at some point they arrive at their destination with everything falling together in an unrecognizable, incongruous union of disparate pasts. Like the three of them – a graphic novelist, a Toronto millionaire/philanthropist, a scientist/psychic hurled together to understand history as it should have been written.

"We must be thinking the same thing," Rose ventured.

Bev smiled. "How different we are, yet here, together to pool our resources to solve a mystery?"

"The mystery of Ben Needham's haunted house. It's a good book title. We need Nancy Drew." Ben tried to lighten the occasion.

"It's much darker than that, isn't it, Ben? You wanted to talk about my mother. I want to hear what you have to say. I know whatever it is, you think I'll challenge you. I'll have to until I can get all the answers I need to accept it."

"We plan on getting them, Ms. Westing. But we need your help. We need your open-mindedness, your trust and your need to hear the truth," Rose said.

"Call me Bev."

Ben felt helpless. "I'm not an expert at protecting people's beliefs or hearts. I don't know how to protect you from the things I've seen."

"Start at the beginning, Ben. It's a good place to start."

"Let's start with a test instead," suggested Rose. "May I have your ring?" Rose extended the palm of her left hand, and Bev placed her wedding ring in it. Rose touched it gently, closed her eyes and softly commented on its genesis and ownership. "The gold is from Southern Rhodesia, the maharatna or precious gems are from central India, the diamond is a rare, Golconda blue diamond, 1760. The ring was given to your grandmother as a parting gift from the new owners of the company your dad had owned. It was given to your grandmother for her great humanitarian work. The ring was said to have been worn by Queen Lakshmi Bai – a gift from her husband, the Raja of Jhansi in the 1800s. Your grandfather gave it as a wedding ring to Alexsis in 1952. Your father, Howard Ingles, removed it from your mother's finger as she was being buried – an afterthought – and gave it to you to keep for your own marriage, but he didn't live to see that. It was then, when he removed the ring that you plunged forward and put your doll in your mother's arms and said, "Sisi will take care of you, mommy."

Rose opened her eyes.

Bev was stunned and stricken and tried to remain composed. "Yes. I had forgotten. I called my doll, Sisi." She couldn't help thinking, when she looked into Rose's eyes, that underneath the calm satisfaction of exposing other people's memories she hid her own. "Thank you for giving me this memory." She turned to Ben. "I'm ready."

"When I'm done you can walk away, never speak to me again, if you want to, but I have to do whatever it takes to make my home safe for Annie and me. I really need you there."

"Sometimes, I hear my mom crying in my dreams. And I don't know why she's crying. I don't know how to help her."

"We don't know either, but we want to find out."

* * * *

Bev listened to everything – all the outrageous, unbelievable details that were like carnivores eating through the linings of her lungs and into her heart. By mid-afternoon, the cold, November light crept between the shutters and fell lifelessly on the autumn guests.

Bill's flight home from Ottawa got in early. He passed the great room and felt that it was ice-bitten in its hard light and silence. He passed once without seeing any signs of Bev, then when he saw the tray and cold pot of tea on the coffee table he poked his head inside and entered.

There was no conversation – not even small talk – as if everyone was stuck in a freeze-frame. He was glad he hadn't missed Ben.

"Run out of syllables?" he joked.

Before she introduced Rose she asked Bill, "Would you do something unconditional with me, if I told you it was the most important thing in my life right now?"

"Not if it's getting rid of the aviary," he joked again.

Bev waited.

"You're not going to tell me what it is, are you? Okay, I'll take a leap of faith."

Bev turned her attention to Rose. "This is Dr. Rose Henhawke. She and Ben and Vienna have invited us to Ben's home this evening for seven."

"Why didn't you say that? All this mumbo jumbo about unconditional devotion and sacrifice. You thought I'd say no, to this? What's wrong with you, woman? I guess I should be asking why Ben's place is the most important thing in your life right now. We do have family visiting. They're pretty important."

"You'll have to wait to find out, but it is."

Ben added, "It's the most important thing right now in my life too." He stood up and shook Bill's hand, while Bev remained seated, trying to conceal that her energy was slowly draining. He had spared no details in recounting the last two months. And as a result, Bev felt weighted in quicksand.

"We should go. Can you come before seven? We'll have all the equipment set up."

"Rose?" Bev asked, "will you touch my husband's scarf?"

Bill laughed. "Have you been into that stuff again, the stuff in your jewelry box in the back of your third dresser drawer? What's going on?"

Rose reached out and slid her hand over the weave and stared into his captive eyes. "It's a Scottish worsted Vicuna from Holland and Sherry, auctioned off after the premiere of *Moulin Rouge*. It would be impolite to tell how much you paid."

"Indulge me," Bill requested.

Rose leaned in and whispered in his ear, "$20,000."

Bill smiled first, then Bev, who knew Rose's price had been accurate.

"I'll see you tonight," Ben said enjoying their inside joke.

After Ben dropped Rose off he picked Annie and Vienna up at school, went to dinner, then to Wendy and Ace's. Ben could see that Annie wasn't pretending to enjoy her mom's company. He could see that Wendy was genuinely thrilled about this new parenting experience. She even had a Yamaha delivered for Annie to play when she visited, and as juvenile as Ace (Wendy's husband) was, Annie somehow warmed to the idea that this University of Toronto, grad, music student was more like an older brother – one who actually took the time to show her a thing or two on the keyboard and on his guitar.

When Annie talked excitedly in hyper-mode, Ben knew he had nothing to worry about. Ace could do this and that. Wendy and Ace wanted to take her here and there - to a concert and to a real recording studio. And when Wendy asked her to stay all week, Annie said she couldn't, that she needed to help Ben with da Vinci and that da Vinci missed her too much, but she couldn't refuse Wendy's invitation to attend the fund raising and gala premiere of *Children of the Glitter War*, an African documentary that Wendy's global charity, *Need to Be More*, was holding later in the week. And that mother and daughter were going to shop in places that Annie didn't know existed in magazines, let alone on the streets of Toronto.

When Ben hugged her good-bye, Annie complained he was squeezing too tight, squeezing her dinner out of her at both ends. And she ordered him not to cry and to give da Vinci a big hug and tell him she'd be home tomorrow.

He promised he wouldn't and he would.

16

He was certain that drivers and pedestrians saw him standing on the sidewalk outside of his house, looking up at the third story window. A compulsive voyeur. It had become a ritual, and today Vienna stood with him until he was ready to approach the locked door. He didn't feel so alone anymore. There was a small circle of believers that had come to his rescue and witnessed his mutating life. And he was thankful Annie was safe.

Six o'clock. He turned the key and entered.

As Rose had requested, they cleared the dining room table, added more chairs and went about freeing up electrical outlets in case they needed them for equipment. Rose had cautioned against using candles, so they let the kitchen light spill into the dining room. Ben found an old alarm clock and put it on the sideboard.

Before the others arrived Ben and Vienna went upstairs for a moment of reflection. He decided to get the tin box from the storage cupboard to show Bev. They walked about and Vienna stared at the centre of the room remembering her ordeal and wondered what was to come. Ben wanted a few moments alone and asked her to take the box downstairs and wait for him. She held him as if her were a preserved relic dug out of some ancient ruin – he seemed ancient and refined, sheltered yet exposed and waiting for resurrection. She left quietly.

He examined the troubled areas of his private space where for a living he invented misfit characters who jumped from his mind, through software, on to pulp, armchair adventures. Then how his world of manic invention had been invaded and offered him an adventure of another kind – an adventure to free someone or something from a prison Ben didn't understand. *I'm not a superhero. I'm not one of my characters in my novels.*

A cold, damp current descended. The moon wall had begun to take shape. *Is that where you are? Behind a wall? In a grave? A cold cell?* Ben shivered and thought that if a mythological devil walked up to him and breathed on him it would feel like this moon wall. He linked his fingers behind his head and twisted his back to the right, then left. He felt awakened as if from a deep sleep.

This is it. Everyone who can help you will be here. You'll have your moment. Take it.

At 6:45 they arrived. Burt couldn't make it – an empty bottle followed by a minor, nervous meltdown kept him under, so Joseph asked Mark if he'd work the hand held video camera. Joseph positioned Emma with the magnetometer, Martin with his thermal imager and Justin with the stationary night vision intensifier. After minor adjustments were made, Joseph seated everyone at the table – Joseph at the head, Ben and Vienna to his right, Rose to his left. At the other end was Bev with Bill drawing close to her on her right. Introductions followed.

"This isn't a Tupperware party, is it?" Bill joked and laughed. He was a non-believer and had to remember not to make a total asshole of himself.

"And you still came?" Joseph smiled. "Let me give you an overview of the anomalous activities in Ben's life." He covered the disturbances, the serology report, Evan Fife's testing, the Holiday connection and their first investigation.

Bev hadn't given Bill details, so she patted his hand to assure him of how appreciative she was. "Thanks for coming with me," she whispered.

Bill didn't care where he was or who was with him. He leaned close to his wife, letting his lips brush against her ear. "I knew three things the first day I met you – that I loved you, that I would walk with you in two worlds – the one I know exists and the one you know exists – and that

I'd follow you anywhere. Here I am." He turned to Ben. "Are you ready?"

"Let's do this."

Joseph suddenly excused himself, disappearing out of the room and returning soon after with Ben's easel, painting and a brush. He set them up behind Ben. "I don't think we'll need the canvas, but, Vienna, would you record any visuals on the canvas if you feel the pull?"

She nodded, took a deep breath, pursed her lips and exhaled slowly.

Rose had brought a large sketch pad and a marker and placed it on the table in front of her. Then reaching to the floor she lifted the toffee box and passed it to Bev. "It was in a storage cupboard in Ben's studio."

"Annie painted the exact figure in art class without knowing the box existed."

Bev stared at the young red-haired woman – a teenager – who could have sold sand to a camel. She clutched Bill's hand. They stared bewildered at the resemblance to Alexsis Ingles.

The bright amber street light suddenly died and the room darkened. Flickering on and off, the kitchen light cast an intermittent strobe on the gathering.

"I have a flameless candle," offered Ben.

"It could be useful," said Joseph and asked Ben to place it in the middle of the table. When it was in place they began.

Rose picked up the marker and moved her hand to the top of the paper.

"Just relax." Joseph's voice was soothingly omnipotent. "Empty your thoughts. Let all your worries drain away like snow in a spring rain. Relax. Relax your shoulders. Let your hands feel weightless. Breathe slowly, deeply. Relax."

The fridge which had been humming stopped. The damp fog crawled along the floor, then slithered up their legs, bodies, to their faces, and through their hair until their scalps felt like corrugated paper.

"Relax. Breathe calmly."

"Should we close our eyes?" whispered Bev.

"You don't have to."

A minute was a long time for the air currents to swirl noiselessly about the room, and by the end of that minute, the anomalous residue from the other plane migrated to the plane of the living and reached out to them. The fragments inside the tin box rattled. Bev thought she heard a soft, child-like cry, muffled inside the box. She felt a mild, electric current spread across her skin, like the sudden warmth of the summer sun appearing in between clouds.

Rose's hand became weighted on top of the paper – she couldn't move it away.

Joseph closed his eyes and spoke, "We're here for you. We're here to help you. To listen to you."

The candle glowed brighter as if the battery experienced a power surge. Unexpectedly, the moon wall drifted toward the candle and started encircling it, like a foggy whirlpool. The tin box rattled toward the swirling funnel and was pulled in. Everyone felt the centrifugal force pulling on them. Vienna felt her ring slide down her finger toward the whirling fog.

Suddenly, the fog dissipated as if the candle absorbed it.

"Are you in this room?" asked Joseph.

Rose's hand slid over the paper. *Yes.* "Yes," said Rose and wrote it out.

Again the street light sparked into existence and shone through the dining room window.

"Are you the woman in the red-striped bathing suit? The woman with the red hair?"

No. "No," said Rose. *No... no... no... no...* The ink scribbled over and over.

The candle brightened, and a buzzing static emanated from its battery as if it were transmitting. Everyone strained to listen to the distant sounds of laughter and music and conversation that faded in and out of the static: *ma cherie... more wine... si... si... grazie... another song...* and then a report... *thousands of fans crowd... the Mars bar... Mary... De Franco...* The static increased and drowned out the sounds.

"Is the woman with the red hair in this house?"

Yes. "Yes," shouted Rose and felt her pulse quicken.

"Did you live in this house?"

A sudden, intermittent clanging in the radiators filled the room. Sounds like beats, like code rang out – one clang, then nine, five, five again, two, one nine, five, eight.

"Did you get that, Rose?"

"Yes."

The sounds shot about like gunfire and crackled with feedback as the team recorded.

Joseph proceeded. "Did you die in this house?"

No..no..no.. "No," said Rose. Quickly she ripped away the paper to the next page as the marker dug in like an engraving tool. *No...no...no.* Rip...rip...rip..

"You said you did not die in this house. Where did you die?"

The street light exploded in brilliance. The wax cylinder encasing of the candle's battery started to melt. As white light blazoned into the room, everyone squinted in its power.

"Are you still alive?"

They felt swallowed in an iridescent iceberg. Their breath froze in their throats as breathing became crystallized.

"Are you still alive?"

The windows rattled, the doors on the sideboard flew open, then banged shut. The table twisted to the right, then left, then vibrated until it left the floor, then crashed down.

Yes... yes... yes. "Yes," shouted Rose. The marker swept across the page in large strokes. *Yes... yes... si...si... yes... yes.*

"What is your name?"

There was no response.

"Will you tell us your name?" Joseph's face felt frost-bitten as he waited for a name. Cold strands of blond hair fell into his eyes. "What is your name?" It wasn't given. Joseph calmed. Took a moment to will warmth into his face. Breathed deeply and calmly. Then, "Who is the woman in the painting?"

The room quieted. Warmth returned. Seductive notes of Harlem Nocturne sounded around them and singing and words: *for you, Lexi, for you.* They heard the words as smoky jazz floated on instrumental purity.

Vienna felt weightless as she moved to the easel. "Ben? What's happening?" her voice choked painfully.

"She'll be okay," assured Joseph.

Taking up the paint brush, colour exploded on to the canvas until the red-haired woman smiled through the colour-soaked threads and she reached for Vienna.

"Wow!" whispered Mark. "I'm getting everything!"

"Ben?" cried Vienna. "She's touching me!"

"Don't be frightened."

Vienna tried to smile, as the woman's energy floated away from the painting – glistening with raw oils, surrounded by the mixed aroma of jasmine and lavender.

Bev stood to face her. "I want to see you."

The presence glided to her, and as Bev studied it, a backdrop between the table and the far wall began to form as if behind a screen – a backdrop of a street in Paris. They could smell Europa, hear the jazz coming through the front door, smell the wine, hear the laughter.

Bev was in awe. "I know that place."

"We've been there," added Bill.

"Paris. The Mars Bar."

Joseph pursued. "Are you the young woman in the ad on the box?"

Yes. "Yes," said Rose.

Bev cupped her mouth, unable to speak as the presence drew closer to Bev and whispered, "Sisi." And she remembered it was a nickname someone had called her a long time ago. She didn't know if she was remembering this of her own will. *"Sisi,"* it repeated and turned around to face Joseph.

Quietly he confronted her. "Did you die in this house?" he asked empathetically.

The marker leaped into action. *I don't love you! I don't love you! I want you to go!* And Rose cried out the words for all to hear. *You have to go. Now!*

"Did you die in this house?" he repeated and stood up, trying to reach toward the pale, cracked form – his hands trembling and weak and on fire. "Did you die in the attic?"

The presence paled as tiny fissures spread over her ghostly skin. *Help me. Help me. Help me.* "Help me. Help me," begged Rose. Rose felt her own tendons tearing in her arm and wrists and hands as the ink ran like a madman's blood over the pages. *"You're frightening me! I want you to leave! Don't!* Breathlessly Rose cried out the pleas as she repeated the presence's words.

From the canvas a small, gaunt, hooded figure floated to the presence. The presence quickly turned to Bev and pleaded for help, knowing that behind her loomed the steel blade she couldn't escape. Her mouth opened. "Help me. Help me, Sisi! The pleas came sharp and clear.

Bev reached toward her. Bill held her back. Tears flooded her eyes. Bill held tightly.

The hooded figure rose like a prison tower over her. Muffled cries sounded slowly from his grey lips. "Run away with me," came words like a schoolboy's pleas. He reached toward the red-haired woman. "Run away with me." And as a thin, mutilated hand holding a steel blade struck down, Bev looked up, into the darkness of the hood at a faded, half-formed face, and seeing the past this close, realized she had been living with lies all these years. She was unaware of the blood rushing from her head, as the shock collapsed her into Bill's arms. He steadied her and lowered her into her chair.

The cloaked figure vanished and the presence sank back into the threads of the painting that spun upward with hurricane force, then plunged downward – the pointed tip of the easel impaling the canvas where the presence's heart opened up in a jagged, bloody hole.

"Stop! We've had enough! Stop this nonsense!" Bill insisted.

"Sh....sh!" Rose cautioned. "Joseph is still engaged. He needs you to remain calm! Joseph? Can you hear me?"

He didn't respond.

Bev opened her eyes and clung to Bill. "I can't breathe."

"I'm taking you home."

"I can't move yet." And she wanted to escape, but was too weak.

"Joseph?" asked Rose again and knew he was still searching the horizon, dividing both planes. "Joseph, I'm here."

He saw in the distance the ancient figure - the one Joseph was searching for, the one he had seen earlier. "Come to us. We need to see you. Will you show yourself?"

Yes. "Yes," said Rose.

Joseph opened his eyes and like a mannequin being postured, he was being pulled on top of the table. Slowly his arms moved, then his body, legs, feet followed, like clay being moulded into a figure. As his form moved into a fetal position he began to change. He became hairless, thread-bare, like an old mop, discoloured with dirt for half a century.

Vienna reached out and touched the bony skull.

"Did you live in this house?" asked Ben.

"Si," answered the reclining man. "Yes."

Ben's heart broke at his helplessness – much like he imagined Jamie would have been in his last moments. "Did you die in this house?" he asked.

"No."

"Are you still living?"

"Si...si... yes... yes."

"Are you the artist?" Ben asked gently and held a withered claw.

"Yes... si."

"Where are you now?" Ben's voice tried for clarity, but was in pain as he looked into the hollow sockets of an old man and saw the place that was his hell. "Where are you?"

"Hospital," he whispered. "Hospital... bride..."

"Are you getting this?" Rose asked Mark.

"Yeah, but I don't fucking believe it."

Suddenly from every pore of Joseph's aged skin tiny rays of light shot outward, then grew into powerful bolts of energy, mutating the helpless form and shifting its posture, drawing it upright until it stretched to the ceiling. Skin became translucent fabric, veins glowed like blue embers and wings were draped with willow-like feathers that unfolded from its side, then folded again like Egyptian fans sending a desert breeze through the room.

"Are you the artist?" asked Ben again.

"Yes," the light proclaimed. "Was...was... was... am... am... am..."

"What is your name?"

The winged creature started to fade, as if its lifespan used itself up in a burst of power. Feathers fell away as the light started spinning out of existence – particles colliding and bulleting to all corners.

"What is your name?" called Rose.

"R.M... R.M.," whispered Joseph as he appeared from a spinning maelstrom of light.

"How can we find you? Help us find you!"

" 28913 X."

The numbers faded breathlessly as Rose committed them to memory. *28913 X...* And Joseph was losing himself in the whirling light. "Joseph, come back!" commanded Rose.

He fell like a meteor on fire. The table cracked under his weight. Quickly Rose felt for vital signs. "He's barely breathing! Emma, get his case!"

Emma froze.

"Now!"

A second to get it, a second to return, and Emma produced the syringe first.

Rose felt his accelerated heartbeat and loosened his clothes drenched in sweat. He wasn't conscious. Administering the thrombolytic drug she waited before preparing to use electrical cardio version, but Joseph revived.

"We need blankets and a cold compress."

Both Ben and Vienna dispersed in different directions and returned with the items for Rose's practised treatment. His breathing strengthened; his shivering subsided.

Joseph's first conscious words were, "I'm not stopping here."

"I know," said Rose. "But we're going to take a break and pick it up at my house where we'll do the analysis. We'll eat, drink and examine what we have. Then decide what to do."

He nodded, as tears flooded his strained eyes. "Time is running out." He had never felt a more urgent call for help than he had tonight. "If we don't finish this soon, they'll be lost for all time."

"I agree," said Ben. "Whatever you need me to do, I'll do it."

Uncontrollably, Bev started crying. "I'm sorry. I'm so sorry. I can't help you. I can't stay. Take me home, Bill!"

She could barely stand, as Vienna rushed to help Bill steady her. He called for their limo, and Ben and Vienna escorted them to the front door.

They didn't speak, but before Bev left she turned to Ben with apologetic pleas. "I can't help you. Don't call me... don't call me!"

Ben was stricken. "I don't understand," he said quietly.

Bev shook her head, as Bill rushed her away.

When Ben joined the others he asked in bewilderment, "What happened? We all saw the same thing. I feel really bad that I did this to her." He shook his hands as if releasing something contagious on them.

"She saw something," Joseph answered. "Something she never could have imagined. And she can't face it. She might not ever be able to." Joseph allowed Rose to help him into his coat while the others packed up. "Ben, we're going to examine this very carefully, then call you, probably in the morning." He looked around. "Mark?"

"Under here." And he waved his hand from under the table.

"You can come out now. Come with us to Rose's."

"For sure. In a minute." And he stayed hidden for a while longer.

Ben called a taxi for Vienna who wanted to stay but couldn't because of Annie. "She needs you all to herself. She'll have a lot to share. And I have school tomorrow. And I'm... I'm... I don't know what I am at this point. Did I dream I was floating? Or was I?"

"I don't know what I saw." He rubbed his eyes. "I think my eyeballs are burned. It's going to be hard switching gears when Annie gets here."

"You'll have to be a dad again."

"I know."

The taxi flashed its lights and Vienna's lips found Ben's for a second of familiar warmth.

* * * *

Emma saw Mark's feet sticking out from under the table. She crouched to see the damage. He was belly down, his face buried in his arms.

"Seriously, you can come out."

"I'm not ready."

"Come on. I'll help you."

He wiggled out backwards, hoisted himself on to his knees while Emma grabbed his elbow and pulled him up.

"You'll be okay. I don't think you're possessed."

"Oh, I'm possessed – just not with Ben's friends."

"I think I wet myself, even though I'm supposed to be used to it."

"Bet you've never seen anything like this? Right?"

"Fuck no! What was that? Tim Burton's wet dream? Are you going to Rose's?"

"Should I?"

"Do you want to?"

"Yeah. I need some closure. I want to know what happened to Joseph."

Ben joined them with a feeling of strange relief – like walking away from the dentist's after days of anxiety. "Still breathing?" he asked Mark.

"I dropped the camera, man!"

"It's okay."

"And I'm going to Rose's."

"Really! That's totally out of character."

"I know, but I want to help you. You should have told me weeks ago."

"I didn't even believe it myself. You're in it now and I'm glad."

They said their good-byes, and Ben set about reassembling his surroundings for Annie's homecoming, decked her favourite music tracks and phoned for some food in case she had an appetite after being on Wendy's starving-to-health-meal-plan for a week-end. *Needham, you're a vindictive bastard. You know that?* He felt that his self-recrimination justified his unjust feelings for his ex. He waited for his daughter in the soft, warm glow of house lights that didn't flicker with someone's distant energy.

17

This Monday night had been like no other in the lives of those touched with a past that was catching up to and bearing down on the present with prehistoric winds of change. Bev had gone home and scurried about as though she were in a labyrinth trying to find an exit, and the only exit she could find was in Bill's aviary with some pot she had found in Mickey's diplomatic immunity dossier. And Bill didn't follow.

She didn't smile as she held the GE enhanced Cannabis ruderalis in her limp grasp. She didn't smile, and she didn't light up. She found the cushioned sofa and lay back under the fifteen foot high dome to stare at the crisp sky - its stars trying hard to get a glimpse of the city below, through the haze. Some birds squawked at her intrusion – how she wasn't the tall one with the deep voice who sweet-talked them. But the air felt frond-fresh, dusted with extra oxygen and soothing on her chapped emotions.

She looked at the joint and wondered if her mind could handle more tricks. She had had enough mind games for one night – for one life time. She thought about what had happened and understood there were three men who needed her to save them: Ben from his paranormal war, the artist from his loveless hell, and Harvard. She couldn't bring herself to face it.

Bill didn't need saving; he was born saved from having to fight for a charmed life. He was simply born charmed. When he joined her after he allowed enough time for her to want his company, he slid under her on the sofa. Two pigmy African geese left their lagoon and waddled over to stare at the couple stretched into each other. They cocked their heads as they wondered if the conversation involved them.

"Are you going to smoke that?"

"Are you going to share it with me?"

"It might mellow the macaws, but it won't mellow a fifty year nightmare."

Bev was as silent as she was on the ride home.

"You're not going to tell me what happened, are you?"

"What's the point?"

"The point is that when we get a handle on this, we can agree on the next step. We all had a major shock tonight and we had to get out of there, but we can't abandon Ben. He's counting on us." Bill moved his chin over her soft, fragrant hair. His arms gathered her closer, pulled her higher on him so his hands curled around her breasts. "I was more afraid in there than I have ever been of falling off one of my new towers. So you're going to help, right?"

She tilted her head back and twisted around until she found his lips and brushed gently against them. "I have to weigh the pain."

"What pain?"

"The pain of the departed with the pain of the living. I have to think about how things will play out if we take the next step, because I know what Ben's going to ask me to do."

"What's that?"

"He's going to ask permission to exhume Alexsis' body."

"Is that a bad thing?"

"Yeah, it is." And suddenly she lifted herself up and walked away with a deep dread sandbagging her lungs, her gut. She felt sick. "I don't want to speak to him if he calls. I have to think of Harvard too. And the kids."

"You'll have to explain things to Harvard."

"No, and neither will you."

"Why not?"

"Look, he's sixty six years old. He doesn't need this now. It's not fair."

"For him or for you?"

She continued walking without answering. When Ben called to see how Bev was doing, Bill played the messenger, delivering Bev's withdrawal from the whole thing. And that he'd let Ben know if anything changed. And that he was sorry.

* * * *

Ben had phoned the Westings moments before Annie arrived home and sat in the soft light, feeling a huge part of the puzzle was dissolving away. He resolved somehow to circumvent Bev's sudden indifference, thought about other channels he could take, but was interrupted when Annie and Wendy crashed through the front door with her back pack and three shopping bags of clothes.

da Vinci who had been locked in a terrifying frenzy in the basement devoured Annie with furry paws and wet kisses until she had to shove him away. Rushing to her dad, Annie gave a non-stop, fast-forward of shopping highlights, girl's day at the hairdresser's, movie night, and future career choices. When Wendy put down the rest of the bags, she asked Annie to get her a glass of water. Annie disappeared down the hall, and Wendy became emotional. A lot more emotional, Ben thought, than when their very first sofa arrived or her first Burberry purchase after she won her first court case.

A momentary shudder took hold, as a tear fell out of her eye.

And Ben tried to rescue her. "Oh, no! It's okay. What's wrong, Wen?"

Her eyes puffed. "I'm sorry. I'm going to miss her so much! I love her!"

"She's a great kid with a few extra quirks than most."

"I really like the quirks. Like how she sets the table..."

"...then changes the seating plan at the last moment."

"I never knew exactly where Adrian and I..."

"...were going to sit. It's part of her list of rituals."

"She doesn't know other people don't do this."

"I think she knows. She's not a recluse. She doesn't care what others do."

Wendy nodded and dried her tears. "This is new to me." From the time Annie was born it was hard for Wendy to accept that something so not 'Grade A' had come from her. Wendy been born and branded with 'A's on her brain and was plugged into a dream machine for cognitive retention by the time she was two. Ben had always known Wendy was a hybrid and seeing her like this alarmed him in a good way.

Annie returned with the water and didn't notice Wendy's distraction. "Is it okay if I go and put my things away? I'll show you everything tomorrow, Dad." And turning away she threw her arms around da Vinci. "Did you miss me, kid? Give me some sugar." And she kept her mouth closed as da Vinci's tongue swallowed her face.

"Annie, I have to go now, sweetie."

"Bye, Mom." She wasn't used to Wendy being there on a Monday night and realized she wasn't staying. She rushed over to her and buried her head in Wendy's chest. "Can I come back next week?"

"We've got the premier on Thursday, right? You're still coming with us, aren't you?"

"Yeah, for sure!" She turned to Ben. "Did you know mom is the Chair for *Need to Be...*"

"*More*," finished Wendy. "*Need to Be More*. It's a global charity that helps in the relocation of African refugee kids, many of whom have been orphaned."

Why Ben felt like holding this woman, like he had met her for the first time and needed to feel how she was fastened together and padded, he didn't understand. Maybe, because she was part Annie.

"Your dad and I'll talk about times for next week – what's good for everyone. But Thursday night should be really special."

Annie smiled and galloped away with da Vinci at her heals.

Ben wondered what happened to Wendy, the workaholic and Wendy, the nor'wester, and Wendy, the back-spinning-fast ball. He was more than thankful for her maternal needs kicking in at this particular time.

Wendy read his thoughts. She was good at that and smiled. "I know. What happened to the old Wendy? I always loved Annie – you know that, right? I just didn't know how to be a mother. Adrian and I have had two miscarriages and we probably won't have our own baby, and I do have a beautiful daughter who needs me. Adrian wants her to be part of our lives. I want to be a good mother – no, a great mother."

"She's lucky to have both of us – I mean the three of us."

Wendy looked at Ben's tired eyes, his gaunt jaw and thin neck. "You've been burning candles at both ends."

"I'm trying not to."

"So if you need me to take her next week-end I'd be happy to."

"Only if you let me take all of you to dinner Sunday evening. Sevenish?"

"I'll have to run it by Adrian." She smiled. "You know he's like a big kid when they hang out. They get along well, but Annie will let you know all about it."

"Yeah, she told me she enjoys babysitting him."

"She did!" And laughed.

It was the first time Ben had heard her laugh in months, years. It was the first laughter he had heard all day.

"So, what's going on? Everything okay? You look overworked?"

"Couldn't be better." He had to lie to her, because Wendy wasn't able to let other people's nightmares enter her world. *Christ, she's just learned to laugh again!* She was incapable of letting unseen and unsavory things in – not da Vinci, not a nightmare, not the homeless, not a dead woman wanting to fly to another place, and not a troubled ex-husband. "Yeah, things are really good. I'm just getting bogged down with work, a love interest, more work, house repairs. Too many things. But Annie always comes first around here."

Wendy nodded. "I'll call this week. Oh, and she got something for you."

"What?"

"I don't want to spoil her surprise."

He walked her out and for what it was worth wrapped his arms around her and held her tight. Then before he was completely embarrassed, he released her. "It's never too late."

18

Rose lived at the Beach in a large semi, left to her by her parents. She owned both properties, lived in one and rented out the other side as a summer house. Her Danish mother created minimalist interiors with no extraneous clutter. From Tasmanian Blackwood floors to a two-way Scandinavian-tiled fireplace, there were very few furnishings, but Rose had warmed it up with pillows and throws, a Spanish bookcase, metal art, candles, a Mexican rug and two prints by Slavic artist Ivan Generalic.

The lake was restless she thought as she listened to it break on the rocks beyond the boardwalk. A November lake. She welcomed the familiar smells and hues of her home and didn't have to introduce Joseph into its comfort. He had been there often.

Joseph insisted on helping with the refreshments and the general ambience that Rose wanted for her exhausted guests – wood in the fireplace, warm candlelight, a couple of trays of finger foods. The rest of the team and Mark were appreciative and had stopped off at Tim's to add another tray of favourites that Mark paid for. Emma and Mark sat on the floor in front of the fireplace, while the others doubled up on the sofa and two wooden chairs; they ate and drank before they gathered in the dining room with their equipment for the analysis.

They sat around an extended teakwood table with seamless leatherette, steel chairs in a spacious, austere room that was crackling with new logs on the fire. Rose prefaced the meeting by commenting on the rarity of Ben's haunting and of her inability in dealing with it, but Joseph disagreed with her feelings of inadequacy and suggested they get on with the analysis, pool their resources and strategize about procedure.

They reviewed Rose's initial token-object testing with the mirror fragment and with the doll. The numbers had formed twice. They agreed that 1947 was probably a date, that 305 perhaps a room number or an address. They needed to be cross-referenced on a data base for their relevance with the Ingles case.

Starting with Martin and Justin, they examined their recorded images of the séance. Both technicians captured a figure that was hovering in a corner and elevated behind Joseph to his right. The thermal imager recorded extreme levels of ambient heat and high levels of infrared radiation and the low-light, night vision equipment, with green phosphor amplification, captured the same image of an aged, decrepit figure watching the gathering like a puppeteer controlling their movements. The magnetometer that Emma used recorded extreme heat emissions in the same area as the taped image. The figure never moved from that space. When they listened to the last numbers that Joseph said – 28913 X – they determined they were being spoken by this figure hovering in the corner behind Joseph.

Rose magnified the shadow. "Did you see that? Did you see what seems to be the mouth area moving in sync with the sound of the letters?"

"Yes." Joseph acknowledged.

Rose took the video recorder and hooked it into her laptop. They watched the footage Mark captured. Before Vienna started painting, the image of the shadow-figure formed identically to the images the other technicians recorded. Barely distinguishable, it was elevated in the corner to the right of Joseph. At one point it turned to Mark, smiled and said, "Find me."

They zoomed into the image and replayed the voice. Mark stared into an old man's face that stared back at him. He never wanted to hold the camera again and seriously wanted Emma to invite him home with her.

They listened three times to the sounds, amplified them, decreased and increased their speeds and made notes. And finally reviewed their own experiences, perceptions, and thoughts, all of which concluded that Alexsis was murdered in the third floor artist studio in Ben's house somewhere between 1955 and 1958. And that the artist, Rigo Molinaro fled for reasons they didn't understand and that he was telling them he was alive in a powerful, anomalous state. Powerful in ways Joseph understood. He believed the artist had harnessed energy to his will, and to his will he wanted everyone to bend.

Based on all their findings they talked about procedure, then made an extensive list: Joseph would contact the police, in particular, Detective Bodhan Jaiteley who was familiar with Joseph's long-standing expertise in his field. He wanted Jaiteley to open a homicide case on Alexsis Ingles' death. Rose was to start checking hospital records in Ontario for a missing person presumed dead from the late fifties. Joseph asked the team to go over their data again to cross check for any other significant happenings they might have missed and to make hard copies for himself, for Rose and Ben. It would be up to Ben and Vienna to approach Bev to enlist her help and also to research any European tours that Billie Holiday made in the fifties.

They had worked until midnight, reviewing all data several times. And when all parties began to shut down verbally, they knew it was time to pack up. Joseph was going to contact Ben and Rose by noon with an update.

* * * *

It had become quiet and starry as everyone made their way to Woodbine Avenue and the Lakeshore. Emma and Mark exited to Queen's Quay to Emma's place in a mutual understanding that both needed someone young and fleshy and mortal to hold on to until morning. And it had entered Joseph's mind for a brief, distracted second how he would have liked to have stayed with Rose, but he'd wait for a colder night, a less fragmented night to ask.

19

Joseph had gone to each team member's place early the next day to see how they were doing, to thank them personally and to collect and collate a full dossier of hard copies of their investigation, after which he made a mid-morning visit to Detective Jaiteley at Police HQ. To Joseph all institutions were primitive, if they weren't science labs with hi-tech interfaces. HQ felt this way to him – a cave filled with cave men and obsolete technical support with a few innovative exceptions. Joseph knew it was a two-way street – he felt he was in the Neolithic period while many at HQ thought he was a remnant from the dark ages and escaped being burned at the stake.

There were sceptics at Police HQ on College, but Detective Bodhan Jaiteley of homicide never challenged Joseph's expertise in matters the police couldn't explain. On two cold cases Jaiteley had called in Joseph who was able to lead Jaiteley's department to viable evidence and murder charges. While he didn't understand the mechanics of Joseph's work, he understood that Joseph's gifts were works in progress, and like all learning opened up new paths. He thought Joseph had an old, intelligent soul – old like the Khajuraho Temples in India that Jaiteley had visited as a boy before his family immigrated to Canada. He trusted Joseph like he trusted ancient architects.

There was a beauty, a sensuality about Jaiteley that glowed in his dark skin and full rose lips that made Joseph feel as though he were at a TV network studio and Jaiteley was the dreamy-eyed detective and Joseph was the acorn squash-gnome-like, less-than-Watson-perfect, side-kick investigator. If Jaiteley were aware of his charisma, he kept it well hidden, Joseph thought.

The appointment was for ten. They shook hands warmly and spent an hour going over the raw data, analyses and implications, while Jaiteley made notes. When the briefing was over, he looked at Joseph and saw the toll this investigation was taking on the neuroscientist's strength. Joseph's voice sounded nervously urgent, his posture seemed brittle with tension. Jaiteley wanted to help him and asked Joseph what he wanted him to do.

"I need you to get a homicide case going. We strongly feel that Alexsis Ingles, wife to the multi-millionaire Howard Ingles was murdered in '58 when she was twenty six. We need an exhumation license from the Attorney General, I need court orders for bank files, CRS records, hospital records dating back to the mid-fifties and any files that the department or the government might have on missing persons, and files on Chiefs of Police in the late fifties. We need forensics to confirm with their own testing what this Ottawa serologist, Greg Miller, substantiated in his report. We need a forensic team to do a full analysis of Ben Needham's home, preferably tomorrow."

Jaiteley was amused with Joseph's tattered stamina given his small, underpumped, stature, his age, and the wear and tear this case was having on him. He watched Joseph lean into every request as though he would jump off of Niagara if he didn't get what he wanted. Jaiteley listened and wondered why after fifty years they should open a case. "Why should the police investigate this death as a homicide? She's been dead and buried for fifty years."

"Because we're convinced a murder was covered up. Because a man went missing, possibly kidnapped – his body never found - and we think he's still alive. Because a murderer was never brought in. Because two souls are lost and can't find peace. Because a man is fighting for the safety of his family and his home, and their lives are in danger. Is this enough?"

Jaiteley considered his options. "Okay, I'll take it to Chief Billings – not a fan of yours as you know - and if he gives me the go ahead, I'll work it with one other detective, but I can only give you a week. That's all I've got."

"I don't think we have a week. This thing, this man that has invaded Ben's home is dying somewhere without anyone to listen to him. He's managed to harness phenomenal power to reach into Ben's life and be heard. We have to move very quickly on this."

"And what if the Chief refuses to make a case?"

"The Chief has to know that Ben Needham's life is in danger and so is his daughter's. I'll do as much as I can to protect them, but I'm not any match for what's in that house. And it's not just confined to that house. We've witnessed its power beyond it. If the Chief wants to talk to me have him call me. Oh, and I've left your number with Ben in the event that anything happens."

"I'll do my best."

* * * *

Ben had lain in the hallway outside of Annie's room all night which had passed in quiet warmth. His whole body had felt like his feet did after a run – gnarled and sore. So he soaked in a steamy bath until it was time to wake Annie. He was thankful for the warmth, the comfort, the relief.

After he had dropped her off at school he spent the morning researching 6 Rue Robert Estienne in Paris – the address of The Mars Club in the fifties and where Holiday sang on her European tour in 1954. He found contact information on the net for the owners - Mr. and Mrs. Lazlo, Americans who retired to the States and were living in a coastal retirement village in South Carolina. He didn't want to lie, had never made it a practice, but he explained that he represented the owner of a Holiday portrait and was looking for any information on the painter, Rigo Molinaro. Mrs. Lazlo was happy to share what she knew.

Rigo was originally from Naples, she quickly remembered, and had an apartment on the same cul-de-sac as the club, an apartment she and her husband were continuously furnishing with odds and ends that they wanted to find a new home for. He made extra money by sketching the patrons of The Mars Bar – writers (Hemingway, Durell, Nin) and painters (Villon, Francis, Kelly), and musicians (Ellington, Holiday, Strayhorn).

She fondly remembered him living with a young Canadian woman with a British accent for a month. A lovely, tall woman with red hair. The woman had met him at the club when she was vacationing from Canada. It wasn't long after they met that they were inseparable. We loved this young woman. She remembered her name was Lexy. Life wasn't fast enough for her, even though she looked frail with that porcelain skin. We could easily see why Rigo would sell his soul to be with her. They had made plans for him to join her in Canada a couple of months after she left.

Mrs. Lazlo remembered his family coming to Paris to say good-bye to him – his grandparents and younger brother. When he stopped coming into the club, the owners knew he had gone to be with her.

She remembered that on the night after Holiday's show, Holiday went with them to Rigo's apartment because he wanted to sketch her. The owner knew this because she and her husband had been invited also, but couldn't go. The next day Rigo gave the owner a tape of a song that Holiday and a sax player recorded in his apartment. Mrs. Lazlo said Rigo showed her Holiday's finished portrait before he sent it to Lexi in Canada.

Ben asked if the song was Harlem Nocturne.

"That's the one. I still have the old tape in a suitcase in the basement locker. I often wondered what became of those two lovers. They seemed so lost to the rest of the world. I could hardly distinguish them from each other. They were more than soul mates. I think Billie Holiday thought they brought a little piece of heaven down to earth. She wanted to be near that. Whatever happened to them?"

Ben told her he thought the artist was still alive and he was trying to find him, but the woman, Alexsis Ingles, died tragically at the age of twenty six.

The woman paused to consider the impact of the tragedy. "Yes, Ingles was her last name. Rigo called her Sisi, because he was always saying 'yes' to her in Italian. Sisi....Sisi. If you think he's still alive, you're wrong. He would have died with her. He wouldn't have been able to have gone on without her for very long."

"You might be right, Mrs. Lazlo. Ben thanked her for her time and asked if he could visit them and bring an old tape recorder to listen to the song. Then as an afterthought asked if the sax player that Billy recorded with were still alive. She didn't know and couldn't remember his name.

Before she hung up she remembered that she had a couple of keepsakes that Ben might be interested in. Sisi had given her a thank you note before she sailed home. She was sure she still had it, because she had written the note on the backside of a thumbnail watercolour that Rigo had painted of The Mars Club. And she also had a photo of the inseparable duo taken at the club by Mrs. Lazlo's husband.

Ben was silent.

The woman knew he wanted to ask for them. "Do you want me to fax copies to you?"

"Thank you very much." And gave her his number. Then told her he really meant what he said about visiting her and her husband in the spring and would keep in touch.

Next on his list was trying to find Molinaro's family. Naples, Mrs. Lazlo had said. He contacted the Consulate General of Italy in Toronto who referred him to the Italian Embassy in Ottawa. Ben hated deceptive misinformation and had cringed when he had deceived Mrs. Lazlo about the portrait. Again he found it distasteful when he told the embassy CSR he was looking for the family of an important Italian painter so that he could return a painting he felt belonged to his family; they gave him a series of numbers to contact.

After spending a couple of hours talking down wrong lines he got a number for Alberto Molinaro, a thirty five year old dentist in Naples. He tried his home number and got him before he went to the office. He learned that Alberto was Rigo's nephew and that his father, Ilario, who was Rigo's younger brother was living in Florence and that Ben should be talking to him. Ben explained about the painting and about wanting the family to have it. Alberto was co-operative and gave Ben his dad's number and told him it was best to call after eight in the evening. Ben thanked him and posted a note for a 3:00 a.m. call to Florence.

These were new sensations – someone else's past like a new family member, a new born – taking root in his life. He felt like he was holding it in his arms, like he did Annie when he brought her home. Newborns – the Lazlos, the Molinaros. When the three page fax came, he rushed it to the studio and placed it on his drawing table like a trophy. *This just came from Mimi Lazlo who owned The Mars Club. I'm leaving it with you. But I need it back to show Bev Westing. I want you to know we're doing what we can. I hope you can see that.*

* * * *

The Chief's office was unusually quiet as the two men reviewed the hard copies that Jaiteley had received from Joseph. The Chief was a young one, a maintenance man trying to maintain a balance between promethean and narcissistic bents within the department. He knew Jaiteley was an expert at stealing holy fire and spreading it around. But he was only a guy with only so many minutes in a day. And even though the Chief was reluctant to share him with

Joseph Hightower, he was fair enough to listen – a bit promethean himself.

"What the hell did we just see?" questioned Chief Billings. "This shit is weird, beyond the fringe. Weird, weird shit," he kept saying as the video footage of the séance played out and the hard copies of the investigation fell limply to his desk. Billings trusted scientists less than he trusted paranormal investigators and Joseph Hightower was both. Changing channels was not something the Chief did well – a known reality on one channel, an unknown one on another. But he had worked with Hightower before with conclusive results, so there was some respect.

"Both of us saw the same weird shit and here's the thing. This guy, Ben Needham who owns the house thinks the red-haired woman in the video is Alexsis Ingles who he thinks was murdered in his art studio in the late 1950s. But what you saw Hightower change into was supposedly this artist, Rigo Molinaro who disappeared in 1958. The police told Molinaro's family, who had come here from Italy to find him, that he was probably dead. They never found the body. And Needham thinks this artist is still alive somewhere and wants us to open a homicide case on the Ingles woman so her spirit can pass to wherever rich women go and maybe we'll find this creepy old man. And it's possible her murderer is still out there."

"Are these people for real?"

"Needham is solid. There's nothing about this guy to suggest otherwise and Hightower thinks Needham and his little girl are in real danger, whether or not they stay in the house. This thing has power beyond that studio. There are witnesses to prove this."

"Yeah, I saw what you saw. So what do you think?"

"I know Hightower. All of this is sticking really deep. He's dead certain about all of it. I want to open the case."

"What do you need from me?"

"I need Eva Biro to work it with me. I need an exhumation license, court orders. I need a week of preliminaries, then we'll talk."

"You have a week; you'll have everything you need by the end of the day. But keep it quiet. I don't want things stirred up among Toronto's top hundred. Keep it quiet."

* * * *

When Detective Jaiteley found Eva Biro, she was on a Health-o-meter upright scale in a staff room. Every twenty or so seconds she took something off – her gun, holster, watch, earrings, jacket, belt, shoes then checked to see how much lighter she weighed. At five three and thirty five years old, she decided that both interior and exterior body parts were becoming bio-hazardous and needed serious attention. She joined the Living for Health group at the station and took her new commitment as dedicatedly as she did her work. By thirty Biro had won The Attorney General's Victim Assistance Award and the next year won The International Police Association's Gimborn Scholarship in Germany.

Jaiteley wanted her on this case and no one else. Unannounced he entered quietly and watched her strip. "Don't stop there," he teased. "It's just getting interesting. What's next?"

She smiled and answered in Hungarian.

"Which translated means what?"

"Come back in a month and lock the door."

He held her holster and .40 caliber Beretta while she dressed. "So, what do you think of the Needham/Ingles case?"

"I got your request, so brief me. From your message this is no ordinary homicide." She was eager to work on the preliminaries with him. She liked his ability to balance his professional and personal styles. It was hard to come by the comfort and trust level she felt with Jaiteley.

He briefed her first then they went through all the documents, and before they left to pick up the court orders, he organized a time the next morning for forensics to do the sweep of Ben's house. They arranged a 9:00 o'clock appointment and asked that Ben be present. Jaiteley agreed to handle the exhumation process and wanted Biro there. He asked her to check into immigration records, and police and government records of Rigo Molinaro's disappearance and find out who the family physician was when the Ingles woman died. They agreed to touch base in the evening.

20

Rose had tried every hospital in metro and greater Toronto, but no one had any admittance records on Rigo Molinaro. She remembered Ben saying he had some information about the artist's disappearance. When Rose called him he told her about the crash site where Molinaro's motorcycle was found near Kingston. He also shared what he had about The Mars Club in Paris and the fax the owner sent. Rose talked him into going with her to the Westings' with the faxes to instill some hope in Ms. Westing.

* * * *

When they arrived, the guard at the gate buzzed the estate, and even though Bev wasn't at home, Harvard invited them in. He told them he had abstained from going with the women and grandkids to the ROM. That he was enjoying some quiet, reminiscent time, while also catching up on diplomatic business.

When Ben introduced Rose to him, she thought he was youthfully handsome for his age. And that it wasn't difficult to fall into his deep dark eyes, and to follow the thick sandy waves of his boyish hairline that framed his smooth, tanned skin and dimpled cheek. She stopped herself before she became too obvious.

But when they shook hands, an uninvited wave of images locked into her viewing mode, as her fingers touched the precious, cold metal of his ring. Her senses crashed into a wall of historic events: the ring that had belonged to his father had blood on it. Blood that had run down the straight edge of a knife, over the swollen veins in his hand and on to the gold ring. Blood stains that Harvard knew had been there, yet wore the ring with humility.

She held on longer than she should have. The pores of her hands like blotters drank the past from the pores of his. She felt taken against her will to distant carnage, as scenes handcuffed her to a viewing chair and made her watch their final moments of hysteria. Made her watch images of innocent people, like millions of drowning sparrows trapped on tree tops, under bloody waters, until she wanted to gag on their hopeless cries. Harvard had seen the chaos; he had been there when the flood gates opened. 1994. Rwanda. He was not among the drowning.

Then one image cut into existence. A black girl, a school girl – sixteen or seventeen - with a jagged, white scar from her forehead, across her right eye and descending down to her chin stood in her uniform. She carried a bouquet of black and white orchids, while a choir somewhere seemed to be singing. Without smiling, without talking she quickly withdrew a gun from within the bouquet, held it up to her head – her fingers shaking as they tightened on the trigger. Rose stared in horror as the barrel pressed more firmly against the girl's temple. The girl closed her eyes, smiled and fired. The shot was silent and final. Rose felt her own head shatter as if she had been dropped from the Tower of Babel.

Harvard saw beads of sweat forming on Rose's face as she jolted unexpectedly and thought he could feel her heartbeat pumping through her fingers he held tightly. "Are you all right?" And he let go of her hand.

Quickly she framed and mounted the images for later reference and tried to smile. "I'm fine. Just one of those gender-specific moments. I felt a little dizzy and tried to steady myself." When she looked at Ben's curious stare, she knew he was acknowledging a reading she had just engaged in. "I'm fine," she repeated.

Harvard was concerned, then, "Let's get comfortable." Warmly he invited them into Provence – Bev's kitchen which was the replica of the kitchen she had studied in, in France as a teenager. He offered tea and some pain au chocolat (French pastries) that Bev and Mickey had made the day before. He made them feel at home, as Rose watched him orchestrate every rhythmical word, like a well-practised politician – a man she was certain had seen more blood in his lifetime than any woman and wondered at what age Harvard went to war.

Ben had brought the fax in an envelope. When he saw Harvard eyeing it, he opened it, removed the three pages and slid them across the table. Harvard took them and looked first at the black and white copy of the artist's watercolour of the Mars Club, then slowly read Alexsis' note. It was an unexpected relic that Harvard held stiffly and read twice – once to himself and again out loud:

"*Dear Madam Lazlo,*

This month has been the happiest time of my life. You have given me music

and poets and the one artist who has taught me to love. I refuse to leave him

in Paris. I'm taking him home with me to new music and a new atelier. He

wanted you to have his small painting of The Mars Club and his new address

so you can write to him: 82 Marion Street, Toronto, Ontario, Canada. If you ever

return to America please visit us. I will take good care of him, my sweet Mimi.

All my love, Sisi

Harvard stared in disbelief at the note, drew in a deep breath as he examined the photo of Alexsis sitting on Molinaro's lap, her left arm flung around his neck, her cheek buried in his chest while she smiled into the camera. Both lovers held drinking glasses raised in a toast to something they wanted to live for. He placed the copies in front of Ben. "How and why do you have this? I'm mystified."

"One of the owners of The Mars Club in Paris faxed it to me, because I phoned her to try to get answers about this artist, Rigo Molinaro and your step mother, Alexsis Ingles. They were lovers. Sisi was a pet name he called her."

"And Bev knows about it?"

"Yes."

"And why are you asking questions, because speaking straight-up, something like this will break Beverly's heart. So, I'm not following why you're doing this."

"Both Bev and Bill are aware of some personal problems I've been having in my home. In fact they have been to my house to see things first hand."

"What things?"

"My house is the same house that the artist, Rigo Molinaro had his studio in. 82 Marion Street, where he and Alexsis met on a regular basis. She was his model, his lover, his partner."

"And?" Harvard turned his palms toward Ben, inviting more info.

"My house is haunted. Professional investigators – Rose is one of them – did two sweeps of my home and have taken their results to the police. We think Alexsis was murdered in my house because of the evidence we found."

Harvard looked at Rose. "And you do what again?"

She was aware of his sudden smugness. "I'm a Kinesiologist and a Geophysicist. And I share research on anomalous psychology with other scientists."

"Two doctorates," added Ben. "She has two doctorates."

"And you think Ben's house is haunted. That this... this artist killed my stepmother?"

"No."

"No?"

"Because this artist, Rigo Molinaro is trying to help us solve what happened."

Harvard laughed and shook his head, a wave of hair falling over his forehead. "I'm sorry, but this artist who is... how old now... maybe over eighty is working with the police?"

"Telekinetically," Rose offered. "He has garnered a power none of us really understands, a power to project himself into Ben's life from an unknown place. We don't know where he is."

"Maybe he and Houdini are partners in paramagic." He shook his head in disbelief. "I'm sorry, but I was sixteen when Lexi died in her bed in our home with my dad lying beside her. There are reports..."

"...that the police will examine. They have court orders and a license from the Attorney General to..."

"... exhume the body. I know who gives what orders, Ben." Harvard picked up the note again. His fingers had moistened and were leaving damp smudges on the page. Rose asked for it back, and when he put it in Rose's outstretched hand her fingers and thumb found the stains she wanted to touch.

And she held the smudged fingerprints under hers and blinked as she watched inwardly a young man sitting beside a bathtub in blood and vomit and excrement. And he cradled a hand enwrapped with a blood-soaked bandage. She blinked again and the image left. Rose studied Harvard carefully and thought he was an artful man – a master of the art of concealment. That he had learned from an early age to smooth over a history of puppetry and to trade in one tyrant for another. She wondered what hell he had entered and if he ever returned. A handsome man with a hollow heart.

She returned the copies to Ben.

Harvard softened, "Ben, I'm not discrediting whatever you've been going through. I've seen some truly, extra-ordinary happenings in Africa. I believe you when you say you've been going through something profound, but I don't want Bev to get hurt. She's had enough pain in her life."

"She needs to know the truth."

He finally nodded in acceptance. "I can tell you she'll want to be at the exhumation."

"I can't stop her."

"I'll help you in any way I can. I know the Attorney General, and I have friends in places that can make things easy for you when the time comes. Let me know how I can help."

"I appreciate it. You can start by showing these to Bev." Ben handed him the envelope. "I'll be home tonight. I hope she calls. Will you ask her to?"

* * * *

It was that time of day when most were settling accounts or getting ready to lock doors, and when Rose dropped Ben off she said she'd touch base with Joseph and start again in the morning to research hospitals in the Kingston area. Before Ben got out of the car he got a call from Joseph saying the police had the exhumation license and that Detective Bodhan Jaiteley had moved quickly to get the disinterment done at 2:00 the next day. He'd e-mail the details.

Rose left Ben with unspoken words of encouragement, like they would soon know everything, and it would soon be over, and soon the truth would hit them like the eulogy of a bitter, fallen god. He squeezed Rose's hand and thanked her.

* * * *

Both Annie and Vienna had slipped back into the warmth of the school's foyer and waited for Ben who was thirty minutes late. He wrapped his long arms around both of them and didn't release them until he found that familiar belonging he needed.

Vienna had worked late into the previous night on art work for her Christmas show. She knew she didn't have to go home, so she packed a few things to stay at Ben's and didn't feel guilty about taking a break.

He was grateful when he saw Vienna's bag and put it beside Annie in the back seat who noticed that Ben was looking a little rough and wondered why. She kept staring at his tired eyes in the mirror and unruly hair that was growing down his neck.

He saw her staring. "I'm going for the Lennon look."

"No kidding. What do you do all day? Can't you trim your hair or go to the gym? When was the last time you went for a run? Even mom's worried about you."

"Okay. How about the two of you taking scissors to this mop tonight?"

"Can I style it?"

"Be my guest."

"Vienna can be my assistant."

After they ate they set up the bathroom as a mini-hairdresser's. The girls gathered shampoo, conditioner, wave enhancer, frizz buster, styling gel and pins. As they washed his hair, Ben luxuriated in their disparate touches – Vienna's like silk worms weaving the sustenance of their fame through his hair, and Annie's like a pup's baby-tooth-love bites, digging into his scalp.

They had given him a shiny side wave, barbered the back of his neck and handed him a mirror. He could easily get addicted to being in the loving hands of the girls he cared for. It held him safely on the fragile side of sanity.

Annie snapped a picture, was too tired not to protest going to bed early and reminded them that Wendy and Ace were picking her up Thursday night for the gala premiere. Annie didn't pretend to be mature, didn't make a conscious effort to be grown-up. She turned out that way and Ben was grateful. Annie felt if her mom was happy with someone else, Ben could be too. She kissed them goodnight and decided that being loved by four special people eased

Annie's pain of losing Nat Newstead, the one person she thought would love her forever. It took her five minutes to fall asleep as she tried to follow him north on the 400.

* * * *

Vienna laughed at Ben's mannequin-like hair that she was afraid to touch in case of breakage. They sat quietly in the invaded house until Ben softly itemized the day's activities, starting with the police opening the homicide case, then the next day's 9:00 am forensic sweep, his conversation with Mrs. Lazlo, the fax she sent, the visit to the Westings with Rose and the exhumation at 2:00 the next day, which reminded him to check his email for details.

Before they turned off the lights Ben called to da Vinci to sleep with Annie. The dog stood outside of the door and refused to enter. Ben did a quick walk through, wanted to curl up on Annie's rug beside her bed, but didn't. He set the alarm on his watch for 3:00, so he could call Ilario Molinaro in Florence about his brother's alleged death.

Vienna knew that if Ben were any less committed he would pack up, take Annie and da Vinci and leave, but he couldn't. She understood he needed to stay and she understood that slowly he was shutting down because of fear. She moved into him like a new dream and together they willed the night to be a blank - void of fragmented reality.

Ben went to sleep, accepting full ownership of his house and his layman's journey into an unknown universe. He had become used to this journey – not loving it, but craving the return trip home, where a mirror was a mirror, a floor was a floor, and a table was a table that obeyed the laws of gravity. Before sleep took him he had waited for Bev's call that never came.

After dining out, Bev and Mickey dropped the grandkids off and went home to Baby Point. Bill had a rare evening appointment that was going to make him late, and Harvard had told the women he would fend for himself.

The women found him sitting in the darkened house by a cold fireplace with an empty wine glass and wine bottle, beside which were three eight and half by eleven scattered pages. He had heard her call his name as she searched the house, finally finding him in a pool of cloud-covered moonlight.

Bev was glad Mickey decided to shower first, so she could spend a few moments alone with Harvard. He was quiet as she nervously approached, draped her arms around his neck then tossed his hair.

"Ouch!" he protested.

"Oh, I'm sorry. My ring caught your hair. Sorry!" And she sat on the plush rug in front of him. "I was calling you." She tried to hide the frailty in her voice.

"I didn't hear. I must have nodded off."

"I'll put on the fire." She found the remote and the fire instantly entertained them. "There's more wine."

"I've had enough."

"What's wrong?"

"Ben Needham was here today. With a friend, Rose. They left something for you."

"I don't think I want to see it."

"I think you should, but if you tell me to throw it away, I will."

She thought carefully. "If it's from Ben, then it has something to do with my past, my history."

"Our past," he corrected. He moved to the edge of the sofa and placed his elbows on his knees. His fingers interlocked while Bev reached out and held his clasped hands. He lowered his head, didn't look at his sister. "Why didn't you tell me about Ben's house?"

"I only met Ben recently over the Holiday portrait that you gave me. It's tying in with the disturbances he's experiencing. I guess he's told you."

"Yes, but he didn't elaborate." He gathered the photocopies and handed them to her. "You should look at these."

She took them and looked at the black and white copy of the painting of The Mars Club first. "Bill and I've been there. It's The Mars Club in Paris."

"This is a copy of a painting given to the owners, the Lazlos, by the artist, Rigo Molinaro. He lived close by and frequented the bar, often sketching its patrons. He met Lexi there."

"What's this?" And she studied Alexsis' note, then read it silently. Pondered the implications. Lingered on the address. "That's Ben's address." Her hands trembled again. Fear overpowered her calm. "I can't stop shaking."

"The Lazlos have been living in the States for some time. Mrs. Lazlo faxed these copies to Ben."

She examined the writing again. "The Mars Club came up in the séance. Bill saw it too. Ben hasn't been able to find ownership records for his property from 1946 to 1962." She waited for Harvard to say something.

He watched Bev run her fingers over Alexsis' wild penmanship. "She invited this artist to move to Toronto, and he ended up in Ben's house. They both ended up there. Why?" She waited and stared into Harvard's distant eyes.

"Dad owned it."

"Did you know about them?"

"Yes."

"Why did he buy it, this house?"

"While he was married to my mother, he bought it as an investment for his mistress and her daughter. She lived on the main floor. She rented out rooms on the second. The attic was empty."

"Alexsis knew about the house?"

"Yeah. I can't remember the exact details, but when dad brought Alexsis home, he sent his mistress packing, probably with a settlement, and re-rented the apartments. Things are fuzzy. I was a kid. When Alexsis died, he closed the rentals. The house was empty until 1962. "I left for the UK in '58, so I don't know much about what happened."

"Mom must have fixed up the attic as a studio for this artist."

"I don't know."

"Did you ever go there, with Lexi, when the artist was there? She brought him back in '54. You would have been twelve."

"I don't remember. I might have."

"You just said you didn't know if Lexi fixed up the attic."

"I'm not sure if it's the same house. There was this gazebo. I stayed there and played with a kid who lived on the main floor. I've forgotten."

"They were there together for four years before she died. You must have known something."

"No. I was in school. I was always in training – tennis, swimming, rowing. I barely was at home. What's with all the questions?"

She shook her head. "It's just that I thought you might know something. What does Ben want me to do with all of this?"

"Call him."

"Not now. In the morning." She looked at Harvard's defeated face. "How are you taking it? It must be really hard. You worshipped her. You were only eight when Alexsis married dad. You were her baby. She was like the Statue of Liberty guarding you. God, the pics we have of the two of you – her arms wrapped around you like a constrictor, or her lips buried in your pink cheek, or the two of you walking hand in hand at our summer place in Picton.

Dancing. Sleeping in the sun. She loved you. I wish I had known her like you did."

"She loved you more."

Bev managed a smile. "I don't think so. She hardly knew me. And then there was her lover, this artist. She probably didn't have any time for me. Probably left me with my nanny."

"No, she didn't. I was there when you were born. She took you everywhere. She'd disappear with you for hours. Never put you down. I had to beg her to let me hold you or take you for a walk in your pram when I had time. She gave you an insane motherload of motherhood."

"Thank you. I remember her only through the photos."

"There's something else."

"What?"

"Ben intimated that the police want to treat Alexsis' death as a homicide."

She knew that Ben had come to tell her this. "And?"

"They're going to exhume her body tomorrow afternoon." He watched a calm take hold of her. It surprised him.

"I was expecting this. It will be anti-climactic compared with the events of the investigation Monday night. I'm more ready for surprises now than I was then."

"I'll stay as long as you need me."

"Where are dad's private papers?"

"In a safety deposit box at the TD on King. You know you have full access to it. Haven't you ever opened it?"

"No. Why would I? The police will want everything. Will you go with me in the morning?"

"I'll do anything you want me to."

At one time she would have believed that, but she didn't now – not after what she thought she had witnessed in the séance. She would have liked to have said, *I don't believe you. I want you to tell me the truth about that day, fifty years ago.*

* * * *

When Mickey joined them they talked about the ROM and the kids, but Bev waited for Bill to arrive to bring everything to the table. He found them chatting up Mickey's few days of grandmotherhood and how she mentored two generations of Rwandan children from a village who needed surrogate parenting. She thought it was a substitute for her own family she missed growing up. Before it got too late Bev asked if everyone could give her a moment to go over important family business and reached to the coffee table for the envelope.

Bill was prepared for it even though he didn't know the details; Mickey was not.

She was in shock as the story unfolded, especially as it involved the Ingles and the Westings. She didn't seem to care much about the Needhams. She refused to believe that Ben had the right to stir up a scandal that would impact on all levels of their lives – from the Rwandan halls of government, to boardrooms, to the kids' school newspapers. The Ingles were high profiled, internationally respected people, and a homicide case could damage their diplomatic ties. A legal investigation was unquestionable. She was furious and didn't hide it. "I want you to stop all of this now. All three of you have the power to stop this before it's networked."

Bev had never seen the flip side of Mickey's serene diplomacy, but understood she was thinking of her son and daughter and grandchildren as well as her family, the Beaulieux. She was enraged that one man's childish nightmare was carving its idiotic threats into the bark of her family's history. She refused to let old photos, old ghosts and a case of nerves destroy her family's reputation.

"Mickey, they already have DNA blood samples from the studio, and forensic team is doing a full investigation tomorrow."

"And you can stop it."

"Ben's life is falling apart. His little girl has been involved - not hurt, not yet, but she's been contacted by these presences."

"Bill, speak to her, talk some sense into her before we're all damaged. Tell her you'll pay this guy to relocate; tear the house down. Everyone wins."

"It's up to Bev. Lexi was her mother."

"Mickey, we'll keep it as quiet as we can."

"You're delusional!" She stood up decisively. "I'm packing. We'll get a flight out as soon as we can. I'll spend time with the family in the morning to let them know what you're doing to us. I want them to hear it from me – not in The National Post." Refusing to waste any more time she excused herself. Harvard followed, leaving the Westings alone.

"Did we both just hear the same thing? I can't believe she's not behind me on this."

"I don't think anyone should have to go through this. It's a horror show. But baby, something is reaching out to Ben to draw all of us together to find the truth. There's no alternative but to grab on, and it sounds like it's really going to happen with or without us. But you want that, right?"

"I don't want it to destroy us."

"That's a little strong."

She turned to look at him with a sadness he was familiar with. A sadness that had hung shroud-like after each of their miscarriages, and now, with the thought that her entire family would be lost.

"What are you afraid of?"

"My past being a lie."

"I'm a big part of that past – over twenty five years now. I'm real."

"I know who you are, but what if my past changes and I'm not the same?"

"Because of what happened to someone fifty years ago? I don't see that happening."

"What if I said I don't want you with me in this?"

"You mean you want me to avoid this as if it were the plague."

"Sort of. I don't want you to see me fall apart – like what happened at Ben's. You don't deserve that."

"Come on! Do you think that was your fault? That you were weak or something? Why do you have to be so fucking perfect all the time? Do you think I'm that narrow? That I can't be strong when you're not? I want to be with you tomorrow."

"I don't want you there."

"We'll talk about it in the morning. It's getting late. And I want you to read Lexi's note, again to me."

"I should talk to Mickey."

"No. She needs some space."

She gathered up the pages and together they quietly slipped past Harvard and Mickey's suite and slid under their warm duvet without their bedtime rituals and read the note again and again. They both knew they were seeing Lexi up close – the other Lexi who had found love like their own.

* * * *

Although the circle of interconnected lives and afterlives had widened around the Needham home, there was an indestructible adhesion around the perimeter. As the night deepened into the darkest sky – its ebony cloud cover blocking out the full, white moon - Ben lay awake, questioning if he'd ever sleep again. In his sleeplessness Ben thought he heard Annie's voice. As he listened more intently he distinctly heard her voice coming from above his room – not across the hall from him, but from above.

Quickly he rolled out of bed and struggled into his joggers. Vienna awoke as Ben ran out of the room. "Ben?" she called as she grabbed her clothes and followed. "Ben?"

The studio door was open. Ben was stunned as the scene hit him like guerrilla warfare on innocent pilgrims. Thin, glowing streams of liquid fire ran in words and numbers down and across the walls and floor. At the opposite wall Annie was transfixed with a writing instrument, dripping lava-like ink down the wall until her hand had blackened, as though it had touched the Arc of the Covenant.

"Quick, the art table...get my camera," he ordered Vienna.

Stepping over the molten images, she grabbed the camera and started shooting. *Find me...find me...find me...1..9..4..7..3..0..5* ran in fiery streams down the walls.

Annie was unaware of their presence and Ben calling gently to her.

"It's daddy, baby. Please stop. Please. Daddy's here."

She turned to look at him. Taking the glowing pen she wrote on her left arm. *Time is running out.* And showed it to Ben.

He knocked the pen out of her burned hand.

"Time is running out!" she growled in a feral, weak voice.

Gathering her up, he took her to the downstairs washroom and ran cold water over her hand, sprayed it and wrapped it. She had fainted in his arms and the writing on her arm scabbed over like dried, reptilian skin. He carried her to her room.

Vienna stayed in the studio to take more pictures, then stepping off the stool she looked around the space and shouted, "You crossed the line, you fucker! Do you hear me? She's a little girl! Things happen to all of us! Deal with it! LEAVE ANNIE ALONE!"

As she turned to leave, a voice, old with decay begged to be found. "Find me!"

They lay on the floor beside Annie's bed until they felt she was safe. When she had fallen into a deep sleep, Vienna wanted to go home, upload the images and make copies for the police. Ben was too traumatized to walk her to the taxi. She hated feeling that the night was swallowing her without him.

He guarded Annie, until his watch beeped. It was time to make a phone call to Italy.

* * * *

Detectives Jaiteley and Biro had met very late over a coffee before they went off duty. Biro went through her reports first: there was no post mortem examination on Alexsis Ingles' body. Dr. Phillip Standern was the family physician who filled out the death report. He gave it to Police Chief, Curtis Knot, who signed and issued the Death Certificate. She died of respiratory failure from asthma and pneumonia – nothing suspicious.

Dr. Phillip Standern was retired and residing in Bronte Village. She made an appointment to see him at 10:30 in the morning. Biro couldn't find any police records on Molinaro's disappearance. She learned that the Police Chief, Curtis Knott, committed suicide in 1958 – reasons unknown. Biro added there were no hospital records for Alexsis Ingles having been admitted for asthmatic attacks. There was no medication mentioned for respiratory illness, and she was not admitted to the hospital on the day of her death.

Jaiteley asked if she made contact with Bev Westing's adopted parents, Thomas and Jane Ingles. When she said she couldn't reach them, Jaiteley offered to try to see them after forensics did their sweep in the morning. He also talked about the archives of the Art Society of Ontario.

Rigo Molinaro's name came up several times - he had shown his works at the Robert Simpson Company in 1957 and had made friends with many of the Group of Eleven - contemporary artists in Toronto. In 1956 he had been invited to show at the Riverview Museum in New York City. For one semester he taught at the Ontario College of Art in Toronto. The man had come to Canada in 1954, had become a Canadian citizen, was a great artist, taught, loved a married woman, then disappeared. Jaiteley decided to put out a Missing Person Bulletin on Molinaro and attach a couple of paintings published in the archives.

Before he forgot, he told her that the exhumation was at 2:00 the next day at Mount Pleasant Cemetery. He wanted her watchful eye – on the family members.

Jaiteley said he got a call from Ben saying that he had contacted Molinaro's family in Italy and that they had kept the police file and the wreckage from the supposed motorcycle accident all these years and that Ben was going to contact Molinaro's only brother later.

They both agreed that the case would move quickly over the next two days from the sweep, to the exhumation, to lab reports, interviews, personal records, to the Molinaro files, and more reports. They had a good feeling about it, and Jaiteley raised his mug of coffee in a toast to their teamwork. Their mugs touched, clinked and lingered.

Putting business aside, Biro softened and relaxed in their booth, waiting for an invitation that Jaiteley wanted to give, but thought inappropriate at this time. She knew it was hard for him to distinguish after hours from before hours – how the day's business kept its hold on his personal time.

She waited, then, "Thanks for asking for me. We're a good fit."

"Yes we are." He stared at her, then smiled. "Time to go." He got up and as he turned he patted her shoulder. "When this is over..." And stopped.

"What?"

He hesitated, "I forgot what I was going to say."

"I'm old enough to fill in the blanks."

"Let's go. Busy day tomorrow."

He left happy. He knew she had waited for something and would have said, 'yes'. And sensed they both would know the right moment to fill in the blanks together.

21

Ben had been too angry to return to the studio. He had been remembering that both his mom and Wendy had had their purses stolen and had cried and said they had felt violated. That a part of their lives had been stolen. He understood now how they felt. Understood that it didn't matter what bad things jack-hammered through your private life, the feeling of complete helplessness was the same.

It was morning and more invaders would come and he didn't know if he dreaded the previous night more or the morning growling at his heels. More scraping, more drilling, more plastic, more banging, more strangers.

He had stayed up after his call to Molinaro's younger brother, Ilario who had never given up hope that someone one day would find something. He insisted on contacting the authorities to have the files and wreckage shipped to Toronto the next day. Their gratitude was mutual and Ben said if Ilario Molinaro wanted to come he'd be welcomed.

* * * *

It was unusual for Annie to sleep in, but a bloodsucking nightmare rocked her into a fitful sleep, then into a deep one when it threw her away. Ben let her sleep and braced himself for an early phone call to Wendy who was already up and seemed eager to talk.

He explained how he was behind in his work because of his girlfriend and how the heating system needed fine tuning and a company was coming in to work on it and how it might annoy Annie. And there had been power outages that needed some inspection. And could she take Annie for the rest of the week.

He was mildly surprised that the inquisitor didn't strap him down and word-slap him silly. He was surprised at her concern when she asked if he was having second thoughts about the old Victorian and listened to him saying that he didn't know floor space could be so challenging. But then he had forgotten she had changed. She was thankful Ben was giving them more time together.

He was seeing Wendy in a new light or Wendy was making herself more visible to him. But he thanked her, and after the call, he found Annie sitting up in bed, examining her bandaged hand and the fingers that extended beyond.

"I don't even know what happened?"

Ben helped her examine them. "You might have been sleep-walking. Maybe you put your hand on the hot rad."

She unwound the bandages and stared at her charred hand that looked like she had been drawing with charcoal. "It doesn't even hurt. Did I put the bandages on?"

Ben grabbed them and kissed them thankfully. "I guess so. Weird, huh?"

"But shouldn't it be red, not grey?"

Ben let go and examined them. "Not if you weren't burned. If it doesn't hurt, you didn't get burned."

"I had a really weird dream last night."

"Oh yeah? You never dream."

"I know, but I did last night. There was this young guy, a painter. He was painting my portrait. He said it was a gift for my birthday."

"You have birthdays? And what happened?"

"Nothing. He just kept painting and said I couldn't look."

"That's pretty weird, but nothing bad happened, right?"

"I guess not. But I saw this guy before in real life."

"Where?"

"I was looking out my window and he was standing on the sidewalk looking up like you do sometimes, I mean, all the time. He waved at me."

"Really? Did you ever see him again in real life?"

"No. Hey, you know it is my birthday next week."

"Is it?"

"Dad!"

"I know... I'm just kiddin' ya."

"I want to do something special."

"Special is the only word in my vocabulary when it comes to you." He changed the subject. "Hey, some people are coming over this morning to check out some things. Your mom called and asked if it was all right if she could take you today until Sunday night. I'd drop you off after school, or your mom'll pick you up. She wants to take you shopping for the gala fundraiser. I said I'd have to ask you."

She had been watching him closely. Tears suddenly flooded her face.

"What?"

"Nothing."

"Tell me. What's goin' on?"

"Are you sick? You look sick. Is that why mom's taking me for the rest of the week?" She pulled out a picture from under the covers of the two of them at the boardwalk in the summer and handed it to him. "That's you in case you don't recognize yourself. And what happened to your hair? It looks like a dead animal! What did you do to it?"

"First, I'm not sick. I'm just worried about the novel, and house problems. Love problems. Can't sleep. Can't write. I think this love thing is either bacterial or viral. And I'm sorry about the hair. It was the way I slept."

She kicked him away as she threw off the covers and jumped out of bed. In frustration she shouted, "I can't take care of everyone!" And left the room.

"No one's asking you to!" he yelled back.

He dropped her off at school and promised to be the old Ben when he picked her up with her suitcase and everything else she needed for the rest of the week. He didn't have time to check his messages until he got home a few minutes before the police and the forensic team arrived.

Vienna had emailed him the enlarged pics she took of the studio walls. Shaking his head in bewilderment he made hard copies and a disc for the police.

* * * *

The doorbell rang twice. First, Joseph and Rose arrived and ten minutes later, Jaiteley and the CSI team.

Joseph and Rose made introductions to Ben who handed over the enlargements that Vienna had taken. Joseph looked at them and recognized similar icons that were present in both his and Rose's transvisitations – the numbers and the pleas. He passed them to Jaiteley and Biro. All four wanted to see the studio before the team coveted it.

The walls and floor were charred as if branded with the darkened images that Vienna had shot. Ben explained to them what had happened to Annie and the dream she had had.

Biro was astonished at the charred handiwork. College had not prepared her for this. Looking at Jaiteley she raised her brows in a question of what the hell were they expected to do with this. She wished Chief Billings could be there. Both detectives drew close to the charred, blistered lines. And smelled them. There was an earthy smell. They couldn't identify any inflammables.

"Why didn't you call us?" asked Jaiteley.

"It happened so quickly. I wanted to get Annie to safety. Vienna went home to do the photos. And anyway, who would you have arrested? The ghost?"

"Our artist is asking for forgiveness," Joseph ventured.

"I can't give it," Ben answered, his jaw rigid with contempt. *Do you hear me? I won't give it until it's over, and maybe not even then. What you did to my baby was a thing of war.*

"Joseph is right," agree Rose. "He needs you to find the strength to forgive."

"Can I go now? Let's go. This place makes me sick."

The team, assisted by the detectives and by Rose's watchful eye, was ready to take control. The whole thing played out like frames from one of Ben's novels. Like robots in sterile white they moved through the house and upstairs taking what they needed. The house had become a specimen, like it had come from another dimension with a hidden identity and agenda, as though it were a second Roswell coming.

Ben and Joseph found some quiet time in the gazebo. They sat facing the sun.

"What will they find?"

Joseph looked toward the house. "Everything. They'll rip up floor boards. Take wall samples, take the toffee container and do what they have to. They'll find everything."

"When will we know?"

"Tomorrow. Are you up for the exhumation?"

"Yeah."

"And Bev Westing?"

"She hasn't called me yet."

"She will."

"How do you know?"

"To her, knowledge is like a magnet drawing her toward disclosure. She's compelled to know the truth. She'll come to the cemetery."

"Rose is coming, right?"

"Yes."

"What if there's no evidence of foul play?"

"There will be. Believe me."

Rose called to Joseph that they were done. When she said good-bye to Ben, he stayed in the gazebo warmed by the unseasonable temperature, his back turned away from the whole, god-damned horror scene.

Jaiteley found him. "You've had a rough month."

"Only because of Annie's safety."

"I just want you to know I trust Joseph, and my partner and I are doing everything we can to investigate thoroughly what's going on. Give us anything you get. We'll work with it."

"I'm not as enthusiastic as I should be."

"Didn't sleep, huh?"

"Not much."

"We're almost done here. I'm going in to help wrap up. I'd try to get some sleep before the exhumation."

Ben bet the house wouldn't let him. When they left, he went into the family room where patches of light were warming the floor. He curled into a ball and grabbed a pillow and a blanket and couldn't remember the last time he had fallen asleep so fast.

* * * *

After forensics had cleared out of the Needham residence, Detective Jaiteley drove east and bumped up onto a Yorkville sidewalk near the Ingles' condo. He guessed that their exclusive, architectural icon would have been a steal at four million. The building itself redefined luxury. When the concierge contacted the Ingles about Jaiteley's business they asked for a security guard to accompany the detective to their penthouse. Jaiteley understood that at some point in the Ingles' ancestry they didn't have all of this. That they had worked hard for it. Like his own parents had. He didn't condemn their excessive lifestyle.

He found them to be co-operative and friendly and genuinely stricken that the police opened a murder case on their sister-in-law's death. He hated to burden them at their age and posed questions as tactfully as he could. They talked about the day of her death, her funeral and things that struck them as odd. They were open about their suspicions of Alexsis' marital situation, Howard Ingles' affairs, enemies he might have had, his volatile temperament.

They had nothing critical to say about Alexsis Ingles. They loved her as everyone did.

Jaiteley didn't like leaving the couple bewildered and worried, but he didn't have anything reassuring to give them. He knew they'd call Bev Westing. Before he met with Biro at Baby Point he reviewed his notes and decided what to question the Westings about and what to leave out.

* * * *

While Jaiteley stayed to the end of the CSI at the Needham residence, Detective Biro left earlier to drive to Bronte Village, west of Toronto where Dr. Phillip Standern had retired. She flashed her credentials at the community's gatehouse and was buzzed in. As she drove along the man-made lake she passed several different architectural revivals – a Cotswold cottage, a Greek temple, a Turkish palace, each on a full acre of sculpted landscaping, until she got to the doctor's residence - a hacienda on a hilltop surrounded with terra cotta urns and statues, wrought iron fencing and gates.

Biro loved this country – how it allowed a minimum waged, grocer's son to climb up the educational ranks to the Dean's list, then to Med school, to graduate with special recognition and become the Ingles' family physician by the age of thirty. She loved how humble origins could be forgiven and forgotten.

Dr. Standern was waiting for her on the wrap-around, arched portico and invited her into the large foyer where he motioned to a chair for her to sit in. He made it clear he was mystified by her visit and by the irrational concerns the police department had about the Ingles family. Howard Ingles, a great philanthropist, was a close friend for a short time.

Biro asked if it was okay to record their conversation.

The doctor was annoyed, but didn't run interference. He knew in advance the standard questions she'd be asking in a homicide case.

"When did you become the Ingles' family physician?"

"In 1958."

"Didn't they already have a family doctor?" She flipped through the pages of her notepad. "Dr. Millcrest?"

"Yes. I recall they did."

"So why did they change?"

"It was over Mrs. Ingles' illness. I was better qualified. Dr. Millcrest agreed."

"To treat her anaemia and respiratory problems."

"Yes."

"I've looked at hospital records and she was never hospitalized for her illness and never took medication."

"I can't remember."

"For being better qualified to treat her, you didn't admit her to a hospital on the day of her death and you didn't prescribe medication. Is that normal?"

"She seemed to be stable, then her lungs imploded..."

"I thought you said you couldn't remember."

"Her lungs collapsed and there was nothing we could do. We were deeply shocked at the turn of events."

"There was no coroner's report."

"I don't recall."

"You were attending when she died?"

"Until the end."

"How old were you at the time?"

"I believe thirty."

"Just out of med school and hungry?" She watched the man mentally connect the dots. "Hungry?"

"You know. For the things you worked hard to get. Hungry to get a foothold in the right circles. I suppose being connected with Howard Ingles got you that foothold. Shortly after Alexsis Ingles' death, didn't you open your own clinic?"

"Where is all of this going?"

"It would have taken a lot of money to have set up shop. Where did it come from?"

"Invested interests."

"Alexsis Ingles was murdered. We've opened a homicide case. We have evidentiary items, DNA amenable."

"It's ridiculous," he said almost under his breath.

Biro thought he wasn't as surprised as he should have been, that he should have been more shocked and less indignant. "It's not ridiculous, Dr. Standern."

"I was there. I saw her take her last breath. You're wasting your time. There is no case." He had enough and stood up to dismiss her.

"I'm not finished yet. I want to know how well you knew Police Chief Curtis Knott."

"Who?"

"He was the Chief of Police in 1958 and committed suicide two months after Alexsis Ingles died."

"I can't recall him."

"Really? I went over the coroner's report and it said you were the attending physician."

"Yes. Oh yes. I remember Curtis Knott. Shot himself. It was tragic."

"Unknown reasons. You didn't know these reasons, did you?"

"Of course not. Why would I? I don't like your tone. I think you better leave, Detective Biro. I won't be talking to you again without a lawyer."

"We're exhuming the body today at 2:00 at Mount Pleasant."

"It's nonsense. You're wasting your time."

"We don't think so." She packed up. "Thanks for seeing me. At some point within the next two days you'll have to make a statement at the station or we can do it here." She handed him contact information. "Phone and make an appointment if you want to." She turned and let herself out.

When her car disappeared down the hill, Standern took out his Blackberry.

* * * *

At nine in the morning the chauffeur had driven Bev to King Street by herself. Harvard wanted to go, but had to stay to finalize packing before he and Mickey went to their son's.

Bev sat in front of the safety deposit box and stared – tempted, but afraid to open it. Then swiped the card. Sliding the metal drawer out of its pocket she stared at a single ledger that didn't belong to Bev's father. It was a ledger that had been kept by the Ingles' family lawyer, Paul Dann. A two hundred page ledger that seemed to be divided into three sections: a diary, a financial record, and an appointment log. Two hundred and some pages of documentation and nothing else.

She was both surprised and disappointed. Quickly she left and went to her office at the Arts Foundation Centre to be alone. She started reading the diary entries first, until it was time to go home to get ready for the exhumation.

When she got home Harvard was there and had told Mickey he was going to the cemetery. Mickey refused to come down to say good-bye. Bev had never known her home to be so uninviting. She felt isolated, as if everything she loved were locked away from her. She knew she had to call Ben.

*****

He had been waiting for her call. He didn't know how she'd sound, but he trusted her to give it to him straight. He was relieved to hear her voice. "Hello Bev. How're you doing?" Ben knew his world had crashed into hers. Finding what you need in life, what you want costs a lot, sometimes. It did for his brother. It did for Alexsis Ingles and Rigo Molinaro. And now for Bev. You pay the price in one way or another.

"How am I? I'm not sure. It's been rough." She knew she hadn't gotten to the critical part; it was the next assault, the disinterment, she was bracing herself for.

"Are you coming this afternoon?"

"Yes. It will be good to see you. How could anyone have known this was going to happen?"

"One person knew."

"The artist."

"Yes. I have a lot to tell you."

"Let's meet tonight. Okay?"

"We need to."

"How's Annie?"

He wasn't sure and lied. "Really good. Enjoying a visit with her mom for a while."

"I'm glad she's all right."

"We both are." Another lie.

The gate signal was beeping on her phone. "Someone's at the gate, Ben. I'll see you later. We'll talk."

They said good-bye knowing that later at Mount Pleasant Cemetery, they would not meet to put someone to rest, but to rattle her bones like witch doctors invoking evil spirits out of a deep sleep.

*****

After Detective Biro listened to her recording and reviewed her notes she drove the QEW to rendezvous with Jaiteley at the Westings'. He was waiting for her at the gate and compared notes on their interviews.

Bev saw the police badges that the dark-skinned man and pretty, black-haired woman held up to the camera; she instructed them to come up to the house. She was surprised that the police were working so quickly. When Detective Jaiteley asked for the contents of the safety deposit box that he had found empty an hour earlier she had prepared herself. When she had arrived home she gathered personal papers and photos that could have been in the box but weren't and handed them over to the detectives. She had hidden the ledger.

"This is it. I needed to see them first. I hope you understand."

"We do." Jaiteley put them in an attaché and thanked her, then he asked if she would help them over the next two days with the archives of the Ingles Foundation. That they would be important in the investigation.

She agreed to help and the two detectives waited, but Bev wasn't going to ask them to stay. When Detective Jaiteley said he had been to see Bev's adopted parents, Thomas and Jane Ingles, Bev wanted to know the details and invited them in for a coffee. Even though the Ingles had called Bev to tell her of the police visit and how upset they were with the investigation, she wanted to hear Jaiteley's report.

Jaiteley scrutinized the room's South Asian decor. He recognized fabrics and motifs, Indian backdrops in photos, topographical maps and was amazed how authentic they were.

"My mother was born in India. Her father was in the export business until my grandmother got sick and they had to return to England. I've kept their past with me."

"It's very impressive. Have you travelled there?" He felt her need of authenticity, a need satisfied with the labour of calloused fingers and stretched ligaments, aching backs and dyed hands.

"We've been to India three times. It's beautiful."

It wasn't long before he brought the conversation back to the Ingles – to how spry and youthful the Ingles were for a late-seventy's couple.

Bev was about to ask what they had discussed when Harvard joined them. She made introductions and explained that Harvard would be staying in Toronto for another week.

"So, how were my adopted parents able to help you?"

"They recalled as much as they could. A couple of things stand out – how they thought it was odd that they weren't allowed to see Alexsis Ingles before she passed. Jane remembered begging Howard Ingles to let her go in and say good-bye, but she wasn't allowed. She wanted to tell your mother that she would help Howard take care of you. That she could rest in peace. And the second thing was how you," he turned to Harvard, "disappeared. Thomas and Jane said they couldn't find you."

"I didn't take it very well. I had lost my own mother when I was a young boy. I was still a kid when my dad married Lexi – that's what we called her – and she was a great mother to me. I remember locking myself in my room and staying there until after the funeral."

"Then you flew to the UK into an early admission into Oxford."

"Yes."

"The Ingles said they weren't allowed to see you before you left. What was that all about?"

Bev was surprised. "They never told me any of this before. Why didn't you say good-bye to Thomas and Jane?"

"I remember not wanting to see anyone. I remember being angry and bitter and you know the Ingles – stiff upper lip and all that bullshit. I was a kid who had lost my mom and best friend. I couldn't wait to get the hell away from there."

"And me?" Bev asked.

"If I could have taken you, Bee, I would have stowed you away."

Detective Biro who had been quiet decided to ask Harvard what he thought about the case and about what Ben Needham was going through.

"I don't know what to think. Ben's a good man, clever, solid. But I was there at Alexsis' bedside when she died. My dad lay beside her holding one hand and I held the other. Our doctor was there."

"Which one?" asked Biro. "It seems you hired an unknown, Dr. Philip Standern, barely out of school to treat Mrs. Ingles. Was that wise? In his care she died."

"It was a sudden turn; she died of respiratory illness. I know you have to exhume the body, but forensics will find there was nothing suspicious. When that happens, there will be lawsuits."

"Harvard," cautioned Bev.

Detective Biro decided to set Harvard straight on a few things. "Forensics have already found evidence, important evidence that something happened to someone in that attic. And that someone has chosen to haunt Ben Needham, an ordinary guy paying down a mortgage, raising a kid, doing a good job. We're listening and watching and investigating because we believe him, and science believes him too."

"Whatever happened didn't happen to my stepmother."

Jaiteley knew there wasn't a lot of time before the exhumation, so he thanked Bev for the coffee and the documents and said they'd see her at the cemetery. Both the detectives left, knowing she hadn't given them the real contents of the bank box.

* * * *

Rose always felt more connected to the multi-planed world, as she knew it, when she was with Joseph. When he arrived, she led him to her rear office with its eastern exposure and warm November light spilling through the large Palladium window. Before she left to get a mid-morning tray of snacks, she flipped a switch controlling a wall of rock and a waterfall to the right of the window; a small, tranquil gurgling fell into existence.

While Joseph listened to the rhythm of the water, he thought how being in Rose's life was not something he nurtured, but something that was inescapable and how she preserved his humanity in ways he didn't think he needed, like being less an algorithm and more a man. Like less a textbook and more a poem. Like more in the mid-plane of life and less in this one or the next, so that the transition between them was smoother. Rose had that effect on him – coaxing him through transitions with soothing energy.

When she joined him, he was sitting in a chair that had become a good friend over the past few years. He was watching her set down the tray of tea and muffins and wondered if she ever missed having a family of her own. Neither of them had kids. He wondered, if like him she was too busy with inter-spiritual fusions and inter-geo-physical visitations to miss the complications of family life. He wondered if she ever loved, had memories of men she thought she loved or knew she didn't. He watched her six foot frame bent at the waist pouring tea and laying out napkins. He watched the breadth of bone structure between her hips that he wanted to reach for.

In his youth he was a planta-genista (a twig of a man) whom women adored and wanted to carry around like a garden ornament. They carried him, piggybacked him, bathed him, fed him and used him – that was before he met his wife, Brit.

He had never loved any of them, before he got married, and since the death of his wife, he thought he might love again, when he met Rose on various cases. Whenever she assuaged his pain, he felt transmutated by some invisible elixir pouring out of her and into his empty veins. He wondered if all lovers felt healed by their partners.

Why not love Rose? he thought to himself and tried being adventurous. "This looks great! A home cooked meal."

"It's just Red Rose and muffin mix. Who has time for recipes?"

"Do you ever think about things like I do?"

"Like the families we never had? I knew that's what you were going to ask because if you're like me, you do think about it. Did you ever want kids?"

"No. We had decided not to. I was experimenting with so much new born stuff that I never had time to think about having a real kid. My wife felt the same. Was there anyone special that you had to pass by or give up because of your career?"

"No."

"I find that hard to believe. Why the hell not?"

"I was too busy trying to understand myself. It's been a major challenge. And one guy after another couldn't deal with my hazy, dichotomous appearance.

"So, who are you?"

"Someone who has totally accepted things as they are and is open for new things."

He got up and joined her on the sofa to look up into her face. An involuntary smile softened his approach. "I really feel comfortable with you. I always look forward to working with you and the time we spend afterwards. Like this. I know I'm a bit older, but there are possibilities, aren't there?"

"Yeah, there are. I understand about all the travelling. No one to come home to. When we're together, like this, we're passionate about our work. We both want to help people. We want to keep on learning and never stop. It's nice having you here. I like to think there are possibilities."

"Yeah?"

"When did you start to have feelings?"

"I was devoted to Brit, but when she passed – it's been five years now – I started paying attention to those other feelings, the ones for you. I think I got engaged to your chair. You wouldn't let me take it home, so I had to keep coming over." Joseph was surprising himself at his easy honesty.

"No one really knows about us, do they? How close we are?" She didn't know why she asked these questions.

"No. But you and I have for the two years, haven't we? Why didn't you say anything?"

"Because I'm a romantic and you're not. Because I've always known about your past. There's a lot of gossip in the lab – Joseph Hightower was seen with this model or that graduate student or that singer, of course, before you were married. I was afraid of you before I met you. Then there was Brit and the love you two shared. I didn't know how you felt after she died. People said you went into a deep depression."

"I loved being married to her. I think marriage made me into a romantic. It took me two years just to be able to sleep again without the nightmares."

"When we worked together, from time to time, I saw the way you looked at me. Compassionately. I was never afraid of your loneliness. I'd catch you staring at me and wondering who and what I was."

"Maybe who, but not what. Your womanhood is stamped all over the place – the way you move, your work, this place. I never wondered about that."

"So, can we file this conversation away until this case is over, then open it again? Go someplace we had a hard time leaving and see what's changed?"

"I can wait for that." He moved closer. "Is all right if I kiss you?"

With her finger she wiped a crumb away from his mouth. "This is a homemade kiss, not a recipe." Her full lips covered his and found what was behind them, for a moment that passed too soon. "I'll be waiting when this is over, but I have something to show you. Follow me."

On her computer, she pulled up articles on a hospital in Kingston.

"What is it?" He drew close and rested his arm on her shoulder.

"These articles are about the Rockwood Asylum for the Insane in...."

"....Kingston, Ontario. Founded in the 1850s. Why is this significant?"

"1958. We haven't been able to get any records of the artist being admitted to any hospital in Ontario, assuming he is still alive as we both believe. So if he was put away and was never meant to be released, what better place than the Rockwood Asylum? His motorcycle was found, or so the police report said, near Kingston. In the séance, do you remember the presence saying he was still alive in a hospital? And he said 'bride'?"

"Yes."

"Rockwood Asylum was built after the Kirkbride model. It's worth investigating."

"Rockwood changed hands in the late fifties and became the Kingston Psychiatric."

"The old building is closed down, but the new one is on the same property. And still treats patients. Look at this article, *Lives of Misery and Terror*."

"What am I looking for?"

"There are files that give patient's accounts of their lives at Rockwood Asylum. Each patient has a number. This man, Thomas James is number 2,685. He was admitted in 1884.

Joseph drew closer. "What were the numbers I whispered in the séance?"

Rose flipped through her files. *28913 X*. "It could be a patient number."

"What's the 'X'? That's unusual. But it's worth looking into. I have to give a lecture at Queen's University tomorrow. I'll do some digging."

They spent the rest of the morning together, not always talking about the case, but about old times – their studies, travels, failures, successes, plans. For old time's sake, they decided to catch a light lunch at the Villa Restaurant on Bloor before they picked up Ben.

* * * *

After Bev's call at noon, Ben decided to pop into the school to see Vienna before the exhumation and found her arranging trays of materials and supplies in the storage closet next to her room. She jumped when he rapped on the door frame, turned around and pulled him into the closet.

Kicking the door closed behind them they were left in the dark, burying their faces in one another's and complaining how much they missed seeing each other.

"Do we have some time, before your next class?"

"Time, yes. Space, no."

Paint tins rattled and brushes toppled to the floor. Sponges and paper towel rolls and empty yogurt containers too. And they laughed and agreed they liked the haunted house better than the supply closet. They knew each other had a lot of heart, a lot of heartache, and a lot of heart-to-heart.

Annie didn't see Ben slip into the staff washroom to clean up on his way out.

* * * *

Ben got two calls on his cell on his way home: Mark, to say if he wanted him to stay at the house – do guard duty on Annie's room or walk the dog – while Ben was at the cemetery, he'd be there for him. And that he and Emma's worlds were fusing, like burning polyester to skin. Ben thanked him for the offer and for the bizarre, figurative language, but declined and said they'd catch up later. And Joseph called to say they were on their way and that Rose wanted a quick look at the attic before the exhumation.

Ben had time to change, open a cooler that he decided he didn't need after all and go up to the attic. It was calm, warm almost, and quiet. The walls were still charred, but there was an emptiness, like a home on moving day. Everything was the same, but Ben felt there were spaces between and among things that were unoccupied and voiceless.

When they arrived, Ben escorted Rose up to the attic, while Joseph asked if he could take da Vinci into the backyard to the gazebo where Joseph had felt stirrings there before. But da Vinci hung back when Joseph called to him. He stood his ground and wouldn't approach.

"Here, boy. Come." The dog refused. "What is it, boy?" When Joseph walked to him da Vinci retreated. "What's wrong, boy?"

The dog's head cocked to one side as he watched a patch of grass beside the gazebo heave as if an invisible spade had lifted it. He started barking as the grass heaved all the way to one side of the octagonal structure.

Joseph focused on the spot the dog was watching. Looking down at a patch of grass, then back at the dog he wondered what the dog had seen. "What is it, boy?"

da Vinci approached and started digging furiously without knowing why.

"Hold on, boy. Ben's not going to like this. Stop. Sit. Stop." But he kept on digging until the soil – a foot deep and four feet long – was dug up, almost to the gazebo. Then da Vinci barked again and ran back to the house, leaving Joseph perplexed about the dog's unstoppable mission. He bent down and touched the soil. It was warm and as he rubbed it between his fingers it turned red.

Joseph let da Vinci into the mud room and made him stay on the mat, while he found Rose and Ben still in the studio.

"It's changed, Joseph."

"What has?"

"The studio."

She was studying the charred walls and knew they had to work fast on the images that had appeared three times now. "The numbers are significant. After the exhumation, we have to cross check them. Dates. Addresses. Anything that could help." And she asked Ben to pull up his novel file and check the frame he knew he hadn't created.

When he did, the frame had faded. The hooded figure had almost vanished. "What's going on?"

Rose noticed the discolouration on Joseph's hands. She reached out and cupped her hand around his.

"The dog went into some kind of digging frenzy and dug up a small trench near the gazebo. When I touched the earth it turned red on my hand."

"It's happening, Joseph." She clasped his hand. Rose's eyelids quivered as she tried to focus. "He's fighting so hard to make us see, and the more he fights, the more he loses this life. We have to step it up." She held on to his hand. "Something is there, buried – ancient, metal, bone – something. "We have to take up the floor boards of the gazebo. Dig up the earth under it."

"What? When?" Ben was bewildered.

"After the exhumation. Jaiteley has to get a team back in here. I don't know what it is, but it's important."

Ben checked the time. "We've got to go."

Before they left, Joseph instructed Rose to take a dirt sample from his hand for Jaiteley. She used a cotton ball and placed it in a lunch baggie. Joseph washed up and while he wanted them to see da Vinci's trench again, they had no time.

22

The vehicles wound their way solemnly through the cemetery, past fountains, past fading fall gardens and rare trees to the Ingles' family crypt. It was flanked by two small ponds with a statue and fountain in the middle of each, and guarded by two Japanese Katsura trees.

Ben knew what it was like to be invaded. He didn't like assuming this role. Invading the tranquility of this soulful, resting place.

A group of people had gathered. The Director of Human Resources, the Executive Vice-President of Cemetery Operations, a medical officer and a health officer along with the forensic team and Detectives Bodhan Jaiteley and Eva Biro who had handed the signed order to the Vice-President. Very quickly the health officer cordoned off the area around the mausoleum and asked all who were going inside to wear disposable, sterile gowns, gloves and masks.

The Westing limo was the last to arrive. Ben was surprised to see Harvard helping Bev out and not Bill who didn't come. Bev squeezed Ben's hand as she passed and let the officials help her and Harvard into their disposable gear. Ben, Joseph and Rose remained outside.

All these years Bev had chosen not to visit the crypt. She paid respect to the living memories of her family, not to dead, decayed corpses. It surprised her that Alexsis' coffin was a simple oak – perhaps there had been no time for a more ornate selection that would have meant something to her mother. But across the top was an intricately woven sari that Bev knew had belonged to her grandmother. She wanted to touch it and decided to wait until the disinterment was over to ask if she could take it home with her.

Both the Vice-President and the medical officer asked everyone to stand back from the coffin as they moved beside it, and aided by two assistants proceeded to open it. Silence. A rigid stillness followed. The men seemed frozen in sculpted watchfulness – immovable and mute. They stared in disbelief.

The medical officer stared into the coffin, while the Vice-President turned to face the gathering. "I'm sorry, Ms. Westing. I don't know how this happened."

The doctor turned around and announced that the body had already been removed. Quickly Jaiteley instructed forensics to do a sweep of the casket and surrounding area and asked everyone to leave immediately.

The parties outside were surprised when they saw Bev and Harvard emerge so soon, followed by the remaining visitors. Bev shook her head as Ben approached and asked what happened.

"Not now; I'm taking Bev home. I told you this nonsense would have a damaging impact on my sister."

Bev released Harvard's hold on her arm. "No. I want to go with Ben. I want to go to Marion Street."

"Bee! It's not going to do you any good going there. Why would you want to go there? You won't get any answers."

"What happened?" asked Ben.

"Her remains aren't there."

"We have to find them," said Rose urgently. "We're running out of time. Joseph, ask Jaiteley to get a team together to dig up the gazebo. Something's been buried there. He'll listen now."

Bev turned to Harvard who had noticeably paled, took his arm and guided him away from the others. With a lowered voice she made herself clear, "Go back to the house, get ready to fly out tomorrow. Don't worry about me. If I were you, I'd start giving some serious thought to how you're going to deal with this."

The pit of his stomach felt jagged and raw. He knew what she was talking about, but pretended he didn't. "What are you talking about?" And for the first time since she had known him, his voice wasn't unalterably sure.

"Saturday, November 29th, 1958. I know you were only a boy of sixteen, but something happened to you that day, the same day that my mother died. You know something. You're hiding something. At this point I really don't want to know. And that's the truth. Whatever happens with or without you here, will happen anyway. What I want is for this family not to be hurt. I want to protect us. You have to believe me. So whatever it is you're hiding, take it with you. And do it soon. I wouldn't stay here, Harvard."

He protested. Wouldn't budge. But when Bev walked away and asked Ben if she could ride with them, Harvard got into the limo and left.

After Joseph had told Detective Jaiteley about the dog incident at Ben's, and Rose confirmed they had taken blood samples, he decided not to accompany Eva Biro, along with the Director of Human Resources, to examine the cemetery records. Jaiteley himself wanted to oversee the excavation at Ben's and had a team ready before he left Mount Pleasant.

* * * *

On the way home Ben filled Bev in on the details of Annie's night walk so that Bev would know what had gone on in the studio. She was genuinely stricken that Annie had been used and had suffered.

By four the crew was extending the trench that da Vinci had dug up to the gazebo. After Rose had handed Jaiteley the sample she had secured from Joseph's hand, she and Bev watched the men pull up the floor boards, one by one and sample each.

Ben had contacted Wendy earlier to see if she could pick up Annie at school and that he'd send her suitcase over in a taxi. Before he joined them he phoned to see how they were doing. All was more than well. Again he was surprised he found comfort in Wendy's assurance that things were good.

By four thirty Vienna came through the front door of Marion Street, found Ben kissing the receiver end of the phone and wrapped her hand around his. Her lips involuntarily formed *I love you.*

He thought this was her best trait – her total acceptance of his mannerisms. She could find him kissing a phone or a potato, or a pencil and know why he was doing it.

"Annie?"

"I'm just sending kisses. And that's the second time you've told me you love me in a week."

"You're counting?" she smiled.

"How do you know it's real?" He had no idea how people decided whether or not love was real. His mom and dad didn't have the Bonnie and Clyde, the Bogart and Bacall, the Parker and Watson kind of love. He never had it with Wendy. So how did people know?

She offered up her thoughts. "Well, in past situations when things didn't go right, I'd eat and eat and eat, like I was replacing the guy with food. But with you, when we're apart, I can't eat. And when I eat, nothing wants to stay down. I feel so empty, so hungry, but I can't eat. I don't even have sex. I'm abstaining. Nothing replaces you."

"Get in here!"

She moved closer until his familiar hold enwrapped her. For an intimate minute his hands moved quietly into the folds of her blouse and pants until da Vinci started whining and howling and barking by the back door. And Ben heard someone call his name. *Mr. Needham! Can you come out here?*

It was Jaiteley waving him closer to the gazebo. Ben and Vienna rushed into the yard – da Vinci hiding behind them and wrapping his teeth gently around the folds of Ben's pants, warning him not to go closer.

"Let go, boy." And Ben shook him off.

While Jaiteley looked on, one of the technicians was using two sets of tongs to remove a discoloured, stained cloth – a shawl, Bev thought – that was rolled around something. They placed it carefully on an examining table, and as they unwound it they took skin and hair samples from the loose weave and took pictures. As they unrolled the last turn, the cloth fell away and exposed the intricate, blood-stained contents.

Immediately Jaiteley recognized the object and turned to Bev who had pressed her hand over her mouth, stopping her shock from cutting the silence. She was visibly shaken. Jaiteley asked Ben to take her into the house where he would join them as soon as he left the team with further instructions.

When they had gathered around the dining room table, Ben asked what it was.

"A Khurkri. An Indian dagger. Three hundred years old. The bone hilt is hand carved of course. I'm hoping for a positive match with the blood on the mirror fragments and on one of the floor boards." He turned to Bev and waited.

"I have a picture of this weapon that was mounted in a glass case on a wall in the Ingles' estate. My dad is standing in front of it."

"It's the same weapon?"

"It was given to my grandfather – Alexsis' father – before he left India. He wanted her to have it when she moved to Canada. One of the many stories my adopted parents told me about my mother's family."

"Do you still have the picture? Forensics will need it."

"Yes. I'll get it for you when I go home."

Rose and Joseph remained quiet to let everything sink in. Jaiteley gathered his thoughts and recapped what they had.

"This is it. We've got a missing body, a mirror fragment, a floor board and a weapon with blood on them, a jealous husband as a possible motive for murder, paranormal disturbances forcing us into this investigation, symbols, words, numbers that a team is working on. We have possible, living parties to this murder cover-up. We've got a missing artist, his younger brother in Italy who is sending the wreckage of Molinaro's motorcycle. We've got data that places Alexsis and Molinaro here in this house. We need to find the body. We need something to lead us to Molinaro."

Rose opened her bag and removed a summary sheet of the symbols that the presences communicated to them and told them to take one. "We think the answers are here."

"Rose and I are going to Kingston in the morning. The supposed motorcycle crash happened outside Kingston. We're going to examine patient records at The Psychiatric Hospital that formerly was The Rockwood Asylum for the Criminally Insane. It's been empty for six years now. They have records that predate the 20th Century. I have a lecture in the morning, but I'll be meeting Rose at the records department at Queens in the afternoon. We've checked every hospital in greater Toronto unsuccessfully and there are no police records of finding Molinaro. Hopefully, we'll turn up something. We'll be back late tomorrow night."

Jaiteley crossed his arms on the table top, and Rose understood his question behind his quiet scrutiny.

"No," Joseph intervened. "I won't let Rose test the knife. It's too dangerous, Bodham. You didn't see her after the first investigation."

"Fair enough, but if you change your mind, we'll work with you in a highly controlled cell. You know that." He took one of the data sheets and joined his team.

And Joseph and Rose excused themselves so they could get ready for their early morning drive.

The other women were quiet while everyone dispersed to various destinations. Then Vienna turned to Bev. "This can't be easy for you. I don't know how to help."

"It's even harder on an empty stomach. I know I shouldn't want to eat, but surprisingly I'm starving. What's in your fridge, Ben?"

"Salmon steaks. We could grill 'em. Toss a salad."

As the trio got things ready, Bev commented on how such ordinary things like a salmon steak and an onion and tomato seemed so unexpected, so surreal while everything else – all the bizarre events - had become the expected.

There was little talk as they ate, then Ben ventured to ask about Bill. "Have you phoned Bill yet?" He waited for a reply.

"I can't. I'm so ashamed of the things I'm finding out about my past. I just can't unload them on Bill. I feel I'm in a cave-in. I'm being weighed down with these enormous revelations. I don't want him in there with me."

Ben understood. "There's been a lot of evidence coming at us so fast. What do we do with it all? Where's it leading us? Still, I think Bill will be hurt if you don't let him do this with you. What's the poor guy going through thinking you don't trust him?"

"I know what you're saying, but maybe I'm waiting for something concrete so I can bring it to him. So together we can come face to face with the truth."

"Do you think her murderer is still alive?" asked Vienna.

"I don't want him to be."

"In my friend's serology report, Greg concluded the murderer must have been small. It couldn't have been your dad."

"I know. Forensics will show that."

"The artist was small. Standing beside Alexsis, he looked like a small man in the picture."

Quietly they agreed, then Bev asked if she could go up to the studio.

"Everything's torn apart and under plastic." When she insisted, Ben took her up.

Bev looked at the debris that had been swept up into organized rubble.

"It's quieter," Vienna commented. "Like it's lost a battle."

"...or won." Bev tried to imagine this place fifty years ago. And for a brief moment thought she heard a child's laughter, like a kid being tickled, rapid-firing giggles. "Is it gone? This thing. This presence. Is it gone?"

"No," said Ben. "I think it's resting. Getting its second wind. Winding up for the final assault. I don't think it needs me anymore. It's just a feeling I have."

Bev looked at the faded writings on the broken walls. "I wouldn't want to be its next conduit, its next catalyst." She looked around the space and tried to remember. "I thought I might have remembered my mother bringing me here. That there'd be something. I want to go. I don't belong here." As she turned to leave, a tiny white corner of a piece of shiny paper caught her eye – a miniscule white triangle. It was lodged behind a window frame on the wall at the end of the room and had partially fallen out when the men had pulled things apart.

"What's that?"

"What?"

"That piece of paper sticking out of the window frame at the far end." She pointed to it.

Ben squinted to see it. "God, you have good vision. It must have fallen down with all the banging."

They went to it and Vienna whose nails were the longest clamped down on the corner and carefully removed it. It was the flip side of a photo with scribbled writing in Italian, *Sisi and me and B, 1956.* She turned it over.

All three stared at a happy trio submerged in the waves at the beach – the short, dark-skinned man, the pale, tall model and a little girl holding on to the man like a life raft.

Bev felt faint. Suddenly sun-damaged. "Who's taking the picture?" she asked. Her voice cracked with unwanted possibilities.

"You knew the artist," Vienna said softly.

"And so did the photographer. I want to leave."

"I'll help you downstairs," whispered Vienna. They left quietly – Bev's trembling hands holding more than she needed to know.

As they sat, Bev mused how this house felt more like hers than it did Ben's. That it somehow felt like home and wondered at the intricacy of events that drew them all together – Annie's music, the Holiday portrait, the party, the séance, the exhumation. And what was to come? She was thankful that Harvard had escaped all this and would soon be on his way home.

"I've only met one person in my life who discovered life-altering things about her past. There could have been others, but they didn't own up to it"

"Who was your friend?"

"She was a woman who in her late thirties found out that her mother who was born in England had been loaned or sold to a farmer near Exeter, here in Ontario in the late forties. She was ten years old when her family literally sold her into a life of servitude. By the time she was fourteen she had had two kids to this farmer and then gave birth to my friend. My friend grew up not knowing the truth about her parentage, the abuse her mom suffered, and that she had two sisters somewhere. I never understood how she handled it. I always thought I knew everything about my family – how my parents loved me, how Harvard adored me and how Bill almost deifies me, at least my cooking. And then this comes along. Who the hell am I?"

"Would it be so hard to accept this other person into your life?" Ben asked.

"Other person? You mean this thing that's destroying all of us? I don't know who I am anymore or what I'm entitled to."

"You're entitled to the truth."

Bev frowned. "It's too expensive." She found her purse and slipped the photo into an unused compartment. "I want it for a little while, then I'll hand it over it. And I do need Bill."

23

It didn't take long for Jaiteley and Biro to hook up at FIS (Forensic Identification Services) on Jane. On the way Biro said she didn't find anything suspicious regarding the Ingles cemetery records that the Director of Human Resources of Mount Pleasant handed over. She was amazed that the murder weapon turned up on Ben's property.

Pete Moore, the DNA Co-ordinator (aka the forensic identification officer and police liaison man) was waiting for them with a full report of their DNA profiling.

"What have we got here?" asked Jaiteley.

"I'll walk you through it," Pete suggested as his stomach did a surround sound rumble that embarrassed him. Everyone present had taken the lab rat survival workshop and knew that work suffered if you didn't eat. To Pete, dedicated DNA profiling precluded eating.

"I feel guilty, Pete. Do you want to grab something or order in?"

"Nah. This won't take long." And tried to talk above his abdominal rumblings. "Okay, from all the blood samples we have one DNA profile – blood from the mirror fragment, cracks in the old pine flooring, and from the weapon. This profile matches skin samples found in the cloth that was a shawl, wrapped around the dagger. We identified another DNA profile from a strand of hair imbedded in the loose weave of the shawl. This matched another skin sample that was on the cloth, different from the first DNA profile. The first profile belongs to a young mother and the second to a young man, short, with a powerful, left hand, downward thrust. We examined your forwarded copies of the art works that Rigo Molinaro did. He was left handed. His brush strokes were aggressive and from his photo he was below average height."

"He was thirty. Still a young man."

"He could be a suspect. We don't have a DNA profile for him."

"The wreckage from his brother should be here tomorrow. Maybe there'll be usable sampling. So you have two profiles – one from a murdered woman and one possibly from her murderer?"

"I'd like Ms. Westing to give us a sample; we'll do an mtDNA analysis to get a positive ID on Alexsis Ingles. But we still need the body. From the exhumation we sampled hair; its profile matched the murdered woman's DNA. There were no other samples from the coffin."

"But the CS DNA profile could be her murderer's?"

"Yes."

"Howard Ingles was an older man, a large man with a weak heart. What are the chances? He had a motive – the jealous husband."

"If Bev Westing's DNA matches both samples, we have a positive ID on both her parents. But our DNA results profile a younger man."

"I'll call her. Good work, Pete."

"Do you want me to meet with you and the Chief?"

"Maybe later."

At headquarters they took some time to review their follow-ups. Jaiteley would contact Bev Westing about arranging the DNA sampling, and Biro would see Dr. Standern a second time in the morning. Jaiteley wanted the Database Specialist to run the numbers and letters from Rose's investigation through the system: the date, 1947, the number, 305, and the letters, CBI. He was convinced something would turn up somewhere.

Biro flipped through her files and caught her notations about Dr. Standern's clinic he opened in 1959. From what she found, there was a donation of $500,000.00 from the Ingles' Foundation given to the Standern Children's Care Centre in Toronto. Gut feeling told her this was a payoff. She wanted to shake up Standern's memory.

Jaiteley told her to go home, get a good sleep, and that he'd update the Chief in the morning, himself.

* * * *

Some welcomed the night – they could retreat to some darkened corner to review their day of successful results or less-than-successful misfires. For Biro and Jaiteley the night often was an extended coffee break. Both went home, didn't sleep much, couldn't go to the places where Ben, Rose and Joseph had gone, so they stuck to the facts, the reports, the speculations.

* * * *

For Bill and Bev Westing the night wasn't so much to be feared as was being alone with each other. She was quiet on the way home and quieter as they reclined on a sectional in front of their fireplace in their bedroom. Bill had motioned her over; she had slid against him.

His hand pushed back her short hair, stroking its soft waves. Then he reached down to unsnap each hidden dome on the front of her blouse, loosening it to make her more comfortable. Then to the bottom of her slacks and up under each leg to pull off her knee highs. He held the collar of her shirt while she squirmed out of it and pulled a throw over the two of them. "Better?"

"A little. I need a shower. I was in a crypt, then in a chewed-up back yard – mud everywhere – and at a crime scene filled with dust and splinters. I feel so dirty."

"Figuratively?"

"Literally. And figuratively."

Bill let it pass and asked about Ben's yard.

"They were digging because Ben's dog was going nuts about something. So they dug a trench over to this gazebo and under it and pulled up floor boards."

"Did they find anything?"

"You bet. Just a dagger that had belonged to my granddad. Given to him as a gift when he left India. He gave it to Alexsis. It had been mounted on a wall at the estate."

"We have a pic of it with Howard and Alexsis standing in front of it."

"That's the one. It was wrapped up, blood and all, in a shawl my mom wore." Becoming emotional she found it hard to go on.

"Sh... you don't have to talk about if you don't want to."

"I don't want to. I want to pretend this isn't happening to me. But it is and I need to talk about it."

"I'm not judging. You know that, don't you?"

"I'm not sure I know that. Family has always been like a building to you. If the structure is weakening, you're not a restoration guy. You're a demolition man. You would rather tear it all down and resurrect something in its place. You've never liked saving someone else's mistakes."

"Not true. This family is strong. We're strong. There are a lot of people in this city who would agree – and not only in this city. Everywhere."

She turned to look at him. "There was blood on the dagger and the shawl. It was the murder weapon. I'm waiting to hear the forensic report. I hope they call tonight."

Bill tried to focus on the import of it. Harvard had told him about the exhumation, that there was no body. He knew how difficult it would be for the police to proceed. He couldn't begin to imagine what Bev was going through. "The police have a good, solid team. Something will turn up." Then he changed the subject. "You were in the attic?"

"Yes. I wanted to see if I remembered anything."

"Did you?"

She closed her eyes and let Bill's fingers make furrows in her hair. She arched her head backwards, then rose, got her purse and removed the five-decade-old photo. She held the shiny paper with its back to Bill.

"It was hidden or had fallen behind the window frame in the studio. I caught sight of it when I was leaving."

"Let's have a look at the writing."

"It's in Italian. It translates, *Sisi and me and B, 1956.*" She turned it over for him to see. "I was one when it was taken. I want to know who took this photograph. I want to know who I was to this man."

"I'd be totally wrong if I thought this man didn't make Lexi happy. Or you. Look at you. You're clinging to him like a puppy. Look at his hand cupping your face. His lips glued to your cheek. And Lexi smiling as though this man was the first dad on this earth or the first man to create this little, frilly bundle he's holding."

"Bill, who's behind the camera?"

"Who do think?"

She started crying. "I think it was Harvard. I think he knew about them."

Bill drew her close and tried to calm her. "Sh....maybe it was Harvard. Sh...but why would it be Harvard?"

"I don't know. Because he loved her. Because if this was the only way he could stay near to her he would. I know him. He's so needy. My dad wasn't always there for him. You've seen the family photos – how Lexi consumed Harvard. They did everything together – biking, swimming, tennis. Then she went away to Europe, fell in love, and came back with this artist. You tell me Harvard wouldn't have been hurt. I imagine he was a diplomat even then, working the opportunity, finding ways to stay close to her."

"What are you saying?"

"I'm not sure, but something's not right."

"Is that why you sent him home?"

"Yeah. Whatever happened that day in Ben's studio, I think Harvard was involved. I think he's hiding something. And I don't want to know. What's the point,

Bill? Fifty years have gone by. We have a strong family, a loving family."

"Except for your mom and this artist who can't find peace, who won't leave Ben's house, who want us to do something."

"Do you honestly believe that?"

"I wouldn't have last week. I do now. I don't want to let them down. I don't want you to either. How can we not help? They need us. We can get through this together. You know we can."

She reached around and parted her lips letting his words slide off his tongue into her mouth. "I'm so sorry for the past couple of days."

"You can have all the space and time you need to sort through this. I'm here when you need me. Just keep in touch like this, from time to time, okay?"

He looked at the photo again. "What do you think?"

They were interrupted by the phone. It was Jaiteley.

Bill watched Bev lower her head in contemplation. Her eyebrows drew together as wrinkles patterned across her forehead. He watched her nod her head while she listened attentively to Jaiteley's report and his request. She had put the speaker on for Bill to hear. Each detail of the report reached raw-ended nerves that Bev found hard to soothe.

"Nine o'clock? I'll be waiting, detective." And she hung up and turned to Bill. "It's so unreal." And turned away.

When Bill heard her shower running he hesitated then rapped on the glass door. Bev thought he looked so alone under the pale yellow light, surrounded by grey rough-cut stone, like he had been abandoned on the moon.

She backed against the wall, let the water work its magic and waited for him. They would shower, dry, get into bed – the three of them: Bev, Bill and the ledger.

* * * *

Before Ben, Vienna, and da Vinci went back to her place which she had prepped for Ben's visit, they drove down Wendy's street, stopping for a moment outside while Ben tried to get a glimpse of Annie through some window.

He missed saying good night to her and walking the dog with her while she sang or hypothesized about her condition and her future. He missed her unexpected witticisms and deeply profound understanding of emotional quotients.

When Vienna gently urged him to go, he pulled away, and da Vinci seemed to be more settled as they left Wendy's street behind.

24

They left before Toronto's morning rush hour – the sun sprinkling its warm tendrils on the silver-back hillsides and Lake Ontario shoreline, and arrived in Kingston by 9:00 am. While Joseph prepared for his lecture at 10:00 and the Q & A that followed, Rose insisted she wanted to go straight to the Records office at The Providence Care Centre, on the grounds of which loomed the abandoned Rockwood Insane Asylum.

Detective Jaiteley had already contacted Kingston Police Department with full disclosure of the Ingles' homicide case and requested its assistance in meeting Joseph and Rose's initial, investigative needs when the time arose. And Joseph informed Meryl Dupuis, the Executive Officer of the Medical Records and Forms Committee of their arrival and asked for an itinerary for Rose that started in the records department and ended with a tour of Rockwood. While Meryl Dupuis didn't like the idea of opening Rockwood's doors, she made the necessary arrangements when Joseph informed her that it was a police investigation.

* * * *

Meryl Dupuis was waiting for Rose and as she escorted her to the Records office, her thin red lips clamped down on a heavy, but eloquent, Quebecois accent. The patient files were in a large modern, cement-walled, filing room with metal shelves finding their vanishing points twelve feet upwards against the walls. On the shelves were filing boxes that contained all patient records that pre-dated 2000. Meryl pointed to the top of the first set of shelves and said the records started there and continued to the bottom shelf then back to the top of the next, and that patient files were in alphabetical order from year 1859 to Rockwood's closing in 1959 and from 1959 with the new Kingston Psychiatric Hospital until 2000. Retrieving a sliding ladder for Rose that she secured in place, she showed Rose how to lock and unlock its base and how to use the intercom by the door if she had any questions.

Climbing the ladder felt like crossing a rope bridge, but at least it didn't sway. With her height and arm extension she rested safely on the fifth rung and tried not to look down. The shelves had no alphabetic indicators, so she had to scale twenty shelves in three different rows before she found the first files starting with 'M'.

Maat, Maybe, MacAdam, MacCallum, MacEvoy, MacLean... She closed the box and opened another, two shelves lower. *Mitts, Mittleholtz, Mitryk, Moch...* Replacing this box she scaled the ladder to the top of the next row. *Modesto, Moffat, Moir, Molasky, Molina, Molson...* Quickly she flipped through the names again. There was no file on Molinaro.

A sudden faintness swept over her – too many pages, too many tragedies. She should have put on her handling gloves. Quickly she grabbed the sides of the ladder as vertigo plunged her into a spin. She closed her eyes and leaned against the shelves, then descended, put on her gloves and searched again. She found the first box of R's thinking that they had gotten his name mixed up, that they could have filed him under the surname, Rigo. Working quickly through five boxes her search ended with nothing.

The intercom buzzed in Meryl's office.

"Nothing showed up, Meryl. I need to know where you keep files on unidentified patients. Are they here, in this room?"

Meryl took Rose to a small room in the basement with a single, five drawer filing cabinet. "They're here; I'd help you, but I have a meeting." She turned to leave.

"So many records," Rose commented as she opened the first drawer.

"Often people left unwanted family members without identification at our doors – family members who suffered from different disorders and didn't know who they were. Children, spouses, siblings. Some were dropped off and threatened with bodily harm if they revealed their names. Others had no memory of who they were and the police brought them here. The files, of course, are in numerical order. Sorry, I have to go. The exit, when you're finished, is through that door, at the end of the hall, turn right."

"Thank you." Rose noticed she had forgotten to remove her gloves, so quickly set about flipping through files - numbers blurring by – 240, 392, 801, 2219, 3759, 15222, 21136, 25476.....until she came to Patient, 28913 X. She pulled it and started skimming.

When she reached the door at the far end of the room, it slowly opened for her. She hesitated, looked around first, then left, knowing he was watching. Before she found the exit, the door closed gently.

Meryl's secretary gladly made three copies of the file, while Rose waited for Meryl to join her to clarify omissions in the file.

Meryl was extremely co-operative in helping. She glanced at the file. "Apparently Patient 28913 X was admitted to Rockwood Hospital on Nov. 25, 1958. He suffered from head trauma, a head fracture, and while he sustained amnesia-like symptoms, there was no physical cause."

"Psychosomatic amnesia."

"Perhaps. In 1959 the hospital became The Kingston Psychiatric Hospital and Patient X was moved to another building." Meryl read on. "There are no monthly progress reports. It's odd that it doesn't give attending physicians' names either. There are no references to patient care referrals or progress benchmarks."

"I noticed that." Rose looked at the last page. "It says he died on May 26, 2004. Where are the medical certificate and the names of the medical examiner and his team? Funeral arrangements?"

Meryl shook her head. "They're not here. I don't have answers," she said apologetically. "I don't understand how this could have happened."

"This is a homicide investigation. I want to know who entered this report. How do we find out?"

Meryl understood the political dynamics of any institution – how some things slipped unnoticed through the system, but she understood the urgency of Rose's request and acted quickly, even though she knew some wouldn't want her to. "I'll make some calls."

Rose continued to re-read the file: how this man was a talented artist, how he gave art lessons to other patients and mentored one patient in particular, Sandra Bolyn who was the only person, apparently, he let into his life, how his paintings still hung in the Rockwood building, how he became obsessed with Angeloloy – the study of the hierarchy of the twelve angelic orders, how his alter-ego took the form of a Throne angel which is the name of an angel from the sixth order – an angel which is near spiritual perfection and called a bringer of justice, how he was known as the angel of light. *I want to know who made these entries*, thought Rose. She read on: Patient 28913 X volunteered as a test subject in Alpha Brainwave Entrainment in 1990 at Queen's. *Joseph would have been here then.* Patient 28913 X stopped eating in 1995. *How could he stop eating and live to 2004?*

When she had read enough she found Meryl on the phone, trying to source info on the missing patient data.

Rose waited until she hung up and asked for two things: that she find out what happened to a patient, Sandra

Bolyn, and that she was ready to tour the Rockwood building. Meryl had already assigned Jimmy Hearns, a security guard, to take Rose through Rockwood and asked him to join her in the lobby of the records building. She asked Rose to see her after, and that she'd try to get the answers she needed.

Before they left, Rose requested one thing. "I need administrative logs. Someone has to have answers and we needed them yesterday. If you have to, you can pass along the fact that the police will have no trouble getting search warrants."

* * * *

Rockwood Asylum was designed as hundreds were, as a facility that supported the visions of Philadelphia psychiatrist, Dr. Thomas Kirkbride. These institutions had come to be known as Kirkbride hospitals. They all had a linear plan that was characteristic of many asylums, some of which were the Athens State Hospital, Cherokee State, Danvers, the Hudson and the London, Ontario Psychiatric Hospital, and of course, the Rockwood Lunatic Asylum that sat back, isolated from the public, on expansive grounds, away from the heart of the city. Rockwood, like many of the others was suffering from neglect and decay, as if misery had sharpened its teeth, eating its way through mortar and brick, like predatory ivy.

Rose wanted to park on the outer drive and walk through the grounds to the main entrance, breathing in the fresh lake air (the property led to the shores of Lake Ontario). As they walked she thought of the article she had read in The Journal, a Queen's University publication. *Lives of Misery, Sadness and Terror.* She didn't have to be told how patients, labelled as deviants, felt so isolated behind such an unforgiving austerity, how they were locked away in small cells, hardly big enough for a single bed and dresser, how female patients first stayed in the stables along with horses and their dung and their flies. Lepers and whores alike shared the disreputable label of being insane. Rose didn't want to know how they survived and knew instinctively she'd have to refrain from reaching out and touching walls, door frames, desks, windows, photos.

She faced the building - its seemingly peaceful exterior that had housed so much turmoil and unrest, so much spiritual emaciation. The core of Rockwood was the central admissions building, flanked by patient wards that were built in tiers. The linear design facilitated segregation according to gender and illness. She followed its deteriorating lines - dark and foreboding like a scarecrow in a desert, hit by lightning.

"If you weren't nuts when you came, you probably were when you left – if you ever left," Jimmy commented. "I'll take you to the far east door, the only one that isn't welded shut." An involuntary shudder shook his stout frame, as it always did before entering Rockwood.

They walked past the barred, dirty windows, the faded, unruly ivy, and as they neared the door, Rose asked Jimmy how long he had been working there.

He did some mental calendar hopping to arrive at twenty two years. He had been there over two decades and had been a guard at the Pen, before asking for a transfer to the Hospital. In three years he'd be retiring.

She asked if he knew Patient X, the one they called the Angel of Light, and if he saw any of his paintings.

He nodded with mixed emotions – a chuckle constrained by a mix of fear and respect, and said under his breath that X was the strangest S.O.B. he had ever met. He went on to describe that on two occasions they had to wrestle him into a strait-jacket, not because he was violent, but because he wouldn't put down his paint brush. Said he needed to find the door and started painting the walls in the admissions office and the floors (they didn't know how he slipped past security). It was heart breaking how he'd cry and claw at the walls in his room as if there was someone hiding in them. And wrap his arms around thin air and rock himself to sleep. Then he added that Patient X started painting angels and never stopped until he got it right, then he'd paint the same one over and over, but bigger and brighter.

"Jimmy, you saw the paintings?"

"They're stored right here. But there's one in the great hall. Looks like Michelangelo did it. I'll show you."

"Did you see him before he died?"

"Who?"

"Patient X?"

"Did he die?"

"His file says he did. Are you surprised?"

He thought about it as he unlocked the door and entered the dark, central corridor with rows of small rooms on either side. "This takes us to admissions. Yeah, I'm surprised."

The hallway was endless. There were myriad smells – moist and medicinal and unhealthy like lingering, old smoke and musty smells like unwashed linens, and soiled, reverent smells, like old bibles hidden behind gritty toilets.

"Is that something you should have heard – that Patient X had died?"

"Sure, even though I don't know half the patients who die. I am surprised. It's just that he had such a high profile here. Someone would have told me. I think it's pretty odd that no one said anything to me."

"You didn't ask about him?"

"No."

"Why not?"

"Because he was moved," he paused to think, "in 2001. I don't know where they took him, but they took him in an ambulance out of the new psychiatric hospital."

"Why did they move him?"

"His age, his condition."

"What was his condition?"

"Not good, but we weren't allowed to see him. They had put him in isolation."

"Isolation! Did you ever hear of a Sandra Bolyn? She supposedly became Patient X's friend."

"Yup. No one to this day ever found out what happened to her."

"What do you mean?"

"Well, she was admitted, high on everything you could think of and cuts all over her arms and legs. A self-harmer. Pulled out her hair too. One day she saw X painting and sat and watched him. It seemed to calm her. He started to let her paint with him, on his canvases. She got really good." He stopped to reflect.

"Then what happened."

"She changed. Not overnight. But it happened. She got better."

"How much better?"

"Cured. Even her cuts disappeared. And the scars. No one could figure it out."

"What happened to her?"

"She was discharged."

"Before Patient X was moved?"

"I...I think so."

"Does anyone know where she is?"

"I don't know. None of us ever heard from her again."

When they got to the admissions room, the guard pointed to the west wall. "That's the last painting he did."

Rose stared at the painting of an angel, a Throne – powerful and winged. The canvas was at least eight feet wide and twelve feet high. "What do you think about it?"

'It's what he wanted to be."

"Do you know why?"

"No. He didn't talk."

"Ever?"

"No one ever heard him talk."

"Did he talk to Sandra?"

"I don't think so. I never heard him."

Rose decided not to put her gloves on. She removed a notepad and pen from her purse and handed them to Jim. "I'm going to touch the painting gently. Write down anything you see or hear. After about a minute I want you to call my name. If I don't respond, I want you to pull me back from the painting, so that I break contact with it."

"I don't think we should be doing this, Dr. Henhawke."

"It's okay, Jimmy." She drew close. "Ready?" Moving toward the bottom right hand corner she found the signature hidden behind a layer of draped light and pressed her fingertips against the 'X'.

The paint fell away like flaking skin to the floor. Jimmy wrote, *paint...blistering...dust falling....* He waited as Rose closed her eyes; he stood helplessly as the doctor started shaking.

Dr. Henhawke is shaking...she can't stop... "Dr. Henhawke?"

Like a battery being drained of its energy, Rose felt all her will being sucked into the signature and from the signature it ran into the threads of the canvas. Knowing her body was becoming a weightless shell, she didn't try to pull away. She could see her energy, like a living ghost, float inside the brush strokes on the canvas. When it had been completely absorbed, she fell like a spiritless doll to the floor.

Dr. Henhawke has fainted.... "Dr. Henhawke?" He felt for a pulse; it was irregular. He tried his radio; there was no signal. He sat by her side trying to talk her into consciousness, but knew that anyone getting that close to the Angel of Light would be powerfully altered.

From inside the painting her energy was enfolded in the wings of the Throne angel. It held her until his power locked her to him – her eyes looking outward at a scene that was playing for an audience of one – for her alone. It was a remarkable scene with surreal clarity - a scene that took her across the ocean to a dry, November day in the land of a thousand hills reverberating with proud drums and reborn voices.

There was a street with dust funnels swirling around three black cars, the middle one of which flew a diplomat's flag with blue, yellow and green stripes and a sun in the top right corner. The first and last cars were like armour surrounding the middle car, beside which were eight soldiers on guard. The street was in front of a school in the heart of the city. And behind the school on the playing field, hundreds of people had gathered to honour a man and a woman who worked tirelessly for the lost children of this war-ravaged land.

Rose saw it play out from all angles as she panned and hovered and tracked, camera-like over the scene. She watched men and women and children standing ceremoniously on the field behind flag bearers and an ensemble of students played drums and stringed instruments as dancers danced the Ikinimba. A choir of boys and girls sang a song of honour and treasure and eternity, while an older boy played the inanga and sang a solo about hope and unity.

It was joyous. Rose could feel her pulse beating to the ingabe drums. It was joyous and sacred, until she panned down the line of dignitaries and came to one student.

There was a black girl, a teenager – the girl Rose had envisioned before - who cradled a bouquet of orchids in her right hand as she stood at the end of the line of greeters. With her free hand she touched a war wound that had branded her face from her forehead, through her eye, over her cheek and down to the corner of her mouth with the inescapable memory of the man who had put it there. She was ready to hand the bouquet to the white diplomat and his wife who had started to shake hands with the Principal of the school and was proceeding down the line to her, the mutilated girl with the perfectly arranged bouquet of black and white orchids. There was a calm in this girl. Her hands did not shake the flower petals, nor did sweat break out on her forehead.

The girl's face turned sideways to watch the man smile as he was greeted by each dignitary. He was a man she had been waiting to meet from the first time she saw him when she was a young girl. She had been playing an adagio by Haydn on her harp, when she heard the guard dogs bark and yelp and her parents scream for help. Racing to her window she saw the limo and this man protected inside of it. He wore sunglasses and stared at her house, while his small army stormed it and dragged off her parents and brothers and did to her eleven-year-old body what they needed to do to get high on power.

She knew he had watched and heard their screams. She knew what he had come for – her father's safe and the diamonds in it, she knew waited for a future.

When the ugly men threw her down in disgust of her rich, doll-like perfection, she bit and scratched their black skins. And one soldier took his knife and ripped open her face, tearing through flesh, and bone and muscle until a curtain of blood covered one eye in darkness. As her body scraped and bumped its way over the road to an armoured truck, she remembered trying to focus on the limo with the flag blowing proudly on it.

The white man got out, removed his glasses and inspected the contents of her father's safe before they put it in the trunk of the limo. He took an envelope from his pocket and walked to the soldier whose one hand dug into the girl's black hair and the other hand was outstretched for his payment.

From the ground she saw the white man's face and his deformed hand holding the envelope. But she knew she'd plan to meet him again, holding a bouquet of orchids on a dry, December day in the heart of the city, and the bouquet would be draped in such a way that no one would notice what it concealed.

Rose felt she was in a daydream – her body leaving its physical surroundings and entering an ur-reality of a world beyond. Her ghost-like essence was not in Jimmy's world, but was in the girl's, witnessing another justice to end all sorrow. She had seen this girl before when she shook Harvard's hand. Rose knew what was hiding among the flower petals. She had seen the cold metal make its way to the girl's hand, as if it had a mind of its own. Rose had no voice in this other world. She wanted to whisper to the girl to save herself, that she was worth more than the flowers she held and their secret.

The white man with the deformed hand stood face to face with the scarred, black girl. He smiled as she started to hand him the bouquet – a gift for his charitable donation to her school – then stopped. He smiled and waited, and in a moment of recognition, in a flash of history as he had orchestrated it, his smile faded. He had remembered the scar like a brush stroke of paint that could have been found in Picasso's *Guernica*. He remembered it and saw in her eyes what was inescapable - that fate knocks more than once. That it can take half a hand or half a life. He didn't even try to say *I'm sorry*, before she pulled the trigger beside her head.

Jimmy looked at his watch. She had been unresponsive for fifty five seconds. He took her pulse again. It seemed normal. "Dr. Henhawke! What do I do? I don't know what to do! If you can hear me, do something!"

Suddenly he jumped as a pressure touched his shoulder from behind. Spinning around he fell backwards, away from Rose and witnessed a long wisp of light fall on the unconscious woman, like it was her ghost repossessing her.

Again, when he tried his radio, there was no signal. "I'll get help," he shouted and ran for the door. It locked as he got to it. Fumbling with his key he couldn't get it to turn the lock.

A shadow, small and shrivelled that had crouched in the ceiling beams above the fallen woman followed Jimmy as he rushed for the door. It fell down behind him; Jimmy could smell it and heard it slide along the floor. He turned to face it. The shadow – its sockets empty and sad – stared at the guard, then turned and crawled slowly away. Jimmy followed.

25

Paul Dann's ledger was divided into three parts – a personal diary, a record of the Ingles finances, and an appointment log. Bev had firmed up their pillows as they lay reading. Both wore reading glasses and Bill was the official page turner.

Paul Dann, Howard's family lawyer, had grown up in the Ingles' circle. When WWII hit, both men stayed on the home front and oversaw the transition of the Ingles' main and subsidiary factories from heavy machinery to arms for Canadian and British soldiers. With their wives, both men participated in the war effort – converting their arms factories into workplaces that the new workforce – the women – could function in. They built housing, installed bowling lanes, and music to keep everyone happy on factory lands.

Examining the figures, Bill drew Bev's attention to the fortune both Howard Ingles and Paul Dann had amassed. They were rich before the war and richer after it. Paul had glued into the ledger all business transactions that were legal and binding between the Ingles business empire and Canadian and British governments.

By the end of the war, Clara Bernard-Ingles (Harvard's mother) had contracted TB and succumbed to it in 1947 when Harvard was five. She was cremated at the Necropolis, Toronto's first crematorium. Bev stopped Bill's finger from turning the page.

"What?" he asked.

"I thought she had been buried. I'm sure Harvard visits her plot when he's here."

"At Mount Pleasant?"

"I don't think so."

"We can find out." Bill cross-checked and found a funeral bill for Clara Ingles' cremation. "It's all here. The arrangements, the billing." He flipped to the appointment log. "Here is the cremation date and time. He certainly was thorough."

"I'm puzzled. I know for certain she has a burial plot and that Harvard wants to be buried beside her. I know this for a fact. I've forgotten which cemetery."

"Maybe there was a plot. Maybe your dad arranged one for her. Maybe she wanted to be next to her parents, then had a change of heart near the end."

"It's possible. Why is everything so complicated?"

"Because we make it. Can I turn the page now or do you want to skim the appointment log? Or the financial statements?"

"God, look at you! You're so tired." Her nose nuzzled his cheek. "You get some sleep. I'll turn off your light and curl up by the fire. I want to read on."

"Are you sure?"

She looked at the clock and Bill's face. "It's after 1:00. I won't be much longer."

* * * *

That morning two women had been busy with the business of discovery. Bev had finished reading at 5:00 a.m., while in the east end of Toronto, Rose had finished eating breakfast and brushing her teeth and getting sunglasses to protect against the flaming eastern sky on her drive to Kingston. Bev uncurled her fingers from the ledger and stretched in front of the fire, while Rose had crunched into her car, her fingers tightening around the wheel she preferred not to be behind. While Rose had stolen sideways glances both at Joseph and at the frost-tipped landscape that gradually melted as Kingston approached, Bev peeked out her window at frost-bitten gardens and was too upset to stick around to witness their revival in the thick morning fire. Two women had set a course in different directions – directions none-the-less steering them to discovery.

The ledger was one of those moments in history that Bev would erase if she could time travel. One of those moments that like a diseased stillborn slides into your hands that are shaking so badly you think you'll never be young again, and life's cruel revelations leave your emotions cratered and scarred. The ledger was like a disease, a cruel revelation. She knew about these moments and how to keep their disease from driving her insane. She made a decision. Going to the basement, she found a carpet knife and a straight edge.

Carefully cutting through three pages in the ledger as close to the spine as she could get, she removed the indicting entries she had found and examined her handiwork. *No one would notice.* She took the ledger and the pages to the library and hid the detached evidence in a locked drawer of her desk, along with the photo she found at Ben's. Not to raise suspicions, she left the ledger on her night table, slid beside Bill and tried to sleep before Jaiteley arrived.

When Bill knew she'd need time to get ready, he woke her at 8:00 – coffee and a scone waiting for her on their four season balcony. She ate and sipped while he massaged her shoulders.

"Any revelations?"

"I almost finished it. Nothing glaring. Nothing to be ashamed of. I put a bookmark in the appointment log. If you have time, take a look at the last twenty pages for me."

"I don't need to read the rest of it."

"Well, there's nothing in it, nothing evidential, but I should give it to Detective Jaiteley."

"Okay. Do you want me to hang around? I can cancel my meeting."

"No. I'll be fine."

He studied her face. Took a moment to reflect.

"What?"

"I always know when you're trying to get rid of me – usually because you have too many things going on up here." He tapped her forehead. "Are you sure you don't want to run away with me? Maybe visit the folks in Yorkville, take 'em out to brunch?"

"I talked with them yesterday. They're just as upset as I am. It wouldn't be good for them to see me. It's better that they think I'm handling this well."

"And what about Mickey? Do you want me to try to smooth things over?"

"Bill, nothing you could do or say, will change her mind about this. She's over-reacting. It's too much. Just go."

"Okay." Bill left her, but before he went to work, he rapped on Harvard's door; no one answered.

* * * *

Jaiteley arrived at 9:00 with two forensic technicians – Leanne Li and Ken Dawes, both of whom had their own testing kits. Bev welcomed them and asked Jaiteley where they wanted to do the testing.

"The kitchen is good," he answered, then introduced her to the team.

Jaiteley decided to use the island and pulled out a stool for Bev to sit on. "Just relax," he encouraged. He went through the procedure, step by step, while Leanne who was taking the first sample removed the contents of her kit.

She asked Bev to rinse her mouth with a solution that she provided. Leanne held two instruments – the first to take a saliva swab, and the second to take a tiny, flesh sampling. It was done quickly and she produced a sterile, cotton pad that she held over the small incision in the inner cheek. "How are you doing, Ms. Weston?"

"Good."

Ken performed the second and third sampling – a blood sample from the tip of her finger and a lock of hair from above the nape of her neck. When storage was completed, they locked their kits and politely declined an offering of tea. They wanted to get the kits back to the lab. They apologized for any discomfort she might have had and left.

"You can't refuse some malty, spicy Assam tea?"

"Of course not." He pulled out a second stool and watched Bev move quickly about the space, reaching for mugs, sugar, milk.

As she placed the arrangement in front of him, Mickey and Harvard entered.

"What's going on?" Mickey asked in French.

Bev made introductions and let Jaiteley provide the details about uncovering the murder weapon in Ben's backyard and the mtDNA testing to identify Alexsis Ingles' blood.

"I know what it is," Mickey said curtly.

"Michelle is a doctor," added Bev.

"What good will this investigation do anyone after fifty years?" she asked coldly.

"A murder was committed; we want to solve it and clear the air, so to speak, in Ben's home."

"You saw it? This thing? This spirit?" she asked.

"No, but I saw what it did."

"Bill and I saw it. It was Alexsis' ghost. And there was this other presence."

"It was some trick that in the end will make us all look like idiots. The limo should be here soon. We can see ourselves out. We'll be with the family at Pearson, until our flight leaves."

"I'll call you tomorrow night."

"Don't." Mickey turned abruptly and left.

Embracing Bev warmly, Harvard whispered, "Call me. I'll be waiting." He left without acknowledging Jaiteley who rose off his stool to say good-bye.

"If you want to wait with your brother, Ms. Westing, feel free to go," Jaiteley insisted.

"No. It's okay. My sister-in-law is really upset. I can't deal with her."

He sat down again and while he sipped his tea, he brought Bev up to speed with a full report of their investigation to date and added if she had anything else that could help, he'd appreciate it.

"There is one thing – a ledger I found in the safety deposit box that I wanted to look at, before I turned it over as evidence."

"A ledger you've had since yesterday?"

"Yes."

"You read it?"

"I'll get it." She excused herself and moments later returned with it. "There's nothing in it. Nothing incriminating."

"We might find something you overlooked. Something that cross-checks with other data we've run. You should have turned it over yesterday."

She grew quiet and looked away.

"What is it?"

"This family – both the Westings and the Ingles – share a commitment to a progressive community that reaches across all the demographic divides to help people."

"I know your family does a lot of good for this city. I don't want this investigation to shake the foundation of what you stand for. We're going to keep this as quiet as we can."

"For what it's worth, I'm glad it's you who is working with Ben. I trust you and your partner to do the right thing."

He finished his tea and said he'd contact her with anything new they might get.

When he was ready to leave, Bev walked him out. The Ingles had gone – Mickey's exquisite French perfume still lingered.

Jaiteley smiled. "Les Larmes Sacrees de Thebes. Your sister-in-law has very expensive tastes in perfume." He said good-bye, leaving Bev to wonder how a detective with the TPD could know that.

Immediately she went to her office, removed the detached ledger pages and reread them. Folding them carefully, she put them into her purse and decided to go for a drive.

26

For some strange reason Ben had felt a definitive calm as he drove down Wendy's street, and leaving it behind, knew Annie was completely safe with her mom. He had felt more welcomed at Vienna's than at any other time in anyone's house, even more than the Westings'. The two of them had curled up in front of Vienna's small LCD with da Vinci's front paws and jaw firmly planted on their legs. They had fallen asleep like that, and when Ben had unknowingly rolled off the sofa, da Vinci had joined him for the rest of the night on the floor.

Ben, wanting Vienna to have her morning privacy to get ready for school, had tugged da Vinci out the door, and went home to shower before he touched base with Detective Jaiteley. When he unlocked the front door, he realized he hadn't stopped to look up to the third story and he hadn't hesitated indecisively with his key. He didn't know whether or not this was a good thing.

More leaves had fallen; more light filled the darker recesses in the rooms. He realized there were no fragrances, in the absence of which he felt more grounded in the 21st Century. He recognized in the low hung light, things that were his and not distortions of them – lights he had bought, rugs, pillows, candle holders, prints, many of which had come from 21st Century merchandise giants. Somehow, seeing what he had bought at the Pottery Barn and Quantum and Home Sense made him feel less trapped in someone's fifty-year-old nightmare. *Are you doing this to help me heal?*

He indulged himself in a twenty minute shower. Every muscle that had been knotted for two months undid under a payload of solar-heated water. When he thought he couldn't feel more relaxed he stood naked under the heat light, letting it dry every steamy droplet. He thought about the price he had paid to be this relaxed. But when he reached to wipe away the steam on the bathroom mirror, he was suddenly jolted into yesterday's vanguard, as words wrote themselves across the mirror in the steam: *I look forward to meeting you.*

The phone rang. It was Jaiteley. He wanted to come over to talk.

By 10:00, Ben was showing Jaiteley the message on the mirror that had somehow managed to stay steamy, even though the fan and heat light had sucked his towels almost dry.

Jaiteley walked around, opening and closing doors and took a look at the studio which hadn't reinvented itself over the past twenty four hours. "You gotta love this house, Ben! It should be one of the wonders of the world, like The Red Fort in India or the Coliseum or the Grand Canyon."

"I don't see it that way."

"Really? It defies all standards." He thought about it for a minute, then let it go and took out a summary of forensic reports. "I want to go over this with you. The guys at the lab have been knocking themselves out to get their analyses and reports done. So, what we have is DNA from Beverly Westing – I took it this morning – that gives us a positive ID for Alexsis Ingles, the victim of a fatal stabbing on November 23, 1958 in this house. We have an unidentified sample of hair from the cloth that the murder weapon was wrapped in, probably the murderer's DNA. We have an analysis of the motorcycle wreckage that was couriered in last night. The wreck had been staged. There was no organic residue or other vehicle residue on any of the parts which had been definitely banged up with man-made devices. There was a button found inside some twisted metal that belonged to a police issue uniform in the fifties. Our data analyst cross-checked the two numbers Joseph had given us – 1947 and 305. Out of thousands of references, they eliminated every source except two relevant numbers."

"What are they?"

"1947 was the date of Clara Bernard Ingles' passing – she was Harvard Ingles' mother - and 305 is part of the Mount Hope Cemetery address where she's buried. It's 305 Erskine."

"Should this mean something?"

"I've already done some checking. Harvard Ingles bought his own plot next to his mother's in 1992."

"And you think the body is buried there?"

"Maybe. It's my job to find out."

"If the body's there, wouldn't that make Harvard Ingles a suspect?"

"I don't know, but I do know I'm heading to the Westings' with a search warrant, after we dig up the plot. My team will be at Mount Hope in twenty minutes."

"Where do you want me in all this?"

"We've got rent control, we've got crowd control, how about some friend control? Ms. Westing is really going to need your support. I'd like you to come."

Ben found an old reliable suede coat, fleece-lined and shiny-elbowed that he put on for old time comfort, while Jaiteley snapped a pic of the handwriting on the mirror.

* * * *

By the time Bev got to Mount Hope Cemetery, she had doubts about why she had come. She didn't know what to expect. Taking out the ledger pages she checked the plot number of Clara Bernard Ingles and made her way through the morning frost to her gravesite, in front of which rested a carved, grieving angel made of sandstone – its arms folded delicately over the inscribed eulogy: *Here rests an angel whose wings flew tirelessly into the hearts of many. May she find peace in her flight to heaven.* Clara had been cremated. Bev had the page to prove it. She didn't doubt this plot had been originally bought for Clara, then she changed her mind about it, but why did Harvard want his plot next to hers? He must have known about the cremation. But Bev knew whenever he was home, he visited it.

A carved bench had been placed in front of the site. Bev sat down and stared at the grave. She wanted to lie on top of it. Put her cheek against the cool grass. Run her fingers through the blades and hold out her fingers for whatever was beneath to reach up and touch her. She stood and moved in front of Harvard's plot. Its granite headstone was rough and uncut and she wondered if Harvard had written his own eulogy. She sat on the bench and thought about how everything had lost its balance, how everything was drunken and disorderly, unable to stand up, unable to speak clearly without slurring the facts.

She looked again at the pages. These were the facts. These were the sobering facts that could make all this drunkenness get sober in a hurry. She had been drunk on illusions all her life, Harvard on power, Bill on her, the artist on salvation. *We all need sobriety. How do I get off the illusion binge? How do I learn to let this woman go?*

She was oblivious to the mini excavator rumbling through the cemetery and to Jaiteley's team who quietly had moved behind her, and she barely heard Ben call her name.

"Bev?"

She didn't move.

"Bev, what are you doing here?"

Finally aware that someone was there, she turned to six people staring at her and waiting for an explanation she wasn't prepared to give.

Ben and Jaiteley approached her, while the first cut was made into Harvard's plot. She refused to look at or speak to Jaiteley, while he attempted to talk to her.

"Your DNA matches the samples we took from Ben's house. The murdered woman was your mother."

Ben sat beside her on the bench and tried to soothe her. "I don't think my world has been rocked like yours, because I can pack up and walk away if I want to. Can you?"

She didn't answer.

"And if you can't walk away, then help us end what's doing this to us. I think we can end this, together. I think we can restore something meaningful for everyone involved."

She turned to face Ben. "Why should we do anything about it now? I think it will pass. Time will run out. He'll die and all of this will go away, if we just wait."

"And who gets hurt while we're waiting. Annie? Me? You? Bill? Your mother was murdered. She's not at rest. She wants us to find her. The numbers in Rose's reading lead us here. What does that tell you?"

She was angered. "It tells me that my mother and this artist were and are selfish s.o.bs. They're selfish," she shouted. "If they want to hurt innocent people just to prove how powerful they are, then they're cruel and hateful. All the things I worshipped – memories, photos, painting, her clothes, her jewelry, even old shoes – have become invalid passwords to my private life. I don't want to co-operate anymore."

A small hill from the plot formed as everyone looked on expectantly, and Jaiteley waited until Bev had calmed. "It's not invalidating your life."

"Then, what's it doing to me and to Bill?"

"Reshaping it, redefining it," answered Jaiteley.

"I was happy the way I was."

The excavating stopped. Two officers climbed inside the gaping hole and poked around. There was nothing. Jaiteley was frustrated and embarrassed and dismissed the team. The operator filled in the hole.

"Are you satisfied?" she asked Jaiteley.

"No. Here's the thing. Forensics found that several pages are missing from the ledger. They were removed with a straight edge so that no one would notice. But our guys have machines that are good. We want them, Ms. Westing. And the other thing is, why are you here? You just felt like visiting an empty plot?"

"I don't have the pages." She stood up and started walking away. Ben followed.

Jaiteley was about to pursue when he got a call from Detective Biro. It was short and alarming and threw the case in a whole new direction.

When Biro hung up, Jaiteley shot after Bev and called out. "Ms. Westing, I need to speak to you."

She halted.

"I just got a phone call." She turned around as he caught up. "...from my partner, Detective Biro. Dr. Phillip Standern has been murdered. Probably between one and three this morning. The coroner's there now."

She felt the blood drain out of her head, as her body fell limp against Ben.

"One o'clock at Baby Point, Ms. Westing, I'll have a search warrant. Be there."

She had neither strength nor voice to object as Ben looped her arm through his. She found comfort in holding on to him, even though Ben knew she was lying about the ledger. He didn't judge her.

* * * *

When Detective Biro saw Jaiteley pull up to the Standern estate she went out to brief him. "Standern was definitely murdered."

"Evidence?"

"We found PSA (pressure sensitive adhesive) residue from duct tape that had been put over his mouth and later removed. His fingers on both hands had dug into his sheets as he was suffocating. He was pinned down across his chest. We have a hair sample that had fallen on the sheet."

"Forced entry?"

"No. The team's finishing up its sweep."

He updated her about Harvard's plot being empty and about Beverly Westing being at Mount Hope Cemetery before they got there. He said he wanted her to accompany him and four officers in their search of the Westing residence at 1:00.

He did a quick walk through, thanking forensics for doing such a thorough job. Without Biro noticing, he stood a moment to watch her cross check notes and procedures. He wondered how he'd get by when the case was over and if he could make this thing he felt for her as important as his work was.

* * * *

When Jaiteley and his team arrived at Baby Point, Bev had locked her purse in her limo and had it driven off the property. She had asked Ben at the cemetery to stay with her until the search was over. Bev had found the balance she needed to be kind to strangers in her home – strangers on a mission to upturn particles of this and that, strands of this colour and that colour, stains with this element and that from the periodic table.

She shook their hands and told them to take their time and if they needed water, she had a pitcher and glasses in the kitchen. Upon request she escorted Jaiteley to the security room where he watched footage of the previous night and early morning, and Biro assigned search areas to the officers – one on the third story, two on the main floor. She was going to do the second floor.

When Biro started her search of the guest suite, she found the garbage emptied and the suite completely cleaned and vacuumed. She found Bev and asked her to show her where the garbage was stored as well as the vacuum. Bev escorted her to a shed to the rear of the main cabana and left Biro to sift through the week's refuse.

When Biro found the bag of discarded toiletries, she lifted and bagged a toothbrush and sanitary, paper cups. She didn't find hair, but found finger prints around a variety of soaps and tubes. She approached Bev in the great room and asked about the toothbrush.

"My brother had forgotten to pack his. We always have extras for our guests. Harvard used that one. I remember getting it for him." *What was I thinking of – not finding it first and getting rid of it.* She felt pinned down by flutters of panic.

Biro found the utility closet behind the guest en suite and set about examining the dusty contents of the vacuum, from which she bagged hair and skin samples. Carefully Biro swept the remaining areas of the second floor, using her flashlight and magnifying eye. All the hardwoods had been washed and shined, the flat Bergama rugs were dust free. The remote that controlled the blinds, fireplace and lights had been disinfected. Biro decided she'd like to hire the Westing maid.

When Jaiteley found Bev, he had copies of the surveillance footage and said he would need her phone records. He also confirmed Harvard's departure flight at 11:00 from Pearson to Rwanda via France. He added that he wasn't up to par on protocol, if they needed Harvard back in Toronto for questioning – he was a Canadian Goodwill Ambassador with immunity. Of course, Bev knew the government protected him.

One by one the team finished, packed up and left silently. Bev asked, "Did you get everything you needed?"

"You know I didn't. What are you waiting for?"

She remained silent.

"The ghosts to disappear? Ben's house to repair itself? To forget this ever happened? I need those pages," he urged softly. He showed himself out, and as he opened the front door, he got a call, listened carefully and rushed back into the great room.

"What's happened?" Bev felt his sudden excitement and urgency.

"That was Kingston PD. Rose Henhawke and Joseph Hightower have found your artist, Rigo Molinaro. I'm taking a chopper into Kingston in one hour. He knew from the sudden light in her eyes that she wanted an invitation. Ben looked at her apologetically. She knew he couldn't fly off and leave Annie, Vienna, and the house not at rest.

27

When Joseph couldn't get Rose on her cell, he went to the Records Office to check in with Meryl Dupuis who had information about Patient X's file that she wanted him to give Rose when he found her at Rockwood. She gave him duplicates with contact info for two people: Dr. Neela Mayur, one of the doctors who treated Patient X and Sandra Bolyn, a patient who was befriended by Patient X and who had been discharged in December of 2000.

Joseph explained he couldn't get Rose on her cell, so Meryl tried Jimmy's radio. He wasn't answering. She tried different channels without luck.

"I'm no technophile, but shouldn't we be able to contact him?" asked Joseph.

Meryl called Wayne Grayson, the head of security at Queens to meet Joseph at her office to assist him in locating Rose Henhawke.

He picked up Joseph, and on their way to Rockwood they tried both Rose's cell and Jimmy's radio again. There was no reception.

The side door of Rockwood was open; the men entered.

It was quiet. There was no trace of either Rose or Jimmy. It bothered Wayne Greyson because Jimmy Hearns would never leave a building unlocked. The men had done a quick search, but had found nothing except the painting. Joseph knew Rose had seen it too.

Greyson paced. "I need to know where Jimmy Hearns is and Dr. Henhawke. It's not like Jimmy to be careless. I have to contact security. Where do you need to be right now?"

"I need to see Dr. Mayur immediately."

They decided to go back to Queens. Joseph contacted Mayur on their way back. She was in a class and would meet with him when it was over. Grayson left him in her office and told him he'd be pulling in some people to help.

Dr. Mayur dismissed her class early and found Joseph waiting patiently, but seemed agitated when she introduced herself. "I don't like shaving my students' instructional time."

She was a wisp of a woman – delicate and dark-skinned, like Jaiteley, Joseph thought, and distinctly graceful – even the subtle movement of her eyes and mouth had a gracefulness in their expression, but she wasn't particularly friendly. Joseph felt she was offended by his intrusion. He didn't apologize and quickly explained why he and Rose Henhawke were there and how Rose wasn't answering his calls and how he needed to know why there were exclusions in Patient X's file, like the death certificate and names of attending physicians.

"I don't know why this information is missing...."

"Were you the medical examiner?"

"No."

"Do you know who was?"

"No."

"But you treated Patient X."

"Yes. From 2002 and until they told me he had passed."

"Who told you?"

"I got a memo that he had passed, and the hospital, of course, was taking care of all the arrangements."

"I want to see his room."

"He was moved."

"When?"

"In 2001."

"Where?"

"Into an isolation unit. I treated him there, because he had stopped eating. And because he had started to change."

"How?"

"He gained power from visualizing, from brainwave training. That's your area, isn't it?"

"Yes. What kind of power?"

"You should know."

"What do you mean?"

"Telekinetic, psychokinetic. He was one of your brainwave training subjects in the '90s. I'm surprised you don't remember him. He would probably have been the only subject who couldn't talk; instead, he painted his experiences."

Joseph went cold, dry-mouthed. He had had hundreds of test subjects over the years. The artist wasn't the most unique, but he did recall him. "I had a large test group; they had no names for control purposes, but I remember him. A short, swarthy man. Handsome. Eyes that seemed to clear paths into what we don't even want to confront in ourselves. He could see these things. I remember how he represented his visualizations, like he had been on a round trip to hell and heaven and back and painted it."

"He was in one of your original study groups and whatever happened there changed his life. He became obsessed with visualization techniques, and this continued until he became so powerful that he had to be isolated. The staff had become terrified of him."

"Where did they take him?"

"To an isolated unit at Rockwood Asylum where he died."

Joseph had to act quickly. "I need to see Sandra Bolyn immediately."

"Should we not contact the police? If Dr. Henhawke is still at Rockwood..."

"Not yet. I don't think it's wise to bring in that kind of containment. Call Sandra."

* * * *

At first Sandra Bolyn wouldn't talk to Joseph, but when he explained about Rose going to Rockwood and that he had lost contact with her, Sandra said she'd take the next ferry over from Wolfe Island to the mainland and meet him at Rockwood.

Dr. Mayur returned him to Wayne Grayson who had instructed a team of guards to meet him at Rockwood. The two men went to the ferry terminal in downtown Kingston to wait for Sandra, the second woman whom the artist had loved and cared enough to heal.

She emerged from the ferry wearing a long Oilcloth coat, high boots, a floppy-brimmed hat and sunglasses. Walking hunched over and examining the walkway as she hurried to them, she waved introductions and didn't speak, as Grayson held the security car door open for her.

While Joseph had been conferencing with Dr. Mayur, Grayson checked the ferry passenger lists and the visitor's list at The Providence Care Center. Sandra Bolyn caught the ferry every Sunday and Wednesday to Kingston and also signed in at the center on those days. He turned to his passenger sitting next to him in the front seat. "When you come to the center every Sunday and Wednesday, do you visit Patient X?"

She had to tell him, but was afraid of the consequences.

"You don't have to be afraid, Ms. Bolyn," Joseph said softly. "We're not here to hurt your friend, but I think you already know that."

She laughed. "Hurt him? I don't think so. You don't understand."

"Then help us."

"I was his experiment."

"What do you mean?"

"He used me to test his powers. If he could make me better, then he'd be able to find a way to get his family back. They were his sole purpose for living. It's what he's dying for."

"How is he dying?"

"How do you think I'm living?"

"Tell me."

"His energy is keeping me alive, keeping me sane, keeping me from killing myself. And when he started all of this business with Ben Needham, he has been draining all of his reserves. He's like a battery that's running low."

"And you think when he dies, you'll....."

"Not exactly."

"I can help you the way he does."

"You couldn't even help yourself, when your wife died. Who do you think gave you the strength to go on? You have no idea the power he can infuse in others to do what he wants them to do."

"I do know."

When they arrived at Rockwood, the side door that Grayson had locked was again opened. They stepped into the darkened hallway and followed Sandra down a flight of stairs to the rear of the building and through an arched, brick tunnel, on either side of which were stalls. She explained it used to be the stables. They arrived at a locked door. She rapped twice.

28

Jimmy Kearns had kept raising the cuff of his jacket to his forehead to wipe the sweat away as he followed the decrepit shadow down the hall to where Rose remained unconscious. Crouching beside her, the shadow fit his arms underneath her back and behind her knees and lifted the long, limp figure effortlessly. They rose slightly above the ground and floated down a stairway, through an arched, brick tunnel to an open door.

Jimmy followed, hesitated before entering, then stepped into the lavender-filled room, the air of which could almost be tasted, like the air hovering above a fresh, spring-fed quarry or the air in a flower shop. One side of the room was dimly lit from a natural light source, without windows or natural vents leading to the open air. But it was natural light, like perpetual morning, Jimmy thought. He watched the shadow put Rose down gently in a chair, then faded into the far corner of the room opposite him that was dark and quiet with something glowing in the middle, like a dying ember. The door closed and locked them in.

Jimmy bent beside the woman and patted her hand. "Dr. Henhawke, you need to wake up, please." He placed his head on her chest. He could hear her heart beat. He wrapped his fingers around her wrist. Her pulse was stronger. "Dr. Henhawke."

"She'll be all right," a soft voice whispered as though it surrounded Jimmy; he panned the room, trying to locate the source. The whisper continued, "She has seen more than she knows what to do with." The voice was unmistakably weak, mildly foreign and unusually eloquent for its frailty.

Jimmy leaned into the direction he thought it was coming from. The voice was an ancient relic that had been dug out of a time-parched throat. Foreign, eloquent, and frail. Jimmy focused on the far end of the room, on a cubicle surrounded by glass. And inside, a dim light glowed like a stationary firefly. It was a small cubicle with some sort of bed or cot in it, around which had grown vines and flowers, most of which were in decline.

Jimmy rubbed his eyes and took a step toward the cage. He saw the cot encircled by a garden and on the wall behind the bed was a mural, painted with leaves and flowers – larger ones in the front that grew smaller as they receded up a hill. Flowers and vines that had caught autumn's demands.

He stepped closer. "Are you in there?"

"I am," the voice teased, the voice that was unsteadily rooted in a decaying throat like an old tent on wobbly pegs, ready to collapse in the winds.

"Uh-huh?" Jimmy strained to see some form, some movement against the mural in the cage, but couldn't. "Do you remember me?" he asked.

"I remember your touch, how you never hurt me, when I had to be restrained, how you spoke gently. I remember your kindness, not like the others."

Jimmy knew that the other attendants and guards had used force that came from somewhere that the job description didn't prescribe. "I know who they were. I could never be like that."

"Would you like me to reward you, Jimmy, with some wings? I could give you wings." And he tried to laugh to lighten the anxiety he had placed upon the guard.

"They might be better than a golf cart, but it might cause a few heart attacks – me having wings and flying over the fairways." And he attempted to laugh too and turned to see how Rose was doing, then tried again to face the patient he couldn't see. "You never talked before."

"When people told me they'd cut out my tongue if I did, it was easy not to, but I found other ways to talk, didn't I?"

"Who are you?"

"A man who needs to find someone before I die. Someone I want to take with me."

Sudden noises in the chair beside Jimmy startled him. Rose was trying to swallow and speak at the same time, as she awakened from her anomalous migration. She reached out for Jimmy's hand, and the voice offered them a glass of water from a pitcher behind them.

Jimmy leaned close to her. "He's here."

"Where?" she asked, trying to moisten her lips.

"In there." And pointed to the glassed-in cell.

Jimmy poured water for both of them and helped Rose drink from her glass. She didn't know if the water was naturally sweet and lemony or whether the artist had concocted it.

She stood up, steadying herself, and walked cautiously to the cell. She had called him a monster. She had felt the invasion of this power as if fuelled by a rogue element. She was cautious. "Where are you?" And she dared to move her face to within a hair-width of the glass barrier.

"I'm here, in my garden."

She squinted, trying to separate light and dark tones. "You don't want to be seen," she ventured. "Do you think that after what I've witnessed because of you, I wouldn't be able to look at you?" There was a slight shift in posture as the old man moved his entangled body. Rose caught the movement. Saw his body art fall out of sync with the wall art. "You've painted yourself."

"Tattooed."

"Did you have help?"

Silence. His body was at rest again, indistinguishable from the twisted, but beautiful mural behind him.

"Are you looking at me?" she asked.

"In my own way I see you."

He had closed his eyes five years ago, deciding to use vision threads that interconnected him with all things. Psychosomatic blindness was a way to re-channel his sight to a higher perceptual plane. "You'd be surprised what I've seen in you and through you."

"Are you Rigo Molinaro?"

"I was, to people who loved me, a long time ago." He moved slightly, fitting himself more comfortably against a pillow.

"I saw you for a moment."

"Describe me."

She needed a poet or Bradbury to do that. "It happened so quickly."

"Like a hummingbird's wings."

"Yes."

"I see myself the way I remember a lover should be, the way a father should be."

Rose caught for a moment the ragged bundle of skin and bones and lines and angles, that had once been beautified by stems and leaves and petals. A bundle of physical impotence, like JEH Macdonald's tangled garden. She studied his cell and tried to see the monster who had forced her into a world that myth-makers like to immortalize. The monster who reached beyond his cage and into the cages of so-called free people.

"Am I or am I not that monster?" he asked.

She doubted his saintliness. "Will you let me come in and sit with you?"

"Yes. But first, take a stroll around my room. I've been scrapbooking for decades."

As she turned around, she saw books, albums, loose photos and sheets of data sitting on shelves.

She went through them, stopping to look at what the artist has benchmarked – newspaper articles, magazine clippings, medical journals (several were written by Joseph), reports and analyses of the artist's visualization tests, art anthologies, architectural digests with Bill Westing's ventures and successes, Beverly Westing's charitable philanthropy, and worldly political crises. The Rwandan genocide was there and Harvard Ingles' diplomatic ties with both old and new regimes – his money didn't turn bad; it just changed sides. Everything seemed to have been carefully stored in chronological order.

All these people had become his family – the good sheep; the not-so-good. The ones he'd reward and the ones he'd punish.

When she finished, she knew he had spent a lifetime learning to speak different languages: better English, telekinesis, transcendence, clairvoyance, art, all of which led him to travel through print and image into foreign debt, and sorrow and tyranny.

She faced the glass and the imploding heartbeat beyond. "It's incredible - all of it! May I come in?" she asked with genuine humility.

"Yes."

Jimmy started to rise, then didn't. He wanted to pull her back, but knew he had no power to. He watched, feeling less a man than the thing in the cage.

She looked for a door, an opening, a handle. "I can't find the door."

"Because you think it's the only way to enter." He sat up slowly.

She saw his body imagery move against the wall - its faded ink stains, old and gritty, like knotted, pine floors. She looked at the glass and knew the artist accomplished everything by merely believing he could. She walked into the glass expecting it to break, but there was no barrier at all. A mirage. A trick. She sat at the end of his cot.

He kept very still. In the dim light he was camouflaged enough to make Rose search.

As her eyes adjusted to the light, she caught sight of his misshapen form, ribbed and brittle and dying.

"I know it must be so difficult to talk, but Joseph and I – we don't understand your power. How you've been able to harvest it, use it."

"You're wrong," he slowly gasped. "Joseph understands, because he loved and was loved." He moved his head toward her, inviting truth and opened his eyes for the first time in five years.

"And you think love has given you this power?"

"It drives me. Not like pain. Pain keeps me focused, fires up my need for justice, but love will give me peace in the end. Release."

"Justice for whom?"

He looked at the woman who never wanted to be a statue, but had become wooden, marble, cast iron. A woman who never trusted in love – who thought it was always a missile on its own destructive path.

He closed his eyes again and looked into that night when this tall sapling of a girl was coming home late from lab work and turned a corner into the wrong touch, into the wrong body, muscled with physical weapons and steel weapons that cut into her and cut up the things that are needed to invite love in. He looked and wondered how she remained so beautiful, yet so loveless.

He answered her question. "I want justice for everyone. For the people who put me here. For the people who buried Alexsis without any truth or dignity and threw her between the divide to suffer for all time." Words came faster than breath. With great effort he managed an inflow of air. He stopped for a moment.

Rose waited patiently, felt him watching her. Then, "You have to tell me what you want us to do. We haven't abandoned you, but we don't know what you want."

"Tell them to come for me. I want to go home to my studio."

Rose understood why he had to go there. "They haven't found her grave yet."

"They will."

"I'll stay with you, Rigo. Jimmy will call the authorities and they'll get you home."

"This man, this Rigo," he said with despair, "I don't know who he is." His words came like a parent watching his only child disappear inside a dream. "He's gone."

She turned around and nodded at Jimmy. "You know what to do."

He stood up and faced Patient X. "I hope you find everything that was taken from you."

As he left, the door opened and the shadow emerged from the darkest corner to help Jimmy through the maze.

29

Two travellers were consumed by urgent business: Bodhan Jaiteley and Beverly Westing. Not until they buckled up for take-off did their constant movement cease. Each had had an hour to set things straight, say good-bye and make apologies.

Before the chopper left for Kingston, Jaiteley headed quickly to the Chief's office with the Ingles' case file and the latest forensics report. Going over it carefully, the Chief was both convinced by the evidence, and alarmed with Standern's murder. The hair sample they analysed from the Standern CSI matched one of the hair samples from the fibres of the shawl surrounding the Krukri dagger found at Ben's. It was a match, and although Harvard Ingles was a suspect and Jaiteley had wanted to bring him in for questioning, his DNA profile from the saliva sample didn't match either of the hair samples. Harvard was not their man.

After the Chief gave Jaiteley more time and more men to investigate both murder cases, Jaiteley told Biro to get the rest of the team up to speed on the files and that he'd be available for updates.

He called Ben to tell him about the DNA matches and to tell him to be cautious.

* * * *

Bev had phoned Bill and asked him to wait for her at his construction site. She took a limo and found him in a quiet office in the design center. She couldn't keep Standern's murder from him. He was dismayed by the implications. Looking at the small woman who was broken-hearted and ashamed at what was happening to them, he wrapped his arms around her and buried his face in her delicate, white neck. She knew they had never been as distant as they had been this past week.

Gently he pushed away. "So, Standern was murdered - when, last night, this morning? And there's this murderer out there with who knows what agenda. And he's probably tied to Alexsis' murder. Right? And you're riding around, meeting me, maybe going shopping after? Maybe going for a manicure? Or to your book club? Not particularly worrying about who's around the next corner? Right?"

"Wrong." She shrugged and teared up.

Quickly he pulled her close, holding on to what he knew he'd get back again - their coupled singularity – that unique union of two that was different from almost everyone they knew. "Stay with me," he almost begged. "I don't want you to be that exposed."

"I can't stay." Her trembling fingers smoothed the furrows on his forehead. Breathlessly, she blurted, "They found the artist. They found Rigo Molinaro after all these years of imprisonment. I wanted to see you before I went to Kingston with Jaiteley. He's there in Kingston, has been, since 1958."

He didn't respond at first, because in some strange way he thought people had lied to her. That she was caught in someone's bad story that wasn't real and had to end the way tragic archetypes ended. He didn't like any of it. "Did they give you any details?"

"No. Just that he was in an isolated, private room. He's not doing well."

"That surprises me – that he's failing with all the power he has. It doesn't fit."

"Rose is with him. They're expecting Joseph."

"Is Ben going?"

"No. He wants to stay in the house when they bring him home."

"This artist wants to come back to the scene of the crime? After all these years?"

"She's still there. You know she can't leave." Her voice cracked with despair.

"But they haven't found her body."

"I know where she's buried."

"How in the hell do you know that?" He almost didn't want to hear.

"It was in the ledger. Paul Dann noted appointments and payments."

"And Jaiteley has the ledger, right?"

"He has the ledger, but I cut out some pages that Jaiteley hasn't seen."

"Christ! You are playing with fire! This isn't like you, Bee. So, where is she buried?"

"Jaiteley found out that Harvard bought a plot next to his mother's, so they dug it up. There was nothing."

"And because you think Clara Ingles was cremated, you think Alexsis' remains are buried in her plot."

"I know she is. There is a cremation document, and Paul Dann paid some men to move my mother's remains to the plot beside Harvard's. There are dates, times, names."

"Why was she moved?"

"You'd have to ask Harvard. I would guess partly because he wanted to remove any evidence that she had been murdered and mostly because he wanted to be buried beside her."

"What are you saying, Bev? That Harvard was involved? He was only a kid!"

"A kid who was passionate about her. He was jealous of Rigo Molinaro. I know he would have been. You have to trust me, Bill. I can't say anymore."

"You have to give the pages to Jaiteley."

"I burned them."

"What? Phil Standern is dead. You...you think Harvard is involved in Standern's murder too? Why are you doing this?"

There were no words to express her fear, her loss, her anger at what was happening to her family, and in her own way she knew she wasn't doing what was morally right, but she thought somehow things didn't mean as much now as they had fifty years ago – that is until Standern was murdered. But it was too late. She did what she had to do. "Their flight left this morning, Bill. He's gone. He has immunity."

"This isn't right. It's bullshit! It's all wrong!"

"I have to go." She turned to him and asked if he'd do something for her.

"What?" he snapped, then tried to tone it down.

"Will you dig up Clara Ingles' plot and keep my mother's remains safe?"

He took a step back, crossed his arms and thought a moment. He shook his head. Looked at this diminutive woman he was so crazy about, fought battles with, sank to the bottom of isolation with, then softened, "It wouldn't be the first time I dug up remains in my career, would it? What do you want me to do?"

"Call Biro. Try to explain that the remains have to be taken to Ben's. No forensics. They can have them after we get back from Kingston. Phone Ben. Tell him you have to bring the remains to the studio. No forensics," again she insisted.

"Okay... okay. When will you get back?"

"Not late. I'll phone you before we leave Kingston. I gotta go."

* * * *

Waiting for Jaiteley to get airborne, Bill took his time getting to Biro, and once he did, she put in the request for another license. The Mount Hope board contacted the Chief with complaints about his department, that they had already disrupted business once, and how many graves did they plan on unearthing in one day. They had to get it right this time.

Biro came prepared with the proper storage unit to help Bill transport the remains. He was grateful she agreed to Bev's request, even though she knew Jaiteley would call her up on this one. The remains would be officially the departments', once Beverly Westing released them.

The excavator rolled up again, and another mound of earth formed beside another grave. When the operator stopped and the machine quieted, Detective Biro, Bill Westing and the Director of Human Resources peered into the cavity at a six foot shroud of green velvet, covering the remains of Alexsis Ingles.

The air enlivened, as if the grave had been holding its breath and needed to exhale. The shroud lifted slightly in the breeze, and Biro waited a moment for the air to calm.

Bill had seen pictures of Lexi, had heard anecdotes about her height, but was amazed at the length of the shroud and how the bony remnants wore the velvet like a tragic mistake.

Biro requested that everyone move back, as she put on proper gear and removed the remains to the storage unit. As Bill watched the young bones being lifted and saw remnants of red hair fallen beside her delicate skull, a shiver took hold and he cried for this woman who didn't live to hear, *I Want To Hold Your Hand* or feel the tragedy of JFK or of the Tiananmen massacre, or the Wall coming down. He didn't wipe his tears; let them fall to the frosty ground.   He stared at the woman who never saw her baby grow up. He paused and closed his eyes. He knew she was finally coming home to a place and a heart waiting so long for her.

30

Ben had enough time to pick up Annie and Vienna, take them to a cafe, then drop Annie off at Wendy's. He was surprised that Wendy insisted they come in and meet Ace and let Annie show off her room and the new Yamaha and the clothes she'd be wearing to the benefit and premier of *Children of the Glitter War*.

Wendy had always known from the beginning that she had to work two jobs – purging society of the bad guys and purging Ben from himself. When he gradually locked her out of his private life, she allowed her career to swallow her and left him to himself and to Annie, who was like one of his fiction characters – there to grow with him, test his imagination, draw him away from the real world.

Wendy had nothing, not even her little girl, to keep her a little more than a machine. Then Adrian came along. She couldn't explain how it happened or what happened. It just did. The machine stopped whirring and acquired home sense with family room vocabulary. And as a result she started to love again.

Ben thought there would have been awkwardness standing in Wendy's house, on her perfectly shined floors with perfectly hung art and puddled drapery, with Vienna by his side and Ace beside Wendy, but there wasn't. He felt at home there with Annie. Wendy made him and Vienna feel this way.

Annie grabbed his hand and Ace's and pulled them to her room where she and Ace played a duet for Ben, and Wendy gave Vienna a tour that ended in Wendy's room where the girls' dresses for the benefit were laid out on the bed in clear garment bags.

Wendy was pleased that Vienna approved of what Annie had chosen to wear to the fund raiser. Vienna had expected that Wendy would have made all of the couture decisions, but she was wrong. She was seeing Wendy in a different light – different from Ben's light source.

They went back to the foyer where they talked briefly about Wendy's global charity, and Vienna told Wendy about her recent meeting with the Ingles whose home was in Kigali, and that they had stayed there through the country's war.

Vienna saw a flicker of doubt, even contempt in Wendy's face as she started to say something, then stopped. "What were you going to say?"

"Just that I know who the Ingles are. Their donations to my charity have built schools, furnished them, bought supplies and relocated hundreds of refugee children to Kigali from the camps near Goma in the Republic of Congo. And one of the schools we sponsor will be honouring the Ingles next month. We're grateful for that, but I've always wondered where the money came from. I've always wondered how Ambassador Ingles worked with one regime and now works for another and why he never left when everyone else was sent packing."

She took a moment to reflect as the trio of music lovers joined them. "Anyway, they are working tirelessly to get the educational system off the ground. Atonement, maybe?"

"Who's being atoned?" asked Ben.

Wendy shook her head, didn't want to talk about it.

Vienna thought it was important. "Wendy knows Harvard Ingles. He has given Wendy's charity loads of money to help educate refugee kids in Rwanda."

"I don't know him personally. I know that he and his wife generously support the education in Rwanda. The school my foundation has been sponsoring is having a school holiday to honour him next month. Lots of festivities. I actually was invited to go."

A sudden wave of anxiety took hold of Ben, inexplicable, deep-rooted, because he knew that, one by one, a circle of people had been drawn together, like they had been cast in a movie, a movie of fated discoveries and corrections. He looked at Vienna and knew she caught what he was thinking. "I've met him twice," he said quietly. "He's connected to the Westings."

"Oh, I didn't know that. Beverly Westing? How did I miss that?"

"She was an Ingles."

"Really. Well, she bought two tickets for tonight. Two thousand dollars a ticket, with another cheque - a twenty thousand dollar donation for our school. I hope she comes."

Vienna looked at Ben who drew in a deep breath to calm himself. He turned to Annie and reaching out, caressed her face, then shook Ace's hand. He leaned into Wendy and whispered, "Keep her safe. At the benefit tonight? Keep her safe?" A sickening instinct in the pit of his gut warned him that the end of this horror story would be nothing like the beginning.

Wendy smiled as her ex backed away. "Ben?"

"Yeah?"

"Annie will be fine," she whispered back.

The last of the autumn leaves were giving up their hold on life as the day dulled into a crisp, November evening. Biro didn't call Jaiteley, knew what she was doing would upset him – transporting remains before they had been tested. Bill Westing carried the containment case while they waited at Ben's door.

Vienna let them in.

He put the case down in the hall. A sudden rush of wind encircled the four onlookers. They felt its warmth, like a perfumed gift on their faces. Unmistakable sighs, like oohs and aahs that came with gift openings, interlaced the silence.

They stared at the box, four feet by two by two, an uncontaminated lab case bringing home an old prayer, a prayer that had reached across the death line into Ben's trust. And here it was waiting to be answered. After minutes of silence, they got busy, doing what they came for and carried Alexsis Ingles' remains to Ben's studio.

31

"Why are you crying?" asked Rose.

An unexpected stream of gratitude took hold of the artist. What liquid he had left in him ran down his face in joy of Lexi's freedom. "Good girl," he gasped quietly, in between sobs. "Good girl."

Rose waited until he could explain. "They found her. She's free."

"Alexsis?"

And he moaned with relief, sighed with anticipation. "She's waiting for me. She's waiting." He curled further into the corner of the bed and wall, again becoming part of the mural behind him.

Rose knew that she had to make her case quickly, before the others arrived. She slid closer to the aged man whose body had ceased to exist in rational, physiological terms. She needed to make him believe her. She moved closer and was drawn into the garden of tattoos that were masterful moments in his history – a flower seen somewhere in a woman's hair in Paris, a bird in some cage in Spain, a statue of a god in Rome, clouds, a raindrop, and a woman with red hair whose lips stayed parted after a kiss had set them on fire. She was hidden under a fern. Rose wondered if he had seen this small tattoo.

She slid closer.

He felt the vibrations in the thin mattress as she moved and heard her clothes swish softly against his covers. "Need a closer look?" he asked, trying to pull air from the bottom of his corrupted lungs. He knew she was poised on the edge of a question or request. "You can try," he offered.

"I want the teenage girl saved. I don't want her to die. I want to save her!"

"You're incapable," he said softly as small spasms shook his throat until it cleared.

"You don't know what I'm capable of."

"You can't save that black girl at the end of a gun, on the other side of the ocean, inside the bloodiest stain on men's hands. You can't save her because you couldn't save the baby inside of you, screaming to be saved. I heard those screams. I heard it claw on the lining of your womb, begging you to listen to it."

"I was raped. And beaten. And raped again," she said coldly.

"Rose, everyone loses something to a taker. Everyone. That black girl did. You can't save her. You don't have enough love in you."

"I do."

"Then I dare you to take hold of my hands." The words came soft like a church prayer, as winding vines with bursts of muted colour moved upward until bony digits reached toward her. "I dare you to see what I've seen for fifty years. Do this and I'll save the girl."

She hesitated, then reached her trembling fingertips toward his. And stopped. Saw the danger. Doubted the reward. Abruptly she left the bed, walked through the phantom glass barrier and turned toward the heap of bones and faded skin. "You're a prick! You don't deserve Ben's charity or a last embrace in Alexsis' arms! She doesn't need you to find peace! What good will the girl's death do to you? Why are you doing this?"

"Because I can. Because I need to."

"Save the girl!"

"She died years ago in the dust beside the white man with the deformed hand. She doesn't want to live anymore."

"Why can't you fight for her?"

"She needs to have her day! I'll be dead in two or three hours. Everyone will be able to work again, sleep, love, count money, count on death and taxes. But not the girl."

He moved slightly away from the mural to see her rage, to smell it. He waited.

"She doesn't have to be a martyr to pay him back!"

"Oh, but she does."

Then suddenly, Rose saw the whole picture. She wondered if the old man enabled it or whether it was her own logic clearing a path through her tangled clairvoyance. She knew now why the girl had waited so long, had become a model student and spokesperson who'd be chosen to carry the deadly orchids and she knew why the artist wouldn't save her.

She turned to face him. "I was right about you! You are a monster!" She rushed the door and banged on it as hard as she could.

It opened. Joseph looked up into her wet eyes and skin that had frowned into itself for reasons he didn't know. He waited while she looked first at him, then at the woman in the dark glasses standing behind him and knew it had to be Sandra Bolyn. He waited until Rose moved to let him in. There were no words to help her. He didn't ask any questions. She stepped aside, then ran past him, out of Rockwood to drive home alone. Rose heard someone call her name, didn't know if it was Joseph or the old man.

She didn't answer.

32

Ben asked himself if this was his place. Standing in his studio, he asked if he remembered buying it, moving in, starting the novel, walking the dog, going to sleep and waking up with Annie across the hall each day. Because standing in the studio seemed like an out of body experience – some place he was seeing for the first time. A place wrapped up in plastic, walls burnt and foul, marks that science left in the name of the law.

Bill set the case down. Biro looked around at the anaesthetic dissection that forensics had performed. Vienna thought it didn't provide the homecoming Alexsis would want.

"What can we do?" asked Ben. "Can we clean it up? I have to clean it up at some point. They'll be here in a couple of hours."

"I don't see why not," Biro said. What can we use?"

"I'll get everything we need."

They didn't open the case and moved it into the hallway while they set about restoring some order to the room. Both Ben and Vienna showed them where cleansers were kept, bedding, an unused rug, candles from other rooms, paint, hammers, nails. Quickly all four of them tore down the plastic membranes, nailed down floor boards, swept and vacuumed, dusted, changed the linens, painted over the hysterical pleas for help that Annie had finger painted on the walls.

They stood back and approved.

Bill got the case and moved it into the room. Biro told him she'd open it for safety reasons. She tried; she couldn't.

"Don't be surprised," Ben said. "When the time comes, it'll open. We're finished here."

33

Grayson had a portable torch and placed it on the only table opposite the cot. When their eyes had adjusted, they saw the cell and the cot in it. Even with the light, they strained to see where the voice was coming from, couldn't discern his body from the wall.

But Sandra could see. She was shocked at his rapid decline – how he had spent so much energy to save a woman who had been waiting so long for him. "There isn't much time. We have to make the transfer here."

"What transfer?" asked Joseph and moved with her through the glass screen into the cell. He watched Sandra let her hat, coat, glasses slide to the floor then move to the middle of the bed. As she extended her arms toward the corner, Joseph saw the body slide from the wall, like an animated garden, into the folds of Sandra's arms.

"Thank you," the old man said.

"I would have come sooner." And she stroked his face. "You've given me a long time to set things straight in this world. I've loved every minute of this borrowed time."

He tried to smile, turned to Joseph and opened his eyes. "You're still the same boy, Joseph, you were twenty years ago when you wired me up and shot me full of possibilities. I owe you so much." A bony hand stretched out for Joseph to take.

Joseph wrapped both hands around it, feeling the paper-thin skin and disfigured joints. He surprised himself by asking about Rose first, then about Alexsis. "Why was Rose so upset?"

"I held up a mirror," he rasped, a thin trickle of saliva running down the corner of his mouth. "Don't leave her alone. She needs you."

Joseph nodded, then let it go and asked where they found Alexsis' remains.

"Beside the grave of a man who killed for her love." Joseph thought the artist was confused. He turned to Sandra again. "What transfer?"

"There are things you don't know."

"I want to know."

She looked helplessly at the old man who relieved her from having to tell the story. He started in, "She was cut up so badly when she came here that they couldn't save her. She had lost so much blood. They did what they could, but they overlooked a nasty poison that got into her and wouldn't go away." He had to stop, open his mouth for more air.

Joseph helped Sandra try to make the old man comfortable as she adjusted his pillow behind his back.

"I died," she blurted out. "I died and Rigo brought me back. He brought me back to a different world I came from. He painted over my scars with his mind. Put paint brushes in my hand and showed me how to survive in a world I created. I evolved into a medical miracle and was discharged, and Rigo faded into his paintings, transformed into light and fire and incomparable energy that he used to make his way back to her. Eventually he had to be locked away."

"They were afraid of me and put me here. Thought I was some kind of religious freak, but we both know religion has nothing to do with it, don't we Joseph?"

Joseph thought about how he turned away from science, when his wife was in her final days, how he turned toward something else, but both practices failed him. He had failed his wife, but obviously not the artist. Maybe he hadn't failed his wife after all.

"I'd still be dead if it wasn't for Rigo."

"What transfer?" Joseph demanded.

"I've been borrowing his strength and so have you. How do you think you've survived your wife's death? Where do you think the strength came from?"

A sudden terror seized him, as Sandra turned to the old man. She placed both hands in Rigo's. "I'm ready."

"You can't do this!" pleaded Joseph. "Don't!"

Sandra turned to Joseph, "If we don't do this, he won't make it home. It's time to pay back my loan." The old hands clasped firmly around hers.

Joseph called Grayson to help, but when he tried to get into the cell, a wall of glass repelled him. And Joseph struggled against an invisible force holding him outside of the energy flowing from the woman to the old man.

The transfer began.

Joseph had witnessed exchanges of power before, but never between a dead person, kept alive by part of a donor's soul, who was returning the energy to its rightful owner. Sandra's skin greyed, lacerations, clotted with blood, marked her body, hair fell in clumps on the floor, teeth decayed and loosened, nails cracked, breath became foul, eyes rolled back, hands, bruised and skeletal and eaten by time fell away from the old man's.

When it was over, he recited words in Latin and kissed her forehead. "Thank you." He had taken enough strength and purpose to take a short trip home. He gathered the girl into his arms and rocked her and kissed her again. "Thank you. You meant so much to me." He turned to Joseph. "We're lucky if we get a second chance. Her second chance was ten lifetimes of happiness – happiness most people don't have for even a second. She knew this day would come. We're wasting time."

"We can't leave her in here," cautioned Grayson.

"She'll be gone soon." He kissed her one last time as she started to fade. "You won't find her when you come back."

Joseph understood what he had done; Grayson didn't, but together they walked the old man out of Rockwood.

34

It was emotional. Bev and Jaiteley standing by the chopper watching the two men hold up the artist and cradle him onto the stretcher in the chopper, where a paramedic tried to give him nourishment he insisted he didn't need. He opened his eyes a second time to look at Bev who had been crying from the time she saw him pull up beside the landing pad, emerge in his frailty and stumble over to her.

"It's all right, Sisi." He had called both of them this pet name.

"I want to remember, but I can't." Her voice cracked with pain. "I found the picture of us taken at the beach. Who took it?"

"You know who did. He went everywhere with us. He loved her as much as I did, and she loved him back in her own way which wasn't enough for him. I'm sorry I couldn't save her. I called for help and held her in my arms until Howard Ingles came with the police. They...they beat me and took me away. She...she..." he started crying.

"Sh...you don't have to tell me."

"She was still alive and called to me and begged me not to leave her. Begged me to find her again. I fought them, but they dragged me away. I didn't stop looking at her and could see her take a fragment of her broken mirror and open her wrists. She never rested again."

"We found her."

"I know." He closed his eyes and could see her waiting, could see her hair wild with youth and jasmine and lavender. He could feel her gentle fingers like the refined sable of his brushes moving over him. He could feel her exotic blood pumping inside her. He could feel summer in the gazebo and that joyous time when everyone loved someone until that day.

She let him remember and refused to let Jaiteley question him.

After transferring him into a waiting ambulance at St. Joseph's in Toronto's west end, his vital signs were stable. Bev rode with him to Marion Street and phoned ahead to tell Ben they were on their way.

Jaiteley and Joseph got there first; Biro updated him on Bev's request not to inform forensics and was surprised that he agreed with their breech of protocol. He leaned in and looked deeply into her eyes. "It's a good thing you brought the unsampled remains here first, because no one should fuck with this guy. This guy," he whispered, "is an accident of human will. I don't understand that kind of omnipotence."

She didn't ask for details.

They were all waiting. Ben, Vienna, Bill, Jaiteley, Biro, Joseph - the haunted, the amateurs, the professionals, the scientists, the artists, the builders. And the one not at rest.

When Ben saw the ambulance pull up, he and Bill went out to help them. The paramedics lowered the stretcher, but Rigo wanted to be unstrapped there, so he could stand and look up at the third story before walking in. He held on to Bev's arm as Bill and the others stood near, helplessly looking at the relic - ancient, primitive, hollow, creased, moss eaten, sinewy, like he had been stripped from the bark of a tree.

The artist raised his head upward and listened. She was waiting for him - had been for fifty years. "Help me?" he asked.

Stepping closer, Ben towered over the small man. "I'm Ben. I'll help you."

Jaiteley and Biro hung back, while the artist grasped Ben's left arm and Bev's right. Vienna went ahead and opened doors and removed things that could make it difficult to walk on or around. And Bill followed Bev so she knew he was right behind her.

As they walked, the artist whose eyes remained closed, moved his head upward toward Ben's face. "I'm sorry. I'm sorry I caused you so much pain."

Ben paled, felt the air stick deep in his lungs, felt that if he breathed he might not hear the voice.

It wasn't the artist's voice. It was Jamie's. "I need you to forgive me, Ben," the old man begged and waited, his head close to Ben's lips. "Please," the voice begged. He waited, then sadly turned away, when Ben couldn't answer.

They escorted him to the foot of the staircase. "This is where it ends," he said calmly. He looked at Joseph, "We both love someone who's not at rest. Don't stay here. There's nothing here for you, and everything, somewhere else, is waiting."

Joseph didn't say good-bye as he rushed away.

Bev clung to his arm. "Let me come with you."

"No. It's not a room for the living." He turned to Ben. "But you'll get it back soon." He looked at Bill and Bev again. "You've...you've..." He stopped, hung his head as tears flowed down the crevasses of his skin. "You've been in my life all these years. I learned how to watch you grow with a different lens." He needed her arms and reached out to her. "I'm so happy I met your mother."

She enfolded him – her cheek gently moving into the hollows of his face. "I wish I could have known you more."

"You will. The hospital has all my art. It belongs to you. Everything you could ever know about me is there." He backed away, took a step up to the attic, as Bev reached behind her for Bill's hand.

Turning, he climbed the remaining stairs alone and when the door opened he said, without turning around, "You have somewhere to be. You should go."

35

Ben felt the blood drain from his head. He looked at Bev. "We have to go!" And pushed past her, frantically colliding with door frames and furniture on his way down to the main floor to get a coat and keys.

"Where?" asked Jaiteley.

"The Palais Royale."

"Why?"

"My little girl's there, and someone's going to die."

"The benefit!" cried Bev.

"There's no time to explain," added Ben as he pulled Vienna out the front door and shouted to Jaiteley. "Take the Westings with you. We don't have much time!"

* * * *

When they arrived, an attendant took Bev's tickets and ushered her and Bill to a table in front of the large screen that had been assembled for the premier of the film. Wendy had reserved the table specifically for the Westings in case they showed. Dinner was over and Wendy and her co-host were introducing the producers and writer/director of their documentary, *Children of the Glitter War* that had taken them eight, impassioned years to make - eight years, wading through historic and emotional rubble to expose hope.

Ben found Annie's table and wrapped his arms around her, and after the introductions and speeches were finished, Wendy joined them and found two more chairs for her guests.

Jaiteley and Biro stayed by the door and waited for whatever had triggered Ben's alarm. They let things play out until things went bad with the film. It had started – timeless and moving as the camera tracked the exodus of children across the Rwandan/Congo border to a camp outside of Goma. Their stories, narrated by journalist Daren

Pascal were deep-reaching, burrowing into those parts of the brain that protected itself from too much reality.

After ten minutes, the film began to experience problems. Pixelated static and sound distortion obscured the images. Erratic volume and mercurial images faded in and out of the interrupted scenes.

Murmurs quickly spread from one table to the next and Wendy left her table to speak with a technician. Then, there was sudden clarity. Crisp. Invasive.

The images became hyper real as the lens fell on one child, a girl whose body was on display inside a glass case, like a museum case. Her breasts, small mounds of innocence on her chest were stripped of clothing and bruised with teeth marks. The audience shifted nervously as the shot lingered on the girl's hideous disfigurement.

Quickly, Ben turned Annie away, and Wendy approached the film makers who were as alarmed as the audience. They had never shot this image. When the technical crew tried to stop it, they couldn't. And Wendy had to make apologies while the camera in the film did a slow close-up of the girl's face.

The director threw up his hands in frustration and faced the guests. "I'm sorry, but these are not my shots. I don't know how they got edited in. We're trying to stop it, but we're having technical difficulties. I'm sorry."

"Daddy, turn off the sounds!" Annie pleaded. She held her ears.

Ben drew her close and tried to calm her, as Wendy joined them.

"Something's going to happen," Ben whispered to Wendy.

"What do you mean?"

"In the film. I don't know what, but something really bad is going to happen. I want Vienna to take Annie home."

"Is this for real? I don't understand how you know this!"

"It's for real."

"Annie, do you want Vienna to take you home?" Wendy asked.

Annie grabbed Vienna's hand and pulled her towards the door without saying good-bye. The noises on the screen made her uneasy, sick to her stomach. Vulnerable.

Jaiteley moved to hold the door open for them; it locked. He tried again, but couldn't budge it. He motioned to Biro to contact management about alternate exits. All were locked. He rushed to Ben's table.

"He's doing this!" Ben shouted over the noise.

"Who's doing what?" asked Wendy, trying to calm her guests who had started to leave their tables to make their way to the coat check. "I'm so sorry," she repeated several times.

Suddenly, the film cut to a school, to the playing field behind it and to the celebration that was underway to honour the white man and his wife who had worked tirelessly to educate lost children – bringing them home, reuniting them with their families, finding homes for the others, finding good schools.

"It's Ambassador Ingles and his wife," Wendy pointed and tried to encourage her guests to sit down. "It's Ambassador Ingles. Please, don't go."

Bev braced herself as she watched her brother walk slowly down the line of dignitaries, taking time to shake each person's hand. The camera dollied back, then closed in on the last person in the line – a black girl, holding a beautiful bouquet of orchids.

Annie had swivelled around when the music and dancing started. She stared at the girl. "That's her. The one with the blood all over her. The one in the glass case!"

Vienna turned her away. "Don't look."

Some of the audience returned to their tables. Others remained, standing by the grand foyer to watch the colourful festivities – the flag bearers, the choir singing, the dancers.

The Ambassador turned to the camera and looked out to the audience as if in 3D. People stepped back as he seemed to float to the woman and her husband at the table nearest the screen. They were amazed at this filming trick and didn't understand it wasn't one.

The white man with the deformed hand looked at Bev, and barely moving his lips, said, "Forgive me." And turned back to the last person in the line – the flower girl.

36

He had come home after all these years of learning that there was a right and wrong way to suffer. That the right way was to turn the pain and anger around and make them his friends, make them knock down doors.

Now, this last door opened for him without the threat of bruising, without being swallowed by emptiness on the other side. He went in, knowing he wasn't there to relive that day, to turn back time, to reinvent a new future. He had come home to die in the arms of a woman who had lived alone in this blood-stained room with broken mirrors and strangers' fears.

When he entered he immediately felt her wonderment at his return. "I'm home." Tears burned his face. He didn't know where they came from – a furnace in his heart, a volcano in his head. He saw the case resting in the middle of the room. The case with a brief history, like a short poem inside of it, but a history that witnessed love at its boldest, its hottest, its deepest passage.

He looked at the bed at the far end of the room, fragrant with fresh linens and oil paint, and imagined her perfumed tresses of hair. He could hear her singing, not always in key, and reciting lines of poetry she had changed to suit her...*I, that had been to you, had you remained, a ghost in marble of a girl you knew, who would have loved you through and through* and *there was never a syllable wasted on air, we rocked to a rhythm, a thought laid bare, and lie in sleep now, our love in a cradle, silently spoken and fatal.* He remembered her words...*silently spoken and fatal...*

He had come home for this English girl from India, this ghost who had stolen his heart from Paris, made promises to him, kept them, had their child, then in a moment of someone else's rage, lost her youth, and waited for him in mourning for fifty years...*their love in a cradle, silently spoken and fatal*. He remembered how sad she was when she spoke these words, wanting to believe they were ambiguous.

"I'm here." He lay on the bed. A savage need to sleep swept over him as if he had been awake for half a century, not only in his conscious being, but also in others like Ben Needham's and Joseph Hightower's, Sandra Bolyn's and Delphine Hakizimana's, who, before her sixteenth birthday, would stand face to face with the man who paid money to another man to rip her fingers from her harp strings, drag her broken body through the dust and throw her on a road that would eventually take her back to him and to the moment she had known would happen, because one old man, who lived across an ocean in a secret cell, overgrown with obsessive intent, said she could.

Like a venture capitalist, he offered all of them a symbiotic state of philanthropy – he gave; they gave. And in the end – freedom.

He closed his eyes and willed the case to unlock. It fell apart. Bones, as though taking cues from a conductor's baton, floated together.

The artist lay still, until Lexi was whole – spiritually alive in an effigy he had created. She understood the brevity of this transformation, from existing as a lost voice and breath in an autumn-sieged attic, to the English girl who spoke French and rode elephants, read Ginsberg in a Paris cafe and held a black singer in an intimate embrace. She understood it wouldn't last, that she had to make peace and die again in a flash of memories, but not alone.

He was waiting.

She heard the shallow breathing and looked to the end of the room and knew he was there, had felt his ancient shadow wandering corpse-like, in and out of Ben's life, taking and giving.

"Rigo," she called, amazed at the words she hadn't spoken since that day.

She said the name again and again and held out her arms.

"I'm here," he whispered. "Waiting for you."

She heard his voice, crushed with longing and started to move toward him.

Holding out her hands, she looked at the smooth scars on her wrists and stopped. Tried not to remember. "I'm afraid." She hesitated.

"Come to me. Let me hold you." His voice was fading. "You've...you've been here too long. It's time." A cold breath licked at his skin. His pulse slowed.

The tunnel of light between them was dimming. His hands reached, his lips parted to say good-bye and stopped.

The silence startled her. She knew what would happen next.

She fled to him, pressed into him, one arm under his head to hold him close, and moved her lips against his. "I'm here. Let go... let go... let go."

She saw them coming as she had fifty years ago.

We're ready. She held on.

37

Rose had peeled off her clothes liked bruised, infected skins on her way to the shower and vowed she'd burn them. She felt as if his cell had dissolved into the threads, and as she drove home, wanted to stop and strip and run into the cold lake to rid herself of him.

The phone rang; she didn't answer.

She removed from her purse the newspaper picture she had taken from the artist's cell. She threw it on her bed as she slid under the covers and stared at it, not wanting to take it in her hands and touch it, but knowing if she did, there might be a gift from him. A gift from a monster who thought he was a lover, a father, a friend. She knew where he was at that very moment, while she stared at his picture and wondered who his god was.

A riveting cry from some place inside her wanted her to touch the face of the young woman whose obituary read: *It is by suffering that human beings become angels.* She looked at Lexi's face and into her eyes, knew she had suffered, knew she was no angel, knew the artist would plead her case when the time came. She looked at the picture and wanted to see beyond the studio, the suffering. She shook her head as if separating her fake motives from the real ones. She felt her pulse explode with urgency. This was her only chance – her only chance to know what had happened to her baby after she denied it an existence. She knew the old man was daring her to step beyond with him and Lexi.

She grabbed the picture and cradled it close. She cried and shook her head. And screamed she was sorry.

The room darkened. A silence fell like that second after house lights dim and a play begins. She waited until out of the darkness, one single thread of light reached into her eye – a single thread of energy sent to her to draw her into it and float on it to the edge of and beyond common belief: that our conscious hours, our waking hours are what make us human. This, she saw, was an untruth. The thread of light drew her energy into it and exposed the real essence of our humanity – that our waking hours (our work, our play) serve only to nurture our sleep, our dreams, where we connect with all energy beyond the great divide, as one living being. That the fusion of energy between those who slept and those who passed was an eternal, natural fusion in which power we could never imagine existed shaped our destiny.

She stood on the edge of this common belief that humans only knew themselves for sixteen hours a day, then forgot their humanity when they slept. She understood that the other side of recorded history, partnered with us in our sleep to make new histories. These threads were all around us, invisible and mapped. This one had come to her from the artist as he began to sleep. Rose held on to Lexi's picture, as her perceptions flowed across the divide.

Rose was in their room on Marion Street. The lovers were asleep in each other's arms – their corporeal substance unravelling among hundreds of threads of energy – not human, not divine – just nature in another form. Energy, turning and turning, like cool, materialized winds, their earth-walking bodies changing, lengthening, liquefying, stretching until they became their own threads of light and energy. He had found his lover, had taken her with him. But even this man, so driven by love, couldn't have known what was beyond. Did not know that love would not endure, and would be replaced by nature's necessity. Without knowing the aftershock, the lovers passed from one existence to the next, completely divorced from what had gone before. But they did pass. They left one world and entered another together, but not one with love.

In her awe, Rose suspended her humanness, had entered this world where the living in their sleep and the dead in theirs co-existed in a massive map of energy. She saw people all over the world at sleep – their energy entwined with the threads of light from the departed. She knew that no one in her world – not her, not Lexi's killer, not a reign of terror, not a gun hidden by flowers, not cancer – had power over life. She knew that all the decisions she had made were only moments, carrying her into one sleep or another. And that Rigo Molinaro's gift – this vision of timeless energy that erased all pain, all guilt, all passion – showed that our lives are times for love. She would never have to search again.

The phone rang. It stopped. It rang again.

She turned away from the picture. The thread receded and disappeared. She didn't see it leave.

Her perceptions quickly returned.

The picture fell to the floor as she reached to get some lights on and heat from the fireplace.

Again the phone rang. It was Joseph.

She answered and apologized for not picking up earlier and listened to his request to go to Ben's with him. He explained everything that happened at the benefit and that Ben and the Westings were all there. She knew they would be; it would have been inescapable. She knew so much more than what she was ready to share. Nothing seemed relevant anymore. Nothing.

38

"I forgive you," Bev whispered as she watched Harvard turn back to the girl. She felt Bill move closer and rest one hand on her shoulder. "It's not really happening." She turned to him and repeated it.

"Don't watch. It's insane what's happening here!" He turned around, trying to find Ben and saw him wrap his arms around Vienna and Annie, as everything seemed to slow down, like moving into a gale and getting nowhere. People were trying to put on their coats, trying to open the doors, trying to stop the film, trying to apologize without getting it done.

Then the sweetest of all voices – sweet with sincerity, smothered in innocence bounced off the screen. Almost singing her name, she introduced herself to the white man, "I'm Delphine Hakizimana, the diamond smuggler's daughter. I've been waiting so long to meet you." She held out the flowers for him to take. She held them high, almost obscuring his eyes. Her hand held the gun tightly until she thought the metal would melt.

Everyone stopped what they were doing and moved closer to the screen.

Harvard paled as he traced her journey on her face - his eyes softening with acknowledgement.

"These are for you." And she smiled as she handed them to him.

His hand brushed her fingers that were wrapped around the stems of the bouquet. The crowd cheered as he bowed to her. Then the first bullet grazed his cheek.

The audience jumped, wondered if the noise was in the ball room or on the film.

"This is from my family," the sweet voice added. She pulled the trigger a second time as blood from both wounds exploded on to the screen.

"We can't stop it," Bill said as he turned Bev away. "No one can stop it."

Everyone heard the third shot ring out and saw the girl fall beside the man, facing each other and waiting for their fear to pass.

The film stopped. The doors opened. Guests rushed out. Others were too weak to leave their tables. The director of the film sat alone, crying and wouldn't talk to anyone. Jaiteley and Biro were circulating to help restore some order.

Wendy went to Bev Westing, and trying to control her hysterics, wanted to apologize to her and ask if she could arrange a limo to take them home.

Speechlessly, Bev grabbed her hand and patted it to console her.

Six people in the room knew something about what had just happened. Wendy was not one of them. Bev told her that there had been recent disturbances in her life that couldn't be explained, and somehow, they were all involved. Bev knew that nothing she was trying to articulate was registering. But she did know what she had seen hadn't happened yet. She also knew she had something to take care of.

"Let's go home," she announced to Bill who didn't question her. She found Jaiteley and asked him to come to Baby Point when he was finished, to pick up something she found that was important for the investigation.

As they passed Ben, they didn't talk. They didn't have to. Both knew it was ending.

Ben leaned towards her. She could feel his sympathy. She reached out to touch Annie's hair and smiled into her distant eyes. Bev nodded in understanding that no one could make her feel better, not at that moment, not even her dad.

* * * *

When Jaiteley arrived, they were waiting for him. Bev greeted him warmly and held out a small, velvet jewellery box. "Open it."

He looked at it, then at her, and asked. "Where are the pages of the ledger?"

"I never took any pages," she insisted. "Open the box."

He did.

A ring, not particularly expensive was inside. A small pearl ring with even smaller rubies on either side. A ring that had belonged to Alexsis. Carefully he held it up to the light. A single hair was caught in one of the claws. Jaiteley looked at it.

"It's Harvard's. I found him sitting alone in the dark the other night. I tousled his hair. He always said he liked me brushing it when I was a kid."

"And?"

"I'd run a test on it. You said the hair samples you tested from both crime scenes matched. That Phillip Standern and my mother's killer are one and the same. I'd check this one out."

"Harvard's DNA doesn't match."

"Harvard has two different eye colours. I know sometimes it's hard to pick that out."

"I didn't catch that." He was amazed he hadn't noticed it. "I know what that can mean. That he has two...."

"He has two DNA codes or strands or whatever your people call it."

"He's a chimera."

"I've heard that name before."

"Why are you doing this?"

"The things in that film haven't happened yet, but they're going to. We have time."

"My partner already made calls. The ceremony we saw in the film - the people, the music, the girl, the flowers, the gun shots, your brother – it's taking place in the

312

morning." He looked at his watch. "It might already be starting. We notified authorities. They said they'd check into it."

She became frantic. "Bill!" she screamed.

He ran for a phone. He tried twice to get connected to Harvard's cell. Then got a signal. "He's not going to answer! He probably doesn't even have it on him!"

"Try Mickey's!"

He tried. "I can't get through!

"Try again!"

It rang.

"Don't hang up until you get someone!"

He let it ring.

She finally answered. "It's Bill."

Silence.

"We can't talk now. We're on our way..."

"I know. To a ceremony at a school."

"How do you...."

"Don't go, Mickey. It's not safe! Something's...."

There was interference. "I...I...can't talk to you right now." Her voice faded.

"No. Listen!"

"We'll talk later."

He couldn't hear her. She left the phone in the limo.

Bev turned desperately to Jaiteley who had let himself out.

39

They wanted one last look at Marion Street. As they stood by the bed and looked down at the lovers, the raw side of reasoning made Joseph and Rose think about the journey these two had taken, since meeting in the Mars Bar in Paris. It had been an ordinary love story that every city had. Two lovers, infidelity, a love child, jealousy, obsession, loneliness, rage, murder. There was someone in every city who snapped, grabbed a weapon, used it, hid it, maybe was caught and maybe not.

They stared down at two people who had been beautiful in each other's eyes and a force in each other's memory. Hideous and misshapen as they were, they held on to each other, their faces buried in shared familiarity. Rose knew that what she was looking at had absolutely no connection to her world – her waking world. She knew their love ended when peace was restored, ended when he stopped breathing, ended before their next journey began. And that they'd never love again.

She couldn't tell Joseph that his wife wasn't waiting for him. But maybe one day, when Rose had loved him enough, he'd stop thinking she was.

They phoned Jaiteley whose team took great care not to separate the lovers.

40

Ben had spent hours trying to console Annie. "It was a cruel, sick joke that someone played on your mom," he whispered. "She didn't deserve this. Don't worry, kiddo, she'll come round. Give her a day or two. She's a Bond girl, remember?"

"It's just you..."

"Sh....." and he pointed to Vienna who was still sleeping.

"...just you she doesn't want to talk to, right now. Not me." She climbed over Ben to get up. "Can we go home? I don't know how da Vinci can live without me!"

da Vinci, he thought. *Must have been a helluva night! It's okay if you couldn't hold your water. Poor son-of-a-bitch!* He turned to Vienna who was slowly waking. All three of them had crashed on Vienna's bed, after the hysterics at the Palais Royale. They had wrapped themselves around Annie who slept, oblivious to walls and charred writings and threads.

Vienna sat up, draped herself over Ben who sat on the edge of the bed, putting on his socks. "There's nothing to say, is there? Let's take Annie home" and she phoned in sick.

* * * *

da Vinci heard them come in, nearly clawed Ben to death to get out.

"Okay! Good boy!" Ben praised him and let him have the run of the front yard.

Vienna mothered. She poured a bath, made it bubbly, helped Annie out of her clothes, which she said didn't make her feel pretty anymore and asked Vienna if she would give them to the Good Will, but wanted to keep the shoes.

"Stay with me?" she asked nervously.

"Sure, but you're home, now. You're safe. You know that, right?"

She nodded as she lowered herself into the jet stream.

"I'll even wash your hair."

When da Vinci had taken the longest whiz on record, Ben fed him and phoned Jaiteley who apologized for not getting back to him earlier. He wanted to tell Ben everything had been taken care of. The coroner had been in and forensics. He had notified Molinaro's family and told Ben that Beverly was taking care of funeral arrangements. And that Joseph and Rose had been there as well, and said the passing had been peaceful. He had his house back.

Jaiteley said he had other news and told Ben about testing the hair sample Bev had handed over. He confirmed a positive match. Harvard Ingles would have been charged with two counts of Murder 1.

"Would have been? Does he have immunity?" Ben asked.

"He's dead, Ben."

"Does Bev know?"

"Yes."

"How?"

"You saw it like I did, like all of us did. Two bullets at close range."

"When?"

"This morning."

"Why did it have to happen?"

"We notified our embassy. They made calls. The police had deployment orders to intervene."

"And?"

"They weren't followed. No one listened. Or didn't want to. Saw an opportunity. Pretended we didn't call. Are you getting the picture?"

"What about the girl?"

"No one saved her."

316

Ben hung up without saying good-bye and went to look for his girls, found them blowing bubbles. "You okay?"

"Annie's going to play for us after we have banana splits."

"Do we have ice cream?"

"Do we?"

"I don't know. If we don't, I'll be back soon. Don't swim away." He closed the door and walked to the bottom of the third story stairway. *This is MY HOUSE!* He waited for some response. He didn't get any. And he went up. He wasn't sure whether or not his house had been given back, but he wasn't going to share it anymore.

He looked around, saw the bed without sheets. Rose must have taken them. He propped up the mattress against the wall and went on line to find a contractor. Things needed to be changed up.

There were two phone calls – one from Wendy who had calmed down and asked if he needed any help with Annie. He told her to come by on Saturday morning as usual, and they'd have a good heart-to-heart. And thought maybe she was grown up enough to handle the truth. Then shook his head.

The other call was from Bev. She phoned to say she had sent him an email. That he should read it without passing judgement. When she hung up, he took his laptop to his chair and sank back into its soft padding. It was Jamie's favourite chair. Jamie had always been in it with some girl on his lap or some book – he liked philosophy. There was still the faint smell of Jamie's hair gel from the back of his head where he rested it on the pillow. Ben closed his eyes, shifted in the uneven padding until he moulded it to his back and looked at Bev's email.

Hi Ben,

I took pictures of some pages in my dad's ledger and uploaded them, before I burned them. It was a ledger written by my dad's lawyer, Paul Dann. Here's what I found: When our family doctor wouldn't falsify documents to cover up Alexsis' murder, he recommended Phillip Standern take care of the family crisis on November 25, 1958. Standern was paid a lot of money for the cover-up. Harvard snapped when he was told he was going off to school in England after Christmas, and in a fit of rage, stabbed Alexsis. He knew about Alexsis' affair with Molinaro and that I was his child. He found out when Alexsis was modeling for the painting, and he waited for the right moment to be alone with her. Molinaro went out for something, and when he returned, he found Alexsis bleeding to death. He called Howard Ingles who sent the police to clean up; they made sure Molinaro would never be found again. As they carried Alexsis out, she found a piece of broken mirror, and with all the strength she could gather, cut her wrists. She was dead by the time she arrived home. Paul Dann listed the names of people who were paid at the Rockwood Asylum to keep the artist silent. Payments were made to both Phillip Standern and the Police Chief to falsify reports of Alexsis' death and Molinaro's disappearance.

Ben, in my heart I know my mother would have survived Harvard's attack, but Standern didn't. I can't believe Harvard is gone. The funeral service for Alexsis and Rigo will be quiet – cremation, one urn, and ashes that Bill and I will take to the dunes in Picton, to happy times. Ilario Molinaro is coming tomorrow. I'll be taking him to Kingston to help me with Rigo's art. I would like you to meet him.

I don't know about the funeral arrangements for Harvard. Michelle won't speak to me. She's gone home to France – I think for safety reasons.

Over the holidays, if you're up for a trip, I'd like to visit the Lazlos. They knew my parents before anyone could ever conceive that my parents' love would never make it past Lexi's 26th birthday. We love you, Ben. Thanks for being so brave. Bev

He logged off.

When Vienna found him, she had never seen him so relaxed. She snuggled into him and sat like that until they heard the piano break the sound barrier and knew Annie's fear had turned to anger over what had happened.

"We better go downstairs."

She turned to look at the attic. "What are you going to do with this place?"

"Change things up. Take out the cupboards, put down new floors. Make it over."

"You need to."

"Yes, I do. Let's go down before she destroys the keyboard."

Ben slid beside Annie and kissed her hands like he always did – like a blessing – and asked her to play her special song – the one she had been working on for the past two weeks. The song she heard Billie Holiday singing.

"I don't know what you're talking about. I don't know any Billie Holiday songs."

"You don't know what I'm talking about?" Ben nodded. "Play me something else."

41

They slept in, didn't have to be at the airport for Ilario's arrival until the afternoon. From the time Bill had awakened, he laced his fingers through Bev's and waited for her ritualistic *Good Morning* and first peck. He loved her most like this – her hair, fallen over one eye and white skin, her lips full and pale like her breasts. He often watched her before she woke, studied her face and hands. She was everything to him.

When she woke up, he was moving his thumb over the small pearl and ruby ring she was wearing that he had never seen on her before.

"Good morning." She slid up to kiss his cheek.

He was still looking at the ring. "I didn't get this for you, right?"

"Right. It was given to Alexsis for her 22nd birthday. A gift from Harvard who said he had saved his horse racing winnings to buy it. He was only twelve at the time. I think he loved her more than my dad, or maybe needed her more. Probably needed her more. He wanted me to have it."

Bill didn't know about the DNA match with the evidence Bev had given Jaiteley. She didn't want him to know. As far as Bev was concerned, the case was closed.

42

Joseph had never witnessed that calm and peace in his dying wife that the reunited lovers shared. He thought about how he'd be able to convince Rose that sometimes waiting for love makes it exclusive when it comes. "Rose, I wish you could have seen them," Joseph said. "You'd never question again what you need to get through this life. Love finds us and goes with us. I'm totally convinced."

"And if it doesn't?"

"Then I feel sorry for anyone who can't find it in this life. But you don't really believe that, right? That love stops when a monitor doesn't register a heartbeat anymore?"

She thought a moment, but couldn't tell him what she had witnessed when she touched Alexsis' face in the photo. He probably wouldn't believe her. She couldn't accept what she was about to say, but said it anyway, "Show me how to love like that, and I'll believe you."

Acknowledgements
Special praise and thanks to editor-in-chief, Nik Morton and the publishing team at Solstice for their ongoing encouragement and professionalism in bringing this debut novel to market. To James Griffin, your sensitive, clear-sighted approach made the editing stage a pleasure.

About the author
Meg Howald says her body feeds on daylight, her heart on reflected light, her mind on absorbed light and her soul twilight. A romantic pioneer, Meg has lived in the light of seven cities, two provinces, and two continents. And of course, by the hemlines of the Aegean, the Bay Fundy, the St. Lawrence, and the Great Lakes. Meg teaches Humanities, Art History, and Writing at Fanshawe College in Ontario, Canada and enjoys the company of exceptional colleagues and students. More than the sum total of all of these, her family constantly reinvents her. She says her novels are socio-psychological mysteries, teased by fate and haunted by irony.

EXPATRIATE BONES

M. Howald

Bounty hunter Leonard Marsland feeds on the hunt, the kill and has been feeding his whole life.

Montreal. Winter. 2002. When Christine Duma, a med student is murdered, Marsland steps closer to the last two names on his hit list, and Detective Austin Del Rio (Montreal PD) steps into the crossfire between Marsland's revenge and a war crimes cover-up.

Detective Del Rio, who likes crime and women to be easy – easy to figure, easy to solve, and easy to forget – is thrown into a runaway homicide with international players on a collision course with death.

And Del Rio finds out that some things can't be forgotten.

Other Solstice Books that might be of interest

THE SCALES OF SIX

Rosean Mile

On assignment collecting relics in Indonesia, independent curator Gail Weaver learns that an ephemeral plant sprouting prolifically on Sumatra can transform all hair types into gorgeous locks. Seizing an opportunity to make a fortune in the cosmetic market, Gail smuggles plant clippings into the US and sways her apprehensive sister Fran to help seek financing for a shampoo she's made with the Indonesian plant. But dreams of impending wealth are quelled by the shocking revelation of the shampoo's horrifying side effects.

Against a backdrop of career and money problems, shady competitors, legal challenges and romance, Fran, Gail and an exotic Indonesian scientist must race against biological, corporate and media forces to save Fran's boss, and a legion of young women whose quest for beauty is transforming them in ways they never imagined.

Testing human greed against forces of nature, *The Scales of Six* blends suspense, intrigue, and surreal circumstance to weave a new story about an old myth coming to life in the contemporary world.

BLOOM FOREVERMORE

E.B. Sullivan

A romantic mystery. Psychology professor Dr. Sonia Wyland seeks a change from her stale routine by vacationing in California. While shopping at a secondhand store, she acquires a diary written by a woman named Margaret. This journal leads Sonia to believe Margaret is in a dangerous liaison with a man who calls himself Alexander.

Detouring from her plans, Sonia attempts to rescue Margaret.

In this quest, Sonia discovers an intriguing man and quickly loses her heart.

OUR LADY OF PERPETUAL VEXATION

John Paulits

It's 1964 and Smitty, Mouse, and Kelso are in their last semester of high school with one thing on their minds—girls.

In their never-ending pursuit of this most elusive quarry, they manage to land themselves in some ridiculous, bizarre, and hilarious situations.

Whether it's the parish dance, a friend's funeral, a wedding reception, or a first sexual encounter, these are engaging, entertaining and sometimes ribald slices of life that will strike a chord or two.

SEPTEMBER WIND

Kathleen Janz-Anderson

Orphaned at birth in 1940, Emily lives the next eighteen years on her grandfather's farm with four thankless men and an indifferent aunt nearby. When the school board forces Grandfather's hand and allows her to attend school, she experiences a beautiful friendship, and the thrill and pain of an innocent young love. Still, there is an underlying loneliness, and a secret she bears alone.

In 1958, the day finally arrives when she prepares to leave the farm forever. Then a tragic mistake thrusts her into a harrowing run for her life. She escapes the horror and hops a train to San Francisco. With a stout heart and a fire in her belly, she fights for her sanity and welcomes the stirrings of a grown-up love.

She arrives in San Francisco wide-eyed and filled with hope. Alone in a strange town, she is vulnerable to a world of crime and those who take advantage of her. Yet, with no one to count on but the rebel inside her, she never gives up even when each turn and every door opened greets her with another unwelcome surprise.

DEATH IS ANOTHER LIFE

Robert Morton

This cross-genre thriller is set in present-day Malta and has echoes from pre-history and also the eighteenth century Knights of Malta.

Malta may be an island of sun and sand, but there's a dark side to it too. It all started when some fishermen pulled a corpse out of the sea... Or maybe it was five years ago, in the cave of Ghar Dalam?

Spellman, an American black magician, has designs on a handpicked bunch of Maltese politicians, bending their will to his master's. A few sacrifices, that's all it takes. And he's helped by Zondadari, a rather nasty vampire. Maltese-American investigative journalist Maria Caruana's in denial. She can't believe Count Zondadari is a vampire. She won't admit it. Such creatures don't exist, surely? She won't admit she's in love with him, either... Detective Sergeant Attard doesn't like caves or anything remotely supernatural. Now he teams up with Maria to unravel the mysterious disappearance of young pregnant women. They're helped by the priest, Father Joseph. And there are caves, supernatural deaths and a haunting exorcism. Just what every holiday island needs, really.

"Dan Brown meets Dracula. Robert Morton's *Death is Another Life* is a fast paced, intelligent read that kept my pulse pounding until the last page. Vampires are certainly enjoying a revival, but Morton's take is entirely fresh, certainly not like those so overdone today. Once I started this, I couldn't put it down." - Heather Savage, author, *The Empath Trilogy*

ANNA'S VISIONS

Joy Redmond

Anna Morgan is a seer, and she sees visions of impending doom for her granddaughter, Tori Hicks, the day Tori is born. Through the years, she experiences more unnerving visions, but she can't put the pieces together and figure out how to save Tori.

Tori is an only child coming of age in a small town in Kentucky where no one locks their doors and everyone knows everyone. From her earliest childhood, she has lived a fairytale life along with her best friend, Jill. When she and Jill enter high school, Tori meets Wesley Asner, the love of her life. But when tragedy strikes, Tori and Wesley find their lives torn apart.

Broken-hearted and desperate for a change, Tori sneaks off to Florida for what she hopes will be a romantic adventure that will take her mind off Wesley. On the beach, she meets Cody Baxter, a handsome young pharmacist who is hiding a dark and dangerous secret...

MURDER ONCE, MURDER TWICE

B.J. McMinn

Detective Julie Hartman must solve a high-profile murder while she combats the chauvinistic attitudes of a small, Oklahoma county's, all male sheriff's department.

She wonders why the sheriff gives her the case until she overhears him and the undersheriff, whom she's nicknamed the 'pissin' buddies', plotting to sabotage her case and use her failure to rid the county of its only woman detective.

Her prime suspects include the husband, his business partner, an ex-lover, a wife abuser, and the undersheriff. When Detective Malloy attempts to integrate himself into her investigation, she suspects him of spying for the sheriff. When she learns of his secret relationship with the victim, he becomes another suspect.

She follows a trail of corporate greed and lust and discloses a thirty-year-old secret. As she her investigation leads to the discovery of the murderer's identity, she becomes the killer's next target…

Reviews

"B. J. McMinn hooks your interest on the first page, with shiver-inducing prose and vivid characters. I hope this is the start of a series."
- William Bernhardt, New York Times bestseller

"B. J. McMinn has done an intriguing job with this tough mystery. Don't miss getting your copy."
- Dusty Richards, Award winning author

THE CURSE OF AKBAR

Troy Bond

Buried deep within a secret chamber, inside a remote Indian palace, is a mysterious manuscript that has remained hidden for centuries.

Dalton sets out from Italy on a dangerous

assignment to the far reaches of an Indian desert where he confronts a fractious group of international scholars, a lissome beauty from Copenhagen, a ruthless private security firm, and the elusive "Omar"—the last person Dr. Ross met after he translated pieces of the Text sent to him by an anonymous source.

Dalton learns that Dr. Ross' translation of the Text fragments revealed a sacred and extraordinary link to the past, which could threaten the very foundation of the Christian faith. But before he can uncover the truth behind the "Text of Akbar", he must be the first to solve the mystery of Dr. Ross's murder, while trying to survive in a palace of easy death.

Made in the USA
Charleston, SC
29 October 2013